AMERICAN OPERATOR

OTHER TITLES BY BRIAN ANDREWS AND JEFFREY WILSON

Tier One Series

Tier One
War Shadows
Crusader One

WRITING AS ALEX RYAN

Nick Foley Thriller Series

Beijing Red
Hong Kong Black

OTHER TITLES BY BRIAN ANDREWS

The Calypso Directive
The Infiltration Game
Reset

OTHER TITLES BY JEFFREY WILSON

The Traiteur's Ring
The Donors
Fade to Black
War Torn

AMERICAN OPERATOR

A TIER ONE THRILLER

ANDREWS & WILSON

This is a work of fiction. Names, characters, organizations, places, events, and incidents are either products of the author's imagination or are used fictitiously. Any resemblance to actual persons, living or dead, or actual events is purely coincidental.

Published by Thomas & Mercer, Seattle

www.apub.com

ISBN-13: 9781503904422
ISBN-10: 1503904423

Cover design by Mike Heath | Magnus Creative

Printed in the United States of America

To the men and women of the Central Intelligence Agency.
"And you shall know the truth, and the truth shall make you free."

PART I

A good teacher is like a candle—it consumes itself to light the way for others.

—Mustafa Kemal Atatürk

CHAPTER 1

Ankara, Turkey
May 4
1330 Local Time

Amanda Allen had a secret.

Keeping it was exhausting.

So far, she'd kept it hidden from her boss, the US Ambassador to Turkey, and from her father—the two most important figures in her life. In the beginning, she'd reassured herself that with time, the burden would grow lighter. Now, four months into her assignment, she wasn't so sure. *I'll give it a year and reassess,* she thought, smiling and nodding while the men talked. Not everyone was cut out for this line of work. If her decision to lead a double life didn't work out, there was always law school. One call from her father and she'd be in, wherever she wanted to go.

Nepotism . . . America's safety net.

The afternoon sun hung high in a cloudless bright-blue sky. Ankara was bustling, almost as if the entire city had silently agreed on taking a late lunch today, and now everyone was hurrying back to work en masse. Since arriving in Turkey, she'd frequently heard people refer to Istanbul as the country's beating heart. If that was true, then Ankara was its calculating mind. Ambassador Bailey had told her that a hundred years ago, the population of the city had numbered only seventy-five thousand. Today, Turkey's capital was home to over five million people. The city didn't feel like home yet to her, but hopefully that would come with time.

Give it a year . . .

She stood with her hands clasped behind her back as her two male companions spoke on the sidewalk outside the charming Aegean seafood restaurant they had just left, which was walking distance from both the US embassy and the Turkish Ministry of the Interior. It was a struggle to stand quietly, patiently—her father had raised her to be a strong woman and encouraged her to speak her mind—but she forced herself. Women's rights had advanced further in Turkey than in many of its Middle Eastern neighbors, but that still put it a half century behind the West. And now, secularism was at risk as Muslim conservatives, led by President Erodan, sought to weave Islam back into law and erase the little bit of progress that had been made.

Amanda listened and tried desperately not to interject as her boss, Ambassador Charles Bailey, engaged in an animated conversation with Halil Demicri. As the acting Director of Migration Management for the Ministry of the Interior, Demicri oversaw Turkey's immigration and asylum programs. The publicly stated mission of his office was to develop "people-oriented policies" for foreign victims of human trafficking who were trying to "harmonize" with the country. However, thus far there had been little discussion of human trafficking, or harmonizing, or even *people-oriented* policies. Instead, Demicri had spent the entire lunch talking about an entirely different kind of migration-management problem—the Kurds.

"If what you are saying is true, Mr. Ambassador, then why does your country continue to support Kurdish separatists in Syria?" Demicri said in his British-accented English. He had reminded them at least three times that he'd earned his degree in international relations in Britain.

"In America, we have an expression, Director Demicri, and maybe you've heard it," Bailey said, "which is that you're comparing apples and oranges. We concur that groups like YPG and PKK are pursuing a terrorist agenda inside Turkey, and we condemn this. However, Kurdish people pursuing cultural recognition, freedom from persecution, and a voice in their local governance are another matter altogether."

Demicri snorted an incredulous laugh. "How can you say such a thing? They are one and the same people."

"Now, Halil," Bailey said, switching deftly to the familiar. "How can *you* say such a thing? Am I to interpret from your comment that you believe that every Kurd is a member of PKK? Take care with your words, or I might misconstrue your statement to mean that Turkey classifies all Kurds as terrorists."

Demicri's cheeks reddened. "Be careful with *your* words, Ambassador, or I might misconstrue your statement to mean that the United States is actively supporting the Kurdish terrorism agenda."

Well, isn't this going just wonderfully, Amanda thought. *Probably time to play peacemaker.*

"Gentlemen, if I could—" she started to say, but not only did Bailey interrupt her, he waved a hand at her to be quiet as if she were a child. Now her cheeks were the ones turning red. Just because they were in Turkey did not mean she forfeited her rights and status as an equal, most especially when operating within their State Department roles. Later, when they were alone, she would tell him so.

The other Amanda Allen, however, the one supporting an entirely different American agenda, was delighted with this conversation. For all its divisiveness, the meeting had been incredibly productive. Demicri had dropped lots of names and been aggressive in trying to control the topics of conversation. Her brain was swimming with details she had not been able to write down but needed to remember for her report to her other boss—what was said and unsaid, her impressions of Demicri, and as much detail as she could collect about the security protocols employed to protect him. When it came to intelligence collection, no detail was insignificant. She was itching to wrap this meeting up; the sooner she could put her observations to paper, the better.

"Clearly this is a sensitive, but important, matter for Turkey," Bailey was saying as Amanda tuned back in. "I think by both of us voicing our concerns today, we've made some headway."

Demicri nodded, a political smile plastered on his face. "Honest dialogue, even when contentious, is an important part of any *strategic* partnership between our two countries. Please convey to the Secretary and President that my government draws a clear distinction between law-abiding Kurdish citizens and Kurdish separatists using terror to pursue an agenda of political unrest and murder. Turkey considers both its native Kurdish population and those seeking asylum from persecution in Syria important and valued minority populations. But we will not tolerate the United States backing any group bent on destabilizing Turkey."

Bailey was gearing up to reply, but this time Amanda shot him a look as she began to speak, daring him to try cutting her off again. "Director Demicri, the United States recognizes that Turkey has opened its borders to more than two million Syrians over the past decade of fighting. We understand this has been a heavy burden, both politically and financially, and we thank you for your generosity and compassion when it comes to refugees."

"That's right," Demicri said, nodding vigorously, his face lighting up for the first time. "You need more on your staff like her, Mr. Ambassador. She understands the sacrifice Turkey has made. It is important for the United States and NATO to understand that for Turkey to remain committed to this strategic partnership, we need financial support from the West. Otherwise, we will have no choice but to explore ways to strengthen our relationships with *other* regional partners."

There's that phrase again, she thought. *Strategic partnership.*

The subtext in Demicri's message was impossible to miss. Either the US stepped up its financial commitment to help Turkey crush the Kurdish separatist movement, or Turkey would start looking to Moscow instead of Washington for support. Amanda would argue that the process had already begun when Erodan met with Russian President Petrov back in April.

"I understand," Bailey said, his tone now placating rather than hard. "I promise you that Turkey's security and stability are of the utmost importance to the State Department and the Warner administration. I'll pass along your concerns and express the financial hardship Turkey faces."

"Please see that you do, Mr. Ambassador," Demicri said, then turned to smile at Amanda. "Ms. Allen, your observations were very insightful. I look forward to our next meeting," he said, shamelessly looking her up and down.

She ignored his lecherous gaze and forced a smile. "It would be wonderful if Azur Basar from the Ministry could attend our next meeting. Her reputation as a champion for women's—"

She stopped midsentence.

Something was wrong.

Her stomach was tight—a feeling she'd come to depend on during her training at the Farm. She shifted her gaze beyond Demicri, aware that he was asking her if something was the matter. Across the street, amid a row of taxis, a black Mercedes sat idling, its driver behind the wheel.

"Is everything okay?" the Ambassador asked.

She ignored Bailey and looked left, her gaze flicking toward the intersection.

The man with the magazine looked out of place. The street was crowded and moving, but this guy was standing perfectly still—not reading, just staring at her. Behind him, parked on the northwest corner, sat a white high-top van with no windows in the rear compartment. The magazine man glanced over his shoulder at the van and then fished a phone from his pocket.

"Oh shit," she said and grabbed Ambassador Bailey by the sleeve of his suit coat.

Her intention was to run, but a massive pressure wave sent her airborne. The heat hit her a heartbeat later, like she'd opened an oven door while her face was too close to it. She never heard the boom. She didn't remember flying through the air or hitting the ground. Somebody closed the oven door, but the right side of her face still felt hot. And wet maybe. Her face hurt, but not nearly as bad as the throbbing pain in her head. When she opened her eyes, the imagery was nonsensical. The white van parked in front of her was pointing toward the sky, climbing a perfectly vertical hill. Booted feet approached, belonging to men running on a wall, their bodies clinging impossibly at a ninety-degree angle. Nothing made sense. Then, something clicked and her proprioception came back. She was lying on her side; that's why the world was askew. She coughed, and the right side of her chest exploded with pain; it felt like someone had just driven a flaming sword between her ribs.

She blinked.

I have to get up.

She tried to push herself onto her knees, but it was as if the earth had somehow turned up the power of gravity. No, not gravity. Something was driving her down, a weight from above, not a tug from below. She saw a black boot beside her and realized that it must belong to a man pressing his other foot into the small of her back. With great effort, she turned her head the other way and gazed into the face of her make-believe boss—Ambassador Bailey. His body lay only inches from her.

At first she thought he was dead, but then he blinked, and a tear spilled from his eye, traveled over the bridge of his nose, and dropped to the dirty sidewalk. She saw there was a boot on his neck. Then she saw the muzzle of the rifle against his temple. He opened his mouth to speak but was interrupted by a flash. The accompanying crack was barely audible—muffled, like a gunshot a thousand yards away. She watched in horror as Bailey's head deflated, his face a balloon squished between two elevator doors, its contents evacuating in a dark pool of blood. Yet he still stared at her—his right eye open, the pupil dilated. A spent casing bounced off the pavement between them, spun in slow motion, and then came to rest by the tip of her nose. A 7.62 rifle-round casing. Was it weird that she knew that detail?

Other muffled gunshots reverberated.

A voice screamed inside her head, *Get up! Run! Escape!* She agreed with the voice. She wanted to do all these things, but she was pinned to the sidewalk by the boot. A boot that pressed with the weight of an F-150 parked on her back. If only she'd been carrying a weapon. Why didn't they let her kind carry weapons on assignment? A voice laughed at this. Would it have made a difference?

Don't be ridiculous, Amanda.

As she waited for the terrorist's bullet to come smashing into her temple, a deep and profound sadness engulfed her.

I'm sorry, Dad. I'm sorry I let you down.

This would devastate him. He wouldn't understand. And worse, he'd never know the truth. She knew how the CIA operated. Despite his prominent status, they would keep him in the dark about what she had really been doing for the United States. They would paint another picture: a selfless young diplomat murdered while trying to make the world a better place.

I guess I don't have to worry about keeping my secret anymore.

The ground began to shake.

At first she thought it was her—her body shaking uncontrollably—but then she smelled the dust and sulfur. The ground shook a second time. Then a third.

More bombs . . . The evil bastards weren't finished yet.

She looked up out of the corner of her eye just in time to see the rifle butt coming down. A sharp pain erupted in the back of her head, and then she felt herself being dragged under—dragged against her will into a deep, dark, and inescapable pool.

CHAPTER 2

Sun Gardens Resort on the Adriatic Sea
Dubrovnik, Croatia
May 5
0040 Local Time

Spotter scope raised to his right eye, John Dempsey watched the inbound luxury yacht *La Traviata*—barely visible on the western horizon of the Adriatic Sea. The air smelled clean tonight, and he could taste a salty tang on the cool, lazy sea breeze. On the balcony, he stood tall, proud, and motionless—an orarian sentinel. He wore a full beard—four months' growth—and his dark hair was as long as he'd ever kept it, long enough to gather into a ponytail, but he preferred to manage the unruly mop with a backward-facing ball cap. His body was strong, rested, and energized. His impending fortieth birthday seemed ten years removed, rather than ten days. His mind operated with a clarity of thought and purpose he could not remember since the day he had decided to become a Navy SEAL two decades ago.

Despite the new life he lived now, he was still doing what he'd been trained to do as a Tier One SEAL. As the head of the Special Activities Division of the covert task force known as Ember, Dempsey's job was to find and dispatch the world's most dangerous criminals, spies, and jihadists. He was a terrorist hunter, a clandestine warrior, a shadow soldier.

He was an American operator.

His current tasking was to disappear Moammar al-Fahkoury—a rising piece of shit in the terrorist underground who seemed to have fashioned himself as an entrepreneur. Although Ember had been watching al-Fahkoury for some time now, they didn't fully understand his operation. For lack of a better description, they'd branded him a "maven" of terrorism. al-Fahkoury was the business equivalent of a savvy and deeply connected information broker—someone keenly aware of trends, new methodologies, and opportunities—hired by death dealers wanting to tap his knowledge and connections. The Director of National Intelligence—and former head of Ember—Kelso Jarvis, had decided al-Fahkoury had been in play long enough.

Ember had been tasked to bring him in.

Dempsey lowered the scope and glanced inside the hotel room at Elizabeth Grimes's lean, muscular frame stretched prone on the dining room table. She had one knee pulled up and her cheek pressed against her sniper rifle as she scanned the horizon through the open sliding glass door. A part of him would have preferred to be on sniper duty rather than quarterbacking the op, but he was only average on the .300 WinMag, as the M91A2 was known in the SEAL Teams. How Grimes would perform was still an unknown. According to Shane Smith, Ember's current Director, her marks at sniper school had been shit hot, but this was her first mission manning the long gun. There was a world of difference between plinking targets and exploding heads. Not everyone was cut out to be an angel of death. Was Elizabeth?

Looking at her, body and weapon merged as if a single organism, he wondered why she'd wanted to go down the sniper path. He thought he knew, but they'd never actually talked about it. The brutal terrorist sleeper attack on the Midrachov in Jerusalem a year ago had affected all of them, but Grimes most profoundly. The AK-47 round she'd taken to the chest had almost killed her. In fact, technically, it had. She'd been flatlined when they'd reached the OR at Jerusalem Medical Center. He remembered her head lolled to the side; her skin gone gray; and her glassy, lifeless eyes. He remembered telling Dan Munn that she was dead and how the SEAL-turned-surgeon had whirled to face him and growled, "She's dead when I say she's dead." By God's grace, Munn's will, or possibly a combination of both, Grimes had pulled through.

On the outside, there was no mistaking Grimes 2.0. She'd always been fit, but over the past year she'd packed on at least fifteen pounds of lean muscle. In fact, that fifteen pounds was probably more like thirty because she'd lost fifteen pounds during her stint in the hospital. She'd cut her postrecovery convalescence short with the most aggressive PT program he had ever seen. The gray tank top she wore tonight advertised the results: defined, muscled arms propping up a lean triangular torso. Her recently trimmed auburn hair was pulled back in a stubby ponytail, except for a too-short strand she had tucked behind her left ear. She was focused—locked on. She should probably be the least of his worries, but she wasn't.

"What the hell are we doing?" Grimes murmured, barely audible.

His stomach went sour at this double-edged sword of a comment. Was she referring to Ember and this op, or was she referring to the wedge between the two of them that had formed over the past year? Dempsey treaded cautiously. He didn't do emotions well—they were just too much damn work, and history had proven there was no return on investment.

"What do you mean?" he asked, keeping his voice neutral.

"I mean, it's been a year, JD." She sighed, her eye still on the scope. "A year since Operation Crusader. Amir Modiri is dead. Justice was meted. We fulfilled our charter."

"Yeah, what's your point?"

"That this is mission number, what, twenty-two, since Crusader? And here we are, chasing down another random dirtbag. This is not Ember. There are plenty of other groups—groups specifically chartered for these activities—that should be out here instead of us. This is not what Ember was conceived for."

"Snatching al-Fahkoury is not the type of op you give to the B-team. This is a direct action mission—exactly what Ember was conceived for."

She disengaged from her rifle and looked at him. "How is taking al-Fahkoury related to surveilling Trugga two weeks ago in Nigeria? Or Mali Haswani in Qatar before that, or Din Tuluk Amin in Malaysia before that?"

"They're all terrorists, Elizabeth," he said, his irritation rising. "That's what we do—we find and stop terrorists."

She shook her head. "They're all *unrelated* terrorists. Can't you see it? Jarvis is running Ember ragged chasing flies. Go here, check on this guy. Now stop, pack up, and go over there and check on that guy. Hold on, change of plans, go watch this other new guy instead. Okay, now shoot him. Thanks. Hurry up, pack your bags, time to surveil the next guy . . . It's ridiculous."

"That's what counterterrorism is," he said, exasperated. "That's how it works in the IC."

"That's how it works for the intelligence community as a whole, but that's not what *we* do—or not what we used to do. It's not why Ember was conceived."

He sighed. "Okay, fine, I'll play along. Tell me, what is it that we should be doing?"

"We should be tasked to longitudinally prosecute whoever is the greatest threat to US national security until that threat is dead and neutralized. Just like we did with Modiri and VEVAK in Iran. I didn't sign on to swat flies, JD. I signed on to slay dragons. What happened to our autonomy? What happened to our focus? We should be hunting tomorrow's bin Laden, tomorrow's Modiri . . ."

"How do you know this guy's not the next bin Laden? In five years, al-Fahkoury could become the type of guy you're talking about. Are you suggesting we leave him in play and wait and see if that happens?"

"al-Fahkoury is definitely *not* the next bin Laden," she said, screwing up her face at him. With a huff, she turned her attention back to her scope. "Never mind."

He watched her for a beat. On the one hand, he understood her frustration. When you were operating at the tip of the spear, sometimes it was hard to see the big picture. Maybe al-Fahkoury wasn't the next bin Laden, but taking him out of the game made the world a safer place by removing a well-oiled cog from the global terrorism machine. Like it or not, "swatting flies," as she'd called it, was part of an operator's job description. And besides, if there was another mastermind of proxy warfare like Amir Modiri out there, then Jarvis *would* give Ember tasking to take him down. If there was one thing in the universe that Dempsey had learned he could trust with unwavering confidence, it was that no matter how complex the problem, no matter how convoluted the details, the DNI saw the threat and knew how best to prosecute it.

He shook his head, not sure what else to say to her, and forced his thoughts back to the mission at hand. Intelligence indicated the meet was scheduled to happen at sea—a prerequisite demanded by the other party. They didn't know who al-Fahkoury was meeting on the inbound yacht, but the mere fact that al-Fahkoury was not controlling the logistics was informative. Dempsey had already concluded that the unknown party in this meet-up was a "money guy." Of course, the money guy himself wouldn't *actually* be on that yacht; that's not how they operated. Money guys hovered above it all, conducting their nefarious business via proxies and lieutenants. Arm's-length separation and layers of obfuscation were the name of the game—these were methods the bad guys had figured out a long, long time ago.

Never do your own dirty work.

The half-moon hanging in the clear night sky provided enough light that he could see the Bilgin 156 luxury yacht without night vision. Even without the moon, it wouldn't have mattered. These guys were operating without stealth in mind—purple mood lights illuminated the main deck, and the green-blue glow of the yacht's Jacuzzi emanated from the stern. Dempsey was surprised he couldn't hear bass speakers thumping. It never ceased to amaze him how often men's carnal desires undermined their OPSEC.

"*La Traviata*, crossing one nautical mile inbound," said a voice in Dempsey's earpiece. The voice belonged to Richard Wang, Ember's resident "all things cyber" boy wonder who was camped out in a room two levels below them. Dempsey pictured the young cybernerd genius tapping away on his computer: a large-diameter parabolic dish sitting beside the sliding glass door, a pile of energy drink cans strewn across the carpet, and a cold mocha cappuccino on the desk.

"Yes, Bronco, we can all see them," Dempsey growled. "But when are you going to have comms up so we can hear them?"

"Damn, you're grumpy tonight," Wang came back.

"He's always grumpy these days," Dan Munn chimed in from a third location—a corner room on the second story with a view of the beach and the access road leading to the marina. Munn had been tapped to lead Charger team—a three-man assault force rounded out by Ember's two new SAD recruits. The plan was to intercept al-Fahkoury's convoy on the access road prior to its reaching the marina parking lot. Taking al-Fahkoury on land was more covert, simpler, and less dangerous for the Ember assault team than conducting a maritime operation. Once they'd positively confirmed the target ship, they could leave it in play. Yachts weren't submarines. They were easy to track and hard to disappear. Plus, it would be interesting to see what the yacht did in reaction to al-Fahkoury's no-show. What communications would follow? Where would the yacht go next? Disappearing al-Fahkoury right before the meeting would incite a reaction, and every reaction was an opportunity to collect intelligence . . .

Shit, Dempsey thought, *Ember has me thinking like a spook all the time now.*

"FleetBroadband, just like I suspected," Wang announced in a victorious tone.

"Say again?" Dempsey asked.

"They're using FleetBroadband on AlphaSat," Wang continued. "You know, if I wanted to be rich, all I'd have to do is quit this rodeo and become a private IT contractor for these dumbasses."

"Get to the point, Bronco," Dempsey growled.

"We've got an arrangement with Inmarsat Maritime. FleetBroadband is their satellite internet service, and AlphaSat is the satellite covering Europe and the Mideast," the kid explained. "And by 'we,' I mean the NSA and me, and by 'the NSA and me,' I mean the NSA."

"And what arrangement is that?"

"That Inmarsat Maritime's encryption protocols are not as awesome as they advertise."

"I take that to mean you're in?"

"Of course I'm in. They've got five computers and a half-dozen mobile phones on the shipboard Wi-Fi network. What a bunch of knobs. I'm just going to turn all their phones into live mikes," Wang said, chuckling. "In principle, we should be able to listen in wherever anybody goes. Even belowdecks. Hell, by the time I hijack all their shit, we won't even need the directional mike I dragged up here."

Despite himself, Dempsey cracked a smile at that.

"Stable, this is Charger One. While we wait on Bronco, has there been any chatter or movement from the primary target?" Munn asked, referring to the al-Fahkoury contingent staying at a guesthouse a few miles away.

"Nothing significant, Dan, or I would have reported it," Ian Baldwin—Stable—answered from his workstation in Ember's Tactical Operations Center in Virginia. Dempsey pictured the tall lanky mathematician turned Ember Signals Director standing behind his two young analysts, Chip and Dale, monitoring feeds from the satellites tasked for the op.

"That's a good indicator that despite the boat's arrival, they're probably not meeting tonight," Dempsey said into the thin mike boom beside his mouth.

"I *did* predict the meeting would occur after sunrise, if you recall," Baldwin said.

"We all remember, Stable," Dempsey said.

"That prediction was based on what again?" Munn chimed in.

"I've tried to explain how the algorithms work, Dan," Baldwin said, using his only-mildly-exasperated voice and eschewing code names as usual. "It's just math."

Dempsey shook his head. It wasn't that Baldwin was undisciplined or sloppy; rather, he was so supremely confident in Ember's comms gear and their encryption protocols that he made a habit of chatting in the clear. On the one hand, Dempsey got it. He'd been more than used to playing by big-boy rules in his Tier One unit, but on the other hand, it just bugged him. Call-sign protocol was born from blood, like so many of the operational methodologies they employed.

"Stable, this is Mustang. Let's try to keep it tight tonight. Call signs only," Dempsey said.

After a cool beat, Baldwin came back: "Copy, Mustang."

"I've got good visuals now," Grimes said to Dempsey, her right eye glued to her scope. "One tango walking the port rail . . . two dudes on the stern, one smoking and one holding a rifle. They look like security." He watched her switch the high-tech scope from night vision to thermal. "On thermal I've got two, no, three tangos on the bridge—ship's captain perhaps sitting in the middle and two others facing him. Belowdecks I have four tangos. Wait, hold on a second—"

The tension in her voice and the way her body stiffened told him something unexpected had caught her attention.

"Make that five bodies belowdecks. Two of the five appear to be captive." She switched her headset to hot mike, and Dempsey heard her talking beside him and then half a beat later echoing in his left ear. "Stable, this is Mustang. Thermals suggest we might have hostages on the boat. Do you have any intel suggesting this meeting could be a prisoner swap?"

"There's been nothing in the previous comms between the parties to suggest that," Baldwin said. "Some of the data suggests a transaction is scheduled for this meeting, but we assumed it was financial . . . I suppose we could revisit the raw data with this new insight in mind."

"Translation—the Professor doesn't know," Munn growled, interpreting for the team. "What do you see, Mustang?"

"Two seated bodies on thermal," Grimes said. "Look like they're bound to chairs."

Grimes adjusted her scope and then looked up at Dempsey.

"Want me to take a look?" he asked.

"Yeah, please," she said, rolling onto her side, away from the rifle scope.

His eyes flicked to the scar below her armpit—still thick and red, but healing up nicely. He leaned in from the other side of the table to peer through the scope.

"I see your five tangos belowdecks—three walking with weapons slung on shoulders, and two seated hostages, side by side . . ." As he studied their postures and the shapes of their thermal signatures, his heart sank. He clicked the zoom detent up a notch on the scope. "And they both appear to be female."

Damn.

Hostages . . . the one and only complication guaranteed to throw their entire operational playbook into the garbage can. He straightened and began to pace. Disappearing al-Fahkoury was the mission objective, not hostage rescue. Hitting the yacht had never been part of the plan, yet his brain had already started working the problem anyway. Revised mission scenarios began populating his mind.

No, he thought, cutting himself off. *We can't let the mission get derailed.*

"Listen up, everybody," he announced on the comms channel. "I realize this changes things emotionally, but it doesn't change the mission. Stay on task. al-Fahkoury is our objective."

"Hold on," Munn barked. "Are you saying we're going to do nothing? We can't just let these assholes keep those girls and float away."

"I'm not saying that, but I'm also not saying we're going to change the OPORD, either," he said, trying to soften the blow. "We need to analyze the situation. I need options and risk assessment."

"Hang on . . . They're moving the girls," Grimes said from beside him, back on her rifle scope. "Five glowing bodies coming up a ladder well . . . the two women, two armed escorts with rifles, and a third dude . . . They're passing through the middeck salon, heading aft to the party deck and the hot tub, I presume."

"Bronco, do you have ears?" Dempsey asked.

"Good ears," Wang said, ditching his trademark sophomoric banter and now all business. "They're talking fast . . . laughing . . . That's not Arabic . . . I'm not sure what language they're using."

"Stream it to me, Bronco," Baldwin said calmly.

Dempsey raised his spotter scope and focused on the party deck. The women stood with stooped postures, heads down, arms hugging themselves. The man in the hot tub tipped his head back as if laughing at something.

"They're speaking Chechen," Baldwin reported.

"Chechen?" Wang asked, his voice tight. "That's weird."

"Stable, can you translate?" Dempsey asked.

"None of us speaks Chechen, but we're running the stream through a real-time translation program. Don't expect better than seventy percent accuracy."

"Fine, just give me the play-by-play," Dempsey barked.

"They look cold. Maybe they need to be warmed up," Baldwin said, relaying the translated audio from the yacht with a several-second delay. "But they don't be having swimsuits . . . That is okay. This we can fix . . ."

Through the scope, Dempsey watched as one of the laughing guards began to rip the clothes off the woman standing on the left.

"No, not that one, the pretty one . . ."

The guard shoved the woman to her knees, while the girl on the right swatted at the other guard pawing at her clothes—choosing instead to undress herself voluntarily.

Smart and brave. Better to get functional clothes back than shredded rags when this is all over, Dempsey thought as she climbed into the hot tub, covering her topless chest.

"Stable, can you get facial recognition from the bird?" Dempsey asked.

"The satellite is overhead now, so the angle is bad," Baldwin said. "Perhaps Elizabeth could—"

"Sending imagery to Bronco now," Grimes said, leaning into her scope, her body visibly tense at the scene unfolding. The scope was wirelessly connected to the tablet on the table beside her and would send digital pictures she snapped to an encrypted file on Wang's computer.

"Got it. Relaying . . ." Wang said.

The girl in the hot tub was sitting opposite her tormenter, as far away as possible. To Dempsey's relief, the heavily muscled dirtbag in the tub was not making a move toward her, just laughing, smoking, and drinking. If he had to guess, Dempsey would peg this jackass as the ringleader.

"Don't tell me we're letting this happen, Mustang," Munn said, his voice a wet fire.

"I could put a fucking round right through his fat face—even from here," Grimes murmured.

"Stay on task, people," Dempsey said, working to keep his voice calm despite feeling the exact same aggravation as Munn and Grimes.

"Well, well . . . looks like I have a match," Baldwin said, his voice taking on the air of a man perusing the jelly aisle at the grocery and finding the last jar of fig preserves.

"Just give it to us," Dempsey said.

"More than ninety-seven percent that is Sarah Bonney in the hot tub. The other woman has her back to us. If she turns, Elizabeth, be sure to get a picture."

"Roger that, *Stable*," she said, emphasizing his call sign to remind the Signals Chief he was slipping again, but Dempsey suspected Baldwin was oblivious to the subtext.

"Sarah Bonney—the British aid worker?" Wang asked.

"Yes. She's a pediatric surgeon. She and an American nurse, one Diana Curtis, disappeared from a refugee hospital run by Medecins Sans Frontieres in Tunisia nearly two months ago."

"Ten bucks says the other woman is Diana Curtis," Munn chimed in.

"A sound bet, statistically speaking of course," Baldwin came back.

"I remember that kidnapping," Dempsey grumbled, ignoring their banter. "Didn't AQIM claim responsibility?"

"Yes, Al Qaeda Islamic Maghreb issued a statement the next day," Baldwin said. "The attack left three wounded and two dead. CIA analysts tracked the group to a camp south of Ajdabiya. A joint French commando and US SEAL team hit the site forty-eight hours later, killing a few dozen terrorists, but Sarah and Diana were not found among the dead."

Dempsey silently cursed Baldwin for identifying these women and sharing their story. Names made it real. Backstory made it real. Staying on mission had been a bitter pill for him to swallow before, but now it was going to be gnaw-off-his-fingers impossible.

"So these girls definitely changed hands at least once," Dempsey said, rubbing his beard. "I'm not aware of regular contact between AQIM and any Chechen terror groups, though."

"I'm inclined to agree with you," Baldwin replied. "This is strange."

"We can't leave them, JD," Grimes said, talking off mike. "We just can't. Let me take the leader out."

With a word, she could send the asshole in the hot tub straight to hell, and probably the pair of guards, too. But even if Grimes was perfect on the WinMag, she wouldn't be able to headshot *everyone* on that boat. The bad guys who survived would cut anchor and run—killing the girls later and then dumping the bodies overboard. On top of that, the al-Fahkoury op would implode. al-Fahkoury would squirt, and it would be months, maybe years, before they got another shot at him.

"What are we gonna do?" Munn asked in his ear.

Dempsey said nothing as he watched the ringleader badger the girl in the hot tub into drinking champagne while the other woman rocked on the deck, hugging herself.

Son of a bitch.

"What is your tactical recommendation, Charger One? You're the strike lead." Dempsey knew Munn would see this as a test, but even a test would reveal where the man stood in his development as a team leader.

"Rescue op. I want to go get them, like right fucking now."

"Understood," Dempsey said. "But I didn't ask what you *wanted* to do. I asked for your tactical recommendation."

He hated the cold-ass son of a bitch he had become. He hated how knowing the big picture had made him a spook—a *Jones*, they would have called him back in the SEAL Teams. At times like these, he wished he was still a door kicker. It was so much easier to hate the higher-ups for making the unpopular call than to have to make the hard call himself.

"If we hit the yacht now, al-Fahkoury will squirt," Munn said in a tight, strained voice.

"That's right," Dempsey said. "But we have satellite coverage. We can track the yacht, notify the Italians, and they can sortie a rescue. It's not a lost cause, people. So unless anybody can convince me of a way to rescue the hostages without jeopardizing the al-Fahkoury op, we stay the course."

Grimes lifted her head and turned to look at him. He met her eyes. She didn't say anything; she didn't have to. He hated himself for making this call, but it was the right call.

"I have an idea," Munn said, his voice suddenly hopeful. "Let me come up and pitch it to you."

Of course you do, Dempsey thought, shaking his head. He glanced at his Suunto watch. Assuming Baldwin was right, which statistically he invariably was, they still had more than six hours until the sunrise meet. "All right. Come up and tell me what you've got."

"We have a positive ID on the other hostage," Baldwin suddenly announced. "Eighty-one percent confidence level she is Diana Curtis, mother of three from Canton, Ohio. Dale has just informed me her husband is a pastor. This was her first trip outside CONUS—a mission trip coordinated through her church."

"Wonderful, just what I *didn't* need to hear," Dempsey mumbled to himself as he began to pace. Whatever Munn's plan was, he hoped it had legs. Because despite the risk, despite the orders, Dempsey knew himself. When it came to making the hard choices, his heart always found a way to fuck things up.

CHAPTER 3

Dempsey glanced at his watch as al-Fahkoury's three-vehicle caravan pulled into the marina parking lot.

0730—right on time.

The driver's window of the lead Mercedes slid down, and June Latif—one of two new Ember recruits—walked up to talk to the driver. *This*, what they were doing right now, was the revised plan—Munn's plan—and it was insane. Insane enough that it might actually work. At least that's what Dempsey told himself. To grab al-Fahkoury *and* rescue the hostages on the yacht, they had no choice but to insinuate themselves into the middle of the bad guys' party. What Latif was doing right now, trying to convince al-Fahkoury that the plans had changed and that they would be playing escort on the water taxi, was the riskiest and most critical phase of the op. Latif had to succeed; otherwise, Ember would have no choice but to intervene prematurely, which virtually guaranteed an unsatisfactory outcome. While Latif negotiated, Dempsey forced himself into the slouch of a weary ditchdigger or tollbooth operator, body language that screamed, *I'm just a hired gun; they don't pay me enough to care.*

"It would appear that they have agreed to the terms," Baldwin said in his ear, summarizing the rapid-fire exchange in Arabic between Latif and al-Fahkoury's driver. A beat later, the rear passenger door of the middle vehicle, a black Land Rover, swung open, and al-Fahkoury stepped out. The terrorist was much younger than Dempsey had expected—no older than early thirties. Unlike so many of his jihadi counterparts whom Dempsey had hunted over the years, al-Fahkoury had eschewed the stereotypical gray tunic for hipster wear. His jet-black hair was coiffed David Beckham style, his beard short and meticulously trimmed. With his Persol sunglasses, expensive black loafers, and gray suit coat over a black T-shirt, the man didn't look like any terrorist Dempsey had crossed swords with before. Was this the new face of terror—a millennial mastermind waging war from an app on his mobile phone?

al-Fahkoury didn't even spare Dempsey a glance as he strode past, briefcase in hand, toward the marina below. Latif fell into conversation with one of al-Fahkoury's men and even managed to get the stern-faced bodyguard to smile at a joke. The former Green Beret officer had transitioned seamlessly into his role at Ember. And for missions like this one, Junayd Abd al-Latif, the only son of parents from the United Arab Emirates, was the perfect fit. Dempsey fell in at the back of the entourage, but immediately one of al-Fahkoury's goons slipped behind him to control the rear of the human caravan.

Three minutes later, the entourage reached the dock. The Damor water taxi had lines reminiscent of a thirty-one-foot Boston Whaler. Like the Whaler, this boat sat high in the water with a closed bow and tall pilot house. From amidships to the stern, it featured a generous open-air seating section, perfect for relaxing or fishing. The layout was ideal for what they had planned. Dempsey glanced up at the pilot house and resisted the urge to give a nod to Munn, who wore a faded blue fishing cap and manned the helm as the boat captain. al-Fahkoury paused on the dock, taking measure of the boat before boarding. Dempsey capitalized on his hesitation, stepped aboard the Damor, and took a corner position near the stern on the port side. Latif followed suit, taking up a mirror image position on the starboard side, and in doing so, they assumed tactical control of the vessel. Like two sentries at the corners of a courtyard, they now owned the space and could not be flanked by al-Fahkoury's men. This was a tactical gaff on al-Fahkoury's part, and the expression on the young hipster terrorist's face showed he recognized as much as he climbed aboard.

Not surprisingly, al-Fahkoury entered the pilot house and sat in the middle of a U-shaped bench seat on the port side. Munn gave the terrorist a cordial nod from where he sat with one ass cheek on the lip of a swiveling captain's chair. al-Fahkoury nodded back, then propped an ankle on a knee and held his black case in his lap. Two of his bodyguards took bookend positions, one on each side, but remained standing, rifles held at the ready. The third goon stood between Dempsey and Latif—a position that would not work well for him shortly. The remainder of al-Fahkoury's security detail stayed on shore—two men walking back toward their vehicles and one remaining on the dock.

Luca Martin, a former Marine who was playing Captain Dan's deckhand, cast off the lines and then hopped onto the bow as the Damor pulled away from the L-shaped pier. Martin scooted backward along the narrow gunwale outside the cockpit, nodding and smiling deferentially at everyone he passed on his way into the pilot house. Dempsey grunted and shook his head at the "lowly deckhand." Then he shifted his attention to the bay, scanning the surrounding water for other boats that might be converging on their position or the yacht. So far, things had gone smoothly—a little too smoothly—and now was about that time in an op when Mr. Murphy liked to throw him curveballs. Who the hell knew what either one of these terrorist organizations was planning? If Ember had unwittingly insinuated themselves in the middle of a trap laid by one party for the other, then they were screwed.

As long as we shoot first, he told himself, *it shouldn't matter.*

The five-minute ride from the marina out to the yacht went by in achingly slow motion. Dempsey had to fight back the need to be at combat ready when his cover required he look bored and nonthreatening. God, how he hated this spooky shit.

"Okay, boys," Grimes said through his earpiece from her sniper nest position back at the hotel. "Here's the roll call. al-Fahkoury is HVT One. His three guards are Tango One, Two, and Three, moving aft to forward. HVT Two is the boss from the hot tub earlier. The two shooters who've taken up position on the stern platform of the yacht are Yankee One and Two, port and starboard respectively. Yankee Three is the guy standing beside HVT Two on the party deck. In the bridge you've got the skipper and Yankee Four and Five. The two shooters with the hostages belowdecks are Yankee Six and Seven."

As Munn closed on the bigger vessel's stern from the starboard side, Dempsey forced himself to look away from the yacht, scanning for waterborne threats as he protected their "guest." The plan worked only if everyone made the proper assumptions—the bad guys on the yacht assumed that he and Latif were part of al-Fahkoury's security detail, while al-Fahkoury and his goons believed they'd been sent to escort him by HVT Two, a man Baldwin had identified as Malik from parsing pirated comms Wang had obtained during the night. Once the shooting commenced, Ember would exploit the precious few seconds of confusion before it became clear to both groups that they were unwanted party crashers.

Munn turned the bow of the Damor west and eased the starboard beam along the diving platform of the yacht, which presented the Damor's stern toward the beach and Grimes in her balcony room in the cliffside hotel. Dempsey noticed that Munn was taking his sweet time docking, giving Grimes plenty of opportunity to set up her shots. Martin moved back to the gunwale and threw the bow line to one of the Yankee shooters on the yacht's stern. The line landed limply on the deck at his feet. Grudgingly, the man released his weapon and bent to pick it up. Then he helped Martin ease the Damor alongside.

"Martin, you'll need to drop flat when the shooting starts to clear my lines," Grimes said, her voice tight. "Okay, here we go . . ."

Dempsey gripped his rifle and tapped his finger on the trigger guard, forcing himself to look anywhere but the yacht.

"Three . . ." Grimes said, starting the countdown.

Martin called for the yacht-shooter-turned-line-tender to take up slack.

"Two . . ."

The man on the platform barked something back in Arabic.

"One . . ."

A bullet streaked inbound, invisible but accompanied by a faintly audible whistle.

The line-tending shooter toppled over, hit the edge of the deck with a wet thud, then fell into the water. Dempsey turned to look aft. Everyone else froze in confusion, except Martin, who dropped low, and Latif, who charged forward into the pilot house. Someone hollered in Arabic. Then came another whistle, and Yankee Two's head exploded in a geyser of red and gray.

"Ahtami! Ahtami!" Dempsey hollered, still playing his role by ordering everyone to take cover. The man beside him, one of al-Fahkoury's goons, clutched at his neck after a .300 Winchester Magnum round from Grimes's death machine tore the front of his throat out. Dempsey felt wet spatter on the side of his face as he took a knee.

"Lines are bad on Tango Two and Three," Grimes said, referring to the guards flanking al-Fahkoury inside the pilot house. "Moving on to Yankee Three."

"What is happening?" one of the guards screamed in Arabic.

al-Fahkoury was on his knees, his case clasped to his chest.

"Take him below," Latif shouted, pointing to the hatch at the front of the pilot house that led to the small sleeping cabin in the bow.

The two bodyguards reacted immediately, pulling al-Fahkoury up and then pushing him toward the hatch. As they turned, Latif moved behind the guard on al-Fahkoury's left and raised his rifle just as Dempsey sighted on the man to al-Fahkoury's right. Latif nodded and they squeezed their triggers, delivering simultaneous headshots. al-Fahkoury whirled to look at Dempsey, his face ashen with shock and dismay.

Dempsey put the iron sight on the terrorist's forehead and smiled. "Mr. Jones, will you escort our guest belowdecks, please?" he said to Martin.

al-Fahkoury's eyes went wide with fear and recognition as he put together the pieces about what had just happened.

"My pleasure," the former Marine said and took al-Fahkoury by both arms, deftly whipped a nylon zip tie around the man's wrists, and then shoved the terrorist headfirst through the hatch and down into the Damor's berthing cabin.

"All right, fellas, let's do this," Dempsey said, whirling toward the yacht.

Munn wore a grin on his face but had fire burning in his eyes. He knelt, opened a compartment under the pilot console, and pulled out three tactical vests and an assault rifle. He tossed vests to Dempsey and Latif. The trio quickly kitted up and then moved in tactical crouches toward the stern while Martin stayed behind to guard al-Fahkoury.

"Two shooters moving aft on the yacht—Yankee Four and Five. HVT Two and Yankee Three are retreating, moving forward," Grimes called out. "My lines are bad. I only have one shot, the skipper on the bridge."

"Take him," Dempsey said. "Before he hits the throttle and breaks our connection."

Dempsey heard glass shatter as he climbed off the Damor onto the yacht's deck.

"Skipper is down. Four and Five are still amidships in cover positions. No shot."

"Boarding now," Munn replied, then, turning to Latif, said, "Call out to these guys. Sound panicked."

"Help!" Latif shouted in Arabic. "There's a small boat. They're shooting at us."

Dempsey took a knee and fired several two-round bursts into the open water. Munn squeezed off a burst as well.

"Eijal! Eijal!" Latif shouted. *Hurry! Hurry!*

"Yankee Four and Five just broke cover," Grimes said.

Dempsey pivoted inboard. One of the two shooters stepped into view, charging around the hot tub and scanning over his weapon but confused about where and whom he should be targeting. Dempsey dropped him with two rounds to the chest. A heartbeat later, the second shooter appeared, and Grimes dispatched him with a headshot.

"Yankee Four and Five are KIA," Grimes announced. "Three and HVT Two are moving through the topside salon. Recommend you pursue before they get belowdecks."

"Charger Three, how is the package?" Munn asked.

"HVT One is secure," Martin answered.

Munn nodded and then fell in beside Dempsey. They moved as a pair across the stern deck toward the sliding glass doors leading to a luxuriously appointed salon. Latif followed a stride behind. Ahead, two figures were fleeing, HVT Two in the lead, trailed by his lone remaining bodyguard.

"Musaeada!" Latif shouted, calling for help in Arabic, his voice tight with fear and panic.

The ploy had the desired effect, with Yankee Three hesitating just long enough for Munn to get off a shot. Munn's bullet hit the bodyguard center mass, sending him stumbling. Dempsey followed a split second later with a headshot, dropping the guard. Alone and with nowhere left to run or hide, HVT Two froze. Raising his hands in the air, the man identified as Malik slowly turned to face the assaulters who had just taken control of his yacht. Instead of fear, however, rage contorted Malik's face.

"Who the hell are you?" he said in English, a slight British accent masking something thicker underneath.

"On your knees," Munn commanded.

Staring daggers, Malik complied.

"I have movement belowdecks," Grimes reported on the comms channel. "One of the shooters is in the stairwell. Get ready . . . No, wait. He stopped . . . He's heading back to the stateroom with the hostages. He's securing the door . . ."

"Cuff this guy," Munn said to Latif, who pulled a pair of plastic flex-cuffs from his pocket. "Then we'll head below and take the others."

Dempsey turned to Munn. "We're gonna need to breach that room. How do you want to—"

A flash of movement in his peripheral vision cut him off. He looked right as the kneeling prisoner's hand snapped out with lightning speed to grab Latif's wrist. Malik twisted, spinning on his knees and jerking Latif off balance toward him. Latif went for his rifle with his free hand, but Malik was too fast and drove an elbow into the side of the young operator's head.

Dempsey surged into action, bringing the barrel of his weapon around for a kill shot. He squeezed the trigger, but Malik spun low, dropping under the line of fire, his body fluid and powerful like a wrestler on a mat. His left palm found the floor and his hips pivoted as if on a fulcrum, and he snapped a kick at Dempsey's leading leg. His heel connected—driving deep and hard into the meat of Dempsey's thigh, just barely missing his knee. The blow knocked Dempsey off balance and sent him pitching forward. As he tumbled, combat training took over. Instead of trying to catch himself, he rolled through the fall and scrambled into a combat crouch.

At the same time, Malik popped to his feet and snatched the pistol from the front of Latif's kit. Latif, still dazed from the blow to his head, didn't even react. Both men, Malik and Dempsey, brought the muzzles of their weapons to bear on the other, with Dempsey juking right as he squeezed the trigger. Malik's pistol discharged. Dempsey felt the bullet streak past his left cheek as his own round found its mark. He squeezed the trigger again and watched as his first bullet tore through Malik's jaw and the second blew out the center of the man's throat. The entire sequence had transpired in less than three seconds but felt a hundred times that long.

"What the fuck was that?" Munn said, surging toward the fallen shooter. Munn put another round through the man's forehead, then turned to help Latif.

The former Green Beret had taken a knee and was shaking his head. "What just happened?" he said through his breath.

"You got schooled, brother," Munn said. "That's what happened."

Munn glanced at Dempsey, jaw set and eyebrows up. Dempsey answered him with a curt nod, reading his friend's mind: the dead man was no lowly proxy for a money guy, the way they'd assumed. Moves like that were a product of experience and advanced combat training. Malik was somebody of consequence, but figuring out who that somebody was fell onto Baldwin's to-do list now. Dempsey had a more urgent problem to deal with—the hostages.

"Everyone okay?" Grimes asked in his ear.

"All good," Dempsey said. "HVT Two is KIA." He turned to Latif. "Take a few breaths, clear those stars, and tell me when you're ready."

Latif did as instructed, pressed to his feet, and said, "Let's do this."

Dempsey turned to his team leader. "How do you want to do this?"

"Mustang, Charger One," Munn said to Grimes. "Gimme the skinny."

"I hold four warm bodies in a stateroom. The two hostages are bound to chairs, and the two armed shooters look to be taking cover behind them," Grimes reported.

"Which side of the ship, port or starboard?"

"I have a broadside view of the yacht and no depth perspective to work with at present," Grimes said. "It's hard to tell with thermals, but if I had to guess, I'd say starboard."

"This sucks, dude," Munn said to Dempsey. "We have to stealth approach through the corridor, we're not positive what side they're on, they're using the girls as human shields so we can't just hose them down on the breach. The bulkheads on commercial vessels are thin. There's nothing to stop them from cutting us to ribbons in the hall, especially if we kick in the wrong door. This is fucking dangerous, JD."

"Yeah, well, it's a dangerous job," Dempsey said with a thin fatalistic smile. "You don't have to tell me. I've been doing this every day for twenty years, and I didn't take a ten-year hiatus to play doctor and dole out pills to kids with VD."

Munn flashed Dempsey a quintessential *You're such an asshole* smirk. "All right, then. Here's the plan . . ."

After briefly conferring, Munn took the lead as he, Dempsey, and Latif approached the oval hatch at the end of the salon. On the other side of the hatch, a narrow stairwell led to the sleep quarters below. Dempsey sighted over Munn's shoulder as they descended, careful not to make any noise. The stairway opened into the middle of a narrow corridor stretching parallel to the keel. He counted six stateroom cabin doors—three port, three starboard—and a single door at the end of the passage.

"That room at the end of the corridor appears to be a bathroom," Grimes said, reading his mind. "Third door on your right, I think that's where they are."

Munn looked at Dempsey, eyebrows raised in query.

Dempsey gave a single nod.

Let's do this.

They advanced, slinking silently over the carpeted passage in a low crouch. As they moved toward the third stateroom on the right, Munn's warning from minutes ago played in Dempsey's head: *The bulkheads on commercial vessels are thin. There's nothing to stop them from cutting us to ribbons in the hall, especially if we kick in the wrong door . . .*

The passage creaked behind him, spiking his heart rate. He stopped and glanced over his shoulder. Latif, who was frozen midstride, wore a pained look on his face, and Dempsey imagined Ember's newest member silently cursing the floor supports. The next three seconds would tell if they would be punished with an enemy strafe through the walls that cut them all down. When it didn't happen, he signaled for Latif to take it slow and turned back to Munn. The doc had maintained his stealth, advanced past the target door, and now stood with his back pressed against the bulkhead. Dempsey moved into position on the other side of the door.

"No changes with thermals," Grimes said softly. "I hold the three of you in the passage and the four warm bodies in the stateroom. The yacht has drifted, and I have a better angle. Confirm starboard side."

In Dempsey's mind's eye, he could see her stretched out on the table, her body one with the sniper rifle as she watched their heat signatures through the scope.

"It's not a wide stateroom," she continued. "The hostages are seated facing the door, chairs nearly pushed together, shoulder to shoulder. Both shooters are kneeling behind them, aiming around the outside shoulder of each woman—the left shooter is far left; the right shooter is far right."

Dempsey double tapped the corner of his jawbone next to his ear canal to send a "double click" acknowledgment via the bone-conduction, wireless earbud. Then he gave Munn the hand signal to set a breacher charge. The former SEAL surgeon silently went to work. After the charge was set, Munn looked up and grinned. It was a grin born from a thousand operations, in a thousand shitty places, where the two of them had narrowly avoided meeting their maker a thousand different times. It was a grin that said, *I love this shit, and it's definitely going to kill me someday, but I don't think that day is today.* And it was a grin that said, *By God, whatever it takes, I'm going to rescue the hostages on the other side of this door.*

Dempsey grinned back.

He held up three fingers and began counting down. On one, Munn detonated the charge. The cabin door exploded, sending shards of melamine and foam core insulation everywhere. Screams filled the air as Dempsey followed Munn through the door and into the room while Latif covered them from the passageway. The scene was just as Grimes had described. One shooter was crouched to the left, holding an assault rifle, using his hostage as a human shield while he squinted and tried to clear his vision. The right-side shooter was armed with a pistol but had taken a different tack. While clutching the woman's torso from behind, he had his cheek pressed against her left ear and the muzzle of his pistol jammed under her chin.

Two loud pops echoed to Dempsey's left as Munn dispatched his target with a double tap to the head. Dempsey fixed his aim on the center of the other terrorist's forehead but didn't pull the trigger. *Not yet,* he told himself. *Work the angle.* He had zero separation between the hostage's and the terrorist's heads. He needed a straight line; every eighth of an inch mattered.

"Let her go," Dempsey said, his voice cool and collected. "If you let her go, I won't shoot you."

"Get out, or I kill her," the man threatened in heavily accented English, his eyes darting back and forth between Dempsey and Munn.

"Everyone else is dead. Malik is dead," Dempsey said, taking a cautious step forward and drifting slightly inboard to get a perfectly straight line. "There's no one left to help you. There's nowhere to go."

"I kill her, I kill her, I swear," the shooter said, sweat pouring from his brow.

Dempsey's gaze ticked to the pistol pressed under the woman's neck, checking whether the shooter's index finger was on the trigger or the guard. Seeing it on the guard, he exhaled, stilled his targeting dot, and squeezed the trigger. His M4 roared, spit fire, and the bullet punched a hole in the center of the shooter's forehead. The terrorist pitched backward; his pistol clattered to the floor.

The hostage on the left, the older of the two women, promptly passed out, going limp in her restraints and sliding partway to the floor. The woman on the right met Dempsey's gaze, smiled, and then began to tremble uncontrollably in her chair.

"Clear," Dempsey hollered.

"Clear," Munn replied.

He moved quickly behind the hostages, confirmed that his bullet had ended his target, and then kicked the pistol to the corner out of reach.

"Hostages are secure," Munn reported over the comms channel.

"Sarah Bonney and Diana Curtis?" Dempsey said, looking at the younger of the two women as Munn knelt to revive the other hostage.

"Yes," she said, a tear spilling onto her cheek. "I'm Sarah. Are you Navy SEALs?"

A nostalgic smile spread across his face. When he'd been with Tier One, they'd had a mantra they used in situations like this, words he hadn't had the joy and privilege of saying in what felt like an eternity: *We're Navy SEALs, and we're here to take you home.* Those days were long gone, but as he crouched to cut off her restraints, he said the next best thing: "We're American operators, and we're here to take you home."

CHAPTER 4

Somewhere . . .

Without explanation or provocation, they beat her.

In the aftermath, she writhed on the floor and wept.

Amanda had never been hit before. Not really. Sure, there was the infamous Allen "spanking incident" when she was six, when her father had lit up her backside after Amanda had defied instructions and run away to play unsupervised in the neighborhood. But this was something entirely different. A man had bludgeoned her with closed fists and kicks, and the acute pain and trauma delivered by each blow redefined in her psyche what it meant to suffer. The pain was only compounded by the trauma she'd suffered from the explosion during the attack in Ankara. In television and film, heroes got pummeled with obscene regularity only to recover moments later with a wince and a glib wisecrack. That was a fantasy. A half hour or more had passed since her bludgeoning, and she was still a wreck on the floor. The pain made it difficult to think clearly, and a primitive reflex had usurped her wits during the event so that she'd cowered like an animal and begged for mercy.

Yes, she would be compliant.

Yes, she would do whatever they commanded her to do . . . so long as the man with the broken front tooth and the dead eyes didn't beat her again.

The two places that hurt the most were her abdomen and her left eye socket. The baseball-size hematoma on the side of her face made it difficult for her to ascertain by touch if the bones of her face were broken. Probably. Her abdomen, however, concerned her more. She had no medical training, but she'd watched enough *Grey's Anatomy* to know that the stuff on the inside—stomach, intestines, liver, pancreas, kidneys—was all pretty important.

Right now, her list of wants and needs was short—not being tortured and beaten again was the top entry, with not dying a close second.

She stopped crying, and eventually she was able to lie still in a heap of misery. More time passed—she didn't know how much—and she managed to sit up. She coughed, cleared her throat, and spit a gob of bloody phlegm onto the floor beside her. She probed the side of her face, wincing as she did. She moved her jaw around and decided that maybe her face wasn't broken after all.

To call the space she was in a room would be an exaggeration; it seemed more like a large plywood closet. The floor was dirty and stained. The dark reddish-brown spots were dried blood, she knew, and the rest, she presumed, had been made by other bodily fluids from previous *guests*. The windowless walls were bare and unpainted. The only light came from a single low-wattage bulb dangling overhead. A dingy metal bucket stood upright in the corner to her left. She was thirsty—so very, very thirsty—and she debated making the short crawl to the bucket to check it for water. But the fly buzzing near the rim told her it wasn't worth the effort. It wasn't a water pail.

She swallowed, tasted blood in her mouth, and started to sob again.

God, my brain is mush . . . I suppose getting blown up and hit in the head repeatedly will do that to a person. I probably have a TBI.

She'd been through a mini-SERE module at the Farm, but the purpose of the training had been familiarization, not preparation. Her diplomatic post was supposed to keep her insulated from scenarios where she'd need to utilize "survive, evade, escape, and resist" methodologies. Yes, she worked for the CIA, but she was not an operator; she was just a Collection Management Officer, whose job was to serve as a bridge between the intelligence "collectors" in the field abroad and the intelligence community back home. Sometimes that meant running her own assets in the host nation, but that activity was not supposed to be dangerous. She wasn't meant to be in situations like this. She wasn't meant to be in places like this.

Footsteps sounded outside. Dread instantly settled over her like a lead blanket. Next, she heard fingers fiddling with the padlock on the metal latch on the outside of the door. She scrambled into the corner.

It's too soon, she pleaded silently. *Too soon for the man with the broken tooth and dead eyes to come back.*

She hadn't told him anything the first time, but he hadn't asked her any questions, either. It was her welcome beating—a little something to set expectations and establish the ground rules. But they would ask her questions. They would try to extract information from her. And they would succeed. Everyone broke eventually . . . everyone.

She heard the lock being pulled from the latch.

Her body began to tremble.

The door swung open and bright light bathed the cell, making her squint. A backlit figure stood in the doorway—medium height, narrow shoulders, wearing a head scarf. This was not the man with the broken tooth and the dead eyes; her visitor was a woman. Amanda's heart rate immediately slowed. The woman stepped into the cell and handed her a bottle of water.

"Drink," she said in Turkish-accented English.

Amanda reached up and took the water bottle. With clumsy fingers, she unscrewed the plastic cap and raised the spout to her lips. She took a tentative first sip; warm water wet her tongue. The taste was odd and coppery, but it was drinkable. She drank a third of the contents while keeping her gaze on the woman. Her stern, cold expression did nothing to warm Amanda's spirits.

"Do you speak English?" Amanda asked between sips. She'd worked hard to become fluent in Turkish, completing the Defense Language Institute immersion course before posting to Ankara. Once in country, she'd hired a private tutor to accelerate her understanding of dialects and colloquial speech. The hard work had paid off, and she was nearly fluent in the spoken language now. She didn't reveal this information to her captors. Their assumption that she was monolingual was one of the few exploits she had available to her.

The woman did not answer. Instead, she kneeled and leaned in to inspect the hematoma on the side of Amanda's face, grasping Amanda's chin between thumb and forefinger and turning it to the side to get a better look.

"My name is Amanda Allen," she said. "I'm an American citizen."

The woman said nothing.

"I work for the US State Department in Turkey."

The woman ignored her as she took out a penlight and shined it in Amanda's eyes—

Checking for pupil dilation, Amanda thought.

"Open your mouth," the woman said.

"What?"

"Open your mouth."

Amanda did so and the woman looked inside.

"You have a broken teeth?"

"No, I don't think so. Are you a doctor?"

"Lay down," the woman said, avoiding eye contact.

Amanda did as she instructed. The woman pulled up Amanda's shirt and checked her rib cage and then palpated her abdomen. When the exam was finished, the woman got to her feet and turned to leave.

"Wait," Amanda said, sitting up quickly and wincing for it. "What's your name?"

The woman stopped at the door, turned back, and stared down at Amanda with callous judgment, as if she were a pathetic creature.

"Will you help me?" Amanda asked. "Please."

"Drink" was all the woman said, and then she closed and locked the door behind her.

Amanda's spirits sank. Was the woman a nurse or a doctor the terrorists had conscripted to check on her? Or maybe the woman was a member of whichever terrorist organization had taken her. ISIS had found some success recruiting women into their operational ranks. Was ISIS behind the attack in Ankara? Her instincts said no. The Islamic State specialized in terrorizing civilians. Its modus operandi was to inflict maximum carnage in public places, thereby inciting fear and chaos. This operation had specifically targeted the US Ambassador and a Turkish Interior Minister. It was politically motivated.

She suddenly felt ill.

A beat later, she vomited. The heaving sent searing pain across her flank and rib cage. *I must have broken a rib,* she thought, buckled over and panting. On hands and knees, she stared at the little puddle of vomit in front of her. It was mostly water. A third of the precious water they'd given her was now wasted, and it made her mad.

I'm going to have to drink slower . . . spread out my sips and pace myself.

When the nausea passed, she eased back onto her haunches and then gingerly leaned against the wall. Staring at the locked plywood door, she resisted the compulsion to zone out. She needed to keep her mind active. Observation, data collection, analysis, and the communication of information and disinformation—these were the weapons of her trade. Despite the pain and the weariness, she had to put her skills to use at every opportunity.

If that woman comes back, I need to try to make a connection, get her to care about me. I need to collect as much information as possible: Where am I, who took me, and why?

That last piece of information was the most critical. They'd killed the Ambassador but taken her. Why? It didn't make any sense. Her mind was sluggish, but eventually the gears began to turn: Scenario one, her kidnapping had been an opportunistic decision. She was young, Western, and reasonably attractive, which made her a valuable commodity for human trafficking. Scenario two, they knew who her father was, which made her a valuable ransom candidate. In both scenarios, their objective would be the same—trade her for money. Every terrorist organization needed to raise capital. It was the most logical explanation for why she, and she alone, had been spared.

But there was a third scenario, one she was afraid to even contemplate.

What if they had taken her because her official cover had been compromised? Because they knew she was CIA?

What if *she*, not the Ambassador, had been the target of the operation?

CHAPTER 5

National Counterterrorism Center (NCTC)
Liberty Crossing
McLean, Virginia
May 5
0230 Local Time

Kelso Jarvis sneezed and barely got the handkerchief up in time to cover his face. "Excuse me," he said as he made his way down the corridor toward the briefing room.

"Bless you," said his Chief of Staff, Petra Felsk. Several others traveling in his wake, including his Deputy Director of Intelligence Integration, Catherine Morgan, echoed her.

"Damn cold," he grumbled and stuffed the handkerchief back into his pocket.

From a SOPMOD M4–carrying Tier One operator to a watery-eyed bureaucrat with a hanky. How the hell did this happen?

This self-deprecating sentiment was a gross simplification of his evolution, however. Jarvis was not just any old watery-eyed bureaucrat.

He was the Director of National Intelligence—the highest ranking official in the US intelligence community, responsible for overseeing the budget, operational priorities, and collection activities of the nation's sixteen separate intelligence agencies. The CIA, Defense Intelligence Agency, NSA, and intelligence departments of each branch of the US military all worked for him, making Kelso Jarvis the second most powerful man in America. Which was why not a day went by since he'd accepted the appointment that he didn't wake up contemplating whether today would be the day he quit.

"The late-spring bugs are the worst," said Reginald Buckingham, the Director of the NCTC, walking on Jarvis's left. "My personal theory is that they've had all winter to fly under the radar and cross-pollinate with all the other germs. They wait until all the regular cold and flu bugs have run their course, then they strike, catching everybody by surprise."

"It's just a cold, Reggie," Jarvis said, suppressing the urge to hack up a throatful of phlegm, "not some virus conspiracy."

Despite the bleary-eyed hour, everyone in earshot laughed.

God, he hated that—the sycophantic fawning that his presence spawned. The jibe wasn't that funny, but because he was the DNI, they laughed—laughed at the Director of the NCTC, a man they would never laugh at under normal circumstances. This was how pecking orders were reinforced. Jarvis had no choice but to capitalize on these innocuous little opportunities whenever they presented themselves. Not because he wanted to, but because he had to. He was the chief. He was the boss. Every little test of his authority needed to be acknowledged and deftly dissuaded. Yet he also needed to engender loyalty, honesty, and respect from his subordinates. Reggie Buckingham was a smart, capable Director. As such, Jarvis would never berate, undermine, or question the man's decisions or abilities in a strategic or operational setting. When it mattered, Jarvis built his people up—leaving occasions like this, when it didn't, to knock them down.

His persona as DNI was different from his persona as Director of Ember, just as his persona as Director of Ember had been different from his persona as a Tier One SEAL unit commander. Quality leadership was like a finely tailored suit, he knew, not a one-size-fits-all garment. What motivated a Navy SEAL operating downrange was very different from what motivated a junior CIA analyst in Langley, which was in turn very different from what motivated a senior "career" civil servant in DC. And Jarvis, while not a psychologist by training, was very much a lifelong student of human psychology and had spent his entire professional career reading people and fine-tuning his actions and behavior.

Jarvis entered the conference room and took the seat at the head of the table. After the doors had shut but before everyone else had found their seats, he said, "I know it's late, and I know everyone is exhausted, but your attendance here speaks volumes. Make no mistake, what happened in Ankara was not just a random act of terrorism. This was a premeditated attack against the United States and against Turkey, our most important NATO ally in the region. US Ambassador Bailey, Turkish Minister Demicri, and dozens of innocent citizens are dead. On top of that, we have an American who is missing and presumed in enemy hands. Every minute counts, people, so bring me up to speed. What are the new developments since the last brief?"

"Unfortunately, sir, we still have more questions than answers," Buckingham began. "No credible source has taken ownership of the attack."

"Has a ransom demand for Amanda Allen been made yet?" Petra asked, seated at Jarvis's right.

"Not yet."

"Do we think this was ISIS?" Jarvis asked.

"Our data suggests that ISIS activity in Turkey peaked with last year's New Year's Eve nightclub attack in Istanbul. We've witnessed a declining taper since then as the multiple active campaigns against

ISIS—ours, Iraqi, Kurdish, and Russian-backed Syrian offensives—have fractured the caliphate and hampered their command and control."

"So are we ruling out ISIS?" Catherine Morgan interjected.

"Not categorically, but operating and loitering in Turkey has become a lot more difficult for ISIS over the past twelve months."

"What does Ankara have to say on the matter?" Jarvis asked. "Have we talked to anyone at Turkish National Intelligence?"

"They're being extremely tight-lipped," Buckingham said. "Not a lot of sharing going on by Turkish MIT at the moment. Relations are strained, and we know it's being driven from the top. Recent personnel changes aren't helping, either. Some of our best allies in MIT have been sidelined or pushed out. Thankfully, Ankara Police are still talking to us—at least until Erodan shuts that down, too. Someone at OGA must have called in a favor with the Ankara Chief of Police because this evening we got street-cam video footage of the attack, which is how we confirmed Amanda Allen survived the blast and was abducted."

"Did anyone pop on facial recognition in the video?" Petra asked.

"We're still working on that."

"If it's not ISIS, I would start with the Kurdistan Freedom Hawks," Jarvis said. "TAK has been active with recent attacks in both Ankara and Istanbul."

"Yes, sir, that's true, and TAK is high on our list of suspects. We're also looking at PKK, YPG, and other armed activist factions pursuing Kurdish autonomy," the NCTC Director said. "As you are undoubtedly aware, two years ago, PKK launched the Peoples' United Revolutionary Movement with the stated aim of overthrowing the Turkish government. By our count, there are no less than nine factions who count themselves as members, including several Marxist-Leninist and Communist terror groups. Even though the individual factions' specific ideological objectives differ, they all agree that the Erodan regime needs to fall. Seventy percent of attacks in Turkey last year were promulgated by these PKK-affiliated groups."

"Both TAK and YPG have disavowed links to PKK," Catherine Morgan said.

"Intelligence suggests otherwise," Buckingham replied with a tight smile.

"The newly completed wall along the Syrian border has been a major impediment to the movement of Kurdish personnel in and out of southeastern Turkey," Petra said, looking from Buckingham to Jarvis. "And the Turkish military has been conducting offensives across the border into Syria, directly striking Kurdish rebel strongholds in Afrin and Manbij. Yesterday's attack in Ankara could be an act of retribution."

"CIA has a well-placed asset in PKK—Barakat, I believe is his name," Jarvis said, looking to Morgan. "Have we heard anything from him?"

"We've not had a report for six weeks," she said, her eyebrows rising with apparent surprise at her boss's by-name knowledge of this asset. "In fact, this is the longest he's ever gone dark. CIA is worried about him."

Jarvis scanned the room, looking for a familiar face from Langley. Not seeing one, he said, "Is everyone here yours, Reggie?"

Buckingham did a quick scan of his own and nodded. "Yes, sir."

"Why is no one from Langley here?"

"Well, it's late. But we've been dialoguing with them from the beginning," Buckingham said and folded his arms across his chest. "I realize this meeting doesn't feel interagency, but I assure you we're talking to all the right people."

"Amanda Allen is CIA," Jarvis said. "Everyone here knows that, right?"

He got nods back from around the table, but no comments.

"Who's looking for her on the ground?" he asked.

"Langley is on it," Buckingham said. "Ground branch is looking for her."

"That's not good enough," Jarvis said, both annoyed and flabbergasted. "Whoever took Allen is going to move her out of country. It might have happened already. This needs to be a coordinated effort so we can bring all the resources of the intelligence community to bear."

"Agreed," Buckingham said. Then, after an uncomfortable beat and an obvious effort not to look at Catherine Morgan: "But to be completely honest, sir, we wanted to see which direction you wanted to take things. My predecessor was let go for overstepping his bounds. Given the highly political and sensitive nature of this event, we weren't sure if you wanted CIA or DIA to take the lead? Or maybe you'd prefer to task that black-vapor task force of yours. NCTC has stepped on all kinds of toes the past couple of years, and I don't want to keep making the same mistakes."

Jarvis resisted the urge to scowl. He resisted the urge to sigh, to curse, to condemn, or to use sarcasm. Reggie Buckingham had just been brazenly honest with him and highlighted the exact reason Jarvis had started Ember in the first place—institutional paralysis perpetuated by bullshit rice-bowl mentalities and supersize bureaucrat egos. The oblique reference to his predecessor's firing by Catherine Morgan during her short tenure as acting DNI was not lost on Jarvis, either. That single act of perceived retribution against his predecessor for protecting Ember had left a mark on Buckingham's psyche. It was astonishing to Jarvis that the Director of the NCTC, one of the top posts in the counterterrorism community, had chosen to handcuff himself rather than face professional admonishment.

In his peripheral vision, Jarvis noted Catherine's jaw set in hard, silent discord. "Your predecessor was put in an impossible situation, Reggie," Jarvis said calmly. "I'm going to try not to do that with you."

Buckingham nodded but offered no other reply.

"All right, folks, let's take a ten-minute break," Jarvis said, pulling out his handkerchief to wipe his runny nose. Then, turning to Buckingham, he quietly added, "Reggie, why don't you give CIA Director Barrett a call at home. Tell him that the DNI was disappointed that neither he nor any of his deputies were in attendance at this meeting."

"Yes, sir," Buckingham said, nodding and red-faced.

"And ask your people to give me, Petra, and Catherine the room for a few minutes."

"Roger that," the NCTC Director said and turned to make it happen.

When the room was theirs, Jarvis exhaled loudly and looked back and forth between the two women he considered to be the brightest and most capable people on his staff, his gaze ultimately settling on Catherine. "What's our exposure with Allen?"

"She's green," Morgan said, not missing a beat. "She's only been in the position four months. From what I can gather, she's smart and early feedback was positive; Clandestine Services had high hopes for her. She's read into most of our operations in the region."

"How big is her stable of collection assets?"

"Pretty big. Her predecessor was Mike Hughes. Do you know Mike?"

"No," Jarvis said.

"Well, he left behind some big shoes to fill. Mike was very aggressive in Turkey, spending most of his tenure developing assets. If she was a hard study and committed her network to memory, it could be a problem for us if they break her."

"That's assuming her cover was blown and she was the target of the operation," Petra interjected. "I find that scenario unlikely."

"So you think she was a target of opportunity?" Morgan asked.

"Not even—I think she was an acquisition of opportunity," said Petra. "A spur-of-the-moment decision."

"There's been no ransom demand yet. Do we think the assholes that took her know who her father is?" Jarvis said.

"The story broke; it's all over the news. If they didn't know before, they most certainly do now," Petra said.

"Has the Chief Justice made a statement yet?" he asked.

"No," said Petra and Catherine in unison.

He nodded. "Good. I want to be in control of the narrative. Petra, can you reach out to Justice Allen and set up a meeting with him tomorrow—er, I mean, this morning? We also need to get someone from the Joint Hostage Recovery Task Force in the loop here. Make sure it's someone good."

"Understood. Will do," Petra said.

"Regardless of the optics, we have to get Allen back. Whoever did this murdered the US Ambassador in broad daylight in downtown Ankara. They're obviously intent on making a very loud statement on the global stage, and I'll be damned if I let them execute Allen on YouTube," Jarvis growled. "It's just us now, so I want your unfiltered opinions. Who do you think took her?"

"My money is on TAK," Morgan said. "They have been the most active terrorist group in Turkey over the past five years, and their MO is bombing police and civilian targets in major cities. Just a month ago, they released a statement reiterating that, and I quote, 'all the cities of Turkey are our battlegrounds,' and that their 'actions will be more intense than in the past.' They've also stated that the recent Turkish offensives in Syria against Kurdish settlements would not go unpunished."

Jarvis nodded, then looked to Petra.

"My money is on PKK," she said.

"Why?"

"They have the most resources, and they have an active intelligence collection apparatus inside Turkey. Despite publicly renouncing the use of terrorist tactics, I think they're escalating. And that's not to say this attack wasn't executed by TAK or one of the other factions, but I believe PKK is driving this bus."

"The common thread I'm hearing from both of you is *escalation*. Erodan is going after the Kurds—no ifs, ands, or buts about it—and the Kurds are fighting back. Still, how TAK or PKK could pull off an attack like this is perplexing to me . . ." Jarvis rubbed his temples. "It would have required dedicated advance ISR—with spotter teams and assets running interference. Maybe PKK has evolved to that level of sophistication, I don't know, but we can worry about the how later. Right now, we need to focus on two things: one, finding and rescuing Allen, and two, figuring out who is responsible and what they're planning next. Because mark my words, something else is coming. I can feel it."

"Agreed," Petra said. "So we have a decision to make. Do we let CIA manage Allen's recovery effort, do we take over and put together a joint task force, or do we simply use Ember?"

Tasking Ember was the most expedient solution. It was the easy answer to a difficult problem, but that didn't make it the right answer. Jarvis sighed with frustration. "Honestly, my immediate inclination is to pick up the phone and conference Shane Smith into this meeting right now. But . . ."

"*But* to ignore the systemic dysfunction we're witnessing between CIA, DIA, NCTC, and State would be a failure of leadership—a failure of *our* leadership," Morgan said.

He met her gaze. Was this the new Catherine Morgan talking or the old one? He knew how she felt about Ember. This was the very woman who one year ago had informed him that her first act, were she confirmed as permanent DNI, would be to disband America's premier black-ops task force. In an ironic twist of fate, the President had appointed Jarvis as DNI, not Morgan. Instead of firing her, Jarvis had made her his Deputy Director of Intelligence Integration. Since she'd been the one complaining most loudly about silo operations and compartmentalized activities within the IC, he'd decided to put her in charge of implementing policies and structures to address interagency dysfunction. Thus far, she'd made very little progress.

Now wasn't the time to rebuke her, so he simply said, "You are correct in saying that a failure to try to bring order and improvement to the current system would be a failure in leadership. But leadership is also about recognizing the difference between emergency surgery and rehabilitation. This is emergency surgery, and Ember is our crash team on standby. I'm sorry, but we don't have a choice. I'm tasking Ember."

He slipped his hand into his pocket, retrieved his mobile phone, and sent a secure SMS to Shane Smith:

Where is Ember SAD right now?

The response came almost instantly.

Croatia. They just nabbed al-Fahkoury and rescued two hostages.

Good. Have you heard about Turkey?

Yes. Do you have tasking for us?

Wrap up, head to Incirlik, and find Amanda Allen.

Roger.

We'll send you all the intel we have, but you have authority to requisition whatever resources you need.

Roger that, standing by.

Jarvis set his phone on the conference table and looked from Petra to Catherine and back again.

"It was the right call to make," Petra said with a nod.

"I know," he said as a grim foreboding washed over him. "But for Amanda Allen's sake, I just hope we're not too late."

CHAPTER 6

***Luxury Yacht* La Traviata**
Adriatic Sea
Twenty-Six Miles Southwest of Dubrovnic
May 5
1130 Local Time

Dempsey stood on the bow of the yacht, scanning the blue depths of the Adriatic as they cruised in open water.

Five minutes, he'd told them. *Just give me five minutes of solitude.*

And they had.

He inhaled deeply and let the energy of the sea recharge his soul. Most people feared the ocean. Few beachgoers ever waded beyond waist-deep, and never at night. When he'd gone through BUD/S, the instructors had made his cohort watch the movie *Jaws* before a five-mile swim in the shark-infested waters around San Clemente Island. The message wasn't to fear the ocean. It was that, for a SEAL, the sea was an ally. It was escape. It was victory. Get to the surf, fin out beyond the break water, and the ocean would swallow you up and conceal you from enemies seeking to destroy you. The nostalgic allure was so powerful, he suddenly felt a compulsion to slip over the railing and disappear, leaving the hamster wheel of missions, responsibility, and killing behind.

It would never happen.

Some dumbass has to run in the hamster wheel, he thought with a chuckle. *Might as well be me.*

"SDV is en route from the *Illinois*," Munn said in his ear from the bridge, where he was once again at the controls playing skipper. "Five mikes."

"Check—Charger Three, bring up the package."

Two double clicks in his ear told him Latif had heard him. Dempsey scanned the horizon looking for a periscope, which he knew was nearby playing peek-a-boo with the rolling waves. The USS *Illinois*—a Virginia-class fast-attack nuclear submarine—was waiting for their arrival. He felt the yacht slow to idle as Munn eased off the throttles. Belowdecks, Martin had been seeing to the rescued hostages, who, despite being a little dehydrated and undernourished, were in physically good condition. Psychologically, however, the women had a long road ahead.

Latif had been assigned to watch al-Fahkoury while they transited. After "the event" with Malik, Dempsey had given Latif the babysitting assignment on purpose—as a show of confidence, but also to make the point never to underestimate an enemy, no matter how benign the perceived risk.

With one final deep breath, Dempsey said goodbye to the sea, turned on a heel, and marched aft. He gave Munn a ball-cap salute as he walked past the bridge and the salon toward the party deck. He circled the hot tub and stepped over Malik—whose body was wrapped like a mummy in a bedspread from the main cabin, held in place by paracord. Dempsey pursed his lips and stared at the corpse. Two decades fighting jihadi terrorists and he had never encountered one who'd transformed like this dude. The speed, the way he'd capitalized on a moment of inattention, the look in his eyes. Malik had executed his escape attempt like a professional soldier. Which was why Dempsey had made the call to hand the corpse over instead of sinking it when they scuttled *La Traviata*.

Dempsey bent at the waist, grabbed several strands of paracord, and dragged the corpse across the party deck and down a few short steps to the stern platform at the very back of the yacht, the dead man's head conking each tread as he did. Once on the platform, he shoved the body against the hull so it wouldn't accidently roll overboard. Behind him, he heard commotion and looked up to see Latif leading a hunched and shuffling al-Fahkoury toward him. The terrorist's wrists and ankles were bound, and he wore a black hood over his head.

"How's our new friend doing?" he said to Latif.

"He has little to say," Latif answered. "Nothing, in fact."

"Well, what a good little soldier of the jihad," Dempsey said, climbing the half flight of steps to join them. He patted the terrorist on the shoulder, and the man recoiled. "We need to get our friend all set for his swim."

Latif looked up at him, brows arched. "We're not going to . . ."

"Yeah, we are," Dempsey said, flashing the Green Beret a sly grin. "So he'll need a HEEDs bottle."

Latif shook his head and chuckled. "Okaaaay, but what if he runs out of air?"

"Then I guess their corpsman will just have to revive him."

Latif gave him a *You're a sick bastard, you know that?* look and then marched off to get the emergency breathing apparatus Dempsey had requested. Dempsey turned his attention back to the sea and scanned for signs of the SDV—the minisub used by SEALs to travel to the target while their host submarine loitered off the coast in deeper water. If he squinted, he thought he could just make out a shadowy silhouette fifty yards off the stern.

"You should have visual on the SDV any second, JD," Munn said in Dempsey's ear.

"Check," he said.

"They'll ask for John. You authenticate 'India' and make the handoff."

Latif returned holding a HEEDs III emergency-egress compressed-air bottle, just as Dempsey was maneuvering al-Fahkoury down to the stern platform. A stream of bubbles surfaced just off the deck, and a beat later, two SEALs in full combat load and dive gear broke the surface. One kicked back a few yards and raised his assault rifle while finning in place. The closer SEAL emerged with a Sig Sauer P226 pistol pointed directly at Dempsey's chest; after a beat, he raised his mask.

Dempsey recognized the man instantly.

At six foot six and 230 pounds, Master Chief Shawn White was one of the largest SEALs Dempsey had served with. His muscular physique and leading-man good looks had earned him the handle Hollywood in the Teams. White was one of only a handful of African American SEALs from Dempsey's generation. He and White had served on different teams most of the time, but they had operated together on several occasions early in their careers and had hung out socially.

Shit, Dempsey thought, adjusting his ball cap, *this could be a problem.*

"Howdy, I'm John," Dempsey said, changing his voice to incorporate a little Texas twang while subtly rolling down his sleeves. The serpentine scar that wrapped his left forearm was the one defining feature that would betray his former identity. After the explosion in Djibouti when the surgeons were putting him back together, the face guy had tweaked his nose, but no amount of work could hide the damage done to that arm.

White spat out his regulator. "Authenticate?" the SEAL boomed in his deep, distinctive voice.

"India," Dempsey said, resisting the urge to rub his shaggy beard. Thank God for the beard and his long hair.

"You have something for us?" White said, all business.

Like a highlight reel in his head, memories of kicking ass side by side on their first deployment flashed through Dempsey's mind. He felt an overwhelming urge to wrap his one-time brother up in a bear hug and trade war stories. But he couldn't. The SEAL named Jack Kemper, the man Dempsey had once been, was officially dead and buried. Setting his jaw, Dempsey pulled the plug on the memories and simply said, "Yeah, party boy here," and then, kicking the corpse at his feet, "and his friend."

He turned and waved a hand at Latif, who guided al-Fahkoury to the edge of the platform. Dempsey took the terrorist by the arm, jerking him roughly to get his attention.

"Listen very carefully. You're about to go for a swim. I'm going to put something in your mouth." Latif handed him the HEEDs bottle—a miniature scuba device only slightly taller and wider than a can of soda, with a black rubber mouthpiece sticking out from one side. Dempsey shoved the bottle under the hood, finding the man's mouth and forcing the regulator in. "Breathe through your nose until you hit the water because you'll only have maybe twenty to thirty breaths in this thing." He felt the terrorist shudder and shake his head. "And bite down hard. If it falls out, no one will know you've drowned until they get you inside the lockout chamber. And no one will give a shit, quite frankly. So don't struggle, and try to breathe slowly."

Watching from the water, White screwed up his face in disapproval. He stowed his Sig and held up a second octopus backup regulator intended for buddy breathing.

Dempsey met the SEAL Master Chief's gaze and flashed him a look that said, *I know, I know . . . just having a little fun with this piece of shit.*

A beat later, White's expression changed and recognition flashed in his eyes. "Do I know you?"

"I don't think so," Dempsey said, his grin fading.

"Yeah, okay," White said, but he looked like he'd seen a ghost. "You remind me of someone I know, er, well, used to know."

"There's a lot of motherfucking Joneses out there who look and talk like me," Dempsey said, amping up his twang and running his tongue between his lower lip and teeth, "if you know what I mean."

White's expression softened, and he actually chuckled at that. "Amen, brother."

Dempsey seized al-Fahkoury by the shoulders and felt the man trembling in his grip.

"They tell me this guy's important, so look after him. His friend is just luggage and won't require any air."

On cue, Latif dragged the mystery corpse down to the edge of the platform and rolled it unceremoniously into the water. The second SEAL finned over, grabbed the corpse, and disappeared under the water.

"Remember," Dempsey said in al-Fahkoury's ear through the hood, "breathe slowly."

Shaking his head, the SEAL Master Chief finned backward a yard, donned his mask, and popped his regulator into his mouth. Then he gave Dempsey a wave signaling he was ready. With a twinge of evil satisfaction, Dempsey shoved al-Fahkoury off the edge of the platform and into the water. The terrorist submerged briefly then kicked furiously to the surface, trying to keep his hooded head above the water. Dempsey watched White wrap thick powerful arms around the man, pull the terrorist beneath the water, and disappear into the deep.

A beat later, an empty black hood floated back up—the perfect metaphorical exclamation point for this unorthodox prisoner exchange at sea. Dempsey and Latif looked at each other and busted up laughing.

As they made their way back to the bridge, Latif said, "Did you know that guy?"

"Nah," Dempsey said. "Why?"

"I don't know, just seemed like the two of you might have been buds . . . once upon a time."

The corner of Dempsey's mouth curled up. "Once upon a time . . . maybe."

He sent Latif down to check on Martin and ready the liberated hostages for their impending EXFIL before wandering to the bridge to caucus with Munn.

"How'd the handoff go?" Munn said, turning to look at him.

"Slick," Dempsey said. "But, dude, you could have warned me."

"Warned you about what?"

"Master Chief Shawn White, that's what. Hollywood was the fucking welcome wagon."

"No shit?" Munn said, grinning. "Well, I'll be damned. How is he?"

Dempsey shook his head. "You're such a dick."

"Did he recognize you?"

"It was touch and go there for a minute . . . maybe."

Munn clasped a hand on Dempsey's shoulder. "Seriously, bro, I didn't know. If I had, I would have warned you or had Latif manage the handoff."

"It was bound to happen sooner or later. It's a small community."

"Yeah, it is," Munn said. "And there's only one Hollywood."

They shared a nostalgic smile, and then Dempsey said, "Is the helo inbound?"

"Yeah, it will be here in twelve mikes. And then Adamo wants us for some new tasking."

Dempsey nodded, then looked around at the beautifully appointed pilot house with a knot in his stomach. "Are we set to scuttle this bitch?"

"All set," Munn replied. "We'll do it remotely from the air once we're clear. I have it set to blow in series so she goes down bow first. Fucking shame, though," Munn added with a theatrical sigh. "I could get used to having one of these. Hell, if I can keep it, I'll even let you call me Captain Dan and drive your tired, ugly ass around wherever you want to go."

Dempsey laughed. "Someday, maybe, but it won't be on a boat like this. We'll be lucky if you and I can tool around in something like that Damor."

"When that day comes, a Damor would be just fine. So long as we have a cooler of beer and some trawling gear so we can go deep-sea fishing together, I'll be happy."

"Hooyah," Dempsey said with a tired smile, and then he turned to go help ready Sarah Bonney and Diana Curtis for their journey home.

CHAPTER 7

Ember's Executive Boeing 787-9, N103XL
Incirlik Joint NATO Airbase
Adana, Turkey
1945 Local Time

"So now we're a QRF?" Grimes grumbled, folding her arms and looking from the image of Simon Adamo on the monitor in the Virginia TOC to Dempsey with an expression that said it all: *See, see what I told you? This is exactly what I was talking about. We've become just another quick reaction force. They've turned Ember into a glorified flyswatter . . .*

Dempsey met her gaze but kept his expression neutral.

"Ember is not a QRF *de facto*, but it is a QRF *de jour*. In other words, Elizabeth, Ember is whatever the DNI needs us to be," Adamo replied with the annoying tone he used when he was exercising his authority while trying not to sound like he was.

"I think what Elizabeth is trying to say," Dempsey said, chiming in for the first time in the brief, "is that we shouldn't even be having this conversation right now. We should be interrogating al-Fahkoury and trying to determine the identity of the dude he was meeting on the yacht. Ground Branch is perfectly capable of extracting Allen, yet you're retasking us to do it. Lately, Simon, it seems like you've got us hopping all over the place. Just when we start digging into an assignment, you pull us off and we have to start from scratch on something new. I think the distinction Grimes is making is important. There's a helluva difference between a *task force* and a *quick reaction force*." Dempsey glanced over at Grimes.

The look she gave back said, *Finally, you get it.*

Adamo pushed his glasses back up onto his nose, index finger and thumb extended in a gesture resembling a finger pistol. "If I'm being completely honest, I don't disagree with the two of you, but there is another factor that I don't think either of you are appreciating . . ."

"Which is?" Grimes asked.

"That the DNI is under an incredible amount of stress. Ember is his Excalibur. Given the choice, he will always task Ember because we're the better blade. So let's table your concern for now and focus on executing our new tasking."

Dempsey resisted the compulsion to argue. The truth was, seeing the former CIA man sitting at Shane Smith's desk and playing Ember Operations Officer irritated him. Probably a product of his twenty years in the Teams, but Dempsey automatically tended to lump people into one of two categories: operators and support. In his mind, Adamo was support—like Ember's Signals and Cyber Division personnel, for example—and was not someone forged for a leadership position. Dempsey worried the former CIA Staff Operations Officer had neither the instincts, the field experience, nor the stones to make the tough life-and-death decisions with the speed and confidence that Smith—as a former Delta Tier One operator—possessed in spades. But with Jarvis's departure to become the DNI and Smith taking the reins as Director of Ember, they were stuck with Adamo as Ops O.

When no one said anything, Munn broke the silence. "Guys," he said, putting on his peacemaker face, "Amanda Allen is out there, right now, alone and in the suck. If I were in her shoes, I would be praying to God that the DNI was sending a shit-hot team to extract me. *We* are that shit-hot team. I agree with Simon. Let's table the OPORD gripe fest until after we get her back."

Dempsey and Grimes both nodded and returned their attention to Adamo as he briefed them on the intelligence collected thus far. Baldwin's assessment was that Allen had been smuggled into Syria by one of the terrorist factions either working directly for or in collaboration with PKK. Also known as the Kurdistan Workers' Party, PKK had been founded with the goal of pursuing Kurdish political autonomy in Turkey. With the fall of Iraq and Syria and the subsequent formation of Kurdish-occupied regions claiming autonomy in those countries, Turkish President Erodan's fear and paranoia about a breakaway Kurdish state in the east had reached a crescendo. Turkey had effectively declared war on the Kurds, and now the United States was officially embroiled in the conflict.

"Why would PKK smuggle Allen into Syria?" Grimes asked. "Seems like a terrible risk."

"I agree. The Turkish-Syrian border ain't what it used to be. The wall changes everything. Border traffic is tightly controlled now. Every crossing is via checkpoint manned by Turkish security forces," Munn said, voicing Dempsey's thoughts while Latif and Martin just sat with their mouths glued shut, taking it all in.

"Valid points," Adamo agreed calmly. "But the heat on PKK inside Turkey is tremendous. There is an argument to be made that smuggling Allen into Syria is actually the lower-risk alternative. Assuming we're right and PKK is the instigator, their leadership does not want to get caught holding an American hostage. This is probably the same reason they have not claimed responsibility for the attack. PKK holds Washington culpable for allowing Erodan to forge and cement his dictatorship in Turkey, but they do not want American special operations elements showing up in country working hand in hand with the Turkish military, thereby speeding their own decimation. If I were overseeing the op for PKK, I'd move Allen to a safe house inside Kurdish-controlled Rojava. I'd stash her somewhere in Afrin, Manbij, or Tell Abyad—somewhere Turkish MIT didn't have eyes watching my every move."

"That actually makes sense," Dempsey said, surprised to hear himself agreeing with Adamo. "But it doesn't address Munn's point, which is, How the hell do you smuggle a blonde American female—whose face is plastered all over the news—across the Turkish-controlled border without anyone noticing?"

"We know PKK has infiltrated Turkish Intelligence. We know they have moles inside both the government and the military. It is possible they utilized this network to facilitate the crossing. Bribes could have been paid to look the other way."

"So what's the endgame?" Grimes asked. "Why kill the Ambassador and take Allen? Especially if what you're saying about PKK is accurate and they have no intention of taking credit for this attack and kidnapping?"

"From the moment we got the tasking, I've been thinking a lot about that question," Adamo said. "I don't have an answer, only theories."

"Well, let's hear them," Munn chimed in.

"All right," Adamo said, pushing his glasses up on his nose again. "Theory one is that they took her for financial reasons—they saw this as an opportunity to kill two birds with one stone. Kill the Ambassador to make a statement and sell back his Chief of Staff to make money. We have to presume they know who her father is and therefore could set a high asking price."

"Who's her father?" Dempsey asked.

Grimes looked up, an eyebrow raised. "Seriously, JD? You've never heard of Supreme Court Chief Justice Henry Allen?"

Dempsey shrugged but felt his face flush. "There are millions of people named Allen in this world. Why would I assume that Amanda Allen is *his* daughter?"

Grimes laughed, enjoying his embarrassment. "I guess I thought we were all expected to keep up with current events in this job. It was all over the press and cable news when the Chief Justice's daughter was assigned to the embassy staff in Turkey a few months back . . . just saying."

Dempsey shook his head. "Been a little busy fighting terrorists lately, if you haven't noticed. I guess some of us don't have time to watch TV whenever we want." But he couldn't help chuckling at himself.

"What's theory two?" Latif asked, speaking up for the first time and looking at Adamo.

"Theory two is that PKK somehow pierced Allen's official cover. They want to know what the CIA knows about their clandestine operations, so they took Allen because she is young and green and they thought they could break her and extract valuable information. When they're done with her, instead of trying to ransom her back to her father or the State Department, they'd probably auction her off to the highest bidder. There are plenty of bad actors who might want to take a crack at a CIA asset with knowledge of the identities of regional double agents and CIA assets."

A chime sounded, and Adamo's gaze shifted from his laptop camera to somewhere else. After a beat, he said, "I'm moving out to the TOC. Smith and Baldwin are ready to jump in."

The big-screen TV in the Boeing's conference room went dark momentarily, and then the feed shifted to a split image: the Ember TOC videoconference camera on the left and a satellite image on the right. The sat image was a crisp bird's-eye view of a small compound comprised of two buildings surrounded by a low stone wall. The imagery zoomed out, revealing that the compound was connected by a quarter-mile-long dirt road to a major highway traveling north of a city.

"Hello, everyone," said Baldwin in a cheerful professorial tone. "This compound lies in Syria, about twenty-four kilometers from the Turkish border at Elbeyli." The screen shifted to a grainier picture of a man and woman talking in a tan desertscape. "The man on the right is Abdul Haq. He was a Regional Commander in PKK in the 2000s, but when the Syrian civil war broke out, he left Turkey to join YPG, also known as the People's Protection Units. YPG is the backbone of the Syrian Democratic Forces fighting to liberate northern Syria from ISIS. We suspect, however, that Haq maintains close ties with his former colleagues in PKK."

"Who is the woman?"

"We haven't made a positive ID, but we believe that is Mutla Birarti, a former YPJ Commander who migrated the other direction, from YPJ into PKK."

"What is YPJ?" Latif asked.

"YPJ is the Women's Protection Units, which is basically the sister unit of YPG. They are closely allied, collaborating and fighting together in all capacities."

"My God, how many friggin' groups are there fighting in Syria?" Latif said. "How the hell do you keep them all straight?"

Baldwin laughed. "I'm not going to lie—we have a spreadsheet."

"What are we looking at here, Baldwin?" Dempsey said, starting to lose his patience.

"This picture was taken in Syria, not very far from al-Bab. The image is only a few weeks old, and it indicates that PKK sent Mutla Birarti to make contact with YPG, leveraging an old association. At the time, we could only speculate about the reason for the meeting, but recent comms intercepts indicate Birarti may have been involved in the Ankara attack. If that's true, then this meeting between Haq and Birarti takes on new relevance."

"So you're saying the woman, Birarti, kidnapped Allen for PKK, and now Abdul Haq is hiding Allen in Syria for them?" Dempsey asked, trying to follow.

"Not Haq or YPG per se, but we believe Haq arranged access to a safe house in Syria for Birarti. It is a business arrangement, not at all uncommon among these cooperating groups motivated by money and the promise of future favors. I'll scratch your back, you scratch mine."

"Why al-Bab? Isn't al-Bab under the control of the pro-Ankara Syrian forces now?" Grimes asked. "Why not choose a safe house in Manbij, a city where YPG has control?"

"Two reasons," Baldwin said. "One, because Haq doesn't want to give Turkish or Syrian forces any justification to launch a campaign against them in Manbij, and second, because since 2014, an American-British coalition has been providing weapons, training, and support to YPG in the battle against ISIS. If they were discovered to be aiding and abetting a PKK faction in a terrorist operation against the United States, then I can't imagine it would sit too well with the coalition. So my guess is, Haq is acting alone on this, making good on some blood debt or other promise."

"Okay, whatever," Dempsey growled. "The point is, PKK took Allen, and now you think Mutla Birarti moved her to this compound in al-Bab?"

"That's what we're attempting to ascertain, John. HUMINT suggests ownership of the compound has changed hands several times. We believe another third-party faction owns this compound presently and that this third party is now involved and may potentially have custody of Allen."

"Oh, for Christ's sake," Dempsey said, feeling a headache coming on. "Is Amanda Allen being held in this compound or not? Answer yes or no."

"There is a high degree—" Baldwin began, but Dempsey cut him off.

"I said answer yes or no. I did not say use lots of words that mean maybe."

"Ah, look, here is Director Smith," Baldwin said, red-faced but bemused, turning on-screen to face Shane Smith as he walked into the frame. "Perfect timing."

"Hey, guys," Smith said, his voice so crystal clear over the sound system in the Boeing TOC, it was as if he were sitting in the room with them. "I couldn't help but overhear the conversation, so I thought I'd jump in."

"Hey, Shane," Dempsey said. "Now that you're here, can we stop playing footsy on this one and you just tell us when and if we have the green light to hit the compound?"

"I realize you're anxious to kit up, John, and go yank Amanda Allen out of the lion's den," Smith began. "But we still have a lot of questions on this one. We suspect PKK was behind all this, but we don't have proof. Normally, we'd wait for confirming intelligence before authorizing any sort of rescue op, but as you know, every hour that goes by is another hour Allen's life is at risk and the information in her head is in jeopardy of falling into enemy hands. So the DNI has authorized us to conduct a small-footprint, kinetic operation in al-Bab. The mission objectives are to A, confirm whether Allen is being held at this compound Baldwin identified, and B, identify the party holding her."

"So you're sending us in?" Dempsey asked curtly.

Smith's gaze took in the whole team. "We're finalizing the mission details and solidifying Dempsey's NOC as we speak—"

"Hold on," Grimes interrupted. "Dempsey's NOC? Don't tell me you're sending him into Syria alone."

"He won't be alone," Smith said. "Adamo is going to embed him in a UN chemical weapons inspection team for a surprise inspection in al-Bab, just a few miles from the compound. Once in al-Bab, we'll use a field asset who can get him close to the site for intel collection."

"And hostage recovery?" Dempsey interjected.

Smith pursed his lips. "If appropriate, John—I trust you to make the call on the ground. But it does Amanda Allen no good if you get killed trying to pull off a one-man insurrection in al-Bab, does it? The first and best option is to gain intel on the facility, stage in place, and we'll pull a team together for a raid. What we desperately need is confirmation she's still alive. I also need you to keep in mind that the other criterion for mission success is gathering intelligence on who is responsible for this and what their next play might be. The DNI and I are both concerned that other attacks are coming, and your ability to gather information to that end is vital."

"Understood," Dempsey said.

Grimes shook her head. "I can't believe you're sending him in alone."

"Agreed. I don't like it," Munn said. "It should be a two-man team, at minimum. Send me with him."

"Having two of you folding in on the NOC raises too many eyebrows," Smith countered. "You'll stand by with a strike team comprised of the rest of Ember SAD, and we will supplement with JSOC assets out of Turkey if required. We can get you in and out by air if things go sideways."

"Simple to say, but what if we can't mobilize an air asset across the border in time to bail him out? What then?" Munn said. "There needs to be some sort of contingency plan."

Dempsey could feel his friend and fellow frogman's eyes on him.

"It's only twenty-four clicks from the border. That's like fifteen miles, Dan. You could practically run and get to me in time. But if it makes you feel better," Dempsey said, turning from Munn back to Smith, "can you arrange support from the 160th Special Operations Air Regiment? That would go a long way toward relaxing everyone here."

"Sure, and if we can't secure an asset from the 160th, we'll use the Air Force's Seventh Special Operations Squadron. They have a detachment at Incirlik right now."

"Pave Lows?" Munn asked.

"No. They're using the B-model Ospreys."

"Shit, that's even better, Dan," Dempsey said, selling it to his friend. "Those CV-22s are a helluva lot faster than helicopters. Even from Incirlik, you're looking at an INFIL under thirty minutes. Hell, if you spooled up the squadron for 'training flights,' you could even shave a couple minutes off that."

Munn nodded, his expression not pleased but at least mollified. "If it's Seventh, see if we can get a couple of PJs from the Wing. Nice to have high-end medical assets for CASEVAC if things go bad."

"Good thinking, Dan. Will do," Smith said.

They were a planning machine now, doing what Ember did better than anyone else.

"How do we make sure the UN inspection team gets across the border, much less with John in tow?" Grimes asked.

"Yeah," Martin said, speaking for the first time. "I just read that Syria has been jerking the inspectors around. They wouldn't let them inspect Khan Sheikhan and then delayed them coming to Shayrat Airbase until it was pointless. Then just this year they refused inspectors access to Douma."

"All true," Smith said from the screen. "But before I address that, I'm dying to know—since when can Marines read, Gunnery Sergeant Martin?"

The room broke into laughter, Martin smiling and shaking his head. Smith was a natural-born leader. The break in tension allowed a pause and for everyone to refocus and come at the problem with a fresh perspective.

"Okay, so here's what you need to know about the state of Syrian chemical weapon inspections," Smith said, now deadly serious. "First, there's renewed world pressure for compliance, and this will give Damascus a great opportunity to show cooperation since we know and they know the Syrian Army is currently in control of al-Bab. The Syrian military will be happy to cooperate because there's nothing in al-Bab. Cooperation is all gain and no loss for them since the UN team will obviously find no chemical weapon signatures. Moreover, the locals will welcome any opportunity to garner more international support for their plight and should be overtly cooperative to a UN team that might report on war crimes perpetrated by the Syrian Army."

"That's smart," Latif said.

"I'm still uncomfortable with this plan," Grimes said. "Who is this asset that's going to be taking Dempsey in?"

"He's with DIA and has been operating for over a year as a chemical weapons expert with the UN. He's made three incursions into Syria under this NOC," Smith said. "I talked to his CO already, and he's a shooter. Don't worry, JD won't be the only gun in this fight if things go bad."

Dempsey had doubts about whether his DIA counterpart was a blooded operator, but if the dude had infiltrated Syria three times and was still going strong, then he had to have skills. Syria was presently the most dangerous fucking place in the world. It was the definition of *suck*.

"So when do I go?" Dempsey asked.

"As soon as possible. While we pull together your NOC credentials and contact your DIA partner to arrange the meet, I advise you folks start prepping everything else we discussed."

"Roger that," Dempsey said, and then, turning to his fellow team members, he added, "You heard the boss. Let's get to work."

He got acknowledgments from everyone around the table, except for one . . .

Grimes was already on her feet, standing by the door to exit the TOC, hand on the knob. "A word?" was all she said and then disappeared.

Dempsey followed her into the Director's office adjacent to the TOC and shut the door behind him. "Yes?" he said simply.

"Are you out of your fucking mind?" she said, hands on hips. "You can't go into Syria and execute this mission alone."

"Where is this coming from?" he said, folding his arms across his pecs.

"You're doing this because of Elinor, aren't you?"

He took a deep breath and then exhaled slowly. "Elizabeth, I have absolutely no idea what you're talking about."

"You've never talked about it . . . what happened in Tehran. Not once. It's been a year, and you pretend like nothing happened. But something did happen, John. You won't admit it, but there was a connection between the two of you."

"No," he said, shaking his head emphatically. "It was all an act . . . a painstakingly constructed, impeccably executed cover story."

"Bullshit," she said. "I saw the two of you together in Jerusalem. I saw the way you looked at each other. You can't fake that. I'm a woman, John. I know what I saw."

He averted his eyes. "For a fleeting moment, maybe there was something . . . a connection between us. But does it matter now? She's dead." Then anger suddenly flared in his chest, and he resented her for riling up his demons. "Jesus. This is fucked-up. Why are you doing this? Is this how you get off these days? Fucking with everybody's head?"

"Is that what you think of me?" she said, screwing up her face. "Nothing could be further from the truth. We're family. I care about you. I'm worried about you . . ."

"I'm fine. I'll be fine . . . Just drop it. Please."

"Look at me," she said and waited until he did. "I know how your brain works, JD. I know that in your mind, you broke the one rule that no SEAL has ever broken. You left a teammate behind. But because you can't live with that, you tell yourself that Elinor was a traitor, that she was a double agent and a spy and that she deserved everything that happened to her. But your heart knows better, and so the end result is that you're stuck oscillating between denial and soul-racking guilt. You can't go on like that. It'll break you, trust me. I know what I'm talking about."

Dempsey felt a lump forming in his throat. "I see her in my dreams," he admitted. "Writhing and bleeding on the floor . . . I left her, Lizzie. I left her to die."

"Yeah, you did. And now you need to forgive yourself for that. There was no scenario, and I mean absolutely none, where you could have exfiltrated with Elinor and survived."

"That's not the point. The *point* is, I didn't even try."

Grimes shook her head. "It's exactly the point. Ember is not Tier One. We play by different rules. We follow a different code. And every member of this team accepts that risk. Elinor accepted that risk. Your executing the mission was not a betrayal. Your escape was not a betrayal." She stepped toward him, her hand reaching out but not touching him. "But it is okay to grieve for her. It is okay to admit that no matter what Elinor Jordan truly was—ally or enemy—a part of you cared about her."

He swallowed but said nothing.

"Going into Syria alone to rescue Amanda Allen is not penance. It is not an act of contrition." She pressed her palm against his chest, over his heart. "No matter how many Amanda Allens you go galloping off to rescue, you can't change the past. All you can do is accept it."

He met her gaze, and her pale baby blues seemed to bore into his soul. He believed her—believed her when she said she cared and was worried about him. But he didn't want someone to care about him. He didn't want someone to worry about his safety or his feelings or the logic of the decisions he was making. He'd lost so many—his entire Tier One team, his identity as Jack Kemper. And those he hadn't lost, he'd either abandoned or let down—including his son and his ex-wife, who could never know John Dempsey. The truth was, caring was just too damn painful. Caring was too hard.

And he didn't want to do it anymore.

"I appreciate your concern," he said, gently removing her hand from his chest. "But orders are orders, and there's an American CIA agent out there who desperately needs our help. So if there's nothing else on your mind, we've got work to do."

Her nostrils flared as she stepped back. "That's the way you're going to play it, huh?"

"I'm not sure what you're talking about," he heard himself say.

"In that case," she said coolly, walking past him to exit the office, "if you'll please excuse me, Mr. Dempsey. As you correctly pointed out, I've got work to do."

CHAPTER 8

Lubyanka (FSB Headquarters)
Moscow, Russia
May 6
1551 Local Time

Arkady Zhukov, the most powerful man in Russia without a job title, watched a live stream on his computer. The feed was from a security camera mounted in the upper corner of a detention cell in Simferopol, looking down at a man seated at a metal table. The man was dressed in a neatly pressed and tailored suit and wore a smug, self-assured grin. Arkady yawned, already bored despite *the show* having not yet started. He knew how this would end; he'd seen it so many times.

"Who is this fool?" Arkady asked, his gaze not leaving the screen.

"Yevgeny Lisovsky," said Arkady's newest acolyte, Yuri. "A Russian human-rights attorney who has begun to make a name for himself. I think he prides himself as the new Sergei Magnitsky, champion of the people and defender of human rights. He stormed down to Crimea a few weeks ago to augment the Crimean Tartar activist Michael

Uramov's legal defense team. We picked him up en route to the courthouse. Uramov's trial is today."

"What time does it start?" Arkady asked, watching as two FSB agents entered the frame. One took a seat across from Lisovsky, and the other walked around and stood behind the attorney.

"In less than an hour," Yuri replied.

"And the plan is to detain him so he misses today's proceedings?"

"Da."

"Is that Boris Bykov?" Arkady asked, squinting at the FSB agent seated at the table. The rear quarter-profile perspective made it hard to recognize the man's face, and Arkady's eyes weren't as good as they once were.

"It is" came the reply.

Arkady groaned with weary aggravation. "He's like toenail fungus, this guy. No matter what I do, he keeps popping back up."

"Lisovsky?" Yuri asked, confused.

"No, Bykov. He's going to fuck this all up. He's going to try to question Lisovsky, but Lisovsky is going to cite attorney-client privilege and tell him to fuck off. This will cause Comrade Boris to lose his temper and get physical. He is not the right man for this interrogation."

"So long as he doesn't mark up Lisovsky's face, what's the problem? Lisovsky misses the trial, knows that the *important* people in Russia are displeased with his actions, and the bruises give him something to think about for next time."

"Right out of the operating manual," Arkady said with a sigh. "But not as effective in the long term as you might think."

"But you practically wrote the operating manual." Yuri laughed, but with good-natured reverence.

"True, but I'm always revising it," Arkady said, turning to look at his prodigy. "Do you have someone on the line with us?"

"*Da.* There is a chat window minimized at the bottom right of the screen. I requested the link so we could send them questions and directives during the interrogation."

"Very good," Arkady said, getting to his feet. "Trade places with me." The powerfully built young Russian did as instructed, taking Arkady's seat at the computer while Arkady stepped behind the chair.

Arkady had poached Yuri from Vympel. Like its sister group, Spetsgruppa A, or Alpha, as it was known in most circles, Vympel was an elite, multimission-capable Special Operations force that worked for the FSB. While in years past Alpha and Vympel had operated with different charters, more recently both groups had been used almost interchangeably for counterterrorism operations and false-flag insurgency missions throughout the former Soviet republics. Like their American counterparts, these Spetsnaz forces operated with relative impunity, overwhelming adversaries with vastly superior skills and firepower. And like the American Navy SEALs, a mythos of godlike invulnerability and superhero status had begun to permeate the zeitgeist. Arkady had always poached the Spetsnaz ranks for suitable candidates for his own ultracovert unit, Spetsgruppa Z, or Zeta.

Almost every Spetsnaz operator had the physical prowess and mental toughness required to become one of Arkady's shadow men. What they did not universally possess, however, was the intellect and disposition necessary for his particular line of work. Intelligence he was able to assess with relative ease during the recruiting process—truly brilliant men, he'd found, distinguished themselves quickly. Disposition, however, was another matter altogether.

Sociopaths and sadists made terrible spies. Identifying them and weeding such men out of the Zeta candidate pool was difficult. They were drawn to this type of work like sharks to blood. But contrary to what the world might think, espionage, and even counterespionage, was about relationships. Effective spies built strong relationships and then exploited them. Sociopaths, while excelling at the latter, failed miserably at the former. So he used them almost exclusively for the only thing they were good at—killing people.

He looked at Yuri, who looked back at him expectantly, still waiting on instructions. Yuri showed great promise—so eager and capable, but still so very, very green. Arkady's gaze flicked back to the monitor, where it appeared that Lisovsky had already succeeded in raising his interrogator's ire. Boris was on his feet now, stalking around the table. "Order Comrade Bykov to stand down," Arkady snapped.

"Yes, sir," Yuri said and quickly turned back to the computer. The chat window populated with text as Yuri's fingers flew on the keyboard. Acknowledgment of the order came back, and a beat later, Bykov turned to look over his shoulder at the door. With a scowl of irritation, he stormed out of the frame, leaving Lisovsky and the other FSB agent in the room wondering what had just happened. A new line of text appeared in the chat window, a request for an explanation for the intervention. Despite the respectful diction, Arkady could practically hear Bykov's indignant fury behind the words. "They want to know why we interrupted the interrogation. What is it that you want them to do?" Yuri asked.

"Go to the file directory on the computer. Find the folder labeled *deviantnoye*," Arkady said.

Yuri did as instructed and clicked to open it with the mouse. Inside the folder were a half-dozen subfolders.

"What is this?" Yuri asked, turning to look at Arkady with surprise. "You already have detailed files on Lisovsky?"

Arkady nodded.

"But I thought you didn't know who he was?"

"I didn't say that."

"But you gave the impression . . ." Yuri's voice trailed off, and then he smiled. "I hate when you do that."

"Do what?"

"Pretend you don't know something to see what I'll say and do."

The corners of Arkady's mouth curled up into a grin, but he simply said, "Click on the folder labeled 'photographs.'"

Yuri turned back to the computer and did as instructed. The folder opened, revealing dozens and dozens of thumbnail images. Most of the images were of Lisovsky, but a good quarter of the photographs were of a woman.

Arkady leaned over Yuri's shoulder and pointed to three different thumbnails. "Open this one, this one, and this one."

The first photograph showed a young blonde woman seated across the table from Lisovsky—wineglasses and dinner plates between them—smiling animatedly at something he'd said. The second showed her in a formfitting tank top and yoga pants, her brow dripping with sweat as she worked out at a public gym. The third and final photograph was a close-up of her asleep in bed, taken with a night vision–equipped camera.

"Is that Lisovsky's girlfriend?" Yuri exclaimed.

Arkady nodded.

"She is beautiful," Yuri said, staring at the monitor.

"I know," he replied. "Would be hard to find another one like this, wouldn't you say?"

Yuri turned to look at him, wordlessly acknowledging the obvious.

"It would be a shame if something happened to her while Comrade Lisovsky was away in Crimea. Moscow is a very safe city, but people have accidents all the time. Sometimes they slip on the stairs and break their necks. Sometimes they trip and fall into the Moskva River."

Yuri nodded and smiled. "You're right, comrade. Accidents can happen anywhere . . . Is that the message you would like me to transmit, along with these three pictures?"

"Yes," Arkady said and then, heading for the door, added, "I need to piss. I'll be back in a minute. Don't let them sever the connection."

He walked to the bathroom, acknowledging nods from colleagues he passed en route. The third floor of Lubyanka was where the important people worked, where the Director of the FSB and his Deputy Directors and Chiefs kept their offices. Arkady had been offered the top post by President Petrov on three separate occasions, and he'd turned it down each time. The people who needed to know him knew him. The people who needed to fear him feared him. That was enough. The last thing he wanted was his name listed on a Wikipedia org chart with a headshot photo and a clickable link to his profile. He was no politico. He was no bureaucrat.

Just like he had shunned promotion, he had also eschewed oligarchy. As one of Petrov's oldest and closest confidants, that path had been open to him. If he had desired so, it could have been him at the helm of Rosneft or Gazprom; he could have been a billionaire robber baron of Russia. But those men disgusted him. They were parasites, draining Russia of her vitality and strength. There was no desire their money could not buy, yet even as American sanctions and falling energy prices crippled the economy, they continued to suck the lifeblood from their countrymen.

It had been Arkady who'd encouraged Petrov to instill trusted allies as the heads of these companies and then use the alliances to take control of the country's energy, financial, and media infrastructure, but never did he imagine this would be the outcome. He'd overestimated their principles and patriotism while underestimating their avarice and self-interest. In the Soviet Union, there had been a wealth gap between the politic and the citizenry, but that gap had been small on both relativistic and absolute terms. He'd expected these men to get rich, but the wealth they'd pilfered exponentially eclipsed what he'd foreseen. Instead of becoming gleaming pillars of a new Russia, men to be emulated and respected, they'd taken the low road, choosing to behave like mafiosos.

Over the past decade, Arkady had helped Petrov round up, break, and stable these wild stallions running amuck. It had proven to be a more difficult task than either of them had anticipated, but by deploying secret FSB resources and tactics, Arkady had gotten it done. Petrov was now, at Arkady's coaching, using his propaganda machine to diminish the perceived importance and influence of the oligarchy—rebuffing talk of *crony capitalism* and rebranding it with the term *state capitalism*. Russian capitalism had stumbled, yes, but now it was remaking itself after the Chinese model, which many economists believed would supersede Western capitalism as the dominant system in the twenty-first century. This was the narrative the Petrov government was peddling, but it was a lie. Despite having wrested functional control of the country's enterprises back from the oligarchy, the oligarchy was firmly entrenched. And recently, a new problem had reared its hydra's head—nepotism.

Over the past two years, Arkady had watched four oligarchs hand control of their enterprises over to their sons. These young barons, the oldest only thirty-two, had grown up in post-Soviet Russia. They had no reverence for the old Communist empire and no respect for Russia's working class—the other 99 percent of the population. None had military service. None had worked for the state. The classrooms of their youth had been nightclubs and yacht decks. They had been socialized in an environment of corruption, drugs, and lavish excess. And they, in concert with their fathers, would take whatever measures necessary to ensure that Russia never transitioned to a true and functional state capitalistic system. The bitter irony of it all was that for all the transformational change and upheaval that Russia had experienced over the past century, under Petrov it'd come full circle back to where it started before the Bolshevik Revolution in 1917. Petrov's Russia was a neofeudal state harkening back to Tsarist Russia—with the oligarchs pledging loyalty to Petrov like feudal lords and paying tribute in the form of deposits in offshore bank accounts. With the oligarchy now under his control, Petrov could stay in power indefinitely. He was rich beyond comprehension, had the Russian army at his command, and his tendrils in every baron's business—Petrov was no longer President . . .

He was Tsar.

Unbeknownst to the world, Arkady Zhukov had been the architect of this grand debacle. He had failed the Russian people, and he hated himself for it. For Russia to survive, Arkady had no choice but to turn his coat.

He'd been a kingmaker.

Now he would have to become kingbreaker.

He flushed the toilet, both his bladder and his conscience voided. He knew what must be done, but how to do it was another matter altogether. One does not slit the king's throat unless all the chess pieces are moved into place, and in place they were not.

Fortunately, he was not alone in this cabal. Secret alliances had been made. Not every Russian in a position of power was a spineless sycophant. There were other men like him who wished to see Russia purged, stabilized, and returned to its former might. The Soviet Union was dead, its Communist corpse too cold and decayed to be revived. But the Soviet empire could be reclaimed and its influence restored. The Chinese model of governance was the key—a disciplined centralized government with tight control of foreign and domestic policy atop a state capitalistic economy in which foreign direct investment could be managed yet innovation could still thrive. In this model, the functional control of the nation would be wrested from Petrov's hands. The Federal Assembly would be purged of his cronies and once again become a functional legislative body.

The efforts were already well underway.

Arkady returned to his office, where Yuri still sat behind the computer. Arkady looked at the monitor and saw that the brash young attorney's bravado had evaporated. He was afraid. No further dialogue or negotiation was necessary. Arkady had seen this look a hundred times. They'd won. Lisovsky was his.

"You see?" Arkady said with a satisfying exhale. "Compliance can be achieved without brutality. No yelling, no punching, no bone breaking. If you want to control a man, all you must do is find something he treasures and threaten to destroy it. He knows the FSB is not an organization that bluffs. We make good on our threats."

Yuri nodded. "So what do you want me to tell them now that he's agreed to cooperate?"

"Tell them that Comrade Lisovsky is to be released immediately. That he is to go to court and try very hard to do his job *just poorly enough* to ensure his client is convicted. Whatever grand defense he has planned should be abandoned; whatever trick he's hiding up his sleeve forgotten. Tell him that if he thinks he can game the system by secretly passing his strategy on to the other members of his legal team so that they can fight while he sits out of the game, we'll know. A guilty conviction is the only acceptable trial outcome. Otherwise, his girlfriend dies."

Yuri passed the instructions to the field agents verbatim, and then they both watched as the message was conveyed to Lisovsky. The attorney listened without interruption, but Arkady saw the man clenching his jaw in restraint. When Bykov was done talking, Lisovsky sat wordless for a long beat. Arkady watched as the anger in the young lawyer's eyes faded to cold compliance. This was the reaction he'd wanted to observe. Had Lisovsky accepted too quickly and without emotion, then Arkady would have known that Lisovsky was playacting and thought the threat idle. But Lisovsky knew better. Everyone in Russia feared the KGB. Everyone in Russia knew the mythos was real. The FSB was the KGB reincarnated, only bigger, badder, and better equipped. The three letters branded on the beast may have changed, but the beast lived.

Arkady's mobile phone rang in his pocket. He retrieved it and checked the caller ID. He took the call immediately.

"Da?" he said simply.

"Are you busy?" said the voice on the line.

Arkady felt a flash of reflux. This would not be good news. "Where are you?"

"Outside. Across the street on a bench."

Arkady pocketed his phone and turned to his young protégé. "Stay here and make sure they don't fuck anything up." He took his heavy black overcoat from where it lay folded neatly on the desk. "I'm going for a walk."

"Is something wrong?"

"Nyet," he said, feeling Yuri's eyes on his back as he shrugged into his overcoat and left. A measure of mystery and uncertainty was good for men like Yuri.

He stepped outside and was immediately hit by a blast of chilly air. It was an unseasonably cold May afternoon, despite the sunshine, and Arkady stood his collar up to block the wind as he set off at an angry pace. He crossed Lubyanskiy Proyezd and made for the park across the street. Face-to-face meetings gave the illusion of privacy—but there were so many ways to eavesdrop, especially here in the Russian capital. Nonetheless, he had trained all of his acolytes to eschew technology and embrace the old ways whenever possible. He dropped heavily onto the bench beside the much younger man, a man diligently climbing the narrow ladder of the Zeta ranks.

"I suspect you're about to ruin my afternoon?" Arkady said.

The man nodded, keeping his gaze fixed across the park. "Malik is dead," he said. "And the yacht is at the bottom of the Adriatic. Imagery captured it being scuttled by a small special operations team."

"The Americans?"

"Unconfirmed, but we have intelligence that they were actively hunting al-Fahkoury. This appears to be a case of very bad timing. I don't think our operation was compromised."

"How can you be so sure? Maybe they took him. Are you positive he's dead?"

"Well, not one hundred percent," the young Zeta said. "But the last ping we received from his tracker was on its way down to the bottom of the ocean."

"Okay, let's hope that's the case," Arkady said and then sat perfectly still in silent thought. This development was a terrible blow. Malik wasn't an actual person, but a Zeta legend most recently occupied by one of his best deep-cover operatives, who had been coordinating a complex series of proxy operations in Turkey. Now he had a decision to make. Let the legend expire and sever all its ties to Russia, or try to salvage the campaign by backfilling it immediately. This was not the first time he'd had to make this decision, and with the Malik legend no less. The man who had been occupying the role was in fact the second man to wear the persona, the first Malik having met his untimely demise after a gun battle with a Chechen rival. There had been few witnesses, so it had been easy to refresh the role. This time would prove trickier. *I don't have a choice,* he decided at last. *The PKK operation in Turkey is in progress. Everything will fall apart if I don't.*

"Are you going to backfill?" the young man asked, reading his mind.

"Yes."

"Who did you have in mind?" the Zeta operator asked, his voice betraying his eagerness for the opportunity. But Arkady knew he wasn't ready.

He needed someone who could put on the legend like an old worn pair of gloves. There was only one Zeta capable of getting them out of this mess—Valerian Kobak. Unfortunately, Valerian was in Abkhazia completing other critical tasking . . . Well, this was the way of things. Valerian would have to wrap that business up quickly and change his skin.

"Patience, my young friend," Arkady said, placing a hand on the other man's shoulder. "You might yet wear the skin, but not today. In the meantime, I need you to stay on damage control. Keep the legend alive until Kobak becomes active. Help him with logistics and comms. We're throwing him into a hornet's nest, and he's not going to be happy. Can you do that for me?"

"Yes, sir," the young man said as they both got to their feet. "I won't let you down."

"I know" was all Arkady said in farewell, and he turned to leave.

I have too many damn balls in the air to juggle, he thought as he walked back to his office.

The FSB was the busiest it had ever been. GRU and SVR were similarly engaged. Arkady could not remember this many simultaneous covert operations being spearheaded by the Russian Clandestine Service since the height of the Cold War. But it was different this time around. The service was much bigger; more capable; and, thanks to Petrov's hubris, emboldened. Petrov's appetite for risk was one of the reasons Arkady had supported the man from the beginning. On this front, he and the President had always aligned. The complexity and scope of the operations they were undertaking put the KGB of old to shame, even with nostalgia coloring his memory.

No, this time was different.

Russia was back.

And this time . . . she was back to stay.

CHAPTER 9

Somewhere . . .

Voices woke her from a dreamless sleep.

For a moment, Amanda couldn't remember where she was. Then the dull pain in her stomach and her throbbing left eye socket reminded her. She was in hell, that's where she was. Other aches and pains, from lesser blows delivered during her beating, made themselves known as she came into full consciousness. Her right hip and thigh, her left shoulder, her left biceps, and her ribs were all complaining now.

She opened her eyes and stared into the pitch-black. Her plywood-box prison had no windows and only a single light bulb, which her captors had turned off. A small gap at the bottom of the door provided a strip of anemic gray light, which made her think it was probably night. The conversation taking place outside her cell, which had begun in hushed tones, was now becoming heated. She recognized the voices—the man with the broken tooth who'd beaten her and the woman who'd checked on her afterward. They were arguing in Turkish:

"We never should have agreed to come here. I don't like this city," the man said. "And I don't like this safe house."

"It was better than the alternative," she replied. "Staying in Turkey was not an option."

"I don't know these men," he growled. "I don't trust them."

"They are brothers in arms. Haq has worked with them for years. He vouched for them."

"They're not brothers in our cause."

"I know, but that's the beauty of the plan. If anything goes wrong, we are not implicated."

"But we're still here!" said the man. "The longer we hold her, the greater the risk we're found. I say we cut her head off, give false credit to Al-Nusra for the attack, and leave. I'm ready to be done with this whole kidnapping business."

Dread flooded Amanda's body, and she began to tremble with fear. *Oh God, he wants to cut off my head. They're going to cut off my head!*

Her heart rate leaped, and panicked thoughts flooded her mind. Primitive, animalistic impulses told her to pound on the door, beg for mercy, offer them whatever they wanted. There had to be something she could offer in exchange for her life. Her body? They didn't have to kill her. They could sell her to a sex-slave trafficker. State would conduct a search for her and they would find her. Then OGA would send in a team to pull her out . . . but if money was all they were after, she could offer to pay a ransom. Her father would pay it.

"You're not thinking this through," the woman argued. "If we do that, we don't get paid. And worse, our relationship with Malik is over."

"Malik," the man scoffed with bitter disdain. "We don't need Malik."

"How can you say that? Before Malik, we were losing. Now we have access to weapons, capital, and information. Without his moles and allies inside the Turkish government, we could have never executed this operation. And the next attack is even more complicated and difficult. Don't you see? With his backing, we finally have the power to incite regime change. Erodan, the puppet of the West, must be brought down.

Only then can we return control of Turkey to its rightful master—the people. The other members of the Movement are counting on us to lead. We must not lose sight of our objective. This was but the first battle in a long and difficult campaign."

Silence hung in the air until finally the man said, "What is so special about *this* girl? What is so special that he would have us kill the Ambassador and take her instead? What is Malik's plan for her?"

"I don't know the details of his plan. That is not the type of information he shares."

"If he ransoms her to the United States, then I think we should be entitled to a share . . . on top of what he agreed to pay us. We are the ones who risked our lives to take her. We are the ones risking our lives waiting with her now."

"I think that would be unwise," the woman said. "He has always treated us fairly."

"Don't be a fool. He's not our benefactor; he's a mercenary. This is a business relationship, and in business, everything is subject to negotiation."

Amanda's panic was ebbing now as she took stock of the information she'd gleaned from eavesdropping on her captors' conversation. First, she now knew she was no longer in Turkey. Her best guess was that they'd smuggled her into Syria—an unfortunate development because the probability of her rescue dropped dramatically. Second, she was being held at a safe house that was operated by a different terror outfit than the one that had taken her.

"How much longer are we meant to wait? The handoff should have already happened. Turkish Intelligence is looking for us. The Americans are looking for us. We can't stay here indefinitely," the man complained.

"I know, I know," she snapped. "But we cannot risk electronic communication, either. The digital spies are always listening. We just need to be patient."

"Something is wrong," he said with an air of anxiety. "I can feel it. Malik is not coming."

"You don't know that."

"I'm telling you, something happened. Something feels off. If we don't receive word from Malik within the next twelve hours, we're leaving."

"And going where, Samir? Back into Turkey? Are you insane? No, we don't dare do this," she argued. "Our instructions were clear. Are you willing to forfeit receipt of payment and the relationship over a few hours? I can assure you that leadership is not. Demîl brokered this deal; we are only his intermediaries. Are you willing to suffer his wrath if Malik cuts ties? I, for one, am not."

"I'm not willing to die for this American or for Malik. Forfeiture of payment would be a devastating loss, but we have fulfilled our end of the bargain. We captured Amanda Allen and brought her to this safe house alive and on schedule. Now we must look after ourselves. Twelve hours, Mutla. Demîl is old and standing with one foot already in the grave. We are the future of the Movement. We are the future of our people. Twelve hours more is all I am willing to wait. If Malik's people do not show up by then . . ."

Amanda heard the big man stomp away and the woman mutter a quiet curse under her breath. Once everything fell silent, she took stock of the gold mine of intelligence she'd collected and even permitted herself a little victory smile. She'd gotten four names from the conversation. The man with the broken tooth was Samir, the woman was Mutla, and they both reported to a man named Demîl.

Demîl, Demîl . . . Where have I heard that name? Could it be Demîl Sinjar—one of the five founders of PKK? That could make sense . . . especially if the "Movement" they kept referring to was the Peoples' United Revolutionary Movement—a congress of terrorist groups bent on overthrowing the Erodan regime. Okay . . . this is all starting to make sense.

There'd been a fourth name they'd used as well. Malik.

This was not a name she'd heard before, but if her translation of the dialogue had been accurate, then Malik was her buyer. Apparently, she was to be sold and handed over to this Malik, but for what purpose she did not know.

A chill snaked down her spine.

Twelve hours, the man with the broken tooth had said. Twelve hours left before she had a new master. But what if Malik didn't come? There seemed to be some legitimate concern over this . . .

She pulled her knees against her chest, hugging them.

If Malik didn't come, what would they do with her?

CHAPTER 10

Office of the Director of National Intelligence (ODNI)
Washington, DC
May 6
1550 Local Time

Jarvis cleared his throat but resisted the urge to cough as he scanned through the subject lines of the absurd number of emails that had populated his inbox. He was just about to click on an email from Simon Adamo when a distinct knock sounded at his office door. Three taps, with a pause between the second and third beats.

Petra's knock.

"Come," he said, his voice dreadfully hoarse.

The door eased open, and his Chief of Staff walked in. Feeling a sneeze coming on, he paused her progress with a hand and a beat later sneezed so hard, it sent a stinger through his rib cage. Grumbling, he pulled the already damp and nasty handkerchief from his pocket. As he raised it to mop up, he noticed his fingers were tingling.

Damn. It's back.

After wiping his nose, he balled the fabric into a wad inside a clenched fist. He noticed Petra's eyes on him, assessing. Not judging, never judging—simply assessing. Always assessing. He'd still not gone to a doctor about his "condition." He'd still not told anyone about the symptoms he was experiencing, but despite his best efforts to conceal his secret, she knew. She knew, and she augmented him accordingly when needed, without ever a word on the subject between them. In meetings, she'd automatically exchange ceramic coffee mugs for his stainless-steel tumbler. She'd accept document folders from outstretched hands on his behalf, precluding him from reaching with a trembling hand. And she seemed almost instinctively to know when that help was *not* needed. Without Petra, Jarvis wondered if he would be succeeding as DNI.

"Yes, Petra," he said at last, forcing a weak smile.

"You have a visitor, sir," she said.

"Justice Allen?" he asked.

She nodded once.

"Is he read into Amanda's OC?"

"Paperwork says no. Shane Smith says he confirmed as much with the Director over at Clandestine Services. But of course, she may have told him in confidence. He is her father, after all."

"Would you have told your dad?"

"No, sir," Petra answered. Then she smiled. "But my dad was a dick."

He chuckled and shook his head. Petra was perfect for this job. Having found her brilliant as an intelligence officer assigned to the Tier One SEAL Team when he had commanded it close to a decade ago, he knew full well the degree of her intellect. Pilfering her from where she had landed at the Office of Naval Intelligence had been one of his first moves when he took the helm as DNI. He'd made her his Chief of Staff and never looked back. They were a team now—trying to tame the multiheaded hydra that was the US intelligence community.

"All right," he said, wiping a drip pooling at the tip of his nose. "Send him in."

"Do you want me in conference?"

He considered this for a moment before saying, "Thank you, but no. I think I'll take this one solo."

"Certainly," she said and disappeared.

A beat later, she returned with Chief Justice Allen in tow. Jarvis stood but elected to stay behind his desk rather than walking around to greet the sitting Supreme Court's most prominent and respected member.

"Chief Justice Allen," Jarvis said with a cordial nod. "If you'd please excuse me for not shaking hands. I'm fighting a nasty cold."

"Noted," Allen said, his demeanor frosty.

Jarvis gestured to one of two empty armchairs on the opposite side of his desk and then looked at Petra.

"Would you like a coffee?" she asked him, but the question wasn't really about coffee. With Petra, communication was a tapestry of subtext. With this single question, she was offering him a "Get Out of Jail Free" card if he needed one, effectively saying, *If this goes on too long, would you like me to interrupt you?*

"Yes, that would be nice," he said with a smile, his own coded reply. *Fifteen minutes, no more . . .*

She nodded her understanding and shut the door.

"We're both very busy men. No point in wasting time with small talk," Allen said, taking a seat and the lead. "Where is my daughter, and what are you doing to get her back?"

Despite the Chief Justice's stone-faced expression, Jarvis could see the anxiety and trepidation in the other man's eyes—a father's dread, a father's worry. This man's only child had been taken by brutal terrorists. And for all the power, influence, and prestige that came with presiding over the highest court in the land, he was impotent to help his little girl.

"The highest probability is that your daughter is in Syria," Jarvis said, giving it to the man straight. "We have some signals intelligence indicating she may have been taken to al-Bab, a city outside of Aleppo, but nothing definitive."

"*May have* been taken? You have the entire intelligence apparatus of the most powerful nation in the world at your disposal. How can you not know with absolute certainty?"

Jarvis took care to keep all sarcasm out of his voice, while flexing and clenching his right fist beneath the desk. "The only certainty in this universe is uncertainty. I know that's not the answer you came here to get, but it's the answer you deserve. Sure, I could sit here and give you false hope and shower you with the platitudes a man in your station has become accustomed to, but what would be the point? After all, you said it yourself; neither of us has time for small talk."

"But how can you not know? Don't you track these groups' movements with satellites and drones? Use the NSA to monitor their communications?"

Jarvis nodded. "We do, but the enemy knows this, and they operate accordingly. They travel at night. They utilize decoys and disguises. They operate with strict EMCON policies, limiting their electronic communications if not eschewing them altogether."

"But you found bin Laden, for Christ's sake. How can you not know where my daughter is being held?"

"Yes, we found bin Laden, and it took a dedicated team of analysts and field assets years, pursuing every possible vulnerability until we finally got an exploit. Right now, I have a similar dedicated team engaged in the search for your daughter. We are using all the tools in our arsenal and shaking all the trees in our underground local network for intelligence, but so far we only have this one lead."

"Then what are you waiting for? Why don't you send a team of Navy SEALs in to get her out?"

"I can't send in a team if I don't know specifically where she's being held. Keep in mind, this is Syria we're talking about. The country is in the middle of a civil war, and this particular region is incredibly unstable, with multiple insurgent groups vying for control. Syria is not Afghanistan. It's not even Iraq. We don't have boots on the ground in country, Your Honor."

"But there must be something we can do!" Allen said, slamming his fist on the armrest of his chair.

Jarvis nodded. "I know this is difficult, but the only thing we can do right now is wait and trust the process."

"I just don't understand," Allen continued as if not hearing him. "Why Amanda? Why murder the Ambassador and take my little girl? Is it because of me? Are they trying to get to me? Yes, I'm Chief Justice, but I'm not a rich man, at least not by Wall Street standards. I could pay a two-hundred-thousand-dollar ransom, but not much more without liquidating my primary residence. Is that what you think they're after? Money?"

Jarvis met the other man's gaze. This was the confirmation he'd been waiting for. Allen didn't know about his daughter's clandestine service. For a fleeting instant, he considered reading the Chief Justice into his daughter's file. As the DNI, Jarvis certainly had the authority to do it, but from a strategic perspective, he saw no benefit from going down that road. Amanda had seen fit to keep her greatest secret from her father, and this was telling. Maybe she didn't want to worry him. Maybe in matters concerning his only daughter, paternal instincts interfered with his ability to make rational decisions. Or maybe she simply didn't trust him with keeping the information secret.

"No legitimate group has claimed credit for the attack," Jarvis said, dabbing at his nose with his handkerchief. "And no ransom demand has been made. As tempting as it is to read into these two data points, a lack of information is usually nothing but that—a lack of information."

"But you must have some working theory as to why they killed Ambassador Bailey but took my daughter."

"I do," Jarvis said, nodding. "I think Ambassador Bailey was the intended target of the attack, and after that objective was achieved, the terrorists at the scene saw a secondary opportunity. Amanda is young, Caucasian, and attractive. They might be planning to ransom her; they might be planning to traffic her into the underground sex trade. They might even want to keep her for themselves. I know that's not the type of thing a father wants to hear, but it's the reality of the world we live in. You need to be prepared for the worst. If they disappear her underground before we can mount a rescue, it will be extremely difficult to locate her. It could take months, maybe longer, and if we do manage to get her out, she won't be the same woman she was before."

Allen shuddered at this comment. Then he sat still for a moment, staring down at his hands. After a long beat, he spoke. "I was born and grew up in a small town—Cottonwood Falls, Kansas. It's a tiny place, not much more than a Main Street, but good people. Like most wide-eyed kids from small towns, when I grew up, I moved away. Later, when my wife, Janet, died, I fell into a dark depression. Amanda was eight, and I, uh . . . I wasn't present for her. I sent her *home* to live with my parents for a year until I could get my head and my act back together. My parents adored Amanda, and they were such wonderful . . ." He paused, and a pained, nostalgic smile spread across his face. "Anyway, she was eight that year, which I think I mentioned, and I came to visit her that fall. It was late October, maybe early November, and unseasonably warm. Every year before the weather turned cold, the ladybugs engage in what's known as a cluster-hibernation. They converge on homes and buildings looking for a sheltered place to hibernate. Sometimes there were so many, my mother would literally sweep them up with a hand broom and dustpan and whisk them back outside, but Amanda . . ."

"Amanda?" Jarvis prompted when the Justice fell silent.

"After every dustpan load of ladybugs was deposited outside, Amanda would painstakingly catch and hand carry the little buggers back inside. For two full days, she chauffeured ladybugs to the dollhouse in her room. When my father asked her what in blazes she was doing filling her room up with bugs, she simply replied, 'They're not just bugs; they're ladybugs, and they need our help.'" Allen chuckled to himself and then met Jarvis's gaze. "I'm telling you this silly little story because I want you to know something important about my daughter. She's compassionate. She cares. She helps. If she finds a beetle stuck on its back, she flips it over. If she spies a turtle trying to cross a street, she stops and carries it to the other side. When she noticed that a kid in grade school regularly had no money for lunch, she took the initiative to pack an extra sandwich every day for a whole year. When she discovered her college roommate was secretly struggling with addiction, Amanda rescued her from the abyss. And when she realized that the world is run by men bent on pillaging the liberties and coffers of the citizenry, she joined the State Department to effect change. You see where I'm going with this? She's a grown woman now, but that beautiful, compassionate spirit she had as a child still guides her in thought and deed." He paused and took a deep breath before continuing. "Over the years, I have come to realize that there are only two types of people in this world: candles and candlesnuffers. In these dark times, my daughter is a light. Please, I beg you, don't let them snuff her out."

Jarvis held the other man's impassioned gaze. He opened his mouth to speak, but a knock came at the door.

Tap, tap . . . tap.

Jarvis looked past Allen to his office door. The handle turned, the door opened, and Petra appeared in the gap.

"I'm sorry to interrupt, but I have your coffee," she said, walking to his desk and setting down his tumbler. "Oh, and I should probably mention, everyone has assembled in the conference room. They're ready for you, sir."

"Thank you, Petra," he said. "Please let them know I'm on my way."

She nodded and walked out, shutting the door behind her.

Jarvis returned his gaze to Allen. Despite the simplicity of the characterization, the man's words had resonated with Jarvis. His own personal view was that most people were unwitting agents of entropy—some bumbling circuitously, others sprinting headlong—but always ignorantly spreading discord and disorder within the system. For every Amanda in the world working tirelessly to right fallen dominos, toppled by moral and natural entropy, there were ten others knocking them over. A woman like Amanda Allen needed rescue, not because she saved ladybugs but because she was like John Dempsey, and Levi Harel, and Petra Felsk, and every other trusted friend and colleague Jarvis held in high esteem. They were cornerstones, pillars, tent poles; they were the men and women who bore the weight of the fragile yet immensely heavy structure built and maintained by society to hold chaos at bay. So yes, Amanda Allen needed rescuing, and that was why he was sending the best operator he had to complete the mission.

"I've tasked my most trusted and capable covert operations task force with Amanda's recovery," he said, leaning forward. He then let the long pause after communicate the unspoken rest of the message: that the operation was underway, that revealing the operation to the media would undermine its effectiveness, and that Amanda's rescue was a top priority.

"I understand," Allen replied with a nod to the unsaid and got to his feet. He made a move to extend his hand but was stopped short with a well-timed sniff from Jarvis. And with that, the Chief Justice of the Supreme Court walked out, having transferred responsibility for his greatest treasure in life to Jarvis.

Petra escorted Allen out but was back a beat later. Jarvis shared Allen's ladybug story with her. When he'd finished, he said, "Pass the details on to Ember—validation material for when Dempsey finds her."

"Roger that," she said, and then catching his eye, she added, "Director Morgan has requested a meeting. Your calendar is full, but I can make room."

"All right. Make it happen," he said, resisting the urge to grimace.

She nodded and turned to go, but when she got to the threshold, she paused and looked over her shoulder at him.

"It's just a head cold," he said, beating her to the punch. "I'm fine."

She responded with a hesitant smile before shutting the door behind her. The time was coming when the proverbial elephant in the room between them would have to be addressed openly, but he wasn't ready.

Not yet . . .

CHAPTER 11

Turkish-Syrian Border Checkpoint
Elbeyli, Turkey
May 6
1540 Local Time

Dempsey sighed and shifted in the front passenger seat of the white Toyota Land Cruiser, trying to find a comfortable position. To his surprise, Adamo had come through, arranging his NOC and obtaining the necessary paperwork in record time. Now here he was, sitting with his three companions in the second SUV of a five-vehicle convoy—each a different white SUV with a large blue "UN" stenciled on the side. A large square of paper with the number "2" hand-printed in marker rested on the right corner of the dashboard beneath the windshield. In the back seat, sitting directly behind him, was his DIA counterpart, traveling as UN inspector Dr. Robert Theobold, a NOC the man had operated under for quite some time. Beside Theobold rode an *actual* UN inspector, a French Canadian named Dubois. The fourth occupant, the driver, was simply that, a German with war-zone experience who had contracted with the UN for the past eighteen months and regularly drove on Syrian excursions.

"What's the delay?" Dempsey said, catching the driver's eye. "We've been idling for over ninety minutes."

The man at the wheel laughed out loud at this—a real belly laugh. "This must be your first crossing with an inspection team," the heavily bearded man said in a thick German accent. "First, we wait on the Turkish bureaucrats. Then, we wait on the Turkish military authorization. Then, we wait on the Syrian Army escort—if there is one, which we usually discover at the last moment. Then, we wait on a smoke break, or a shift change, or maybe the rain. There are so many reasons to wait. I have waited to cross for almost one full day before."

Dempsey clenched his jaw and forced a thin smile.

"So . . . what is this new technology you are bringing with us today?" the German driver asked, fixing Dempsey with a curious smile.

"You'll have to ask the scientist," Dempsey said, gesturing with his thumb over his shoulder at Dr. Theobold. "I'm just the security for the equipment."

"And for the equipment operator, I hope, Peter," the DIA man said with a good-natured chuckle. Dempsey relaxed a little in his seat. The spook was a natural in his NOC, a skill that was more innate than acquired.

They all chuckled as Theobold fielded the question. "The device is a chemical sniffer not unlike the last generation of detectors, but what makes it different is that we don't search for residue signatures alone. Instead, we sample air and soil looking for changes in the organic signatures that would be present even *after* the concentration of the target chemical residuals has dropped below a conventional detection threshold. What we have discovered is that the overall organic chemical signature of, say, soil will change after it has been exposed to, and therefore reacted with, chemical weapon agents. In this way, using baseline samples taken in expanding concentric circles, we can generate a fingerprint for any region. Any future variations from the baseline fingerprint would suggest exposure to a chemical agent. These changes are measurable for many weeks after the residue from the chemical may have degraded. As such, delays in sampling become much less important when using this instrument." Then, with a broad smile, he added, "But don't tell the Syrians this."

The German was smiling still, but his glazed-over stare told Dempsey he'd already lost interest.

"Fascinating," Dubois said in accented English. "How long after exposure can you accurately predict the prior presence of the chemicals?"

"It is highly variable," Theobold said. "It depends on the target chemical, of course, but also on the local background signature. This is our first real-world test. On the average, we anticipate we'll extend the detection period by around twenty to thirty days, but with the right background, it could be up to sixty days."

"Very impressive," Dubois said.

"Scientists," the German said, grinning, and winked at Dempsey.

In his peripheral vision, Dempsey saw that the lead vehicle in the convoy, a white Toyota Hilux SUV, was pulling away.

"Oh, we're moving now," the German said, putting the Land Cruiser's transmission into drive. Two heavily armed Turkish soldiers were waving them forward and through the border gate nestled between two sloping gray walls with guard towers atop. The driver kept their SUV in close single file and stopped briefly to receive their stack of four passports—two American, one German, and one French—from a guard. A moment later, they were through the gate and driving over freshly poured asphalt that funneled them past a fence barricaded with concertina wire and onto the southbound spur of a four-lane highway. Two minutes later, the five-vehicle convoy was in Syria, speeding south toward al-Bab.

A CB radio sitting on the console between them burbled something incomprehensible, and the German driver answered the transmission with an equally incomprehensible retort. Then he chuckled and glanced over at Dempsey. "A short wait today. Much shorter than usual. And no Syrian escort, which is good. But don't be surprised when they are checking us constantly during the inspection."

Dempsey nodded and said, "Can I get my passport back?"

"Oh yes, my apologies," the driver said, slipping his own passport into his breast pocket and then handing the remaining three passports to Dempsey. Dempsey pulled the blue passport with his picture and the name Peter Marks inside and handed the other two over his shoulder. He looked briefly at the stamp that had been added to the visa for entry into Syria for this diplomatic mission.

"Thanks," Dempsey said. "How long until we get to al-Bab?"

"Not long to al-Bab," the German said. Then, over his shoulder to Theobold, he said, "We will have less than twenty-four hours on-site to see if your device works. After that, our diplomatic visas will expire, and we must return to Turkey."

"That should give us plenty of time," Theobold said. "And even if we find nothing, every real-world fingerprint we add to the database will aid future collections, so the trip is a worthy endeavor regardless of the outcome."

Ahead, Dempsey spied a lone truck traveling south. The vehicle looked at least forty years old, chugging along in the left lane. As they closed the distance and prepared to pass, he tensed. Were they in western Iraq, this would be the classic setup for a vehicle-borne IED ambush. He had no reason to believe that a UN convoy in this area of Syria would be targeted, but weirder shit happened. Only once their Land Cruiser had sped past the truck without incident did Dempsey exhale in relief.

"You were a soldier," the German said.

"Yes."

The man nodded. "I spent many years driving trucks in Iraq as a contractor, so I recognize my own fears in you." Then he slapped

Dempsey on the shoulder and laughed his big belly laugh. "But we are in the peaceful paradise of Syria, yes? So what could possibly go wrong?"

Dempsey flashed him a wry smile and shook his head; he liked this German dude.

The miles clicked by until Dempsey recognized a turnoff from the northbound lanes on the other side of the median, a gravel and dirt road that turned to the east and disappeared over a low rise. It was the access road to the target compound, which was less than a mile and a half away from their current position. The urge to commandeer the SUV and head there now, kill the bad guys holding Amanda Allen, and get her safely home was almost overwhelming, but he forced himself to take a deep breath and slip deeper into his NOC.

"Dr. Theobold, do you have a sampling plan?" he asked over his shoulder.

"Of course, Peter," the DIA man said, reminding Dempsey of the real-life Baldwin, who was probably eavesdropping at this very moment via the micro-earpiece deep in Dempsey's left ear canal. "I want to begin with taking some baseline readings in central al-Bab with the rest of the group, especially around the hospital and government complex where the fighting is said to have occurred. Then I would like to head north of the city; there are several olive groves which might prove excellent areas to collect residuals."

"I am not a scientist, but I would concentrate on the hospital area, as this is the block where the chemical attack was reported after the last skirmish," the German said. "We will have precious little time for our inspection and interviews as it is, so I would focus on urban collection."

"Certainly, certainly," Theobold said. "But it is important to sample in multiple locations. I can travel to the areas in the north after the curfew tonight."

"I would not recommend this," the German said. "It is still very dangerous here. Many factions secretly vying for control. It's two years since Operation Euphrates drove ISIS from the city, but not all the terrorists have left, and some sneak back to al-Bab. It is a big town, over a hundred thousand people living here—it is quite easy for terrorists to hide, and not just ISIS. And be careful going on the farms. A farmer might try to shoot you, confusing you for a thief or mercenary opportunist."

"I will be quite safe with Peter, I assure you," Theobold said. "And I need only one of the interpreters with us."

Dempsey shrugged at the driver, adopting the air of a put-upon foot soldier who had been through all this before.

The German nodded but looked worried nonetheless.

As they entered the city, the lead convoy vehicle stopped before two parked trucks angled to partially block the road ahead. The German pulled in behind the lead SUV as Syrian soldiers encircled the convoy. Dempsey felt the Sig Sauer P226 pressing into the small of his back, a subconscious reminder of his tactical disadvantage. With feigned disinterest, he watched the Syrian soldiers through the windshield as they interrogated the lead SUV. After checking papers and inspecting the interior of the vehicle, the lead soldier barked something at the driver and waved them through the checkpoint. Wearing a cross expression, the soldier turned to face their Land Cruiser and beckoned them forward with a curt wave. The German driver idled forward and eased to a stop. He rolled down his window, but the soldier jerked open the door anyway. Dempsey noted that the German kept both hands firmly on the steering wheel, and Dempsey followed suit by placing his own palms on the dashboard. It would be tragic for Amanda Allen to die because a nervous soldier got the wrong impression and started a gun battle at a checkpoint.

After they'd been waved through, the German parked the Land Cruiser behind the lead SUV on the side of the road to wait for the rest of their convoy to clear the checkpoint.

"They certainly don't seem happy to see us," Dempsey said.

"Yes, well, our very presence is an accusation, isn't it?" the German replied. "We are not here to prove that the olive farmers were using chemical weapons. The Syrian Army is the accused party, and they believe they have a right to fight ISIS and defend their sovereign cities by any means they deem necessary."

"Even with chemicals that kill their own children?" Theobold said from the back, anger in his voice.

"I'm not saying I agree they have such a right," the driver said. "I am merely explaining their irritation and suspicion at our presence."

That same irritation and suspicion was going to make tonight's work that much more dangerous for Dempsey and the DIA agent. Apparently, not only did they have to worry about ISIS sleepers in the city who would love to kidnap and behead them, but the Syrian Army was chomping at the bit to make an example of them, too. Should they overstep their bounds and get caught—say, for example, sneaking off from the group to "take samples" in the north—then Dempsey and his DIA counterpart could find themselves in a Syrian detention cell . . . or worse.

If the operation were simple, he mused, *then the DNI would not have sent me.*

Dempsey blew air through his teeth and looked out the window as their UN convoy was finally cleared and got underway. The town of al-Bab had the same shade of brown dirt and the same shade of brown stucco buildings commonplace through much of the Middle East. The roads were paved, and he spied the occasional pop of green. Unlike Aleppo, in al-Bab, not *every* tree and park had been bombed into oblivion. Children and young adults waved at the white trucks with their blue stenciled letters—the same trucks with the same blue letters that had brought food, medicine, and support to them during their time of greatest need. With the battle for the city now over, much of the local population had returned to restart their lives. But the scars of the yearlong battle with ISIS were evident in every direction he looked. So much loss, destruction, and misery . . . yet there was still hope.

When they'd reached their staging area—a small dirt parking lot—the drivers parked in a loose semicircle, and the team members exited their SUVs and assembled. A Syrian military truck that Dempsey had observed following them pulled up onto the sidewalk and parked fifty meters away. Dempsey eyed the soldiers, most of whom seemed disinterested, dragging on cigarettes and chatting with jocularity. One soldier, however, met his gaze with hard eyes and didn't look away.

"All right, everyone, check your gear s'il vous plaît, and then divide into the sector teams as briefed," said a stout balding man dressed in a black shirt and khaki cargo pants. He spoke English but with a heavy French accent. "You must wear your UN vests at all times; this is for your safety."

"And to clearly mark us as targets," said one of the bearded security men. Everyone laughed, the scientists among them nervously, and the "contractors" with the fatalism common in all former military men, regardless of nationality.

"Yes, well, it's not a joke," the Frenchman continued with a hint of irritation. "*Tu vois*, the Syrian Army is watching us. Don't break the rules; the consequences to the UN are severe if we fail in this. Okay, so we have three inspection teams and one testing team." He paused briefly to nod at Theobold. "Dr. Theobold, it is my understanding that you will not need additional security because your assistant serves in this role . . . *ça va*?"

"Yes, that is correct, but I will need an interpreter."

"Of course, of course," the Frenchman said. Then, looking around, he said, "Kadir, I believe you have the assignment?"

A thin dark-skinned man standing nearby raised his hand in acknowledgment.

"Good, good," the French team leader said. "Okay, everyone, gather into your teams; check and calibrate your equipment. Then we divide and conquer. The objective is to collect all the necessary data by morning and be on our way. Good luck and let's get to work."

Dempsey followed Theobold back to the Land Cruiser and opened the tailgate. As he did, a man dressed in a gray shirt and dark trousers approached.

"I am Kadir," the man said, walking up to Theobold first. He extended his hand in greeting. "It is my pleasure to be working with you."

"It is our pleasure, Kadir," Theobold said and shook the interpreter's hand warmly. The DIA man played his role as the genial scientist to perfection, with no hint of familiarity or recognition. Dempsey suspected, however, that Kadir had been a by-name request for this operation—probably an asset he'd run for years. "And this is Peter," Theobold added, looking at Dempsey, "my assistant."

"Ah yes, the rock," Kadir said and extended a hand.

Dempsey shook it but raised his eyebrows. "Sorry?"

"Your name—it means 'the rock,' yes? Like the Christian apostle who formed the church? You actually look like a rock, my friend," Kadir said with a genuine laugh. "You are a large man—a boulder maybe? I have many Christian friends. You should know this."

"And I owe my life many times over to brave Muslim men and women who were partners in the field like we are today," Dempsey said, smiling warmly.

"Very good. I think we will be friends in no time," Kadir said, grinning. Then, turning to Theobold, he asked, "Do you need my help with that?"

"Nah, I got it," Theobold said, sliding a large silver case toward the edge of the tailgate. He indexed the thumb-size wheels on an integrated combination lock and then opened the lid. Neatly positioned inside, secured in precision-cut gray foam cradles, sat a chemical residue detector, three different "sniffer" wand attachments, multiple battery packs, and a tablet computer.

Dempsey resisted the compulsion to lift the fake bottom out of the massively oversize case and survey his own equipment—three short-barreled assault rifles, a half-dozen fragmentation grenades, eight IR strobes to mark locations and themselves if they needed the cavalry, and a sniper rifle broken down into three compact pieces. The SEAL in him desperately wanted to conduct an inventory, but that was impossible here and now. Until nightfall, he'd just have to be satisfied with the knowledge that he'd packed the case himself and it had been in their possession ever since.

Theobold made a show of waving one of the wands around, then connected the tablet to another cylindrical wand, which he stuck into the dirt behind the truck. Some more tapping on the tablet and then he announced, "Excellent. This is truly amazing technology."

Watching him work, Dempsey almost forgot that the DIA man was playacting. Theobold probably knew no more about physics or chemistry than he did, but the man sure knew how to put on a show. Dempsey turned and scanned the two dozen UN workers as they performed their own baseline calibrations. Why anyone would want to be a scientist was beyond him. He was here risking his life to save Amanda Allen; they were here to collect samples of dirt.

Oh well, he thought, *different strokes for different folks.*

He sighed and resisted the urge to check his watch.

Just a few more hours of playacting, and then they could finally get to work doing what they had actually come to do—find Amanda Allen.

CHAPTER 12

Vacation Villa of Sergi Kartevelian
Sukhumi, De Jure Capital of the Autonomous Republic of Abkhazia
Northwest of Georgia on the Black Sea
1851 Local Time

Valerian Kobak selected a Medjool date from the bowl on the table. Using his thumbnails, he split the date lengthwise and extracted the oblong pit. He put the dried fruit in his mouth and slowly chewed, savoring the sweet caramel flavor while his three hostages sat gagged and bound to chairs across the table, watching.

"Mmmm . . . nature's candy. Why everyone is buying cookies and candy when they could just be eating dates—makes no sense to me. What do you think, Sergi?" he said, fixing his gaze on the middle-aged Georgian media tycoon. On Sergi's right sat his wife, handsome, dark-haired Melania, and on his left his mistress, young blonde Makayla. Sergi nodded nervously and grunted, unable to speak because of the ball gag strapped to his face. Valerian cocked an eyebrow at him. "What did you say? I couldn't hear you."

Sergi tried again, articulating nothing but nonsense while emoting desperation quite admirably.

Ordering gagged hostages to speak was juvenile and callow but so damn amusing that Valerian couldn't help himself. In his line of work, opportunities for levity were few and far between. Moments like this helped him retain his humanity. Whenever he made himself a blunt instrument of the trade, that's when "the feeling" came back . . .

The hollowing.

The desolation.

On the one hand, he had to hand it to Sergi. The old sly dog was boning two remarkable women—albeit remarkable for entirely different reasons—while running a billion-dollar media empire. On the other hand, he'd been dumb enough to pick a mistress whose name started with the same first letter as his wife's. How he'd managed to keep their names straight in bed defied logic. Unfortunately for Sergi, this would be the last time he got to be with both the women he loved at the same time.

With a theatrical sigh, Valerian pulled a small black zipper case from his back pocket and set it on the table next to the bowl of dates, drawing attentive stares from all three of them. He unzipped the case and folded it open, revealing a hypodermic syringe and several glass vials of liquid.

He picked up another date and held it up for inspection. "I'm sure the three of you are wondering why I gathered you here. I realize it's awkward, but keep in mind, there are no secrets in a love triangle, only lies," he said, pitting the date and then setting it uneaten on the table. "Fortunately, once a lie is exposed to the light, it withers and dies; it cannot crawl back into the shadows. Nod if you understand me."

He looked at them each in turn. Sergi and Makayla both nodded, but Melania just glared.

"What is important to understand is that relationships, even dysfunctional love triangles like this one, can be surprisingly stable . . . so long as lies don't erode their foundation. Now, Sergi, you've been telling lies. Lots of lies. Lies to Melania. Lies to Makayla. Lies to your friends and shareholders. And lies to the public. Most of your lies are inconsequential and of no concern to us, but some are very troublesome, particularly the lies your newspapers, magazines, and television stations are spreading about Russian corruption and President Petrov's agenda. You have made a dangerous game of undermining Russia's interests in this region, and the Kremlin has taken notice. You see, Sergi, this is not the only love triangle you've managed to involve yourself in. Your media company, Kartevelian Enterprises, is trying to disrupt the love triangle between Russia, Georgia, and Abkhazia. You must know we cannot possibly tolerate this."

He walked over and stood behind the trio, where he placed the palm of his left hand on top of Sergi's head and his right hand on top of Melania's head.

"In this metaphor, Sergi, you are Russia, and Melania is Georgia. Makayla, over there, is Abkhazia. Georgia thinks Russia is too controlling and has decided to distance herself from her one-time partner. Georgia's callous rejection has wounded Russia, and so because of her disaffection, Russia naturally sought congress with another willing partner."

On that cue, he turned both their heads to look at Makayla.

"And that willing partner is Abkhazia. Now I know what you're thinking—Abkhazia is not a separate country; it is part of Georgia. But Russia says no. Ukraine thought it owned Crimea, but Crimea wanted to be with Russia, not Ukraine. It is the same with Abkhazia. The problem is, Georgia refuses to let Russia have a separate and loving relationship with Abkhazia. Georgia thinks it can control Abkhazia and tell Russia what it can and cannot do. This cannot go on."

He removed his hands and walked back to the table, where he turned to eye them again as a group. His expression turned grave, and he shook his head.

"The media outlets owned and controlled by Kartevelian Enterprises have been very vocal and active in their editorial support for Georgia. To speak so disrespectfully of Russia is annoying, but to try and place a wedge between Russia and Abkhazia is intolerable. This cannot stand. Fortunately, it's not too late," he said, his mood suddenly brightening. "It's not too late to reverse course and start telling the truth. So here's what's going to happen. Kartevelian Enterprises is going to cease propaganda operations in Abkhazia and sell its local holdings to a Russian buyer who will contact you in the coming days. It's time to let Abkhazians make decisions of sovereignty without Georgian interference. If Abkhazia wants to follow Crimea and rejoin Russia, then you have no business trying to stand in its way. Do you understand, Sergi?"

Sergi nodded and mumbled something.

"Very good. It appears we've reached an understanding," Valerian said, nodding back. Then he paused and raised his index finger, as if having an epiphany. "When I was new at my job, I would often leave a negotiation such as this believing that an understanding had been reached, only to later find out that the other party had lied to me. In those cases, I had no choice but to return and start the negotiations over from scratch. The terms were never as agreeable the second time, and everyone parted with bad feelings. So now I do things differently. Now I make sure that my clients have a very clear understanding of the agreement. I make sure they don't forget the terms, and I make sure I don't have to come back. In my experience, the most effective way to accomplish this is by taking away something my client loves. That way, the understanding is cemented in their memory, and the client understands the future consequence if I have to return."

Valerian paused. He could see their fear now, practically emanating like a vapor he could inhale. What came next was his favorite part: *the choosing*. It wasn't really a choice—he already knew whom he was going to kill, but they didn't know that. To properly control Sergi moving forward, there could be only one choice.

"Sergi," he said, meeting the mogul's eyes, "because of the lies you've told, because of the way you have mistreated Russia, today you must pay a consequence. One of these women you love dies. You decide who."

Sergi's eyes went wide with panic, and his pupils darted right, then left, in a frantic, blubbering panic.

Interesting . . . He looked right first. His heart is still with Melania after all.

"I agree with your choice," Valerian said, turning his attention to the black case. He selected the glass vial and filled the syringe with a lethal dose of fentanyl. While he prepped the injection, Sergi thrashed against his bindings, sobbing and begging.

Valerian set the syringe next to the pitted Medjool date and then walked over to Melania and undid the straps of her ball gag, releasing it from her mouth. Then he stood in front of her. "Do you have anything you would like to say to me or your husband before you die?"

With composure the likes of which he rarely witnessed, she said, "I know you, son of Georgia. Proud chin, strong jaw, slate-blue eyes—you are one of us, except you . . . you are a *moghalate*." The corners of her lips curled up into a defiant smirk, and she added, "You think they will accept you? You think they will let you rise? You will never be Russian. You are their dog. A pet. Nothing more."

Valerian nodded. "All true, except you are wrong on one detail, proud, beautiful daughter of Georgia. I'm Abkhazian." Her eyes went wide at the admission, and it left her speechless. He picked up the date and the syringe off the table and said, "Do you have any parting words for your husband or his whore?"

Melania swallowed and then looked at Sergi. "You loved me once. Remember that, and remember why we started this company. My murder changes nothing. Find your courage, husband. Protect our homeland."

Sergi nodded to her, crying.

"Okay, it's time, Melania," Valerian said. "Would you like one last carnal pleasure before you die? Something sweet to savor as you leave this world?"

She looked at him aghast but then hesitantly opened her mouth and accepted the piece of fruit. A tear ran down her cheek as she chewed and he injected her with the powerful synthetic opiate. Sergi and Makayla watched the execution in stunned, helpless silence.

Melania Kartevelian died ten heartbeats later.

Valerian packed the syringe away, closed the zipper case, and stuffed it back in his pocket. He selected a date from the bowl for himself, removed the pit, and popped it into his mouth. Chewing, he looked at Sergi and said, "Melania died from an opiate overdose, an addiction she has been struggling with for a long time. You've kept this hidden from the world, of course, but now the secret will come out. You will mourn her for an appropriate period of time. After that, you will propose to and marry the very beautiful and very Russian Makayla here. With time and a newfound understanding, your views on Georgian-Russian relations will change. Russians and Georgians are strongest when we work together, just like man and woman in a healthy marriage."

Sergi stared at him, red-eyed murder in his gaze.

"Sergi, remember what I said about our agreement. The first terms are the best terms. If I have to come back to renegotiate, you won't like it. Nod if you understand."

This time, Sergi nodded.

"Excellent," he said with a smile. "Good day, comrade. And I'm truly sorry for your loss."

Valerian walked out of the villa, stepping over the dead bodies of Kartevelian's security detail. Once outside, he powered on his mobile phone and sent a message to a cleaner to dispose of the bodies and untie Sergi and his soon-to-be Russian bride. With that chore complete, he saw that he had a secure message waiting:

MALIK IS DEAD. BACKFILL REQUIRED. CONFIRM RECEIPT OF NEW TASKING. STANDARD DROP. SHORT TIMELINE.

Valerian sighed and climbed into his rental car.

Damn it, I don't want to be Malik.

He had come to hate Middle East operations. Yes, he was good at it, and yes, his "appetites" were easily sated in that world. But he'd grown weary of playing the Islamic terrorist legends. And it wasn't because he had been raised Roman Catholic or because he harbored religious prejudices. No, it was because these Middle Eastern terrorists were such savages; they were murderers of civilians—women and children no less—barbarians lacking any real culture or class.

But it didn't matter what he wanted. There was no point in asking Arkady to find someone else, because the answer would be no. The answer was always no. That was his penance for being the best.

That was his penance for being Zeta Prime.

CHAPTER 13

Ember's Executive Boeing 787-9, N103XL
Incirlik Joint NATO Airbase
Adana, Turkey
2145 Local Time

Grimes paced the Ember mobile TOC.

Alone.

Munn, Martin, and Latif, along with the two PJs they'd requested, were kitted up and waiting inside the Air Force Special Operations CV-22 Osprey, parked beside the Boeing on the skirt. Munn had encouraged her to wait with them. She'd declined. Dempsey was moving on the compound north of al-Bab where they believed Amanda Allen was being held—no way in hell was she going to hang out in the belly of the Osprey shooting the shit with those guys while their quarterback had the offense inside the red zone. She needed to know what was going on.

She needed to watch.

The plane was warm. They had temp power from the base, but the Boeing's AC units weren't running, just the fans. She hooked her left thumb into the shoulder strap of her body armor and just let her arm hang there. Ever since she'd taken that round to the chest, it just felt better to have her arm like this when she was standing kitted up. She stared at the imagery streaming in a four-way split screen on the monitor mounted on the bulkhead. In the upper-right quadrant, a live satellite feed streamed in green-gray night vision. On the other side of the world, in an underground bunker in Virginia, Simon Adamo was watching the same feed. She could see him sitting at a workstation in the Ember HQ TOC via a wide-angle feed displayed on the monitor's bottom-left quadrant.

"What are those vehicles doing?" she said aloud, talking on her open mike. A three-vehicle convoy appeared to be heading north from al-Bab on the route to Turkey . . . the same route that passed by the target compound.

"Not sure," he said, the timbre of his voice hinting at his own displeasure with the development.

"There's not much north of al-Bab after the target compound," Grimes said, aware she was stating the obvious. "It's only fifteen miles to the border, and there are no authorized crossings after dark."

"That's not entirely accurate," Adamo said. "Our UN convoy, for example, would be permitted to cross at this hour. And there are several small clusters of houses north of the compound that these vehicles could be traveling to."

She resisted the urge to point out that these three beat-up cars were not UN vehicles with special crossing permission, nor were they likely to be a group of friends returning home after a dinner party in town. This was al-Bab, Syria, not some suburb of Chicago. She watched the vehicles slow as they approached the access road leading to the compound.

Damn it. I knew I should have pushed Adamo harder to have the Osprey airborne when Dempsey arrived on the X *at the compound.*

"I'm concerned about these vehicles, Simon," Ian Baldwin said, stepping into frame on the Ember HQ feed.

"For good reason," Simon said, turning to look at another feed off frame. A beat later, his attention was back on the night-vision sat feed. She watched him enter several keystrokes on his workstation keyboard, switching to the operational frequency that included Dempsey. "Atlas One, this is Olympus . . ."

"What's up, Olympus?" Dempsey answered after a beat, his voice a soft whisper automatically augmented by the gain-management software Baldwin's team had programmed into their comms suite.

"Atlas, we have a group of three vehicles headed toward your position. They just turned off the highway and are running dark," Grimes said, beating both Adamo and Baldwin to the punch. She glanced at Adamo, and despite the thousands of miles separating them, he appeared unfazed by her leapfrog.

"Check . . . Stand by," Dempsey came back, his voice calm and cool. Strange how a man who was so passionate in the TOC, an absolute mush of a teddy bear on his back porch drinking a beer and manning the grill, could be absolute ice in the field. All SEALs, she supposed, were like that, but Dempsey operated on a different plane. Outside the wire, Dempsey was unflappable . . . He was a machine of war.

Her gaze ticked to the upper-left quadrant, the feed displaying satellite thermal imagery, and she watched Dempsey's yellow-orange silhouette creep west along a shallow culvert. His movements were smooth and fluid—a jaguar stalking prey. Moments later, another image began to move east—the DIA agent operating as Robert Theobold. The man moved like an operator, but there was only one John Dempsey. A third image stayed put, seeming to cower lower in the culvert. That could only be the interpreter asset whom the DIA man was managing, Kadir.

She felt an overwhelming need to dash from the Boeing, board the waiting Osprey, and swoop in to assist. The arrival of the new vehicles had changed the tactical picture. They needed to act. They needed to take control of the situation before it deteriorated. She glared at Adamo on the monitor, willing the order to flow from his lips, but he just kept watching the feed. *Why is the default state always to be reactive? We need to be proactive. We need to take control of the situation right fucking now!*

This compulsion to take control, to be in control, had become more acute after her near-death experience in Jerusalem. When that bullet tore through her chest and she felt her life slipping away—it changed her. She realized that life was not something she would let happen "to her" ever again. That was why she'd rebuilt her body to be harder, stronger, and more flexible than before. That was also why she'd insisted on sniper training. On the WinMag, behind that scope, she was a god—a god with the power to mete justice with the tip of her index finger. But she wasn't on the long gun now. She was watching this whole damn mess unfold on TV.

The three vehicles approached the five-foot wall of the two-building compound just as Dempsey reached the corner, perhaps only twenty yards away. In her mind, Grimes found herself calculating angles on the compound from the south, where one of the buildings had enough rise to give her a reasonable shot. If she'd insisted on being inserted covertly to cover the op—to give overwatch—she could have been resolving those shots in real time.

"Got 'em," Dempsey whispered. "Three vehicles. How many signatures?"

"Only three," Adamo said, this time answering first. "One driver per vehicle."

"Shit," Dempsey said through his breath. "They're gonna move her."

Grimes cinched the waist panels tight on her body armor and validated the loadout on her kit.

"What are you doing, Elizabeth?" Adamo asked. "I can see you kitting up."

"We need to go get him." She looked at the Ember Ops O through the screen with wide eyes that said there was no other possibility. "Obviously."

On-screen, Dempsey crept up the shallow rise and settled in behind scattered rocks only a few yards from where the vehicles had parked in a loose cluster. Three figures disembarked in unison and walked toward the larger of the two buildings.

"We still need to confirm the package, Boeing One," Adamo said, assigning her a local call sign. The subtext of this was not lost on her. She wasn't going anywhere . . . not yet, anyway.

"Atlas One attempting to confirm the package now," Dempsey said softly in the familiar computer-augmented whisper. "Worried I might be out of time, though."

"Can we at least get our bird up and in slow orbit on our side of the border?" she said.

"Give it a few minutes. We need to confirm the package," Adamo said, his voice an anchor.

A few minutes could be the difference between life and death for Dempsey and the hostage, especially if things went bad now. She slung her compact Sig Sauer MCX Rattler assault rifle across her chest and the case with the .300 WinMag sniper rifle over her shoulder. This was a no-brainer. They needed to be in the air so when JD needed them, they'd be mere minutes from heeding the call.

"I'm gonna wait in the bird," she said, her hands flying across her kit, confirming her extra magazines for the assault rifle and the pistol on her right thigh, as well as smoke and fragmentation grenades at her left side.

Adamo turned to the camera, looked straight at her for the first time. "Confirmation was always the plan, not extraction. We let Atlas One make the call from the *X*. You and your team are the short-fuse QRF on hot standby at the—"

Before he could finish, and before she could protest, a tremendous *whump* rocked the Boeing. She gripped the conference table as the aircraft shuddered and the screens in the TOC flickered.

"What in the holy hell was that?" she barked, looking around. "That felt like an explosion."

As if in answer, a second explosion, this one closer, shook the big jet. A beat later, gunfire erupted outside. What the hell was going on? This wasn't Al Assad Air Base in Iraq or Bagram in Afghanistan. Incirlik was a sprawling NATO base in the middle of Turkey. They couldn't possibly be under attack. This had to be something else—an accident.

"Get me eyes on Incirlik," Adamo said to Baldwin on the monitor, his voice tense but controlled.

"One moment . . ."

"Atlas One, hold," she said.

"What's up?" Dempsey said, his orange-yellow thermal silhouette going still on-screen.

"The base appears to be under attack," Baldwin reported.

She'd rarely heard the Signals Chief sound anything but relaxed, a tone she had once mistaken for indifference. But right now, his voice was tight and even had a tenor of concern.

"That's impossible," Adamo said, echoing her thoughts.

"As improbable as it is, empirical video evidence suggests otherwise." A new satellite feed appeared on her monitor, bumping the Ember HQ TOC from the split. Hastily scrawled white lines overlaid the aerial imagery of the base as Baldwin annotated the scene like an NFL announcer marking up an instant replay on TV. "We have multiple perimeter breaches—here, here, and here—and three groups of assaulters. The largest force is—"

An explosion rocked the jet, throwing Grimes against the table and then to the ground. The TOC went black as she groaned on the floor. Her right elbow had hit the table so hard, her fingers were tingling, and her left hip had taken the brunt of her fall and was complaining loudly as well. She swallowed the pain and got to her hands and knees just as acrid gray smoke began to fill the cabin. A strip of LED lights illuminated along the floor, marking the emergency exit route.

Time to go.

In the dim light, she collected her Rattler and the WinMag from the floor and scrambled to her feet. Hunching low below the cloud of noxious smoke, she followed the lights toward the front of the aircraft. As she moved forward, the smoke became thicker.

"The Boeing appears to be Tango Uniform," she said, coughing. "Shifting command and control to the Osprey."

No one answered.

Shit.

The Boeing had been serving as the comms hub for this op. It was possible that she might still be broadcasting even if she was not receiving, but she doubted it. If the Boeing truly was fucked, then that meant she was blind, deaf, and mute as well.

And so was Dempsey.

Ducking lower, she moved along the passageway until she reached the wide-open cockpit door. Through the cockpit windows, she could see angry fires blazing behind a nearby hangar. A hand on her shoulder made her spin around, her assault rifle coming muzzle to chest with a middle-aged man. He wore a gray T-shirt with "NAVY" emblazoned in blue, running shorts, and flip-flops.

"Whoa, whoa, it's me—flight crew," he said, his hands going up.

She recognized the pilot immediately and lowered her weapon.

"What the hell is going on?" he asked.

"The base is under attack," she said. "I think this plane's on fire. Which means we need to evac to the Osprey and get up in the air ASAFP. We've got a mission on the ground in Syria that needs our support."

"Shouldn't we try to help rebuff the attack on the base?" a new voice asked as the copilot materialized.

"This is a major NATO base. Base security personnel will handle it. If we intervene, we risk getting shot. We need to stay on mission."

"Well," said the copilot with a Georgia drawl, "this plane is definitely on fire, so I agree with swapping assets."

With sudden urgency, the pilot pressed past her and entered the cockpit.

"What are you doing?" she demanded.

"If the fire's in the fuel system or engines, I can extinguish it from up here," he said, slipping into the left seat. "If I can contain the fire, I can save the plane. You guys go; I'll be right behind you." He spun around and looked at her over his shoulder. "But if you get clearance to bug out in the Osprey, don't fucking leave me behind."

"Understood," she said, and then a new thought occurred to her. "Is there a way to destroy the plane and our gear and crypto if things go south?"

The pilot turned and raised his eyebrows in surprise. "Are you saying you think we might lose the base?"

Grimes shrugged. "I don't know what the hell is going on out there. Is there a self-destruct hardwired in?"

"Yeah," the copilot behind her said, his voice tight. "But we can detonate remotely."

"Even without comms or power?"

"Yes," the pilot answered. "It has its own power source and satellite uplink."

"Okay," she said. "Meet us at the Osprey. You've got five mikes and we're going."

The pilot nodded and turned back to the cockpit controls.

"Let's go," Grimes said to the copilot.

He swung the handle, unlocking the main cabin door, and then moved onto the rolling stairwell, but she stopped him at the threshold with a hand on his shoulder. "Are you armed?"

"No," he replied.

She pulled the pistol from her right thigh holster and handed it to him. "Fifteen rounds in the magazine and one in the chamber," she said. "I'll lead."

She slipped past him, crouched, and descended the stairwell, sighting over her Rattler. As she neared the bottom, a gunshot rang out, accompanied by a loud ting as a bullet slammed into the metal frame of the air-stair. She took a tactical knee and scanned for a target. She saw figures running across the tarmac in front of the burning hangar, which was now fully engulfed in flames. Her index finger tensed on the trigger, but she held her fire, uncertain if the figures were assaulters or base security.

"On my mark, we make a run for the Osprey," she shouted.

"That's a nonstarter," the copilot barked over his shoulder. "The Osprey's fucked."

She angled her head right and looked under the nose of the Boeing and beyond to where the Osprey sat at an unnatural angle. The aircraft's left main gear was gone, and the left wing was pressed into the tarmac, two of the proprotor blades bent at unserviceable angles. Smoke rose from the shattered cockpit windscreen.

Oh God, my team's in there . . .

She pounded down the last few steps, ducked around the corner, and broke into a run toward the Osprey. She hadn't gone ten yards when she spied Munn sprinting toward her, left hand up, right hand clutching an assault rifle. As he met her halfway, he scanned the tarmac for threats, droplets of blood flicking from his chin as he looked right and left.

"You okay, Lizzie?" he asked.

"Yeah . . . You?" she replied, eyeing the blood slick down his right cheek running from what looked like a scalp wound.

He nodded and took a tactical knee beside her, checking her six. She did the same as they shared info.

"One of the Osprey pilots is dead and the other is fucked-up—I don't know if he'll make it."

"And Ember?"

"We're okay," Munn said. "Luca has a chunk of shrapnel in his left shoulder, but he's in the fight. I got just this little nick, and June smacked his head pretty good but seems okay. Sounds crazy, but I think we took direct fire, Lizzie . . . We're off the flight line, so it couldn't have been random mortar fire. I mean, Christ, our QRF bird took two hits, and then we saw a rocket hit the Boeing. I think the comms package is fucked."

She glanced back over her shoulder at the Boeing and was relieved to see that the plane was not visibly on fire—at least on the outside—but the hump on the top of the fuselage housing the plane's command and control antennae arrays was damaged. "Are you saying that *we* were the target?"

"I don't see any other planes on this side with smoke pouring out of them."

"How is that possible?"

He shook his head. "I don't know. But they hamstringed us pretty bad."

Grimes gritted her teeth. "What do we do? We can't talk to Olympus and we can't talk to Dempsey."

"I know there's a Harris 117G Multiband Manpack somewhere in the Boeing. I saw Dempsey pack it. If I can find it and get it up and running, and if Baldwin can line up SATCOM UHF, then we're back in business. Until then, we're stuck with line of sight only."

A burst of gunfire erupted to the east, closer than before. They both whirled, weapons trained in the direction of the sound.

"We need to get in this fight," she said, scanning for high ground, somewhere she could set up overwatch.

"Agreed," he said, glancing back at the Osprey. "But we need to move our wounded first."

"And protect the Boeing." She pointed to a second hangar beyond the one on fire behind them. "See that hangar over there?"

"With the C-130 sitting out in front of it?"

"Yeah, I'm heading up top. I'll be your eyes," she said, tapping the sniper rifle at her side, "and thin the herd as best I can."

Munn smiled tightly and turned on the IR strobe on his kit that would mark him as a friendly to NATO forces. "I recommend you do the same."

"Check," she said. Then, meeting his gaze, she added, "Good luck, Dan, and be careful."

"You, too."

She reached behind, snapped her helmet off her kit, and pulled it on. Then, she swung her night vision goggles into position in front of her eyes and held the power button until the NVGs blinked to life. The night instantly came alive in bright monochrome green. With good eyes, she set off toward the far hangar. As she ran, she reached up and found the black circle on the shoulder of her kit, rotated it a quarter turn, and heard the soft click . . . click . . . click indicating her safety strobe was flashing, invisible to the naked eye but a bright light to any friendlies on night vision. Sporadic gunfire echoed in pockets around the base, but for the moment, nobody was shooting at her. Was Munn right? Had the Boeing and the QRF bird been targeted? How was that possible? Ember was black. Nobody outside a very tight circle knew who or where they were and what they were doing in Turkey.

Two new explosions echoed to the south, away from their position. As she ran, she saw flames and smoke rising from several other buildings across the flight line. Apparently, Ember wasn't the only target. Munn was being paranoid. The base itself was under attack.

She reached the hangar and slowed. Chest heaving and pulse pounding, she dropped into a low tactical crouch, scanning over her Rattler for threats as she scouted the perimeter of the building looking for the roof access via an external ladder. She found it, all the way on the back of the building. From this vantage point, she could see where the perimeter road turned north, away from the series of single aircraft "ready alert" hangars, two of which had A-10 Thunderbolts parked in front. So far, these aircraft had not been targeted. The gears in her head started churning: *Is this a terrorist attack or a military strike?* Incirlik was a large joint-operations NATO base with a significant US military presence. For a state actor to attack the base would be a declaration of war against Turkey. Hell, it would be a declaration of war against NATO. This had to be a terrorist attack; no regional actor was that brazen . . . or that stupid. But what was the objective? Her gaze drifted toward the B61 vault—a heavily fortified base within the base where ninety B61 tactical nuclear bombs were kept.

They couldn't possibly be going after the nukes . . . could they?

I've got to get up on this damn roof, she thought, returning her attention to the ladder. Access to the ladder cage was blocked at the bottom by a hinged metal panel padlocked in place. She looked up and saw she could squeeze between the safety cage bars if she climbed above the panel, just six feet. She slung her rifle, jammed the toe of her boot into the gap between the metal rail and the panel, and started to climb—shimmying up the outside of the cage like a monkey climbing the trunk of a coconut palm. A year ago, she might have struggled with this climb, especially with the added weight of her gear, but her upper-body strength was dramatically improved since then. A victorious grin curled her lips as she climbed above the security panel and squeezed between the narrow cage bars. Once inside, she scampered up the thirty-foot ladder to the roof, silently praying that no bad guy would see her climbing and shoot her before she reached the top.

Sirens began to wail, base-wide, just as she was about to climb off the ladder and onto the roof.

About fucking time.

Obviously, base security drilled for this sort of thing, but this attack had caught everyone off guard, including Ember. A direct land-based assault on the base was certainly a contingency in the training manual, but probably one assigned an infinitesimal probability of occurring.

She climbed the last few ladder rungs, slipped silently over the ledge onto the roof, and scanned over her rifle for anyone who might have had the same idea she had. Using her left thumb, she clicked on her IR target designator, and a green laser swept across the roof in her night vision. She moved swiftly left and forward, circling the air handler in a low combat crouch, finger poised on the trigger . . .

Clear.

She squatted and craned her neck to sight into the crawl space under the machinery.

Clear.

Satisfied, she slung her Rattler, pulled the .300 WinMag off her left shoulder, and moved to the north side of the roof. She wished like hell Dempsey were at her side to help her find targets and keep her six clear. Hell, right now she'd take any spotter.

What would Dempsey do? she thought. *He'd set up in the corner so he could use his peripheral vision to detect any bad guys coming up the ladder.*

So that's what she did. The two-foot ledge surrounding the perimeter of the roof was just high enough to prevent her from lying prone to take her shots. She wished she had a box or table she could pull up to the ledge so she could stretch out, but instead, she spread the legs of the attached bipod and set its feet on the ledge. Then she took a knee in a combat crouch behind her weapon. Next, she powered on the high-tech, oversize gunsight and switched it to infrared mode. Then she tipped her NVGs up on her helmet but kept the goggles powered on in case someone came for her. Through the scope, she ranged to the tail of the Boeing on the tarmac—still not on fire, thankfully. She adjusted her magnification and then ranged again to the far east side of the base's perimeter road.

Ready.

She tried to relax her muscles and become one with her weapon.

"Boeing One is now overwatch in position. Boeing One is now Zeus. Anyone up? Olympus? Titan One?"

Silence.

Adamo had been Olympus in the Ember HQ TOC, and Munn had been Titan One on the Osprey when they were Dempsey's QRF in standby. They'd lost comms with Virginia, but line-of-sight comms should still be working.

"Titan One, this is Zeus. Do you copy?" she said, trying Munn again.

No answer.

Shit.

She scanned the tarmac through her scope and spotted Munn and the rest of the Ember QRF moving their wounded from the Osprey toward the Boeing. They were making very slow progress. Two of the crew needed to be carried. She mentally assigned numbers—One for Munn, Two for Martin, Three for Latif, then Four through Six for the two PJs and the wounded Osprey pilot.

Who's the seventh, hmmm? Copilot from the Boeing, she decided.

She scanned slowly across the eastern edge of the perimeter road, identifying a US military HUMVEE and an APV behind it traveling north on the road. She raised her head above the scope and saw that the south end of the sprawling base was mostly in the dark, except for a building beside the flight line and another farther to the southwest, which she assumed were on independent generators.

Whoever planned this attack knew where to strike because they knocked out the power.

She dropped back on the scope and moved her scan to the burning hangar to the east—the fire was now raging completely out of control, and it washed out her IR. She moved off the blaze and scanned the second building. Movement caught her eye, and she clicked her magnification up two ticks. She exhaled and watched, fixing her aim at chest level above the ground. A head appeared, half-hidden by the corner of the building. She ticked up on the magnification again.

Male, bearded . . .

The face pulled back.

She pursed her lips. A bearded fighter sneaking around Langley Air Force Base in Virginia would be suspicious, but in Turkey, a beard meant nothing. Incirlik was a true international base with soldiers from different countries with different codes of appearance. On top of that, coalition SOF teams frequently operated out of this base. Operators in this part of the world—US operators included—wore beards most of the time. She decided her rule of engagement would need to be predicated on aggression. She would not fire on a target unless the target fired first on her people or on soldiers she'd already identified as coalition personnel.

Gunfire echoed and muzzle flares erupted at the corner of the building she was watching. Return fire came from the direction of the Boeing. She shifted her aim back to the building and spied four bearded men running around the corner from the other side to take up a more defensible position along the wall facing her. More defensible against the Ember shooters huddled on the tarmac but completely vulnerable to her.

Well, hello there . . .

She lifted her head and felt no wind at all. She ranged in, consulted the handwritten numbers on the Velcro wristband on her left forearm, and made two fine adjustments on her sight. The lead shooter on the ground took a knee and sighted around the corner, raising his rifle to shoot at Munn's team. Grimes placed the tip of the green targeting arrow in her scope just above the shooter's left ear. Time slowed . . . She became aware of her cheek pressed against the butt of the WinMag, her index finger resting against the trigger, her heart calling the cadence slow and steady in her chest, and her breath synchronizing for the moment.

Exhale . . . stillness . . . squeeze . . .

The rifle burped. Her right shoulder, primed and ready, absorbed the recoil, and she felt a dull, mechanical kiss on her right cheek. Through the scope, the shooter's head spit green-gray onto the wall behind him, and his body crumpled to the ground. The three remaining shooters immediately pulled back. She jerked back the slide to eject the spent cartridge and then pushed it forward again, chambering the next deadly projectile. Two of the three remaining shooters were now looking in her direction, but neither was looking up. She centered the next headshot and slowly exhaled . . .

Good night, bitch.

Trigger squeeze, another head exploded, another body crumpled.

She picked up her cadence. Two more shots in as many seconds and all four terrorists on the near side of the building were dead on the ground.

Then three loud, successive explosions rocked the night. At the same time, the lights in the intact building on the main flight line flickered and went dark as power to the rest of the base went down. Gunfire erupted in multiple locations. She pulled back from her scope and looked in the direction of the Boeing in time to see Munn and his crew all hit the deck. Bouncing headlights to the north caught her attention; she lowered her night vision goggles, looked toward the B61 vault, and saw multiple vehicles racing in that direction.

Oh my God, they really are going for the nukes! she realized.

The base was under attack; the Boeing was disabled; their QRF bird, the CV-22 Osprey, was out of commission; Dempsey was stuck in Syria without comms and backup; and Munn was pinned down on the tarmac. All hell was breaking loose, and she was right in the middle of it with no comms and no spotter. She couldn't imagine the situation getting any worse, and that's when she heard a metallic tink . . . tink . . . tink behind her.

Her heart rate spiked and she looked left—staring at the ladder she'd used to climb onto the roof. She waited and watched, keeping her body perfectly still and her ears attuned, listening for the sound of feet on ladder rungs. Several agonizing seconds passed, but she didn't see or hear anything. *Maybe it was just my imagination,* she thought and turned back to check the scene below. No sooner was her eye on the scope than she heard it again.

Tink . . . tink . . . tink . . .

The noise was back, but louder this time.

No, it wasn't her imagination. They were coming for her.

CHAPTER 14

Compound North of al-Bab, Syria
2215 Local Time

Dempsey tapped his earbud.

One minute Grimes and Adamo had been jabbering like jaybirds about whether to launch the QRF Osprey, and the next they had gone quiet. On the one hand, it saved him the trouble of telling them to shut the fuck up, but on the other hand, losing comms was shit.

"Two, One, you copy?" he whispered.

"Check," came the DIA man's reply.

"I think we lost OTH comms."

"Roger. Concur," Theobold said, seemingly unfazed—a reaction Dempsey would have expected only from a fellow operator. Hopefully that meant Theobold was good in a firefight. Dempsey had a sneaking suspicion it might come to that.

"We're on our own for now. Assume no QRF en route," Dempsey said, just making sure they were on the same page in case everything went to hell before Baldwin unfucked whatever had happened with their comms.

"Check," Theobold said, still unfazed.

The corner of Dempsey's mouth curled up. *I'm starting to like this dude.* He crept around the low perimeter wall until he got to a point where the putrid stench of garbage was wafting over. *Looks like I found the trash heap.* It was as good a spot as any to take a peek at the compound, provided he didn't gag from the odor. The half-moon hanging in the clear sky overhead gave him plenty of visible light; he didn't need the night vision for this. The downside, of course, was that if he didn't need NVGs to see, then neither did the bad guys. He popped his head up for a two-second look about and thankfully did not get his brains blown out. Lights in the main building were on, but the other two smaller buildings were dark. Two sentries were standing watch at the front gate, twenty yards away, beside a weighted arm that served as a gate in a span of wrought iron fence at the front of the property.

"Two, do you have eyes on building two on the east side?"

"Check," Theobold said. "No line of sight inside. The windows of this one are blacked out. No movement in or out. Matches what we expected from imagery." The genial scientist persona of the last twelve hours was nowhere to be found. Kadir—Theobold's managed asset—was still an unknown in Dempsey's mind. They'd left him in the ditch near the vehicle. Hopefully the man wouldn't opt to save his own skin and abandon them if it came to a firefight . . . There was just no telling how a person would respond when their life was on the line.

"Okay, come back. Let's discuss," Dempsey whispered.

Dempsey skirted the compound in a low tactical crouch, keeping his head below the top of the stone and mortar perimeter wall. He moved swiftly, his feet all but silent on the dirt as he swept north. At the corner, he met up with the DIA agent, who gave a nod as they crouched beside each other to caucus.

"So whadaya think happened to our comms?" Theobold asked.

Dempsey shrugged. “We still have local comms, so it ain’t us. Our mobile TOC was acting as the comms hub from Incirlik, so they must be down.”

“So you’re thinking no cavalry?”

Dempsey nodded. “Can’t count on it.”

“So try to confirm the package and we wait?”

“They brought three vehicles. I think that’s all the confirmation we need,” Dempsey said.

Theobold cocked an eyebrow at him. “How ya figure?”

“The only reason to bring three vehicles is because they’re planning to move her, which means she’s here. This wasn’t some entourage of VIPs for a meet; it was just drivers. I’ve seen this game before. They know we’ve got eyes in the sky watching the compound, so they’re going to make things difficult. Mark my words, two of those vehicles will be decoys. They’ll simulate loading three hostages, and all three vehicles will depart simultaneously and go in different directions. We’ve got to act now, or we’ll lose her.”

“Even with comms down, your guys are still watching on satellite, right? They can track them to the next safe house, or if comms come up, we can even hit them on the road somewhere. That’s safer than me and you hitting these assholes alone. We’re seriously outnumbered, bro.”

Dempsey took a long breath. Since Kennedy had formed the Teams in the early sixties, not one SEAL, living or dead, had been left behind on the battlefield. He might not be a SEAL anymore, but that didn’t mean he was willing to abandon the ethos. A flash of memory—Elinor Jordan writhing on the ground in a pool of blood—hijacked his mind’s eye as he spoke his next words. “Right now, one of our own is being held hostage in that fucking shack fifty meters away. I am not leaving without her.”

Theobold pursed his lips and scanned the compound.

“Look, man,” he said, appearing to choose his words carefully. “I’m inclined to agree with you. My gut says she’s in there, but my gut also says that you're rushing this. If your guys saw what we saw, then they'll likely come to the same conclusion we did and dedicate more resources. And if for some reason they actually did lose the satellite, wouldn't they launch a QRF on the assumption we needed them? I mean, that's what I would do."

Dempsey flushed with irritation. "I get what you're saying, bro. But we're not part of some Joint Special Operations Task Force in Afghanistan. My team is small and elite, but we are also deep, deep dark. Only a handful of people know about this mission, and if the TOC at Incirlik is in the blind, then we have to assume that we're on our own. That QRF bird is our only backup. There's no calling the Rangers or Marines in."

"Let's give it another five minutes," Theobold said firmly. "If comms come back up, then we can validate the aerial resources at our disposal. And if the decision is to move on the compound, then we can get your QRF bird in the air and inbound. That would be safer for everyone, including the package."

Dempsey took a deep breath, then said, "Are you a father?"

The DIA man nodded.

"Then I guess the question we should be asking ourselves is this," he said, taking a different tack. "If you were stuck in CONUS right now and that was *your* daughter being held inside that hellhole—what would you want the two operators on the *X* to do? Would you want us to wait and watch while they move her to another compound and risk, with very high probability, that a second opportunity to rescue her never comes, or would you want us to man up and get her out while we still can?"

Theobold let out a slow breath through pursed lips. He held Dempsey's eyes. "Who are you guys? I mean, if I'm gonna go all Butch and Sundance with you tonight, I oughta at least know who I'm taking bullets with."

Dempsey started to give the man the standard ambiguous "spook speech" he'd memorized for these situations, but he stopped midsentence, deciding instead to play it straight.

"I'm John Dempsey," he said, extending a gloved hand to Theobold. "I lead the direct-action arm of an ultrasecret task force run directly by the DNI. I can't tell you much else, except that in a former life, I was a member of a tight-knit Tier One SEAL team. The group I'm with now is just as honorable and every bit the brotherhood as the one I left behind. The only difference is, there's some tasking that needs to happen against the darkest of dark adversaries by operators who don't exist on any org chart—the type of missions, I suspect, *you* might be uniquely prepared to appreciate." Dempsey realized it was true—that Ember was as much a combat team family as his Tier One SEAL team had been.

The DIA man gripped his hand and shook it, his face breaking into a tight grin.

"I'm Sean," the man said. "And I was Delta for a decade before I came to the group I'm with now."

"So what do you think, Sean? We doing this or not?"

"Yeah," he said, nodding slowly. "Let's go get this girl."

"Okay," Dempsey said, suddenly feeling electric. The adrenaline floodgates were now open, and the anticipation of battle and victory was rising inside him. He scanned over the wall. "So just the one door on building two?"

"Yeah."

"We both agree that's the highest probability structure for where they're keeping her? Thermals showed one figure in the back room, two guards in the front room."

"Agreed."

"And we've got the two guards out front, one roving patrol. Plus the three drivers and the five other signatures we had before the drivers arrived—that makes eleven possible responders. So we need to take her fast before the rest of these assholes mobilize and get their act together."

"How about this," Theobold said. "I take position at the door. You take position by that window on the south side. You breach the window and kick off the shooting—firing south to north, please, since I'm at the door. Hopefully you can put bullets in both shooters before I breach and enter. If not, we finish the guards in a ninety-degree cross fire. I secure the girl, bring her out, and we EXFIL over the wall and haul ass south to the truck. We have Kadir man the driver's seat now and start the engine the moment shooting begins."

Dempsey grimaced. "I don't know. We might need that extra gun. Would be nice to have him provide cover fire for us on the egress to the vehicle."

"Roger that, but I doubt he would engage. I trust him as an intel asset, but he's no shooter. To be honest, we just need to pray he doesn't bug out and leave us."

Dempsey grumbled at this but nodded. Just the two of them versus roughly a dozen enemy combatants . . . What could possibly go wrong?

"Okay," he said. "That all sounds good, except I think you and I should swap roles. You take the window; I'll breach the door."

There was no way he was letting anyone else breach a room alone. That burden was on him.

Theobold nodded. "Okay, fine, it's your op."

Dempsey popped his head above the wall, scanned the compound, and then dropped back down. "Those two guards by the gate will be on us quick, almost as soon as we kick it off."

"I thought of that. While you're breaching, assuming I've already dropped the two assholes inside, I'll move to the corner and take them on their approach. Cool?"

"Perfect."

Dempsey signaled go, and Theobold slipped silently over the wall. Dempsey covered the DIA operator as he sprinted across the gap to the outbuilding where Amanda Allen was being held. Theobold took a knee beneath the south window, sighted over his own rifle, and signaled to

Dempsey that he was ready to cover. Dempsey slipped over the wall and advanced low and quiet in a tactical crouch. He vectored toward the north-side corner to maintain a better angle on the two sentries smoking at the front gate. Their backs were turned, their gazes and attention fixed on the access road leading to the compound, allowing him to reach the outbuilding without detection.

Taking position in front of the door, Dempsey exhaled a long controlled breath. Then, clutching his assault rifle, he counted down in a whisper, "Three . . . two . . . one . . . *Go.*"

CHAPTER 15

Twenty-four hours?

Thirty-six?

She couldn't have been locked in the plywood cell any longer than that. She was pretty certain she'd been through only one day and one night. She'd been served only one meal—a bowl of rice that tasted like the blood in her mouth, compliments of her beating. She was leaning heavily on the instruction she'd received at the Farm. The mini-SEER module had been a blur, but they'd packed a lot into her head over those three weeks. They'd taught her to keep track of details, to keep her mind active and aware. In captivity, an agent's wits were her only weapon. Yet despite knowing this, despite trying to prepare herself for the onslaught, without punctuating events to give structure to the day—like scheduled appointments, regular meals, and the rising and setting of the sun—her mind was beginning to feel untethered. She was a kite with a cut string, sucked into the black amorphous maw of a thunderhead.

Floating and tumbling.

Lost in a room the size of a closet.

She didn't like it.

Before, in her old life, time was a reliable dancing partner. Not now. Not here. Here, it undulated and slithered around and beneath her—unpredictable and serpentine, with neither direction nor cadence.

It felt wrong and unnatural.

She closed her eyes, despite the darkness. Using two fingertips, she traced the skin and structures of her face. She started with her forehead, and then over eyebrows, roughing the hairs by going against the grain. Then she lightly caressed her eyelids, then her nose, finally settling on her lips—caressing the Cupid's bow of her upper lip back and forth. Back and forth.

Some part of her brain informed her this was a self-stimulating, self-soothing behavior—a coping mechanism in response to her captivity. *The first of many,* she thought, and decided not to judge herself too harshly.

No matter what happens, I have to preserve my core spirit. They'll try to break me. Depending on their methods and their brutality, they will undoubtedly succeed in breaking many parts of me. And I can let them break the parts because the parts can be put back together. But I have to protect my spirit. Lock it away in their presence and let it shine when I'm alone.

Gunfire erupted outside, jolting her from the confinement-induced stupor toying with her wits. Adrenaline flooded her bloodstream and her senses sharpened. Fear blossomed in her chest, along with uncertainty and hope. *Yes, hope.* Were the Navy SEALs here to rescue her? The timing made sense, executing the rescue before the terrorists could move her.

Glass shattered, and a loud volley of automatic weapon fire reverberated nearby. Reflexively, she shrank into the corner, making herself small, wondering if an errant strafe would send bullets ripping through the plywood walls of her cell, killing her accidentally. A pair of volleys answered, but this time the sound was muted because they were coming from outside the house. She heard boots pounding and men shouting just outside her cell. More glass shattered as bullets raked the walls and windows of the safe house. The intensity of the firefight increased, with more shooters seemingly joining the fray. She dropped to her stomach and pressed herself flat to the floor. She waited, lying perfectly still, listening. Her heart pounded fast and hard against her ribs as the battle for her liberation raged all around her. Then, as suddenly as it had begun, the gunfire stopped.

A lump formed in her throat.

What's going on now? Is it over?

She heard a crack, followed by three gunshots—single trigger pulls, not a volley this time.

"Amanda Allen?" a man's voice boomed, baritone and hard.

Electric anticipation washed over her, and she popped up to her knees. "I'm here," she tried to call, but her voice faltered.

"Amanda Allen," the voice called again, this time closer and louder. "This is a hostage rescue, and I'm with the United States government."

She swallowed hard and tried again. "I'm here," she cried. "I'm in here."

"When you were eight years old, you lived with your grandparents. What was the name of the town?" he shouted.

The non sequitur caught her off guard. "I don't understand," she called to him.

"Authentication protocol to confirm you're actually you."

"Cottonwood Falls."

"And what type of animal did you go on a crusade to save that autumn?"

"Ladybugs," she said, a satisfied smile spreading across her face. "I tried to save all the ladybugs." Then, without warning, she began to weep uncontrollably.

"Are you injured?" he asked, but before she got a chance to answer, fresh gunfire erupted. Two bullets punched holes in the facing wall of her cell a mere foot above her head. Twin shafts of light streamed through like miniature spotlights as she dropped back to the floor and covered her head.

"We've got a problem, dude," she heard another male voice call.

"No shit," the first man cursed. "Where are they?"

"They're firing from the other building," the other man answered.

"Then we EXFIL back out the south window."

"Negative. We've got shooters flanking south. They're going to try to catch us in a cross fire."

"Stay low, Amanda," the first man barked. "We've got some bad guys to kill before we can get you out of here. I'll be back."

"Don't go. Don't leave me!" she heard herself cry out, but her plea was drowned by gunfire.

Gunfire raged on for what felt like an eternity, but she didn't trust her perception of time. Then she heard someone yell, "Grenade!" and a beat later, a deafening thunderclap shook the ground. Shards of shrapnel punched fresh holes in her plywood prison, adding a half-dozen new rays of light streaming into her cell. Forcing herself not to panic, she performed a quick self-assessment—no acute pain, no burning, no wetness.

The firefight resumed, but now the tenor of the weapons firing from inside the house had changed. She was no weapons aficionado, but from her time at the Farm, she knew that every weapon had a unique sound signature that was a function of its design as well as the type and caliber of ammunition being fired. As she listened to the staccato pops, her stomach suddenly soured.

Something's wrong, she thought.

She heard footsteps, and someone started fiddling with the lock on the door to her cell. The heavy padlock clanked as it was dropped on the floor. The door flung open, and a hulking figure stood backlit in the doorway. She squinted, fixing her gaze to try to make out the man's face.

"No," she gasped, her fragile hope shattering.

"Get up," the man with the broken tooth barked.

She tried to scuttle backward away from him, but he stepped into the cell and grabbed a fistful of her hair. She yelped as he jerked her to her feet. Limbs flailing, she accidentally knocked over the full pail of her urine. It splashed on her left leg and foot but also onto his boots. Cursing, he threw her out of the cell onto the floor and kicked her several times. Then, grabbing her by the hair again, he dragged her toward the front of the house. She clutched his powerful wrist as he pulled her, lest he pop her head right off her shoulders. The female terrorist was waiting for them at the threshold of a door leading to what looked like a dirt field beyond. The woman held a black hood in her hands. The man with the broken tooth released Amanda's hair, and as quick as a serpent strike, the woman brought the heavy fabric bag over her head.

"Nooooo," Amanda screamed, clawing desperately to free herself, but two powerful arms picked her up off the ground. There were several more bursts of gunfire, and she felt her hope rise again.

"Kill them," hollered the man with the broken tooth. His calm confidence snuffed that hope out.

Another burst of machine gun fire, this one followed by another and another. She tried to struggle, but the arm holding her across the terrorist's shoulder was an iron vise. The man with the broken tooth carried her outside and threw her into the back seat of an idling vehicle. She was blind inside the hood, and she could barely breathe, but she fought anyway. She heard the door opposite her open. This was it, her last and only chance. Someone climbed into the back seat next to her. The woman probably. With a feral scream, Amanda lashed out—punching, clawing, and kicking. She tried to scramble out the other side of the SUV, but a hand jerked her back. The engine roared and she felt the SUV lurch. A heartbeat later, something smashed into the side of her head.

There was an explosion of pain.

And then nothing.

CHAPTER 16

Dempsey performed a quick self-assessment.

He'd felt the heat, felt the concussive blast, but had managed to dive out the window a split second before the grenade detonated. His right shoulder stung with pain from the awkward impact on the ground, but he didn't appear to have taken any shrapnel. He scanned for Theobold, but the former Delta operator was nowhere to be found.

"Two, this is One," he said, scrambling to his feet. "Do you have eyes on the package?"

No response.

Had Theobold been hit in the barrage of AK-47 cross fire that had pinned them down and prevented the egress they'd planned? And what had become of Amanda Allen? He advanced to the corner of the outbuilding and took a knee. A volley of AK-47 fire strafed the building just feet away. A beat later, he heard return fire nearby.

Dempsey popped around the corner, fired several short bursts at the main house, and shouted, "I'm coming, Sean." He didn't have to go far; Theobold was collapsed against the side of the outbuilding, trying to return fire from a dreadfully indefensible position. Dempsey grabbed him by the straps and dragged him around the corner.

"How bad are you hit?" he asked, inspecting the operator.

"I took a round in the flank," Theobold said, wincing, "but I'm in the fight."

"Where's Allen?" Dempsey said. "Did you see what happened?"

"They dragged her out, threw a bag over her head, and tossed her in the back of an SUV. I tried to go after her, but there were too many of them."

"It's okay," Dempsey said, moving back to the corner. "I'll get her back."

He sighted around the corner and fired a volley at the main house, then scanned the access road. An SUV was already tearing away, the right front tire crushing the head of one of their fallen terrorist comrades like a grape as it accelerated toward the closed gate. A second vehicle, a pickup truck, spun tires and accelerated in retreat as a fleeing terrorist dove into the open bed.

Well, at least that's one less bastard shooting at us, Dempsey thought as he watched the lead SUV smash through the gate, skidding and weaving before straightening out to speed down the access road toward the highway. He shifted his attention from the SUV bugging out with Amanda Allen inside to the enemy fighters in the driveway. Two shooters stood behind the remaining car, a sedan, holding assault rifles and raining fire down on their position. He positioned the red dot of his holosite center of mass on one of the shooters, squeezed the trigger, and the man collapsed in a heap by the rear bumper. He tried to shift his aim to the other shooter, but a volley of AK-47 rounds splintered the wood inches above his head, driving him back to cover.

After a three count, he popped out to fire another volley, but something terrible caught his attention: a figure stood backlit in the open door of the main house, pointing a rocket-propelled grenade launcher directly at him.

"RPG," he shouted.

A bright flash burned away Dempsey's night vision, and the glowing projectile sailed toward them, dragging a serpentine trail of smoke behind it. Dempsey sprinted clear and dove as the RPG slammed into the side of the outbuilding. He experienced the all-too-familiar feeling of the universe being compressed and the air being sucked away, and then the tinny, head-full-of-cotton feeling that told him he had survived as debris rained on and around him.

Groaning, he turned to look back at the main house and saw the doorway was now empty and the shooter was fleeing toward the idling sedan. Rage and fury drove him to his feet, and without a second thought, he pursued. His weapon was up, and in that moment, it became an extension of his consciousness. His red targeting dot found the middle of the fleeing shooter's back and two rounds flew, connecting and pitching the man forward, his back arching violently as he crumpled to the dirt. Dempsey shifted the red dot to the next target—a bearded fighter, rifle coming up—and squeezed the trigger. The round entered the man's forehead and spit his skull's gory contents out onto the trunk. The final shooter saw this and immediately panicked; he dropped his weapon and fumbled with the rear driver-side door as Dempsey charged straight at him.

Three more strides and Dempsey would be there.

The driver whirled to look at Dempsey through the rear glass. Dempsey saw terror in the man's eyes, and a heartbeat later, the engine roared to life. The car's tires sprayed sand and pebbles in a rooster tail as it fought for traction. It fishtailed wildly, knocking the panicked fighter to the ground. The young terrorist screamed as both of his legs went under the car, where they were promptly crushed by the car's spinning rear tires. Dempsey put a bullet through the man's throat as he ran past. He let his rifle fall against his chest, secured to his torso by a combat sling. He sprinted, arms pumping, as the car lurched forward. He willed his legs to pound the dirt just a little faster and then dove awkwardly, trying to land on the hood—his plan to shoot the driver through the windshield.

He didn't make it and succeeded only in hooking his left arm around the sideview mirror as his legs dragged along the dirt. He pulled the mirror into his left armpit; it creaked but did not rip off under his weight. His head smacked against the driver-side window, leaving a greasy, bloody smear across the already cracked glass. Their eyes met. The driver screamed and then went for his AK-47 on the passenger seat. At the same time, Dempsey cocked his right arm and smashed his gloved fist into the driver-side window.

He felt a sharp pop in his hand as the glass exploded into a thousand shards. His fist kept going, however, and struck the driver just behind his left ear. The driver grunted and clutched the wheel with both hands. He glanced at Dempsey, then at the stone wall along the drive. With a malevolent grin, he accelerated and pulled the wheel left, apparently intent on smashing Dempsey into that wall, but Dempsey was too quick. He hooked his right arm around the man's neck, pulled the driver into a headlock, and then let go of the mirror with his left arm. His boots skidded and kicked in the dirt as he pulled and twisted. He felt a nauseating crunch as the bones in the man's neck gave way under the wrenching twist of his full weight. Then he let go, tossing both arms up and over his head a beat before he hit the dirt. The left rear tire whirred past, missing his face by mere inches as he rolled clear. Metal shrieked and groaned as the sedan plowed into the wall and scraped along until it came to a stop.

Dempsey allowed himself one more roll and then used the momentum to propel himself back to his feet. A beat later, he was sighting over his rifle and advancing on the vehicle. Through the passenger-side windows, he could make out a figure slumped over in the driver seat. He flung open the front passenger door and looked inside. The terrorist's head was leaning against the steering wheel, his eyes open and wide with terror. The rest of the man's body, however, was flaccid and limp in the seat, muscles no longer receiving commands from his brain, thanks to the torn spinal cord in his neck.

The driver's bloody mouth moved in a plea: *"Fadlika . . . Idrukni." Please . . . Leave me alone.*

Dempsey fired a single round through the man's forehead. Then he grabbed the back of the dead man's collar and pulled him roughly out of the car. Unslinging his rifle, Dempsey slid into the driver seat. He put the transmission in reverse. Metal screeched as he accelerated backward, until he managed to steer off the wall. He whipped the sedan through a 180-degree turn, shifted into drive, and piloted the old Peugeot back to the compound, where the outbuilding once housing Amanda Allen was now a smoldering pile of rubble. He put the gear shifter in park, climbed out of the car, and sprinted to where he'd last seen Theobold. Spying a booted foot, Dempsey waded through the debris and began frantically clearing chunks of broken lumber.

The leg moved.

"Sean!" he barked. "You alive?"

A hand came up and pushed aside a hunk of corrugated roof panel to reveal a bloody, soot-covered face. Theobold blinked twice, and then his gaze came into focus. "Fuck me," he said. "Did I just get blown up?"

Dempsey grinned tightly, his hands now flying over the battered body beneath him looking for mortal injuries. "Yeah, afraid so, brother. Where are you hit?"

"Right flank, or maybe right chest. Just outside my body armor. Can't tell now. Hurts everywhere."

Dempsey felt Theobold's wet shirt, soaked with blood. Then he quickly checked his pulse. The man's heart was pounding fast—but strong—meaning he'd not lost too much blood . . . yet. He was talking and breathing fast but not gasping, which meant the right lung wasn't collapsed.

"I'm gonna get you home, Sean."

"But the girl."

"They got away," he said through gritted teeth. "I'm gonna take care of you first. Then I'm going after her."

He dragged Theobold out of the rubble and then tried to raise Ember: "Boeing One . . . Olympus . . . This is Atlas One. Anyone up?"

No response.

"Kadir, check in," he barked.

No response.

Over the rear wall of the compound, he could see the taillights of the two fleeing vehicles on the horizon, just now disappearing from view. Based on the vector, Dempsey decided they were probably headed to Raqqa. It was a guess, but where else could they go? If he hurried, there was a chance he could intercept them. If he hurried, he could still save her.

"Kadir, I know you can hear me, asshole. Answer me or I will come find you and shoot you myself."

"I am here. I am in the vehicle."

"Where?"

"Right where we left it."

"Come to us."

"There is no road."

Dempsey was growing irate.

"The terrain is fine. The SUV can handle it. I'm moving toward you now."

Sean's eyes were still clear, his jaw clenched in pain.

"I gotcha, man," Dempsey said. The urge to tear after Amanda Allen's kidnappers was pulling at him, but one way or another, he'd get his chance. For now, he focused on his commitment to the Special Warfare ethos.

No man gets left behind.

Dempsey looked down at Theobold. "I'm going to get you up into a carry."

"All right," the operator said.

Dempsey executed a Ranger roll—grasping the injured man's arm and leg and pulling them together across his chest with his own arms as he rolled over the top of the reclined operator's torso. He grunted and pressed up onto his feet, Theobold up and in a fireman's carry position across his shoulders. He moved rapidly toward the wall and slipped over it with the man still on his shoulders, smoothly dropping to a knee on the other side.

"Fucking ouch," Theobold said.

"I know, bro. Hang tough."

He could see headlights tearing toward him, bouncing up and down. He wished Kadir had the sense to turn the headlights off, but it didn't really matter anymore. The bad guys at the compound were all either dead or gone. Moments later, the white SUV with the blue "UN" emblazoned on the side skidded to a stop nearby.

Dempsey opened the passenger door and set Theobold as gently as possible on the seat.

"What happened?" Kadir asked, his brow furrowed.

"He got shot. That's what happened," Dempsey growled. "Do not go back to al-Bab. Do you understand me? You need to go north, back to Turkey through the border crossing at Elbeyli."

"And cross how? How will I explain this?" Kadir asked, terrified.

"You tell them Dr. Theobold was shot during an ambush while we were taking samples north of al-Bab. That's a story the UN team leader will know, and it's what you stick to," he said as he removed Theobold's body armor and pulled the NVGs from his head. "The NOC will hold up. Get him to medical care."

"And what about you?" Theobold asked, his expression pained.

"You tell Turkish officials the last you saw me, the bad guys were dragging me off towards a truck. Tell them you think I'm dead. But when *my* people get in touch, tell them the truth and that I'm headed east towards Raqqa. Tell them I'm gonna get Allen back or die trying."

"You're headed to Raqqa alone?"

"I've got to. They know we're coming for her now. She probably doesn't have much time left," Dempsey said, put a hand on the man's shoulder, and smiled. "Thanks, Sean. For being the warrior you are. And I'm sorry the op went to hell. Looks like you were right after all. Shoulda waited."

The man shook his head. "No, man, I'm sorry. I'm sorry we didn't get her out . . . We were this fucking close," Theobold said, holding his fingers up in a pinch.

Dempsey nodded and turned to leave.

After a beat, the former Delta operator called out, "Hooyah, frogman."

A smile crept across Dempsey's face, but he didn't look back.

Hooyah, brother . . . Hooyah.

CHAPTER 17

Heart pounding, Grimes rolled away from the sniper rifle, scooped up her Rattler, and moved swiftly toward the air-handling unit on top of the hangar roof.

She could hear voices.

Someone was coming for her.

Taking cover behind the stout metal structure, she dropped to a knee at the corner. She adjusted her NVGs, and the green targeting laser streaming from her weapon reappeared. Exhaling to calm her nerves, she sighted around the corner and put the green laser a foot below the top of the ledge where the ladder cage accessed the roof.

She waited . . .

Tink . . . tink . . .

A face materialized and peered over the ledge—male, bearded, no NVGs. In high-resolution green-gray night vision, she watched his eyes scan the roof. The decision she had to make would likely determine her fate. Did she shoot him now and prevent him from gaining access to the roof, or did she wait? Killing him now was the easier option, but she didn't know how many others were behind him, and killing the leader would alert them to her presence.

And I have to be sure he's not a friendly . . .

If she'd thought to come up here for base defense, then other coalition SOF operators might do the same.

Damn it.

Her pulse was pounding so loudly in her ears, it was all she could hear. She watched as the man slipped over the ledge and went into a crouch. He was dressed in dark pants and an untucked shirt, not a uniform and not unmarked tactical clothing. A rifle strap angled across his chest. She could see the end of the muzzle sticking above his left shoulder, but she couldn't discern the make or model. Seemingly satisfied that the roof was clear, he turned and called out to someone behind him in what sounded like Arabic, but she couldn't be sure. A beat later, another head appeared over the ledge. This dude was wearing a *keffiyeh*—a long patterned scarf—and had it wrapped around his head, neck, and mouth in the style common to Middle East fighters. Her finger tensed on the trigger. *Is it enough to make the call?*

No.

She had worn them on Middle East operations, and Dempsey typically wore a keffiyeh when he was embedded. The second man dropped onto the roof and then looked back over the ledge and motioned to someone else farther down the ladder.

Shit. How many are there?

The second man was standing now. He began walking toward the north side, when he abruptly stopped—his gaze fixed where her sniper rifle rested, propped up on the ledge by its bipod. The man hollered back at his companion, who quickly brought his rifle around—an AK-47.

All the data considered together was enough to act.

She dropped the first terrorist with a two-round volley to the chest. As he crumpled to the ground, she shifted her aim to shooter number two, the one whose face was hidden by the shemagh, and dropped him with a headshot. She sighted back to the ladder egress, ready for a third insurgent, but she didn't see anyone. She surged to her feet, advanced around the corner of the air handler, and sprinted to the ledge. She resisted the urge to peer over, lest she get shot in the face. Instead, she drifted right, giving herself an offset. She took two quick breaths, sighted over the ledge, and spied four dark figures lined up inside the ladder cage like a column of soldier ants climbing the building. But these guys weren't climbing; they were furiously retreating back down the ladder, the top fighter shouting in panic.

It was fish in a barrel . . .

A moment later, they were all corpses. She squeezed off a few insurance rounds into the bodies, then knelt to peek over the ledge and scan the grounds on this side of the hangar, looking for movement and additional threats. Seeing nothing, she jogged to the WinMag and settled back into position behind her long gun. A firefight raged to the north, near the B61 vault, and she saw additional vehicles screaming across the base in that direction. But in this corner of the base, everything seemed to have gone abruptly quiet. She looked right, toward the Boeing, to check on Munn and the QRF contingent but didn't see any people or vehicles on the tarmac. A rush of panic washed over her.

"Where'd they go?" she mumbled, scanning around the Boeing and the damaged Osprey but not finding anyone. A knot began to form in her stomach.

Damn it.

She was overwatch. She was Zeus, the WinMag her thunderbolt. As with her other default sniper call signs—God and Mother—her role on the team was to watch over and shield the operators on the ground. The implication was not subtle; a sniper's job was to dole out death with absolute discrimination from on high. Protecting Munn, Latif, and Martin was her responsibility, and she'd failed them. She had a perfectly valid excuse, of course, but that didn't change the fact that when they'd needed her most, "God" had been busy.

"If I just had fucking comms," she grumbled, "I could at least—"

A figure appeared on the top landing of the Boeing's air-stair, then turned and waved in her direction. She switched her optics from thermal to night vision and saw that the figure was Munn. She exhaled with relief. He waved for several more seconds, then just stared in her direction. She wondered how to signal him, but then he made it easy for her by raising a handheld scope to his eye and looking at her. She waved and stood up enough that her IR strobe would be visible to him. It worked because he waved again, then gave her a thumbs-up. Next, he cupped a hand to his ear and gave her *another* thumbs-up.

"Did you fix comms?" she said, feeling a surge of excitement, hoping that her earbud would come alive, but Munn's familiar voice did not greet her in response.

He was still spotting her with his scope, so she cupped her hand to her ear and then dragged a straight index finger across her throat. Munn nodded in understanding, then gestured for her to come down. She screwed up her face.

What the hell? The base is still under attack.

He traced his index finger in a circle in the air above his head and then made a gesture with a hand shooting out toward the horizon, which, combined, she took to mean: *Wrap it up; we're bugging out.* She gave him a thumbs-up, and he disappeared back into the Boeing. Certainly the plane wasn't fixed. Maybe he'd gotten the portable comms unit up and running. Her thoughts went immediately to Dempsey: Did they have comms back with Dempsey? Was Amanda Allen confirmed at the compound? Had the terrorists tried to move her? Had Dempsey intervened? Did he need the QRF? Were they already too late?

She shook her head.

I'll know soon enough . . .

She was about to pack up the WinMag when she noticed a white pickup truck heading down the tarmac in the general direction of the Boeing. She leaned in for a look on the scope and increased her magnification. It was hard to tell in the monochrome world of night vision, but she thought she could make out a winged United States Air Force emblem painted on the side of the door. She clicked the magnification again. Two men were seated in the cab. They didn't look like American servicemen, but again, on this base, that didn't count for much. She swept left, back to the air-stair, and saw Latif carrying a load of gear down to the tarmac. Martin was already at the bottom setting down two large duffel bags. A beat later, Munn stepped out of the plane, arms burdened with a full load of gear. None of them appeared to notice the truck, which was approaching from the other side of the plane. None of them seemed alarmed. They must be expecting it. Made sense; they were going to load their gear in the bed and hitch a ride to whatever air asset Adamo had procured for them.

Satisfied, she eased back on her haunches . . .

But something still didn't feel right.

She shifted back into shooting posture and assessed the truck through the scope. *These guys should be slowing down.* She increased the magnification and looked through the windshield at the men's faces. *This is all wrong. Trust your instincts,* she told herself. After that, she stopped thinking, and the sniper took over. She selected her target—the engine block—but it would be a tricky shot. The vehicle was coming in at a narrow angle, and its speed was hard to judge. She did the math in her head, corrected for wind and speed, and aimed.

She exhaled.

Trigger squeeze.

The WinMag kicked. She chambered a new round. At first she thought she'd missed, but as she corrected for her next shot, steam suddenly erupted from the grill and corners of the hood. The truck veered right toward the Boeing and then stopped. Two men hopped out, pulling AK-47s with them. The passenger was wearing something bulky under his shirt and held something small in his left hand. A detonator? She increased the magnification another tick, zooming in. Yes, she was sure. She needed to drop him now, at barely a safe distance from her team and the Boeing.

Exhale.

Squeeze.

The man's head spit gray and black out behind him and he crumpled to the ground. His partner opened fire in the direction of Martin, Latif, and Munn. She prayed they'd taken cover behind the air-stair. She closed her eyes to protect her night vision from the impending boom.

A dull whump echoed from the tarmac.

She counted to three and then opened her eyes.

The suicide bomber was gone—completely evaporated. The second insurgent was on the ground, writhing in pain from the injuries sustained when the dead man's switch had blown his partner to bits. Then, with an apparent surge of adrenaline and renewed purpose, he lunged for his AK-47.

Grimes sighted.

Exhaled.

And sent him to join his friend in hell.

"Clear," she said, even though no one could hear her, and scanned left. She counted one, two, three operators—all intact and on their feet. Munn turned to face her and gave her an appreciative salute. Feeling redeemed, she scanned the entire tarmac one last time before packing up and heading to the Boeing to rejoin her team.

"Thanks a lot for taking out our driver and blowing up our ride," Munn said with a toothy grin as she jogged up to meet him several minutes later.

"I thought I told you guys never to call an Uber."

With a laugh, he wrapped her in a big bear hug, which she returned awkwardly. "You saved our asses, girl," he said, releasing her. "That was some fine shooting."

"Thanks," she said, the corner of her mouth curling up. Then, looking over his shoulder at the still burning hangar behind him, "Now if you don't mind, what the fuck is going on, Dan?"

"Terror attack," he said simply. "A big one."

"They went after the nukes, didn't they?"

"Yeah, but I just heard on the radio that the offensive has been put down."

"I don't understand. The nukes are in a vault. Even with an assault force this big, they'd need artillery to get in there. And even if they got in—"

"I'm going to stop you right there," Munn interrupted her. "The nukes aren't our concern. We have direct and immediate tasking from the DNI. There's a *second* attack underway right now. A CIA compound fifteen clicks from here. Our conventional forces here on base are tied up, obviously, and the Turks have shut down all US action outside Incirlik—which leaves us. Our tasking is to save the compound and EXFIL the ten-man team pinned down there. They're rigging their sensitive equipment for destruction, but the situation is desperate. If we don't hurry, we could have another Benghazi on our hands."

"What are the Turks doing to help?"

"That's the problem. Apparently, we neglected to inform them about the existence of this particular facility. Now that they are aware of it, Erodan is irate. His supposed response to President Warner was, 'How can Turkey help protect a facility that does not exist?' The DNI did get a back-channel promise from the head of Turkish Counterterror that they would mobilize in an hour—but that probably means five. Our guys will all be dead in half that time. We're leaving now."

"Okay," she said, nodding. "But what about Dempsey?"

"For the time being, at least, Dempsey's on his own. The DNI made this priority one."

"He's alive?"

"Yeah."

"And Allen?"

"I'll explain what I know in the air," he said, looking up and over her shoulder. That's when she noticed the faint beat of helicopter rotors on the wind. "We have two Jordanian Air Force helos inbound, so I hope you're ready to kick some more ass."

The corner of her mouth curled up into a crooked grin, and she tapped her WinMag. "Always."

PART II

To contemplate is to look into the shadows.

—*Victor Hugo,* Les Travailleurs de la mer

CHAPTER 18

M4 Highway
Eighteen Miles Northeast of al-Bab, Syria
May 6
2315 Local Time

The horrible rattle that had plagued the battered Peugeot for the last twenty miles was now accompanied by a loud hiss.

"Looks like I'm going to be walking soon," Dempsey grumbled and then cursed the car and his luck like a proper frogman, using every possible variant of the F-word—noun, verb, adjective, and adverb.

Fortunately, he'd made it past al-Bab, and now he was headed east toward Ar Raqqa. By the time he'd gotten on the road from the compound, the SUV with Amanda Allen was long gone. And since he had no comms, he wasn't able to validate with Baldwin to see where the target vehicle had gone. His instincts told him Raqqa because it was a vile place occupied by vile men—the perfect spot to torture or trade an American female hostage if you were in the business of terrorism. Picturing the map of the region he'd studied during his pre-op prep, his mind's eye visualized two possible routes—one going southeast of Lake

Assad, the other circling northeast. The former was faster, but the latter went through Manbij, which would give the terrorists an opportunity to swap vehicles or get supplies.

Dempsey had decided to take the road through Manbij for similar reasons. The cloud of steam streaming over the windshield told him he wasn't going to make it. He felt the car begin to slow, pressed on the gas, and the vehicle promptly coughed and died. Grumbling, he steered it off the road and then, while the diminishing momentum allowed, into the shallow roadside ditch.

"Shit."

He climbed out of the steaming piece of junk and grabbed his night vision goggles. He scanned the barren, rocky terrain in all directions: no movement, no headlights, no nothing. A dim aura winked on the horizon to the east. Manbij. He sighed and slung his kit over his head, the familiar weight on his shoulders comforting. He tapped a finger on his remaining magazines—four, which meant 120 rounds on top of the magazine already in his rifle. Two extra magazines for the Sig Sauer pistol on his thigh meant another 45 rounds. He had two grenades and one frag in the pouch on the left side of his kit. He slung his Sig 716 assault rifle over his chest in a combat carry and set off toward the lights.

His first priority was to find a place to hole up before morning light. He was deep in "Indian country" now, traversing a dangerous crossroads in the middle of a country embroiled in the greatest war of factions the world had ever seen. The Syrians, the rebels, the Turks, the Kurds, the Israelis, the Iranians, Al-Nusra, ISIS, the Russians, and US coalition forces were all playing in this bloody sandbox . . . and the Syrian people were paying the price. During his two decades in the Teams, he'd seen the type of death and misery up close that would make most Americans vomit, but Syria was spiraling into a tragedy of epic proportions.

His thoughts drifted to Amanda Allen.

"I was so close," he mumbled. "So fucking close, I almost had her."

They're going to kill her. They know we're coming after them now, so they're going to cut off her head, make their YouTube video, and scatter like the roaches that they are.

Uncertainty was the worst part of his job. The worst part. Outside the community, people assumed it was the repetitive violence, or the physical abuse, or the emotional trauma, or maybe the impact to personal relationships that was the hardest part of being an operator. Yeah, those things were a bitch, but the uncertainty in moments like this was worse. Everyone on the inside knew it, felt it. That's why intelligence collection was the cornerstone of special operations—to systematically remove uncertainty. But in the field, at the tip of the spear, alone without comms and without data, an operator had only two weapons to combat uncertainty—hope and instinct—both of which Dempsey was leaning on heavily at the moment.

What he wanted more than anything in the world was Baldwin's annoying professorial voice in his ear. He wanted the Ember Signals guru to launch into one of his long-winded explanations about how some solar flare had jacked their comms; he wanted to listen to him babble until he couldn't stand it anymore and then snap at the man to get to the point; and then he wanted Baldwin to say that despite the snafu, they had maintained satellite coverage throughout the assault, had tracked Allen to a safe house just two clicks away, and that Munn and the rest of Ember's SAD were en route in the Osprey to join the fight and take them home.

That was not going to happen.

He was on his own. He would have to find these assholes by himself. He would have to rescue Allen by himself. And he would have to figure some way to get them both back across the border into Turkey by himself.

Easy day.

Then he heard Munn's voice in his head—*The only easy day was yesterday, dude*—and he started to laugh. That was the motto he'd lived by in the Teams. He'd just never believed it could be as true as it was now.

He mulled this over in his mind until a dim light ahead caught his attention. *This could be an opportunity,* he thought. An opportunity for new wheels. His right hand drifted to the grip of his rifle, ready to bring it up into a firing position in an instant. His finger tapped the outside of the trigger guard as he closed on the light. After a hundred meters, he could make out a small house—more of a hut—surrounded by stacks of wood in a makeshift fence. As he got closer, he saw that the "fence" was little more than an impediment to keep two goats penned in. He peered through a sheer fabric curtain hanging behind an open window and saw an old man asleep in front of a dying fire. He scanned the grounds but saw no vehicles—not even a beat-up farm truck or dilapidated motorcycle. He did, however, spy a bicycle with a bent tire leaning against the fence, and for a moment he contemplated stealing it—but it was such a piece of shit, it would probably slow him down. Anyway, the thought of getting killed while pedaling that ridiculous thing was more than he could bear. There was no question John Dempsey would depart this world in a painful death . . . but not like that.

Dempsey slipped over the pile of stacked wood and moved to the left of the house. One goat ignored him completely. The other looked over, stretched out its long pink tongue, and then farted and turned away. With a wayward scowl at the offensive creature, Dempsey walked around the hut until he spied a tattered square of burlap fabric tarped over a half cord of firewood stacked beside the house. He took the tarp and quietly balled it up under his left arm. Beside the wood pile rested an ax with a burgundy-colored keffiyeh draped over the handle. He grabbed it and wrapped it around his neck, gagging at the smell as he did.

Jesus, this thing smells worse than the goats.

He slipped back over the makeshift fence and resumed his trek toward Manbij. As he walked, he pulled his SOG knife from the scabbard on the front of his kit and cut a foot-long hole roughly in the center of the gray-brown tarp. He replaced his knife and pulled the improvised poncho over his head. *There, at least now I don't look like a kitted-up operator at a hundred meters.* Suddenly feeling empowered, he picked up the pace—double-timing it now toward the lights.

"Atlas One, this is Olympus . . . Do you copy?"

Dempsey stopped and took a knee, wondering if his mind was playing tricks on him or if he really had just heard Baldwin's voice in his ear.

"Olympus, this is Atlas," Dempsey said. "How do you read?"

"Yes, I know . . . I know they want it back, but tell them we just found our man and politely inform them we need a few more minutes," Baldwin was saying.

Dempsey rolled his eyes and grinned. "Say again, over."

"Sorry about that, Atlas. We're dealing with asset-management issues today," Baldwin said. "But we read you Lima Charlie. Stand by . . ."

"Atlas—Olympus—SITREP?" said a new voice in his ear. Shane Smith, and he was all business.

"Atlas does not have the package. My assets are both back across the border, or should be by now. I am solo and in pursuit."

In pursuit? That was probably a stretch . . .

"Atlas, we believe we have you on imagery. Confirm you are twenty miles east of the original target and north of Highway M4?"

Dempsey hesitated a beat, swearing under his breath at how ridiculous his situation and his plan were now that he was forced to report on them. "That is my position," he said.

"Confirm you have a location on the package?"

"I do not have a confirmed location on the package—yet." An uncomfortable silence hung on the air. When Smith didn't say anything, Dempsey said, "Were you guys 'eyes on' during the firefight? Do you have imagery you can use to confirm the package EXFIL from the original compound?"

"What firefight? Are you intact?"

Dempsey shook his head in annoyance.

"We confirmed the package was at the compound, but before we lost comms, three vehicles arrived to move the package. We had to act before the window of opportunity closed. We were unsuccessful, but I am intact. Do you have imagery from the event?"

"Negative. There *was and is* a major situation requiring our imagery assets. We will have to pull historical data and use whatever we can find to reconstruct."

"Roger. I have a strong lead on the package but need time for ISR to confirm. Headed east of current position."

There was a long pause, and Dempsey scanned his surroundings in the silver moonlight while he waited for the reply. The night was perfectly still and benign, not even a single vehicle moving on the highway a half mile south of him.

"Atlas, are you five by?"

Was he? Physically he was five by five. He was armed and now had Ember in his ear. Emotionally? That was another matter.

"Yes. I'm five by five. I may be able to confirm package location by next nightfall." Now that was a complete fabrication. He had no leads other than seeing the target SUV heading east when it first bugged out from the compound. Allen could be anywhere. "Are you keeping eyes on?"

"Negative, Crusader. And we are going to lose comms again."

"Wait a minute. We're not back up on UHF SATCOM?"

"Negative. We borrowed a drone from our friends in Tel Aviv, but we spent all the time we had looking for you. Now they want it back. Once the situation in Turkey is under control, we'll get dedicated satellite or drone coverage back."

"What situation in Turkey?"

“No time to explain,” Smith said. “Advise you find a location to shelter in place and wait until we contact you. By that time we should have reconstructed data and the QRF stood back up and ready to assist. Good luck, Atlas. Olympus out.”

Dempsey got to his feet and pushed east at a fast clip. What was the “situation” in Turkey that had taken Ember’s eyes and sidelined the QRF? Why hadn’t they scrambled the Osprey when they lost comms? That’s what he would’ve done. Something must have happened.

Something bad.

That was the only thing that explained Smith’s frosty demeanor, and why the Ember Director was seemingly unfazed by leaving Dempsey to his own devices in the middle of Syria.

“Olympus, Atlas . . . Is everyone all right?” Dempsey heard himself say, praying the Israeli drone was still relaying his comms. “Olympus . . . Olympus?”

CHAPTER 19

Lead Jordanian MH-60 Blackhawk Helicopter
Call Sign Sword One
Low, over the Girne Bulvari Highway, Four Miles East of Merkez Park
Adana, Turkey
2335 Local Time

Grimes tightened her grip on the sniper rifle slung over her shoulder as she watched the ground whiz by beneath the low-flying Blackhawk. Despite all her field operations with Ember over the past two years, she'd never fast-roped into combat. Next to her, Munn looked so relaxed, completely in his element. He smiled at her, and for a moment, she saw her dead brother staring back at her. Funny how far down the rabbit hole she'd tumbled. The Tier One massacre two years ago had derailed her life, it had birthed Ember, and now she was an operator. Not a SEAL, but close. If her big brother could see her right now—kitted up for a mission that his unit could have been tasked to fulfill—would he be proud? Would he be mortified? What would he think of her becoming a sniper? Would he look at her differently knowing she'd killed a dozen men in the past twenty-four hours?

"Two minutes," Munn said in her ear. "Remember, we're dropping on building three. You're overwatch, and the rest of us are going in to extract the staff. Can you manage without a spotter?"

"Sure," she said. *I did it before . . .*

"Okay, focus on the park to the east—that's our biggest vulnerability—but also keep an eye on the southern approach. Thermal imagery shows GRS staff has taken a defensive position along the west wall. We're going in but coming back to building three for EXFIL by helo. If that plan goes to shit, we will retreat west, and you'll have to follow. Copy?"

She gave him a thumbs-up. "You call the move if you need me to reposition."

"Roger," he said. "Any questions?"

"How many of the ten are GRS?" she asked. The GRS, the CIA's Global Response Staff, was a security team of contractors comprised primarily of former Special Forces operators. They would augment the rescue party—Munn, Martin, Latif, and the Air Force PJ who had insisted on coming along—and help cover the retreat.

"Four. One has a minor injury but is reportedly still in the fight. All of that could change by the time we get there. That leaves six organic CIA personnel who may or may not be helpful in a running gunfight, depending on their background."

She nodded. This facility was a Clandestine Services compound, so unlike Ground Branch safe houses, it was not manned entirely by former operators. The crew needing to be rescued was a mixed lot—some were shooters, and some were luggage.

"One minute."

She rolled her neck, aware the motion was becoming a reflexive habit, and took a long, deep breath. Then she leaned out the open door of the Blackhawk and looked at the scene unfolding below. "My

God," she said through her breath. Two of the compound's three buildings were in flames; the building at the far northwest corner was fully engulfed and belching black smoke into the night sky. A park just east of the compound was packed with rioting demonstrators, burning cars blocking access to the gathering from the street. The southern half of the U-shaped compound was an open courtyard filled with trees and secured along the perimeter by a wrought iron fence. If the rioters decided to swarm the compound, this was where they would do it. Seeing this, she decided she would set up on the southeast corner and cover the mob in the park and the southern approach simultaneously.

She felt the nose of the helicopter pull up as they flared twenty feet over the roof of the southeast building. Metallic pings reverberated around her, and it took her a moment to identify the sound—bullets fired by the mob were hitting the Blackhawk's fuselage. In response, the Jordanian door gunner answered with a burst of fifty-caliber machine gun fire. She winced, worried at first he was mowing down the crowd, before seeing that his strafe intentionally fell short. It had the desired effect, however, panicking the crowd and causing a commotion.

Munn disappeared out the door, which meant she was up.

Adrenaline surged in her veins as she shifted forward and clasped the thick rope. She twisted her hands to tighten her grip, locked the rope between the insteps of her boots, and slipped out the door. She slid fast, praying a bullet wouldn't knock her off the rope as she descended toward the roof deck. Another tongue of flame from the door gunner kept any shooters in the park down. A heartbeat later, her boots hit the roof, and she was sprinting toward her corner. In seconds, the entire team was down, and the Jordanian Blackhawks were powering up and away.

She dropped to a knee, snapped open the bipod on her WinMag, and powered on the night-vision function on the sight. She started by scanning the park for active shooters. The scene was chaos, a mob in every sense of the word. And the mob was dangerous, to be sure, but in the same unpredictable way a forest fire was dangerous. For the moment, it was acting without purpose or organization. For the moment, they were rioters, not assaulters . . . but this could change.

She took this opportunity to sweep her gaze south, scanning along the fence and inside the tree-filled courtyard for movement. Finding none, she called in.

"Zero," she reported, announcing she was in position by using a simple numeric call sign as the DNI had instructed them to do. The intention had been clear—no echoes of Ember on this joint channel. No paperwork, no familiar call signs, no clues in the recordings.

She shifted her attention back to the park.

"One is moving down the stairs. EXFIL in five or less." Munn sounded calm and controlled.

"Air in orbit," the Jordanian pilot replied, acknowledging. The same two birds that had dropped them would also haul the fifteen of them—Ember, the PJ, plus the ten CIA compound staff—off the *X*. The plan was to EXFIL to the aircraft carrier USS *Ronald Reagan* in the Med, getting everyone who wasn't supposed to be in Turkey out of Turkey to regroup and effect Dempsey's rescue without Turkish restrictions and oversight. Worry bloomed in her chest at the thought of Dempsey and how they'd been forced to abandon him in Syria.

Dempsey can take care of himself, she chastised herself. *The mission is here. The mission is now.*

She trained her scope back to the park. The crowd, which she estimated at fifty to seventy-five people, was riotous. They were yelling, pumping their fists in the air, and throwing whatever they could get their hands on. That was when she noticed that almost the entire crowd was unarmed . . . *everyone except for those guys.* She zoomed in and began to count. There were about a dozen men armed with assault rifles who seemed to be working in concert to whip the crowd into a frenzy. One of them turned and fired a volley at the compound. Then another followed suit, and then another. After each volley, they shouted and pumped their fists.

They're trying to rally the mob to swarm the grounds.

Instantly, she understood what was going on. Grimes sighted in on the man she deduced to be the ringleader from the way others were occasionally looking his direction. She ranged the target, adjusted for wind, and then sighted on the man's chest. A barrage of bullets hit the northeast corner of the building below her. She held her finger gently against the trigger as noncombatants—aka rioting civilians—danced in and out of her line of fire. This situation was different from the attack on Incirlik. At the air base, a terrorist assault force had breached a military facility housing tactical nuclear weapons. Authorization to use lethal force in defense of those assets was implicit. Here, the compound was located in a neighborhood, and the perimeter had not yet been breached. On top of that, "the compound" wasn't even supposed to exist. The rules of engagement from the DNI had been clear: use of lethal force was permitted only as a last resort. The revelation of a secret American CIA compound was damaging enough; if reports came out that American personnel were shooting civilians in the streets of Turkey, this would become an international crisis not seen in decades.

"Damn," she breathed, unable to get a clear shot. Frustrated, she scanned south, clearing the most vulnerable approach, but this time she saw activity. Two, no three, figures emerging from an alley.

"Zero—One. We're moving across the compound grounds to the west wall," Munn said in her ear. "I'm up on channel two with GRS. We will have one urgent surgical and two minor nonsurgicals."

"One—Zero. I have three possible tangos on the south side outside the wire. Could be preparing to breach."

"Check."

The three men ducked behind a parked vehicle, knelt in a huddle, and began pulling equipment from a large duffel bag.

Her heart rate picked up. "One—Zero—they're setting up a mortar."

"We won't be out in time. Take them."

Grimes sighted in on the man assembling the equipment, his hands flying expertly as he connected the tube to the tripod. She made her corrections and then . . .

Exhale.

Squeeze.

The man pitched over backward, dead.

The other two men stared at their friend in horror and shock. Then one of them leaped to his feet and sprinted back down the alley. The second screamed at him but, instead of fleeing, resumed construction of the mortar.

Exhale.

Squeeze.

His hands went to his throat, and he collapsed next to the tube, convulsing. She fired a second round, putting this one above his left eye; it killed him instantly.

She swung her barrel south, but the squirter had escaped.

"Mortar threat neutralized," she reported.

She scanned the fence and inside the courtyard looking for ambush threats.

"Courtyard is clear for your EXFIL," she added and then swung her attention back to the park. The ringleader had stepped up onto a wooden crate and was shaking his fist and rallying the crowd into a frenzy. A beat later, seemingly sensing the mob's consensus to swarm the compound, he raised his rifle and screamed a battle cry.

Sighting in, she found her line of fire clear—her target now standing head and shoulders above the crowd.

She exhaled.

And squeezed . . .

CHAPTER 20

Situation Room of the White House
May 6
1450 Local Time

"Did that sniper just kill that man in the park?" said Ted Baker, the newly sworn-in Secretary of State. "Is that sniper a woman? Who are these people?"

"Yes, the sniper is a woman," Jarvis said, irritated that the circle of people who knew of Ember's existence had just increased threefold. This exigency in Adana was not something he'd either planned on or anticipated using Ember for. "And that man," he continued, "just to be clear, is a terrorist insurgent, not a civilian."

"But how can we be sure?" he asked. "He's just one in a crowd of people."

Jarvis was about to answer when President Warner swept into the Situation Room with all the subtlety of a battering ram.

"What the hell is going on at Incirlik?" Warner barked, striding to his chair at the head of the conference table. Jarvis watched the President grip the headrest, each of his eight fingertips making angry depressions in the padded leather cushion. Warner glanced at the live feed of the rescue underway before scanning the faces in the room. All the heavy hitters were assembled, including the Vice President, SecDef, the National Security Adviser, the Secretary of State, the Director of Counterterrorism for the National Security Council, the President's Chief of Staff, and several members of the Joint Chiefs. The President's gaze ultimately settled on Jarvis.

And so did everyone else's.

Under the weight of the collective scrutiny of the most powerful people in the US government and the military, Jarvis did not wilt; he did not falter. He simply said, "Mr. President, we have two critical incidents underway in Turkey as we speak. First, we have the infiltration at Incirlik. Second, we have a coordinated attack on a CIA Clandestine Services compound in a neighborhood in Adana. We have confirmation from the base commander that the attack at Incirlik has been rebuffed, the base is on lockdown, and damage and casualty assessment is in progress. Equally pressing, we have a covert rescue operation underway at the CIA compound as you can see on the live feed."

"You authorized the rescue operation without consulting me or the Secretary of State?"

Warner's voice was firm, and he held Jarvis's gaze, but there seemed to be no overt condemnation. It was a question—for now.

"Yes, sir," he replied. "The opportunity to effect a rescue was on a remarkably short fuse. If I waited, we would have had another Benghazi on our hands. If I have overstepped my authority, it was well meaning. I know you would never allow ten Americans to be left unaided under fire. Additionally, the rescue involves deeply covert assets not appropriate for discussion with all members present—all due respect."

Secretary Baker's face suggested he felt no such respect. "Are you suggesting I don't have clearance to—"

Warner held up a hand, silencing him.

"You made the right call," Warner said, but his eyes told Jarvis there would be another private discussion about this. What Jarvis could not discern was what the nature of that conversation would be. The President took a seat and focused on the live feed. "What am I watching here?"

Jarvis glanced at the monitor and saw Grimes repositioning on the roof, the sniper rifle now slung, and sighting over a smaller assault rifle. *She must be covering the movement of the rest of the team back to the roof for EXFIL,* he thought, meaning the team might be only minutes away from a successful rescue.

"We inserted a covert team by helo with coalition assistance. We have a sniper on the roof providing overwatch and a team of operators to augment the four-man CIA GRS team on-site. The compound is under assault by what we believe is a mixed force—terrorist insurgents and Turkish civilians they've incited to riot."

On the screen, Grimes took a knee at the east wall, set her rifle, and scanned the crowd. The image rotated slowly on a central axis pinned to the center of the roof. The live feed stuttered, froze, and then refreshed, having panned out to a wider view. To the west, Munn led a line of personnel running toward the building where Grimes was. Eight shooters protected the central cluster, arranged as pairs in a diamond formation. The two shooters at the rear of the group were firing almost continually. Hearing this, Grimes swung her rifle south and began to fire.

"We've got shooters coming over the wall," someone said.

Jarvis didn't look to see who had stated the obvious, but they were right. After Grimes had dropped the apparent leader of the insurgency with a headshot for all the crowd to see, the mob had quickly disbanded—the *civilian* portion of the mob, that is. The remaining armed insurgents had not given up. They'd changed tactics and were attempting to breach the courtyard from the south, attacking the fleeing pack of Americans. The tension in the room reached a crescendo as dozens of tracers zipped through the night, and for a moment, the escape party looked like it was in serious trouble. But then, slowly and methodically, the Americans turned the tide as Grimes picked off one insurgent after another with her WinMag.

"My God, there is gonna be one helluva body count," the Secretary of State muttered as insurgent bodies began to pile up along the southern perimeter.

"But no Americans were executed on live TV only to have their corpses dragged through the streets of Adana," Jarvis said. He looked at President Warner, who held his eyes and then gave him a subtle nod. When he turned back to the feed, Jarvis saw the last two operators ascending the stairs to the rooftop where Grimes was still mopping up. A black helicopter passed beneath the drone video feed, blocking the view of the roof, as the first load of evacuees was whisked off the *X*. A second chopper followed suit, picking up Grimes and the Ember QRF shooters next, and thirty seconds later, they were looking at an empty roof. Jarvis felt his secure mobile phone vibrate in his pocket. He retrieved the device and read the EXFIL report from Ember Director Smith.

"All personnel are secure, sir," he said to the President. "Two casualties with survivable injuries, two minor nonsurgicals, and all staff and rescue team personnel are accounted for."

"Good work, Kelso," Warner said.

Thank you, Ember, Jarvis thought as he slipped his phone back into his pocket. Then, breathing easier, he turned to the room. "I'll share insurgent casualty data and a compound damage assessment as they become available, but from everything we just witnessed, this was a successful rescue operation. Now on to Incirlik."

Everyone but Secretary Baker and Catherine Morgan gave him full attention. The brand-new Secretary of State, who still looked unnerved by what he'd just watched, was leaning on an elbow toward Morgan, who was whispering in his ear.

Jarvis paused a beat, then continued despite their private powwow. "We've confirmed the details of what was a large-scale terrorist incursion at Incirlik Air Base. This was remarkably well coordinated, sir. Four separate teams executing four separate but synchronized breaches. They used vehicles to breach the perimeter fences, used mortar teams to target air assets on the tarmac and in aircraft hangars, and deployed suicide bombers against the main security building as well as the main operations center."

"Casualties?" Warner demanded.

"Unknown yet, sir, but most definitely the number is high," the Secretary of Defense said, joining the conversation.

"Like Beirut barracks high?" the President asked, referring to the terrorist attack on the Marine barracks in Beirut, which had left 241 American and 58 French peacekeepers dead in 1983.

"Not that high, but it'll be a real number."

The Chairman of the Joint Chiefs, four-star Air Force General Peter McMillan, jumped in. "The attack has been rebuffed, Mr. President. But our security forces will be engaged for several hours or more making sure that none of the assholes who infiltrated the base are hiding and preparing to hit us again when our guard is down during cleanup operations."

"I'll want a breakdown of the casualties by nationality. This won't scare us into leaving Turkey, but not all of our partners share our resolve."

Jarvis decided the time was right to share the rest of the "good" news. "Sir, we believe they were going after the B61s."

Warner's gaze shifted back to Peter McMillan. "Just to confirm, Pete, for everyone in the room, the ordnance Director Jarvis is referring to are nukes?"

"*Tactical* nuclear weapons," McMillan clarified. "But yes, sir, that is correct."

"But we have no evidence whatsoever to suggest that's the case." The Secretary of Defense scowled. "We're still getting a handle on this thing. We don't know anything."

"Actually, sir, we do," Jarvis said smoothly. "By coincidence, I had a covert operations team on-site at Incirlik—they were providing command and control for a completely unrelated operation we have underway nearby—and they were able to confirm an organized and obvious force movement towards the Thirty-Ninth Squadron compound."

While the existence of these weapons in Turkey was not a secret, it was not something DoD advertised, either. In Congressional defense budget documents, the phrase *special weapons* operated as a pseudonym for *tactical nukes*. Presently, sixty Cold War–era B61 Mod 7 nuclear gravity bombs, with adjustable yield capability, were maintained by the Air Force's Thirty-Ninth Squadron in Incirlik—a mere seventy miles from the Syrian border. Seventy miles from the greatest proxy war in history, with Russia fighting against NATO efforts through their support of the Syrian regime, and the highest concentration of paramilitary terrorist groups on the planet. Possession of tactical nuclear weapons would instantaneously transform the balance of power, turning any one of those extremist groups into a regional superpower.

"That's ridiculous," Secretary Baker said. "No terrorist group would be foolish enough to think such an operation could possibly succeed. The B61 compound is a base within a base protected by a regiment of heavily armed security forces—some of our best—inside an underground vault. Even if they killed every allied soldier on base, breaching the physical security to access the B61s would require bunker-busting ordnance. Trying to 'steal' the B61s is an impossible endeavor."

"I don't disagree with your assessment of the security, sir." Jarvis had his own theory on what had motivated a clearly futile attempt, but this was not the venue in which to share it. "Perhaps not all terrorists are as insightful as we think."

The SecDef made a *pffft* sound and shook his head.

Since becoming DNI, Jarvis had already participated in three different discussions about the risks and rewards of continuing to maintain the B61 stockpile in Turkey, where the political landscape was shifting like sand beneath their feet. The arguments were compelling on both sides, but thus far, those in favor of leaving them in place had gotten their way. After today, Jarvis imagined gale-force winds of change would begin blowing in the other direction. But he was getting ahead of himself . . . crisis management before strategic management. He shot Catherine Morgan, his Deputy Director of Intelligence Integration, a look that required no translation: *Where the hell is our data stream from Incirlik?*

She responded with a tight-lipped grimace and subtle shake of her head.

A series of unfortunate and ill-timed events was contributing to the chaos. The classified electro-optical geosynchronous satellite the US kept in position to monitor Iraq, Syria, and Iran was not responding to retask orders because of an unknown software error. Communications were down on the NATO base, and an already-paranoid President Erodan, fearing the attacks were part of a second coup attempt by the Turkish military, had cut off power to the base and initiated a no-fly zone overhead. Jarvis glanced down at his secure mobile phone, willing a call from Smith or Baldwin with real-time information.

"Where's the real-time battle-space feed?" Warner said, gesturing to the large flat-screen monitors at the other end of the conference table still displaying the presidential seal.

"We are working on that, sir," Morgan offered. "NSA tells me any moment they will have us online. Communications are difficult, due to the Turks shutting everything down on their end. They're not authorizing any NATO activity except that required to defend Incirlik."

"But that doesn't apply to the paramilitary response we just watched that left stacks of dead bodies on the street?" said Secretary of State Baker. "You said you were trying to prevent another Benghazi, but what happened in Adana will not go unnoticed. If relations with Turkey were already shaky, this 'rescue' operation was an earthquake."

Jarvis exhaled slowly, trying to control his anger. He got it; he really did. Baker was not a career politician, nor was he former military. He was a CEO of a Fortune 500 company whom Warner had drafted in an attempt to bring "fresh blood" and a "fresh perspective" to international relations. Before two weeks ago, Baker had never held a security clearance. Before two weeks ago, the only special operations the man had ever witnessed were those he'd watched in movies. He was a man whose publicly stated mission was to negotiate America back to greatness. He wanted to reimagine political relationships as business relationships. Secret CIA compounds and dead protestors in the streets of Turkey did not fit his mold.

"No, Mr. Secretary," he said, his voice measured and even. "Another Benghazi would have meant that we abandoned our people and let the bad guys win, neither of which happened tonight."

"Enough," Warner said.

Everyone followed the President's gaze to the small screen that still showed black smoke billowing above the burning remnants of the CIA operations center. There were a few men now on the roof of the remaining building, rifles in the air in triumph at having "captured" the American CIA compound, while the dead bodies of their terrorist brothers littered the street below. After a long solemn pause, he addressed the room: "All right, people, let's get back to the broader discussion of Incirlik and this nightmare in Turkey. We need to find out who hit us, why they hit us, and then we need to start planning our response. And if that wasn't enough, we need to figure out what the hell I'm supposed to say to President Erodan before this thing spirals completely out of control . . ."

CHAPTER 21

In an SUV
Somewhere . . .

Amanda jerked awake with a gasp.

Her first thought was that she'd gone blind, but then she remembered the black hood. She felt its fabric against her nose and forehead. She sat up. A hand immediately grabbed her, fingers fully encapsulating her biceps and triceps muscles with a grip so strong, it felt like her arm could be yanked from the socket with ease.

"Don't fight" came the gruff instruction in heavily accented English.

The man with the broken tooth.

As her brain ramped up to full consciousness, status reports from her body flooded in. She was seated inside a moving vehicle. Her hands had been bound while she was unconscious, and tightly so. From the way her inner wrists were pressed together and the way the strap dug into her flesh, she identified the binding as a heavy-duty plastic zip tie. Unlike handcuffs, plastic ties could be cut, but not easily. She moved her legs and was relieved to confirm her ankles had not been lashed together. The top of her right ear throbbed, and her skull ached where she had been struck. Her throat was dry, and she had trouble mustering any saliva to swallow. She needed water. She needed sleep. She hurt in so, so many places . . .

She slumped back into the seat.

There was nothing she could do. Nothing assertive, anyway.

She closed her eyes; inside the hood, it didn't matter. She devoted all her mental resources to her other senses. She was sitting in the middle seat of the passenger compartment. The man with the broken tooth was sitting on her right, the outside of his muscled thigh pressed against hers. Someone was sitting on her left, confirmed by occasional shoulder contact when the SUV jostled over bumps and potholes. Probably the woman terrorist.

They drove in silence for a while. Then the vehicle slowed and made a left turn. Not long after, ambient noise picked up. She heard a car horn blare in the distance and a motor scooter zip past. She thought, perhaps, they'd been driving on a highway at first, but now they seemed clearly to be in a town or city. To her relief, she didn't hear any gunfire or artillery shells exploding. She tried to memorize each turn and count the seconds between maneuvers by inventing a mnemonic, but it proved to be a pointless exercise. The mnemonic was awkward and too long. Her mind was so sluggish, she felt like she was wading through molten wax. Periodically, the wax would cool—coagulating and trapping her impotently in the moment. She needed to restoke her fire, burn bright, melt the wax so she could move. So she could escape.

But she ached, and she was so tired.

And thirsty.

The SUV jerked to a halt, and a flurry of conversation erupted in Turkish. No, not Turkish . . . Kurdish? Kurdish had three dialects, and Amanda didn't speak any of them. The conversation ended as abruptly as it had started. The left passenger door opened, and Amanda was shoved toward it by the man with the broken tooth. She complied, scooting over to the opening. She smelled body odor and urine and, with horror, realized it was her. Blinded by the hood and hands still bound, she tried to cautiously exit the vehicle, but a second shove from behind sent her pitching forward out the door. She stumbled and fell headfirst into the dirt.

She yelped with pain, then struggled to get to her knees.

Another flurry of conversation erupted above her, this time a heated back-and-forth between the man with the broken tooth and another man. Someone helped her to her feet, two hands gripping her under her armpits.

"It's okay," a male voice said in accented English. "I help you."

She stood.

A little sprite of courage sparked inside, and she pulled her slumping shoulders back and stood up straight—a subtle recalcitrance. Then she tightened her stomach and readied her core muscles for a punch to the gut. The man with the broken tooth would put her in her place for this, she knew.

But the punch never came.

"I guide you," said the voice belonging to the man who'd helped her up, and he linked his right arm with her left.

As she let him lead her, Amanda wondered if this was to be her final destination. Was she being handed over to the man they had called Malik? When her captors had been arguing, this was the name they had mentioned. This was the man they both feared and respected.

Malik . . . There is something familiar about that name, she thought again. *Where have I heard that before?*

She was led inside a building, but with the hood still on, she couldn't tell what type of structure it was. She felt the surface underfoot change from tile, to carpet, then tile again. *Probably a house.* Her escort stopped and released her arm. The air smelled of cigarette smoke and another scent she couldn't identify.

"You wait here," he instructed. "Don't move, just wait."

She heard him step away and a door shut behind her. Her respiration rate picked up, and her pulse quickened. Despite the quiet, she knew she wasn't alone. The hood suddenly felt thick and heavy, making it difficult to get enough air. Not being able to see where she was, who was with her, and what was about to happen was terrifying. She had been released from the plywood holding cell, but now she wore her prison—standing blind, bound, and clueless, she felt more vulnerable than ever.

She heard a sharp crack, reminiscent of the sound of kindling snapping underfoot. The sound came from inside the room, seemingly in front of her. A beat later, she heard another crack, this one more muted but still emanating from the same direction. Then someone exhaled a long tired sigh.

Her body tensed.

"Amanda Allen," a man said, his English flavored with an indiscernible accent. "At last we finally meet."

Not Turkish, not Arab, not German . . . maybe Armenian? Croatian?

She didn't answer.

She heard another sharp crack.

Whatever happens next, she decided, steeling herself, *whatever torture is about to be done to me, I cannot confess I work for the CIA. I cannot make myself any more valuable to them than they already think I am, or they will disappear me down a hole so deep and dark, I'll never escape.*

"How have you been treated?" he asked with a note of legitimate concern.

"Poorly," she said, surprised at the confidence she heard in her voice.

"Hmmm, I'm sorry to hear that," he said. "But I suppose it is to be expected . . . To my colleagues, you are a prisoner of war."

"A prisoner of war?" she repeated, her voice ripe with sarcasm. "For me to be a prisoner of war would require two things. First, I would need to be a soldier, which I am not. And second, I would need to be fighting in a war, which I also am not."

Another crack echoed, this one a tad duller than the previous one.

"That's where you are mistaken. There are many types of soldiers and many types of wars. You are a spy in the world's greatest war—the war for American global hegemony."

"I'm not a spy," she said with conviction. "I'm a diplomat. I work for the US Ambassador to Turkey . . . Well, I did work for him, before your people executed him in cold blood."

"That's your official cover. We know you work for the CIA," he said, and the next crack made her flinch. "And I'm going to be honest with you now. In dying on the street for all the world to see, the Ambassador fulfilled his purpose. Now that we know who you are, you will be afforded the same opportunity."

"And what opportunity is that—to die in captivity with a black bag over my head?" She laughed, an involuntary reaction she found to be both absurd and liberating. "You've gone to such great lengths to kidnap me and bring me here, but you have it backward. You should've killed me on the streets of Ankara and taken Ambassador Bailey. I'm nothing but a glorified personal assistant. He was the one with the information, the connections. I've only been in Ankara for a few months."

"In that case, it appears we have a mutual problem," he said.

"And what's that?"

"You spelled it out yourself. If you do not work for the CIA, as you say, then you are of no value to me. And if you are of no valuc to me, I have no use for you. And if I have no use for you, then, well . . . We both know how that story ends."

His words were like a punch to the gut. Had she just made a grave tactical error? By denying her CIA pedigree, had she diminished her value to the point where she wasn't worth the trouble of keeping alive? *No,* she thought. *I can't break cover.* She knew the case studies; things did not end well for agents who broke cover. There were worse fates than a bullet to the head. She'd seen pictures at the Farm of the alternative—nauseating pictures, inhuman pictures. *But I have to give him something . . . something to drag this out. Yes, that's the strategy. I need to buy myself more time. The SEALs tried to come for me once. They'll try again.*

Maybe it was time to pivot and play the ransom card.

Until now, she had successfully compartmentalized all thoughts of her father, keeping them locked away from her captors but also from herself. The bond she had with him was the strongest and most important relationship in her life. The death of her mother when Amanda was a child had dealt a blow so unexpected and devastating, it had almost destroyed her father, but he had emerged from the darkness and become the rock in her life. His accession to Chief Justice of the Supreme Court had surprised many people, but not Amanda. There was no man more honorable, no man more stalwart. She missed her father. She needed him now . . . desperately so.

She jumped at the sound of the man's voice behind her now.

"So that's it? You have nothing to offer me?" he said.

"Are you Malik?" she asked boldly, ignoring his question.

"Where did you hear that name?"

She detected a new undercurrent in his voice. *Irritation? Concern?*

"I heard them arguing about you. The woman and the man with the broken tooth," she said, straightening her back defiantly. "They were in a disagreement about whether they could trust you. Whether this mission was worth the risk and money you paid them."

It was dangerous what she was doing, trying to sow seeds of dissension in the ranks. It might only serve to earn her another beating, but she had to try to exploit every crack. She desperately needed information, and stimulating dialogue was the only means she had left to that end. If she could get them to talk to her, any of them, she might coax some detail or tidbit she could leverage. So far, she didn't know which group had taken her or where she was. She didn't know what their ultimate objective was, nor had she discovered any clues about their next operation.

"Thank you for bringing this matter to my attention," he said simply, and then she heard a click.

She tensed, wondering if this was it. *Is this how I end? Is this how I leave the world, shot in the back of the skull with a bag over my head, never seeing the face of my murderer?* Her heart pounded wildly in her chest, as fast as if she were running a race. She felt suddenly cold, and her knees began to shake.

Another click.

"I'm going to give you some time to think, Amanda. While I'm gone, I want you to contemplate the reality of your situation here. I want you to think about the advantages and disadvantages of cooperation so that when I return, we can have a productive discussion about the two paths available to you."

He placed his hand gently on her shoulder, left it there for a beat, and then walked away. She heard door hinges creak on the open swing and then again on the closing arc as the door slammed shut. From the sound of that thud, she suspected that her present enclosure was significantly more robust than the plywood box she'd been kept in before. Just when she was about to sit down, the latch clicked again and the door swung open. Dread roiled her stomach—the man with the broken tooth. Despite the hood, she knew it was him. She could identify him by scent now.

She felt something cold and hard slip along the inside of her forearms.

A knife, oh shit, a knife.

The blade settled against the plastic tie binding her wrists, and he began to saw back and forth. When the binding popped free, a glimmer of hope welled up inside her, but that hope turned to dread a heartbeat later. His hands became an angry flurry—grabbing the lapels of her blouse and ripping it open down the front. Buttons sheared and stitches tore as he violently ripped the garment off her. She clutched her arms about her chest as he stalked behind her. His fingers slipped under the bra strap arcing over her left shoulder; he pulled it away from the skin and cut it. He did the same with the right shoulder strap. Then he pulled the center clasp apart and ripped the bra free from her chest and threw it on the floor.

She cowered, covering her breasts with crossed arms.

He stepped up behind her, pressing himself against her. She could feel him panting in her right ear, smell his rank breath despite the hood. One hand wormed under hers to cup her left breast while the other found her abdomen and slipped inside the waistband of her pants. Anger, fear, and adrenaline surged through her body.

"No!" she screamed and thrashed with all her strength to get free from his grip.

He laughed and said something in that language she didn't understand.

She uttered a seething "Fuck you" and then slammed the back of her head into his face.

He grunted, but instead of letting her go, he picked her up and threw her. She hit the tile floor hard and let out a wail. The impact sent flares of pain up in too many places to count, but adrenaline was the best analgesic, and she scrambled to her knees despite the agony.

The door latch clicked and hinges creaked behind her.

What sounded like a reprimand was barked at the man with the broken tooth in a language she didn't understand. That same Kurdish dialect, she thought, but she really didn't care. The man with the broken tooth said something back, and the rebuke that followed was more vehement. Next, she heard the broken tooth man stomp out of the room, and a few moments later, other footsteps entered—lighter footsteps accompanied by a soft swishing sound.

She felt a presence beside her.

Ah yes—the female terrorist was back, playing nursemaid once again in the aftermath of her male counterpart's bludgeoning. Amanda knelt, unmoving while feminine fingers deftly untied the knotted string of the hood and pulled it off her head. She squinted, the world reluctantly coming into focus. She fixed her gaze on the female terrorist.

"You're a woman," Amanda said, her voice half whisper, half croak. "And you would let him rape me?"

The woman stood and looked down at her with cold malice in her eyes. "I would have him rape you and watch it be done. Just as you have watched my people raped by your government. I will see Turkey returned to the people," she said and then spat on Amanda. She gathered Amanda's ruined clothes and underwear off the floor, balled them up in a heap under her arm, and walked out.

Amanda shut her eyes and concentrated on her breathing.

She understood what was happening. Stripping her naked was part of the process. Humiliation, deprivation, and sexual domination were tools to weaken her resolve and break her spirit. Nothing broke a hostage—man or woman—faster than such ultimate violation. Malik, if that was in fact his name, had stopped the rape this time . . . but make no mistake, rape was on the docket for later, should she require additional motivation.

She rolled onto her side and curled into the fetal position.

And as she began to shiver on the cold, hard tile of her new prison cell, she spied a little pile of something on the floor by the opposite corner. She squinted, trying to make out what she was seeing. *Looks like a pile of walnut shells . . . with walnut pieces stacked in a little pyramid. So that's what Malik was doing while he was talking to me, cracking walnuts . . . a little offering to build trust and endearment. Well, asshole, it won't work.*

As she stared at them, her mouth began to salivate.

Her empty stomach growled.

But she did not move.

I bet he's watching me right now. He's measuring my willpower. Waiting to see how long it takes before I crack under his pressure . . . crack just like one of those walnuts.

CHAPTER 22

CAG's Sensitive Compartmented Information Facility (SCIF)
***USS* Ronald Reagan**
Mediterranean Sea, Seventy Miles North-Northwest of Lattakia, Syria
May 7
0400 Local Time

Grimes watched the Admiral's complexion with great interest, wondering just how red a person's face could turn before he lost consciousness from lack of blood flow to the brain. He was pissed, and she wasn't exactly sure why . . .

"My first instinct is to throw your asses out of here and let you wait this out in the Dirty Shirt Wardroom up front," the Commander of the Air Group barked. The sleeves of the CAG's flight suit were rolled up, displaying thick muscular arms that, she presumed from the winged insignia on his chest, had once expertly piloted some of the most advanced tactical aircraft in the world. Apparently, he did not like being displaced from his SCIF.

"I understand, sir," Munn said. "And I want to assure you—"

"Shut your cakehole, Smith or Jones or whatever fake-ass, spooky fucking name you're using today."

Munn did as he was told, clasping his hands in front of him.

Clearly, the Admiral needed to blow off steam, but now that the Adana rescue mission was complete, she and the rest of Ember desperately needed to get back to their original tasking—finding and rescuing Amanda Allen. Dempsey was alive, that much they knew, but that was all they knew. With the Boeing grounded, their Osprey out of commission, and the Jordanian Blackhawks gone, they were effectively prisoners on the floating city that was the USS *Ronald Reagan*. This man controlled all the aircraft, and that meant that this man was their only ticket to flying the friendly skies into Syria. She had to try to reframe this situation and win him over.

"Sir," she began. "If I may—"

"Shut it, Sheila," the Admiral barked. "I'm up to my neck in combat air patrols and direct air support following an attempt to steal tactical nukes from a NATO base in Turkey. And to make matters worse, we have Russian, Turkish, French, Iranian, Jordanian, and Israeli aircraft, and drones I might add, all flying sorties in Syrian airspace. It is a clusterfuck of epic proportions and one collision away from kicking off a war in the Middle East. Everybody wants a piece of Syria, and now it looks like Turkey might be next. So whatever spook-ass shit you're up to is a distraction from my mission." He held his hand up as Munn tried to speak. "However, as this request comes from the DNI himself—a friend and shipmate from the Academy and one of the finest damn human beings I've had the privilege to serve—I will permit you to turn *my* SCIF into your spooky war room." The Admiral leaned in, and for a moment, Grimes saw a twinkle in the man's eye that betrayed his bluster. "But don't fucking push it, son, or you and your merry band might find yourselves traveling by inflatable lifeboat to your next target."

"Thank you, sir," Munn said.

The Admiral handed a radio to Munn. "Call if you need anything from me. And give me a heads-up when you need to bolt so I can work you into a very chaotic flight deck schedule." His gaze ticked to the massive hematoma decorating half of Latif's face and then to Martin's blood-soaked shirt. "I'll send the doc up. That one looks like he needs stitches."

The Admiral spun on a heel and headed for the door.

"Jeez, what a prick," Latif said.

"Not hardly," Munn said, laughing. He shared a knowing look with Grimes.

Munn sat at a computer console, then tapped an access code on the keyboard to bring up the Joint Worldwide Intelligence Communications System, the DOD's top secret version of the internet.

"Is that smart?" Grimes asked. "Who else can see that?"

"Nobody, I hope," Munn said. "But what other choice do we have? We need a channel to talk to the boss and a portal for Baldwin to send us the latest imagery—provided he has imagery to send us."

She frowned. JWICS was secure but widely used by the rest of the intelligence community. She hated when they were so damn exposed to the world. Ember worked because Ember was invisible. For now, though, she supposed this was as good as they could do.

"What took you so long?" Baldwin said a millisecond after his face appeared on-screen. "We've been waiting for you to initiate a JWICS channel."

"We've been a little busy," Munn said with a chuckle, "or hadn't you noticed?"

"Hey, guys," said Smith, stepping into the frame as Grimes, Martin, and Latif crowded around the computer. "First, JD is alive and still trying to prosecute the package. Long story short, he and his DIA counterpart, Theobold, tried to take the compound and extract Allen."

"Of course they did," said Munn, shaking his head.

"And the op went bad," Smith said.

"Of course it did," Munn added.

"Theobold was badly wounded, and he and his asset crossed back into Turkey. He's in surgery now, and last we heard, he should make it."

"Why didn't Dempsey EXFIL with them?" Grimes asked.

"Because he's Dempsey and because he seems to have forgotten the meaning of the word EXFIL," Smith said.

"Don't tell me he's trying to recover Allen on his own?" she said.

"Oh yeah, that's exactly what he's doing," Smith said, and his live video feed was replaced by drone imagery. "The image on your screen shows him fifteen miles south of the Turkish border, traveling on foot west of al-Bab paralleling the M4 Highway. He's heading into the city of Manbij as we speak."

"Why?"

"They moved Allen. And he seems to think she's there, or at least that he can conduct ISR and figure out where they took her after leaving the compound."

"Do you have imagery to support his assessment?" she asked.

"We reconstructed the terrorist's escape route as best we could, and yes, the vehicle carrying Allen did appear to travel toward Manbij," said Baldwin's voice. "As you know, thanks to a series of unfortunate events, we've been resource limited for some time now, but I assure you we are about to solve this problem. I will have a dedicated Reaper in the air over Manbij in one hour. No one can take it; it's ours. And in eighty-eight minutes, we'll have SATCOM UHF back up, giving us redundant BLOS comms back."

"So have you talked to Dempsey?" she asked, her irritation tempered only by the news that comms were coming back up very soon.

"Yes, and he was instructed to hole up and lay low until we can plan his extraction and resume the hunt for Allen," Smith said.

"Yeah, like that's going to happen." Latif laughed.

"Any ransom demand yet on Allen?" she asked. "Any claims of responsibility?"

"Strangely, no," Smith observed. "We'd expected to hear some chatter on this, and Ian is working with our friends at NSA and OGA, but there's nothing credible so far."

"Credible?" Martin asked.

"Glory hounds," Munn explained. "There's always some group or individual who'll step up and claim responsibility. Sometimes that makes it hard to sort out what's real from what's bullshit."

"Precisely," Baldwin agreed.

"Well, as interesting as this recap has been," Grimes said, "when are we going to be wheels up to go get JD? Clearly Dempsey is not going to find Allen on his own. We need to regroup and do this right."

"As soon as we get the Reaper in orbit," Smith said, "we'll reestablish comms with Dempsey, validate his position, then get you guys in the air. But understand, the world has gotten exponentially more complicated in the past three hours. Turkey has Incirlik on lockdown and has established a no-fly zone inside Turkish airspace. We're not sure if we can set up a FARP in Turkey for you guys—we'll either have to break the no-fly or cash in some chits with the Israelis. Adamo is working all the options, and he needs a little more time. We're gonna try to get you another Osprey, but no promises. Just hang tight a little longer."

Grimes looked at her hands. How much more time did Amanda Allen have before her captors decided she had become more of a liability than an asset? How much more time could Dempsey survive on his own in war-ravaged Syria? Time was the one thing neither of them had.

"How are you guys?" Smith asked, scrutinizing them via video feed. "Latif, you're looking a little rough, brother. Everybody five by?"

"We're good. The ship's doc is going to get Martin and Latif patched up," Munn said. "In the meantime, ping us when you have something. We'll be percolating in hot standby."

And with that, Smith signed off.

A perfectly timed knock sounded on the door to the SCIF. Munn closed the videoconference window and said, "Come in."

The door cracked open, and an unfamiliar face poked in. "I'm Doc Rainey. The CAG said I should drop by, say hello."

Munn flashed a smile and said, "Nice to meet you. I gotta couple of Smiths here that could use a patch job. Mind if I send them with you?"

The Navy doc's eyes shifted to Martin and Latif, and he waved a hand. "C'mon, fellas, let's get you checked out and stitched up."

Ember's two newest operators hesitated.

"You heard the man, get moving," Munn said. Then, with a wry grin, he added, "Don't worry, we're not gonna leave without you."

With the rookies gone, Munn knitted his fingers behind his head, leaned back in his chair, and let out a whistle. "Been a helluva night," he said, looking at Grimes. "You doing all right?"

"I'm fine," she said and set to work rubbing her temples.

"You sure? You seem stressed, Lizzie."

"Yeah, well, this situation sucks. God only knows how much time Allen and Dempsey have left. Seriously, Dan, we need to get our act together and take fucking control. Either you own the chaos, or the chaos owns you."

He fixed her with a disarming, easy smile.

"What's that look for?"

"You and I are about a decade apart," he said, rocking slowly in his chair. "You wanna know what I learned in that decade?"

"Sure." She shrugged. "Knock me out."

"That people like us, folks psychologists like to call Type A personalities, we're programmed to think we can control everything. But life doesn't work that way. At some point, you realize *control* is an illusion. Once you shed the illusion, suddenly your entire perception of the world changes dramatically. It is liberating, let me tell you."

She screwed up her face. "That is the biggest pile of horseshit I've ever heard."

Munn chuckled. "How so?"

"It's the sort of advice I'd expect to hear from a Buddhist monk on a mountaintop, or a surfer dude smoking reefer after an evening set."

"And your point?" he said.

She laughed at this. "In case you haven't noticed, monks and surfers do not participate in the world. They've opted out. When's the last time a monk rescued a hostage? Show me a surfer who stopped a terrorist attack. Sure, it's nice and liberating to take the *Chill out, dude* approach, but it's the coward's philosophy, the quitter's philosophy. The only way to make a difference in this world, the only way we separate ourselves from inanimate objects, is through agency. It's why I stayed on at Ember, because Jarvis understood this—hell, he embodies it."

"Is that why you went to sniper school?" Munn asked, his tone without animus or judgment. "Because you needed to feel more in control?"

She hesitated, caught off guard by the targeted poignancy of the question. Then she rolled her neck and exhaled, as if setting up for her next shot. "When I first came to Ember, I was of the opinion that Jarvis and his band of shadow operators were in desperate need of intellectual supervision. Before our first op, I'd already decided that my job was to make sure the Neanderthals knew exactly which rock to break before they stepped out of the cave. But once we were in the field, I quickly realized that I had grossly misjudged my teammates. Tier One operators might not have PhDs from Harvard or MIT, but they've earned the functional equivalent of one—in this world, Dempsey's tactical prowess, operational knowledge, and strategic insights trump my analytical contribution nine times out of ten. In this world, I was the one who was deficient. I was the one who was a liability to the team, because I didn't have the firearms proficiency and operational experience to pull my weight on a tactical team."

"That's not true," Munn said. "You're a badass in the field, as good as any operator I've ever worked with."

"Oh really? Then why was I the only one on the team who got shot in Jerusalem?"

Now Munn was the one who screwed up his face. "Yes, we're operators, but that doesn't mean we're omniscient. It doesn't mean we're perfect. This was my point exactly, Elizabeth. There are just some things we can't control."

"You're wrong," she insisted. "I had a bead on the asshole who shot me in the Midrachov. I fired first, Dan, and I missed. I nearly died that day because I didn't make a shot I should have made. And if he hadn't shot me, he would have shot one of you. One of you might be dead today . . . When I came back, I made a decision that if I was going to stay at Ember, then I needed to be better. I'll never be able to challenge a six-foot-two, two-hundred-twenty pound operator in hand-to-hand combat; it's just biology, and there's no wasting time pretending otherwise. But overwatch—now that's a different story. That's a function I realized I could perform at a level equal to or better than anyone else on the team. And if we're being honest, it was a void at Ember that needed filling. That's why I went to sniper school. And when I'm up on a rooftop, cheek pressed against the WinMag, right eye looking through the scope, I *do* have control . . . the ultimate control."

He stared at her, apparently at a loss for words.

"Well, aren't you going to say *something*?" she asked, resisting the urge to fold her arms across her chest.

"I understand," he said, his gaze going to the middle distance. "That's why I stepped away from the Teams and became a surgeon. I reached a point where enough of my brothers had died from battlefield injuries that I decided to take control of the situation. I was a damn good 18-Delta SOF medic, but it wasn't enough. No one else was going to bleed out on my watch. I would decide who lived and who died, not the enemy . . . not the Grim Reaper. I would alleviate the Almighty of that burden. I would shoulder that burden."

"So I have you to thank for cheating death, not God," she said quietly, meeting his gaze. And when he didn't say anything, the corner of her mouth curled up. "I knew you were like me, at least a part of you . . ."

They sat in silence for a long time. When Munn finally broke it, he said, "You did good today, Lizzie, up there on the roof. You did real good."

"'Good' might not be the best choice of words," she said, looking at her lap. "I took a lot of lives today, Dan. Somehow, it doesn't feel like a whole lotta good."

"That's one perspective, I suppose," he said, reaching out and giving her hand a squeeze. "But it's not mine. Yes, you took lives today, but the question you need to be asking yourself is this: By being up on those rooftops, by doing what it is that you do, how many lives did you save?"

CHAPTER 23

Manbij, Syria
0430 Local Time

Would I kill for a cup of coffee?

Yes, yes, I would.

Even one of Wang's foo-foo coffees loaded with whipped cream and sugar . . .

These were the thoughts going through Dempsey's head as he advanced on the warehouse, trying not to look suspicious. Beneath his makeshift poncho, he clutched his Sig assault rifle, holding it tight against his chest. His helmet and NVGs were clipped to his belt. He was looking for a safe place to hole up, just like Smith had instructed. How long he would heed this instruction was up for debate. He scanned the perimeter and windows of the unlit building for movement. Finding none, he scanned the row of two- and three-story buildings down the street—storefronts on the ground level with apartments above. He saw one, and only one, vehicle, a black BMW sedan of all things, parked on the street. The 7 Series looked to be early 2000s vintage and was beat to hell. The windows and tires were intact, however, despite bullet holes dimpling the bodywork.

A BMW 7 Series in Syria, he thought. *Somebody thinks he's the mack daddy . . .*

The blackout tinted windows prevented Dempsey from seeing inside the cabin. Just in case, he pulled the spotter scope out of his kit, switched on the thermal function, and raised it to his right eye. The engine compartment glowed an angry orange, the heat suggesting the car had been recently driven. More interesting, the car was occupied, a single thermal image sitting behind the wheel.

Dempsey replaced the scope in his kit and pursed his lips.

Unlikely this guy was a pastry chef waiting until dawn to open his bakery. Probably local Mafia waiting to confront a local business owner and bully his weekly tribute. *Dirtbag or not, I can't afford to get involved,* Dempsey told himself and decided to circle back south around the warehouse and look for a way inside. He was surprised Baldwin hadn't gotten comms back up yet. What the hell was going on in Turkey, anyway? He desperately needed intel on Amanda Allen. Trying to find her alone had been a stupid idea. Really, what was his plan . . . walk door to door and ask every person who answered, *"Hi, I'm John. Never mind the assault rifle under my poncho. Have you seen the kidnapped CIA agent I'm looking for?"*

As he rose from his combat crouch and began to back out of his hide, the BMW's engine roared to life. Dempsey dropped back to a knee and made himself small. Had he been made by the jerkoff in the sedan? But despite the running engine, the driver kept the headlights off and the car idling at the curb. Then, in his peripheral vision, Dempsey noticed headlights approaching from the south.

Maybe this is a meet?

His mind started playing out a fantastical scenario—maybe the dude in the BMW was a sex trafficker. Maybe he'd bought Amanda Allen from the terrorists and this was the swap. *Don't be ridiculous,* he scolded himself. *This is what happens when you don't sleep for two days.* Besides, coincidences like that just didn't happen. Yet despite knowing this, his body was creeping forward anyway. He advanced until he reached a large gray power junction box and crouched behind it. He strained to see whether the approaching cars—two of them—were the vehicles that had left the compound with Allen. His right hand found the grip of his Sig Sauer rifle, and his index finger slid to the ready position on the trigger guard.

His heart rate spiked when he saw that the approaching vehicles were indeed an SUV and a pickup, only to sink a beat later when he confirmed the late model Nissan Qashqai SUV and Toyota truck passing by were not the vehicles that had fled al-Bab. Despite this, his curiosity was piqued, and he couldn't help but raise his spotter scope for a look. The cars drove past the parked BMW to the next intersection. The SUV kept moving north, but the pickup braked in the middle of the intersection, parking at a forty-five-degree angle to block any future traffic from all directions. The driver then exited the pickup, climbed into the bed, and picked up an AK-47, which he held at the ready across his chest.

Shit, what's all this about?

Dempsey zoomed in and watched the shooter, who had fixed his attention squarely on the BMW, trying to peer through the tinted windows to check for occupants just as Dempsey had done. Beyond, Dempsey saw the brake lights of the SUV light up as the vehicle stopped farther down the road. The gunner in the truck shifted his attention from the BMW to whatever his colleagues were doing just up the street. As Dempsey pondered what the hell was going on, he heard the roar of an engine and the squeal of tires. The shooter in the pickup heard it, too, but by the time he'd whirled around and taken aim, the black BMW slammed into the side of the truck, sending the man flying out of the bed and onto the pavement. Dempsey winced as the dude hit hard, headfirst—a landing he suspected the man would not be getting up from. The BMW's tires squealed again, this time in reverse as the driver expertly backed up and then whipped around the pickup to head toward the Nissan up the street.

Next thing he knew, Dempsey was up and moving toward the pickup.

What are you doing, John? he asked himself, but the SEAL didn't answer. The SEAL didn't like this scenario for some reason, and the SEAL was getting involved. At ten meters from the pickup, he flung the front flap of his poncho back over his left shoulder, like something from a Clint Eastwood movie, and brought his rifle up. He glanced at the body in the street, saw a pool of dark blood leaking from its skull, and glided past the dead shooter. He ducked behind the truck bed as small-arms fire echoed up the street. A burst of automatic rifle fire answered a beat later and he knew it was on.

He took a knee and sighted around the corner of the bed.

The driver's door of the BMW was open, and a bearded man stood defiantly a half step out of the vehicle, pointing an assault rifle at a cluster of people on the sidewalk in front of a storefront apartment. Two bodies lay on the sidewalk, and a man was holding a woman hostage at gunpoint. Dempsey lowered his rifle and raised his spotter scope to his eye, just to be sure.

"Dark hair, almond skin, wearing a maroon robe . . . She's young, fifteen or sixteen tops—definitely not Amanda Allen," he mumbled. "Fuck, I can't let this happen."

Dempsey advanced, keeping to the left side of the street and out of the BMW driver's peripheral vision. A shouting match was in progress between the two armed men, presumably over the fate of the teenager. Dempsey closed ground quickly, flanking the BMW. The man on the sidewalk saw him and his eyes went wide. He released the girl, dropped his pistol, and ran north up the street. BMW man kept his rifle raised, pointing at the girl—or maybe at someone inside the doorway to the shop beyond. He hollered something in what Dempsey thought was

Kurdish. The quivering teenager took a tentative step toward the black sedan. The driver barked something at her, prompting her to cover her ears and run toward the front passenger door. Dempsey arrived just as she reached for the door handle. The driver became aware of his presence, but too late. Dempsey ambushed him from behind, releasing his rifle at the last moment, and pulling the pistol from his thigh holster instead. He smashed into the driver with his torso, knocking the man's AK-47 to the ground. With lightning speed, his left arm snaked around the man's neck. He then bumped out his hip to tilt his adversary off balance and pressed the muzzle of his pistol into the man's temple.

"Stop right now, asshole," he commanded, letting the muzzle of the pistol do the translating for him.

"Are you kidding me? Let go, dickhead," the man wheezed, struggling in Dempsey's grip. The distinctively New York accent shocked Dempsey, but he kept his choke hold firm. "I gotta get this girl in the car and motor before the assholes inside come out."

Dempsey shifted his gaze and saw two new and important developments altering his perception of the situation. First, the girl was already climbing into the car of her own free will. And second, an angry-looking shooter with an AK-47 had appeared in the doorway across the sidewalk. The girl slammed the front passenger door shut.

"Let go of me," BMW man said over his shoulder. "You're gonna get this poor girl murdered."

As if in confirmation, the shooter in the doorway shouted and strafed the side of the car with a volley. Dempsey released the driver and dropped to a crouch, taking cover behind the cab of the sedan. The driver did the same but didn't waste any time. He picked up his rifle, tossed it into the car, and scrambled into the driver's seat. Before shutting the door, he locked eyes with Dempsey.

"You got two seconds, bro. Come with, or stay here, but we're leaving."

It was an easy decision.

He flung open the rear passenger door and dove in headfirst as the big black Bimmer laid a strip of rubber and rocketed forward. The girl screamed, and Dempsey ducked as more rounds pinged the side and back of the sedan. Two starbursts appeared on the rear passenger-side window, but by some miracle, the rounds didn't penetrate the glass.

"Talk," Dempsey demanded, pressing the muzzle of his Sig Sauer into the back of the driver's seat, center-of-mass position. "What business do you have with this girl?"

"I'm rescuing her, asshole," the driver said and laughed. "That's my business."

Dempsey hesitated, unsure what to say or do. The paradox of this dark-skinned, heavily bearded Kurd talking with a thick Bronx accent and driving a BMW through the dark streets of Manbij made him momentarily wonder if he was dreaming, his body asleep back at the warehouse.

"Who the hell are you?" Dempsey finally said. "And why are your windows bulletproof?"

"My friends call me Raz. I'm sort of a guardian around here," the driver said, flashing Dempsey a genuine smile in the rearview mirror. "This girl is Jeza, a Kurd who was kidnapped by a group of Syrian thugs. They were taking her to sell her—probably to some ISIS shitheads—as a sex slave. Human trafficking is big business around here these days. I'm the guy trying to stop it . . ." His voice trailed off. "When I can."

"You're American?"

"Yeah, and so are you," the man said, his dark eyes meeting Dempsey's gaze in the mirror again. "So what happened? Did your buddies leave you behind when they pulled out last week?"

Raz was referring to the recent departure of US coalition forces from Manbij after years of supporting the Kurdish Syrian Defense Forces in the battle against ISIS. The US presence in Manbij had been a major thorn in US-Turkish relations, and so with ISIS's caliphate broken now, the Warner administration had made the decision to withdraw, thereby ending the *unofficial* and rarely reported-on policy of keeping a limited number of US boots on the ground in Syria.

"Something like that," Dempsey said.

"Well, then you can report back to your bosses what's happened in the aftermath."

"And what is that?"

"Same thing that always happens when a power vacuum is created," Raz said, the good humor evaporating from his expression. "Bad guys stream out of the cracks to fill it. This place has gone to hell since our boys left. Kidnappings, lootings, assassinations—all back."

They tore around another corner, and only then did Raz finally ease off the gas and slow to something below white-knuckle velocity.

"What about SDF? Can't they keep things under control?" Dempsey asked.

Raz laughed. "They try, but they got their fucking hands full, man. The Syrian military is gunning for them, and so are the Turks. It's not a good time to be in Manbij, bro. Word is the Turks are going to strike any day. So why is it you're here again? I don't think you ever answered my question."

Dempsey squinted at the face in the rearview mirror, and a memory sparked. He'd heard stories about this guy, Amraz Demir—a real-life, no-shit, crime-fighting vigilante. He'd earned himself a helluva favor chit when he saved several Navy SEALs with his up-armored BMW in Iraq. "I know who you are," Dempsey said, the corner of his mouth curling up. "You're Amraz Demir."

"In the flesh."

"I thought your bat cave was in Iraq?" Dempsey said, subtly holstering his Sig.

"It was, but I follow the action."

"Oh c'mon, there's gotta be more to the story than that."

Dempsey watched Raz smile wanly in the mirror. "I spent six years in the Navy, serving as a combat medic with the Marines in the Second

MEF. Saw a lot of terrible shit . . . You're a shooter, so I know you can relate. Anyway, it chewed me up and spit me out. I got out after my tour and went back home to New York. My dad always wanted me to be a doctor . . . I tried, man, but Iraq gets under your skin, ya know . . ."

"Yeah, I know."

"My parents are Iraqi Kurds, but I was born in America. When I showed them pictures, they didn't even recognize Iraq anymore. Anyway, when the drawdown happened and ISIS blew up, it pissed me off. The shit these guys do to other people . . . it's just disgusting. I'm not a religious guy, but I have a moral code. I don't know, man, I couldn't just hang out in the Bronx and let innocent people get slaughtered. I decided to go back, but not with the Navy. Too many restrictions; if I was going to do this, I needed to do it my way. I talked to some of my buddies and eventually found a dude to come with me. His name was Danny Weidner. We made our way to Irbil, joined up with the Kurds there and started kicking some ass. Then it got rough for a while. Danny got plinked and he didn't make it. Once Iraq settled down, I joined a group that headed into Syria to rescue a group of schoolgirls those ISIS bastards kidnapped. Kind of a crazy suicide mission, I guess, but we pulled it off. That's when I knew."

"Knew what?"

The man smiled at him and laughed.

"That this was my true calling—rescue ops," he said.

They turned east, heading deep into the city now.

"How long have you been in Manbij?"

"Just over a year. I ran some rescues in al-Bab when the fighting was really bad back then."

"And you do this shit alone?"

Raz laughed. "Everyone else either died or moved on. I got the Batmobile here right after we rescued the schoolgirls in Al Qaim. Bought it off a guy, who bought it off a guy, who acquired it from a former Saddam-era General in Fallujah. It's badass, right? Up-armored, bulletproof glass, plate-steel undercarriage, two fuel tanks, run-flat tires . . . practically fucking indestructible."

Dempsey nodded. "Yeah, definitely badass."

The Kurdish girl, Jeza, who until now had been staring like a statue out the windshield, turned to Raz—words and tears spilling from her in a torrent.

Raz answered her and gave her hand a squeeze.

Dempsey couldn't pick out much of the exchange, but he gleaned an apology and a promise to take her home.

"So far, I've done all the talking," Raz said. "What's your story?"

"I'm looking for someone," Dempsey said, debating how much he was willing to share. "I happen to be on a solo rescue mission of my own, but unfortunately, I had to leave my Batmobile at home."

"Ahhh, so you think your hostage is in Manbij?"

"I lost the trail outside of al-Bab, and I was hoping to pick it back up here," Dempsey said. "So you're pretty wired here, I imagine."

"Yeah, you could say that. The Kurdish community trusts me, obviously, and feeds me very well by the way."

Dempsey nodded.

"Just ask, bro," Raz said, shaking his head with a chuckle. "It ain't like we're dating."

"Maybe you could ask around," Dempsey said. "See if anybody knows anything about an American smuggled into or trafficked through Manbij in the last few hours."

"Under one condition," Raz said, with a sly grin.

"It's a deal."

"You didn't even hear what I want."

"You help me save this girl, and I'll get you *whatever* you want, brother."

"In that case, if she's here, we'll get her out," he said and pointed to a series of hash marks carved into the BMW's dashboard. "We're doing this together now, by the way. It's not every day I get an opportunity for a two-fer."

Dempsey laughed. He liked this guy . . . Raz kinda reminded him of a young, well, him.

Raz reached up and pressed a button on the garage door opener clipped to his visor, just as if they were in the suburbs back home. Dempsey watched as a heavy steel gate opened, allowing access through a stout compound perimeter fence topped with razor wire. Raz piloted the BMW into a single-car garage attached to a modest single-story stone house and then closed the door behind them.

"I need an hour to get this girl to her family, and then we can get to work. In the meantime, I've got fresh water, coffee, lamb stew, and fruit you can help yourself to. And if you need to catch some shut-eye, I got a spare mattress."

A giant smile spread across Dempsey's face.

"Heaven to my ears," he said and opened the door to climb out.

Perhaps there was a God who heard the prayers of lost souls like him after all.

CHAPTER 24

The "Demir Compound"
Manbij, Syria
1130 Local Time

Dempsey stretched across the mattress on the floor and let out a satisfied groan.

In his bone-weary state, this might as well have been a Four Seasons hotel. He considered removing his boots—the downrange equivalent of a spa massage—but couldn't even muster the energy to do that. He had a full belly, and for the moment, he was safe. He closed his eyes and let his mind wander to all the default and dangerous places an operator's mind tended to go when he let down his guard. He began by contemplating the hell Amanda Allen was probably enduring right now. A failed rescue—and especially one with a high body count—would not endear her to her captors. She would be punished for his failure. Every hour that passed meant more scars she would have to carry for the rest of her life. And that was on him.

Eventually, his thoughts drifted to Theobold and the wounds the DIA man had suffered during the failed raid. After that, he thought of Grimes and their parting discussion on the Boeing, and then . . .

"You left me," a familiar voice said sometime later, a woman's voice.

He opened his eyes and found a beautiful woman straddling his chest. She wore simple slacks, a white linen blouse, and a turquoise scarf tied loosely around her head. A dark red pinprick appeared on her blouse midchest, then began to blossom before his eyes.

"Elinor?" he said, his voice catching in his throat.

"You left me," she said, her face contorting with anguish and rage. "You left me . . . to . . . die!"

Her punches came furiously and without warning, fists pounding his chest and face as she cried tears of blood.

"I'm sorry," he screamed, trying to shield himself from the maelstrom of blows. "I'm sorry, Elinor."

He woke with a start, sitting bolt upright, chest heaving. Wild-eyed, he looked around the room, but of course, it was empty. "God, I fucking hate that dream," he sighed and then collapsed back onto the mattress. He ran the back of his hand across his forehead, wiping the sweat away. It had been a year, and still he couldn't get the image out of his head—her writhing in pain on the dirty floor of an underground hookah bar in the Grand Bazaar. That was how he had left her. *Left* her to die.

And in doing so, he'd broken his creed.

In the Teams, no one gets left behind.

But in the gray world of spies, did that creed apply?

Elinor had betrayed him, personally and professionally—of that there was no doubt. Yet a part of him simply couldn't shake the feeling that in the final moment, she'd stood with him. She could have turned her weapon on him. But she hadn't. And that's what haunted him. They'd been teammates; they'd shared a night together. She'd presented him to her dying father as her husband. Was it all self-serving? Had she ever been more than a very good adversary?

Only Elinor had known who she was—traitor or teammate—in those final minutes.

And she'd taken that truth to the grave with her . . . because he'd left her.

He stared at the cracking paint of the nicotine-stained ceiling.

"Atlas, this is Olympus. Do you copy?" said Baldwin's voice in his ear.

"Of all the times you could have restored comms," he said, grinning to himself, "you wait until I'm asleep."

"My apologies, Atlas," Baldwin came back. "So I presume from your answer that you are not being held captive in that compound where we hold you on the outskirts of Manbij."

"Check."

"That's good because our Reaper holds a black sedan arriving at your location," Baldwin said. "Thermal imagery confirms the driver is alone."

"Check."

"Who is your new friend?" Baldwin asked. "We're all very curious."

"Amraz Demir," he answered, his eyes still closed.

"No shit" came Smith's excited voice on the line. "That dude's a local legend."

"He's shorter than he looks on TV," Dempsey said with a laugh, and then with a groan, he sat up and said, "I should probably get up . . . What's the skinny? You have any new intel for me?"

Baldwin was just beginning to babble about intersecting lines and confidence intervals when the door burst open to Dempsey's room.

"I know where she is!" Raz bellowed, standing in the doorway, arms crossed proudly on his chest and his eyes on fire.

"Whadaya got?" Dempsey said, popping to his feet and following Raz to a small folding table in the kitchen. His new partner retrieved a beer—a longneck Budweiser of all things—from the fridge and offered him one. Dempsey shook his head, energized by the news.

"This community continues to impress me," Raz said, tipping his beer back. "The Kurds have eyes and ears that probably rival the satellites and drones that the NSA has overhead, maybe even better because they *talk* to one another."

"Agreed," Dempsey said with a *Get to the point* stare.

"The vehicles you described were spotted arriving in the city last night. They traveled to a compound used by a YPG commander named Haq. He's risen in the ranks of SDF, but I've never liked him. Rumor is, he came over from PKK. Most of the Kurds like and trust Americans, but not all of them. I would put Haq in the latter category. Anyway, whoever this woman is, her arrival caused quite an incident."

"What do you mean, an incident?"

"Infighting in YPG."

Dempsey rubbed his beard. "Maybe it's time I read you in . . ."

"No, Atlas," Smith said. "Absolutely not."

Dempsey ignored Smith, looked at his young partner, and said, "Raz, I have a confession to make."

"Here it comes," Raz said and took a long pull from his beer.

"We're not alone right now. I've got my people on the line and a Reaper in orbit overhead."

"Hello, John's people," Raz said, looking at the ceiling.

"You told him your name?" Smith sighed. "C'mon, you gotta stop doing that."

"Olympus, let's take a look at the compound Raz just reported on with the Reaper. It would be nice to know how many shooters we're dealing with and see if you can confirm a thermal signature that looks like it belongs to a hostage. We need to keep eyes on that compound continuously in case they try to move her again."

"What about us?" Raz said.

"Let's go for a drive. I'd like to survey the compound and see what we're up against."

Raz laughed. "I admire your ambition, and you know how I roll, but not even I would try and pull someone out of Haq's compound alone."

"Like I said, we're not alone, Raz," he said, clapping a hand on his new partner's shoulder. "I have an entire team of friends standing by to help—friends I have a feeling you're going to like very much."

CHAPTER 25

Situation Room of the White House
Washington, DC
May 7
0300 Local Time

Contrary to its name, the current incarnation of the Situation Room was not a room at all. Rather, it was a massive permanently staffed command-and-control complex built under the White House. This was the longest stretch Jarvis had spent in the world's most famous op center during his professional career.

It was not a record he intended to make a habit of breaking.

President Warner caught his eye and gestured for him to join him.

Well, here it is. I'm either a hero or a failure to the man who hired me. Time to find out which.

Jarvis headed toward the door, weaving behind and around agents at workstations directing men and women in crisis from thousands of miles away. As he watched them work, loyal extensions of the President, he wondered if he had done the right thing mobilizing the rescue mission without authorization. The question was not whether his decision had been morally and tactically prudent—of that he had no doubt—but had it reflected the President's policy?

He was about to find out.

Warner shut the door softly behind him.

"Have a seat, Kelso."

It wasn't an offer but an order, so Jarvis sat in the large and comfortable leather chair in front of the small desk. President Warner took the seat beside him instead of behind the desk.

A good sign.

"You look like hell," Warner began.

"I'm a little under the weather," he said.

"When is the last time you slept?"

"I don't know," Jarvis said with a sigh. "A couple days."

"When things calm down, I want you to get some rest," the President said. "There are sleeping accommodations down here, as you are undoubtedly aware. I'm directing you to use them. That's an order."

"Yes, sir."

"All right, down to business. I'm assuming it was your Ember team that executed the rescue in Adana?"

"Yes, sir."

"Fortuitous that they were in theater. I assume you had them engaged in the hunt for Amanda Allen?"

Jarvis nodded. "The team was parked in Incirlik, where they were providing command and control for an operator I had in the field conducting ISR on a compound where we believed Miss Allen was being held."

The President nodded and then crossed his legs at the knees. "Any luck?"

Jarvis paused and thought about how best to answer. He viewed providing the President plausible deniability as one of his most important roles. "We're not sure, Mr. President. The operation was interrupted by the attack on Incirlik. Our air asset was damaged and we lost comms with my guy. It made sense to retask Ember for the rescue operation in Adana. Ember is now back on the Allen mission, and I expect an update on their progress in an hour or so."

President Warner nodded and then stretched his back. "Let me ask you a question, Kelso."

Jarvis waited quietly.

"Did you have a concern that I would not offer my approval of the rescue mission? Is that why you launched without discussing it with me? I know why you didn't involve Secretary Baker—who is going to be a great Secretary of State, by the way—but I am at a loss to understand your decision to exclude me."

Jarvis flashed back to his last one-on-one with Warner a year ago, on the day the President had made him the DNI. The more he interacted with the President, the more the man surprised him. Warner's everyman demeanor was a carefully crafted façade, and behind that façade was a tenacious, nimble mind. Warner was the ultimate politician and high-stakes poker player. Even in the absence of data, the President knew when to bluff, when to hold, when to raise, and when to fold, regardless of the complexity of the situation. Warner's mind did not work like his. Where Jarvis relied on logic, analytics, and risk-reward calculations, the President rapidly aggregated recommendations and inputs from trusted channels, sussing truth from fiction with astounding accuracy. Fortunately, Jarvis had not lied to the President, and he had no intention of starting now.

"Sir, I meant what I said. I know that you would never leave our people behind, no matter the political fallout. I believe that, or I would never have accepted the DNI position. If I had doubts about the mission's approval, I can honestly say that I was not conscious of it. However, sir, while I work to execute my job on behalf of the American people, I have an equally important responsibility to you and your administration. When I decide that the best way to execute your policy is to use the completely clandestine, black ops unit we created—the unit that exists outside of legally mandated oversight—I feel obligated to do so on my own and provide your office with plausible deniability. In this case, the risks of the operation were manageable, but high enough that the political fallout from a potential failure weighed heavily on my decision. Within minutes of the compound being attacked, Erodan became aware of its existence, but the media didn't. Plausible deniability was still on the table in the public realm. Also, I was not about to let this become your Benghazi. Taken together, it seemed prudent to make the responsibility for the mission wholly my own."

The President chuckled. "So you saw yourself as taking a bullet for me? Is that it, Kelso?"

"Yes, sir," Jarvis said, nodding.

"Harry Truman famously said, 'The buck stops here.' I'm the President of the United States, Kelso. You don't need to worry about sheltering me. That's not what I signed on for. Moving forward, I need to be in the loop on these types of decisions, though I want you to retain the autonomy to get the job done when the luxury of consultation is not available. In those cases, provided your decision was just and prudent, you can count on me to have your back. Is that fair?"

"Abundantly, sir," Jarvis said. He watched the President carefully—the subtle smile despite the level of crisis all around him, and the eyes that told him the words were not bullshit.

"For someone who hates politics and bureaucracy, you seem to be developing a knack for it," Warner said. "Perhaps one day we'll find you sitting in my chair."

It was Jarvis's turn to laugh now. "Not much chance of that, sir."

There was no conceivable situation in which he would ever be America's Politician in Chief. A sudden numbness in his left leg reminded him that, even if he were willing, FDR was and would always be the country's only wheelchair-bound President.

Warner stood and Jarvis moved to get up.

"Oh, we're not finished," the President said, walking to take the seat behind the desk. He picked up the desk phone and said, "Send in Secretary Baker, please."

Clenching his jaw, Jarvis settled back into his seat.

"Time to put those budding politician skills of yours to work, Captain," Warner said with an entirely-too-pleased-with-himself smile. The Secretary of State appeared at the door a beat later, and Warner waved him in. "Have a seat there next to the Director of National Intelligence, Mr. Secretary."

Baker flashed the President a deferential smile and sat.

Warner eyed them both before finally breaking the uncomfortable silence.

"Well, gentlemen, it looks like we have an international fucking catastrophe on our hands, and it is going to take the combined efforts of all three of us to sort it out. We all see the writing on the wall—we're losing control of Turkey. Erodan is not an ally we can trust or depend on. Before this attack on Incirlik, I'd already harbored unspoken fears that by the end of my term, Turkey would be a NATO member in name only. NATO members do not foster strategic alliances with Russia like Turkey is doing. NATO members do not endorse Iranian 'diplomatic initiatives' in Syria like Turkey has done. And NATO members do not establish an underground railroad for Islamic State fighters inside their borders, nor do they supply guns and resources to regional al-Qaeda affiliates. Erodan's neo-Ottoman reorientation is not a subtle policy shift, gentlemen; it is a hard pivot away from the West. Turkey is rebuffing the EU, and the ground work is being laid for its membership in the Shanghai Cooperation Organization—Moscow and China's answer to NATO. I don't have the solution to the Erodan problem, but we desperately need a strategy. This will take a three-pronged approach if we want any chance of success—political, economic, and strategic—and the three of us are going to begin drafting it right now. Tell me your thoughts, theories, and fears. I want your honest, unfiltered opinions, and don't hold back."

"At his core, I believe Erodan is an opportunist," Secretary Baker said. "He's shopping for the best deal, and he's going to play both sides against each other to get it. So far, Petrov has given him the best deal, lifting Russia's tourism ban on Turkey and committing to two major energy infrastructure projects—the Turkstream natural gas pipeline, which will allow Russian natural gas to flow into Turkey, and this Russian-made nuclear power plant Turkey intends to build in Akkuyu. Russian rubles are flowing into Turkey, and unless the US and EU are willing to provide economic incentives that eclipse those from Moscow, then Erodan will not change dancing partners."

The President nodded and looked at Jarvis. "Kelso, your thoughts?"

"I agree with the Secretary's assessment. Turkey just purchased Russian S-400 missiles, a move that would have been unthinkable two years ago. As you said, Mr. President, this is not the type of behavior expected from a NATO member. Any and all current initiatives for Turkey to purchase F-35 fighters need to be tabled indefinitely. I think it's abundantly clear the minute Erodan gets his hands on an F-35, the weapons system will be compromised. God only knows what design information will be passed to the Russians and Chinese. Hell, I wouldn't be surprised if Erodan let his new buddy Petrov take one for a spin. On top of these specific concerns, there's the broader and more troubling matter of Turkey and NATO. As we saw today, Erodan's duplicity is now impacting coordination and readiness. And just last month, Turkish and Russian Naval forces conducted joint training exercises in the Med for the first time in my career. My point is, Turkey is no longer a reliable NATO partner."

"Then we should just expel them," Baker said.

"It's not so simple," Warner replied. "There's no simple mechanism in NATO to expel member states. NATO is run by consensus."

"Ironically," Jarvis said, "Turkey remaining in NATO could pose more of a threat than its excommunication."

"How so?" Warner asked.

"Like you said, Mr. President, NATO is run by consensus. A corrupted, misaligned Turkey could effectively act as a Trojan horse, paralyzing NATO into inaction. Imagine a scenario where Russia moves to annex Ukrainian territory or, God forbid, one of the Baltics and Turkey torpedoes NATO consensus, forcing the US to act unilaterally or build an outside coalition. Crimea happened fast, and it proved that Russia doesn't need to beat NATO to achieve its reunification agenda. It just needs to outrun it."

Warner sighed and ran his fingers through his hair. "Listening to the two of you has confirmed my fears. So to start, what do we do about Incirlik?"

"Well, the first order of business is to get those B61s out of there," Baker said. "I've already been discussing this matter with Deputy Director Morgan. She and I are of the strong opinion that we can't continue to give a man like Erodan access to a cache of tactical nuclear weapons."

So that's what the two of you were whispering about during the brief, Jarvis thought.

"Do you agree, Kelso?" the President asked.

"I don't know, Mr. President," Jarvis said. "On the one hand, the B61s are like a pair of handcuffs. They're our weapons; so long as they reside in Incirlik, Erodan is bound to us. He is brazen, but not so brazen as to risk provoking the full might and power of the US military by seizing a nuclear asset that does not belong to him. On the other hand, their continued presence on Turkish soil sends a message to the world that we support Erodan and trust him implicitly enough to give him a nuclear weapons cache while he betrays and embarrasses us by having a very public affair with Russia. Maybe divorce in this case is merited."

"The minute we pull those nukes, he'll boot us off the base and suspend NATO operations in the country. Losing Turkey as a base of operations and handing it over to the Russians would be a serious strategic blow in the region," the President said.

"And we can't forget about Israel. Without a US presence in Turkey, Israel becomes even more isolated and Iran more emboldened," Jarvis added, wondering what his friend and mentor Levi Harel must be thinking right now.

A chill descended on the office as the three most powerful people in the American government brooded in silence. After a long beat, Warner's expression hardened. "I refuse to be the conductor who lets this runaway train drive off the tracks. No, not on my watch," he said. "So pack your bags, gentlemen, because we're going to Turkey."

CHAPTER 26

Wherever . . .

Amanda sat in the corner clutching her knees, naked and shivering.

She'd eaten the walnuts, eaten every last crumb, and she didn't feel guilty about it. She was so fucking hungry; she needed every morsel of protein she could scavenge. For the past several hours, they'd ignored her. Malik was letting her stew and fret, just like he'd promised to do.

Was it working?

Yes.

It was important to be honest with herself.

Being naked stripped her of her dignity. Being cold made her feel weak. Being in solitary confinement made her feel alone. Not "alone" as in "by herself." That was obvious. But alone in the world—disconnected, without love, support, or allies.

Naked, cold, and alone—it was a powerful triad of deprivation.

But as long as I recognize what is being done to me, I can take steps to counter the psychological and emotional effects. I have to keep talking to myself. When they break me down, I have to build myself up. I'm the only person who can do it. I'm my only friend. I'm my only ally.

Eventually, she felt the need to urinate, but she didn't move. She held it. She was so dehydrated her lips were wrinkled and chapped. She knew kidneys cleaned the blood to make urine, but she wasn't well versed in the mechanism. She knew the process happened automatically in the background, regardless of how thirsty a person was, but she wondered if by holding her pee, her body would maybe slow that process down . . . save more water. It was probably a stupid thing to do. It probably didn't matter, and all she was doing was making herself unnecessarily uncomfortable.

You're not a camel, Amanda, she thought, talking to herself in third person. This made her laugh, something she needed desperately.

"Fuck it, this is stupid." She sighed and got to her feet, stiff knees and hips protesting as she did. She stood there for a moment, letting the pins and needles subside as blood flow got moving again in her legs. Then she limped over to the metal pail in the corner and squatted over it. The door opened, startling her just as she began to relieve herself.

Jesus Christ!

Malik appeared in the doorway, holding something in his right hand. His gaze went immediately to her crotch and stayed there as her stream of urine made the dingy metal reverberate beneath her.

"Enjoying the show?" she asked, trying to find strength in this humiliation.

"Actually, yes," he said, the left corner of his mouth curling up. "I like it immensely." The look in his eyes wasn't sexual lust—it was something else. Something far more frightening.

She snorted in wordless disdain and glared at him.

"I'm a man of strange predilections," he said with a shrug. "That's probably one of the reasons I gravitated to this line of work in the first place, rather than becoming, say, an accountant."

Knees shaking as she finished, she stood and stepped away from the bucket. She watched his gaze shift immediately upward to her breasts.

The urge to cover herself and run back to her corner was overpowering, but she resisted with every ounce of strength she had left.

"Is a roll of toilet paper too much to ask for?" she said.

"No, it is not," he said, then shut the door behind him. "I will see it done."

He gestured for her to sit. Then he unfolded the thing in his right hand, which she now recognized to be a collapsible, three-legged camping stool with a hammock-style seat. He sat.

With all the dignity and courage she could muster, she headed back to her corner. Try as she might, she couldn't stop her knees from shaking as she walked. She was too tired, too weak, and too scared. This man absolutely terrified her—terrified her more than even the man with the broken tooth. The man with the broken tooth was an ogre—primal and carnal. Malik, however, was something else entirely . . . a cerebral predator.

Something born of nightmares.

She sat in her corner, pulling her knees to her chest and keeping her ankles and calves pressed together in front of her to block his view. He looked at her, lips pressed together but tipped up in a half smile. The expression was patronizing and unduly familiar, one that translated to, *Oh, Amanda, what am I going to do with you?*

She didn't like it; it made her angry. She held his gaze in what soon morphed into a staring contest. "What do you want?" she said at last, breaking the silence but not the eye contact.

"I want the truth, Amanda. The same as before."

"I gave you the truth. You didn't believe me."

"Hmmm," he said, nodding. "Are you cold?"

"I'm shivering. What do you fucking think?"

"Are you hungry?"

She narrowed her eyes at him.

"Thirsty? Uncomfortable?"

"Yes," she finally said with a sigh. "All those things."

"Do you want to go home?"

"Yes."

"Then talk to me, and this can all be over," he said. "I'll get you some new clothes. We can drive to Beirut, just you and me. I'll get you a hotel room. You can take a bath, get some rest, and then we'll have a nice dinner together. After you tell me everything, I'll take you to the airport, and you can go home and put this terrible experience behind you."

"And if I say no?"

"Then I leave and Samir comes back in here to beat and rape you until you talk. Either way, the end result is the same. The choice is so simple," he said, then began to laugh with incredulity and formed his hands into the arms of an unbalanced scale. "Easy way, hard way. Why so many people pick the hard way, I will never understand."

"They pick the hard way because it's all bullshit!" she hissed.

"What is bullshit?" he said, leaning in, elbows on knees. "Amanda, I think you understand by now that this is not my first interrogation. This is what I do for a living, okay? This is my profession."

"I know," she said, laughing now herself. "Which is what makes this whole charade so laughable. I'm not an idiot. Hard way, easy way, it doesn't matter. This ends with my murder, regardless of how much information you extract and how you extract it. Stop pretending otherwise."

He pursed his lips at her and looked like he was about to scold her but then did something else instead. He leaned to the side so he could retrieve a plastic Ziploc bag from his pants pocket. He opened the bag and pulled out something oblong and brown. She watched him split it lengthwise with his thumbnails, extract a brown pit, and then pop the fruit in his mouth. He tossed the leftover pit at her piss pail; the throw was short, and it clanged off the side.

"Medjool date," he said, chewing. "Do you want one?"

"Yes," she said.

He fished another date from the bag and tossed it to her. She caught it, and he watched her intently as she pitted and then devoured the date. It was delicious . . . quite possibly the most delicious thing she'd ever tasted.

"Good, huh?" he asked.

"Yeah." She nodded, licking her lips and then her fingertips.

He flashed her that *What am I going to do with you, Amanda?* look again.

The words just tumbled out. "My father is Supreme Court Justice Allen." No sooner had she said them than her stomach turned to acid. *What the fuck am I doing?* she thought, horrified. *Why did I say that?*

"I know," he said, nodding.

"You do?"

"Yes, of course." He pitted another date for himself and ate it. He tossed the pit at her piss pail, and this time it landed inside with a clang.

"You can ransom me for money," she said, her voice hopeful and pathetic. "He will pay."

He frowned. "This is not about money," he said. "We took you for two reasons. First and foremost, for the intelligence stored in your brain. And second, to make a statement."

"And what statement is that?" she asked, deflating inside.

"That America is not invincible. That America is not welcome in Turkey. And that we can get to anyone, anytime. Even to the American Ambassador and the CIA agent who pretends to be his assistant."

"Who is 'we'?" she asked, suddenly terrified by the confidence with which he perfectly described her role.

He smirked at this and said, "Time's up, Amanda. Have you made your decision? Will it be a cordial dinner with me, or pain and defilement with Samir?"

Jaw clenched, she stared at him. She studied the bone structure of his face, the shape of his eyes and nose. His hair was black and he wore a beard. His skin was tanned a rich brown, but this man was not an

Arab. He could be Turkish . . . maybe Armenian? From where she sat, his eyes appeared to be espresso brown, but earlier she'd noticed he was wearing contact lenses. Were they *colored* contacts? This man was not who he pretended to be. He was no Islamic terrorist, and his name was certainly not Malik.

Terrorists don't talk like he talks. Zealots don't behave like he behaves.

She swallowed, gathering her courage. "Why don't you do it yourself?"

"Do what, Amanda?"

"Torture me. If that's my fate, then why not do it yourself? Why send your thug in here to do it for you? Is it because you don't have the balls for it? Because you don't want to get your hands dirty? Or is it because you want to watch?" She was shaking as she yelled at him, trying to get under his skin. Why she was taking this tack, she didn't know. All she knew was that she had to keep him in the room. She was terrified of Samir and what he would do to her. He would break her; she was certain of this.

She dropped her arms to her side. "Here I am, Malik. Do with me what you will."

He narrowed his eyes at her, his jaw set in anger now.

"Be careful what you ask for, Amanda," he said, getting to his feet and folding up his stool. "Samir is a monster, but I think you would find the experience with me to be much more unpleasant. I enjoy my chosen profession more than you can know."

A cold chill snaked down her spine as the realization of who and what she was dealing with once again hit home. She wrapped her arms around her knees, hugging herself tightly.

"Please," she said, all the strength gone from her voice. "Please . . . don't do this."

He ran his tongue over his teeth and then, fixing his eyes on her, said, "I gave you a choice, Amanda. I gave you a way out of all of this, but you opted to insult me and call me a liar. I can be reasonable and decent until the time for being reasonable and decent has passed."

Her throat felt tight, like she was being strangled by unseen hands. *So this is what it feels like to be choked with fear,* she thought. *Oh God, he's really going to let it happen. He's really going to have me raped, tortured, and beaten until I break.* Cold rivulets of sweat began running from her armpits over her ribs. *I've got to buy more time. Shit, shit, shit!*

"I'm sorry," she blurted. "Please. Please, give me another chance," she begged, disgusted with the sound of her weakness.

He reached up and massaged his temples for several long seconds and then said, "Here's what's going to happen. I'm going to bring you a pad of paper and a pen. You have one hour to produce a list of ten names—ten American agents or assets in Turkey. I want real names, along with pseudonyms, code names, details about their legends, roles, and responsibilities. If you do this for me, you earn another hour-long reprieve, during which you will produce another ten names, and so on and so on."

"And what happens when I run out of names?" she asked.

"Then I change questions."

"And what happens when you run out of questions?"

"That, I suppose, depends on your answers." He turned his back on her and knocked on the door. A latch clicked, and someone unlocked it from the other side. A few minutes later, he returned with a woven basket. From within, he retrieved a paper notebook and a stubby wooden pencil, which, after a moment's reluctance, she accepted. Next, he retrieved a roll of toilet paper and handed this to her, too.

"Thank you," she said.

The next thing out of the basket was a can of Coca-Cola. He held the iconic red-and-white can up and showed it to her. Like a Pavlovian dog, her mouth immediately began to salivate, but she resisted reaching for it. He studied her for a moment, then bent at the waist and set it down next to her left foot. As he did, she sneaked a peek inside the basket and saw one remaining item—a gray and white–striped blanket folded into a tidy rectangle. To her astonishment, it was woven from Angora wool and looked to be of the finest quality. She'd seen artisan blankets like this at the bazaar in Istanbul advertised for hundreds of dollars. Why these monsters would own a blanket of such refinement was a mystery to her.

"Would you like a blanket?" he asked, his eyes surveying her nakedness with an interest that seemed somehow clinical.

"Yes, thank you," she said, snatching it from his outstretched hand and immediately cradling it to her chest.

"One hour" was all he said in reply.

She nodded and watched him turn to leave for the second time in as many minutes. When he reached the door, she said, "What should I call you?"

"Excuse me?" he said, his back to her.

"I know you're not Malik. So what should I call you?"

She thought she saw his shoulders tense, but in a heartbeat, it was gone. "Ten names," he said plainly and then left her alone to the business of betrayal.

As soon as the door slammed shut, she unfurled the blanket and wrapped it around her. She huddled there, eyes closed. She knew what he was doing to her. She knew exactly how this worked. She had been cold, so he gifted her a blanket. She had been thirsty, so he gifted something to drink. She was tired and weak and demoralized, so he gave her something sweet with sugar and caffeine to give her a temporary lift before she set about her task. She inhaled deeply through her nose and blew the air in a slow, measured exhale through pursed lips. Then she opened her eyes.

She looked at the can of Coke.

Then she looked at the pencil and paper.

The truth was unavoidable.

There was no one coming for her. The SEALs or Army Special Forces or whoever had tried to rescue her had failed. If the American team had been able to track them when they left the last compound, she would be either dead or free already. There was no cavalry coming for her. She would live or die based only on the decisions she made. And if she had to die, then so be it, but she would not quit. She would be prepared to kill every one of these bastards if that's what it took.

"Damn," she said with a sigh, picking up the notebook and setting it on her lap.

Ten names . . . You can do this, Amanda, she told herself as she began to write. She'd made her decision. The battle lines were set. The only question remaining was how long it would take before he figured out her list was bullshit.

CHAPTER 27

Moscow, Russia
May 7
1930 Local Time

Arkady lit a match and touched it to the paper.

Holding the sheet between thumb and forefinger, he watched the corner curl and burn. A line of fire spread and crept upward, leaving a delicate charcoal remainder in its wake. He held it until the flames licked at his skin, then dropped it into the empty metal trash can at his feet. The blackened, crinkled remnant fractured into a hundred wisps of ash and ember as it hit the bottom of the pail—its message digested, transformed, and forever lost.

In the spy business, paper was back in fashion.

The document had been prepared by Catherine Morgan—his mole in the Office of the Director of National Intelligence—but sent by a proxy in Amsterdam. Catherine—his lovely insider since she was twenty-five—would have followed his directions to the letter, despite the time-sensitive nature of the information, and gone through two blinds to get the message to their courier in Europe. There it would have been converted into the embedded message now contained within the 397-page United Nations OHCHR report on human rights abuses. That report had been sent via a diplomatic courier service and marked "Urgent and Time Sensitive" to the Secretariat of the Moscow International Model UN at Moscow State University, where it had been picked up by an FSB courier and personally delivered to Arkady. The new generation of spies relied entirely on electronic communications and touted speed. Yes, the paper method had taken fifteen hours, but it was immune to electronic intercepts and digital snooping. In almost every scenario, he'd trade time for security. Morgan was his most valuable spy within the US government, and her unmasking would be devastating to his current and ongoing operations. There was no scenario where that risk was acceptable.

Upon receipt, Arkady had extracted ten pages—any one of which might contain the hidden communication—and *developed* the pages in a solution of manganese sulfate, hydrogen peroxide, and other trace reagents. The process activated the cerium oxalate ink impregnated onto the back of page 212, revealing the hidden text in burnt-orange handwriting.

Using "invisible" ink to send top-secret messages had been practiced for hundreds of years, but it reached its pinnacle during the Cold War, with a chemical formulation used by East German Stasi agents and their KGB counterparts. The chemistry behind the technique had recently been cracked by the West, but Russian chemists had tweaked the formulation at Arkady's request. Only with the new and improved development reagent could the ink be oxidized to give up its secrets.

"What to do, what to do . . . what to do?" Arkady said as he read, rubbing the back of his neck. His mind churned through the implications and opportunities born of this new development. The message confirmed that Arkady's recent false-flag offensives had achieved their goals. In targeting the B61s at Incirlik and unmasking the hidden

CIA operations center nearby, he'd created doubt concerning America's operational strength and integrity in Turkey. In her own words, his top spy had written:

> *The situation with Turkey is deteriorating quickly. POTUS has decided to travel to Istanbul to talk America back into Erodan's good graces and instructed the DNI to accompany him on the trip.*

"What did the paper say?" Yuri asked, shaking Arkady from his fugue. For a moment, he'd forgotten his young acolyte was in the room.

"I'm sorry, Yuri, this one is above your pay grade, but I wanted to show you how the development process works so you can employ this method when the time comes. I've been told the Americans are very close to achieving quantum decryption capability. When this happens, none of our electronic transmissions will be secure."

"Regardless of the size of the RSA key?" Yuri asked.

"Yes," Arkady said, nodding. "Our top mathematicians are working on postquantum cryptography protocols, but I think there will be a gap during which we will be vulnerable. There may come a time when we have to rely exclusively on face-to-face communication or sending chemically encrypted notes by courier for all our most sensitive transmissions."

Yuri nodded.

"Tell me about the lawyer, Lisovsky," Arkady asked, abruptly shifting topics. "What did he do after we let him go?"

"He went straight to the trial."

"And then what?"

"He did exactly what we told him to do," Yuri said with a self-satisfied grin, as if he'd been the architect of the plan himself. "Lisovsky sat on his hands during the trial. The defense was weak, and Michael

Uramov was convicted and taken back to prison. It's over, problem solved."

Arkady shook his head. "You only told me half of the story—the first half. What happened next?"

"I . . . I don't know," Yuri said, confused, searching Arkady's expression for a clue.

Arkady sighed. *This one is not as smart as I'd hoped . . .* "What did Lisovsky do after the trial?"

Yuri paled. "I don't know."

"Well, I do. He called Alexei Nalvana."

"Nalvana the activist?"

"No, the tennis player," Arkady scoffed. "Of course the activist—don't be stupid."

"I'm sorry."

"Lisovsky told Nalvana everything that happened, and when they hung up, Nalvana called Brouder in London. He asked Brouder if he would use his contacts in the British government to pursue political asylum for Lisovsky and his girlfriend. Brouder said he'd try. Lisovsky then bought two tickets on KLM from Moscow to London. One in his name and one in his girlfriend's name, leaving tomorrow."

"He's running?"

"Obviously."

"So what do we do? You want me to kill them?"

"Fuck no," Arkady bellowed, his face incredulous.

"But I thought . . . I mean . . . Don't tell me we're just going to let them get away?"

Arkady nodded. "Yes."

"But why? I could take care of both of them; it's not a problem."

"Let me try to explain this to you with a metaphor I think you'll understand," Arkady said with an exasperated sigh. "Pretend, Yuri, that you are walking to get a cup of coffee when you come upon a small, fresh, steaming piece of dog shit on the sidewalk. It smells, it is ugly to look at, but it can't hurt you. Sure, you could try to clean it up, but in doing so, most likely all you will end up with is a dirty, smelly mess on your hands. Alternatively, you could just ignore it and walk on, confident that the masses behind you will be trying to do the same—everyone not wanting to look at or risk getting dirty from touching the little piece of shit. Do you understand what I'm trying to tell you?"

Yuri nodded, trying and failing to suppress a grin.

"Who plays Lisovsky in this story?" Arkady asked.

"The little piece of shit," Yuri said.

"That's right," Arkady said, clasping the young man's shoulder and facing him. "So in conclusion, what is the lesson from all this?"

"That our response to a problem must be commensurate with the threat the problem poses."

"Wrong!" Arkady slammed his fist into the young man's solar plexus. Yuri doubled over at the waist in agony, gasping for air. "The lesson is that *you must pay attention*," the spymaster chastised.

Yuri tried to speak, but all he could manage was to look up at Arkady with red incredulous eyes.

This one is too slow and too trusting, he decided, scowling at his soon-to-be ex-pupil. *What I need is another Valerian . . . another who can go from Georgian thug to Malik the Middle East terrorist in the blink of an eye. Valerian has the gift.*

"I'm late for a meeting," Arkady said, turning his back on the hunched-over operator. "I've decided you're going back to Vympel. You're not cut out for the type of work we do in Zeta; tell Veronika to draft your transfer orders when you get your breath back."

At that, Yuri managed to croak out a "Yes, sir," and forced himself to stand up straight. "Despite my failure . . . thank you . . . for this opportunity."

Arkady gave the big operator's shoulder a farewell pat and walked out of his office. When he stepped out onto Lubyanka Square, one of Petrov's personal drivers was waiting in an idling black Mercedes G-Wagen. The official vehicle of the President's motorcade was an armored Mercedes S-class limousine, but Petrov preferred to ride in SUVs and maintained a fleet of six G-Wagens—two armored and four decoys. This, Arkady surmised, was one of the decoys. The ride to the Kremlin was brief, taking less time than clearing security and waiting for Petrov. An hour had passed by the time he finally sat down opposite Vladimir Petrov in the Russian President's private office.

"Tea?" Petrov's secretary asked Arkady with a smile.

"I'll have a coffee," Arkady said. "If it's not too much trouble."

"No trouble at all, Director Arkady," she said and hurried away.

Arkady looked at Petrov and found the President looking down his nose at him.

"What?" Arkady said with a chuckle.

"What's wrong with tea?"

"I hate tea. It tastes like dirty water."

Petrov made a *pftttt* sound, blowing a little puff of air through pursed lips to show his disagreement.

The President disliked coffee, shunned tobacco, and generally refrained from alcohol, save for obligatory toasts when his refusal would either emasculate his image or offend an ally of repute. He also avoided prescription medication, once commenting to Arkady that prescription pharmaceuticals were a coordinated conspiratorial campaign by the West to create dependencies in the populace. He went on to claim, in one of his more bizarre paranoid episodes, that the ultimate goal was to wean Russians off state vodka and turn them into mindless slaves of the West hooked on prescription meds. Thinking of this exchange still made Arkady chuckle. Paradoxically, however, Arkady had heard rumors that Petrov had begun dabbling in nootropic cocktails over the past several months, combining pharmaceuticals and herbal supplements. This was a very Petrov thing to do; he was always looking for a way to elevate himself above those around him. In the past, his weapon had been discipline, but as his mind and body aged, discipline alone was not enough. Today, Petrov looked as sly and sharp as Arkady could ever remember; maybe the program was working.

Petrov's secretary was back a beat later with Arkady's coffee, and then Petrov dismissed her with a wave of his hand.

"You look well rested, my friend," Arkady said, taking a cautious sip of the very hot brew.

Petrov despised small talk and reminded Arkady of this with a wordless, irritated glower. "Ivanov was here this morning, complaining about you."

"Uh-huh, that sounds like Ivanov. What did he say?"

"He asked me if I had authorized you to conduct covert operations in Turkey and then failed to inform him about it," Petrov said.

"And what did you say?"

"I reminded him that the SVR works for me, not the other way around, and that I didn't like the implication that I needed his permission to do anything."

Arkady nodded. "Ivanov likes org charts with dotted lines, forms with boxes to check, and decisions that are only black and white . . . He needs to relax, or he is going to have a heart attack."

Petrov took a sip of tea and then set down his cup. "Mixed in with all the whining, he did mention something that caught my interest. Amanda Allen—Ivanov says she's CIA and that you have her."

"Did he?" Arkady chuckled. "Well, it's true. She is CIA, and I am in the process of readying her for transport."

"Transport to where?"

"Grozny."

"Well, Ivanov wants her."

"Only after we're done with her. He can do as he pleases with what's left."

Petrov contemplated this in silence for a moment and then said, "Fine, what else?"

"I have some very big news and a crazy idea . . ."

This finally earned him one of Petrov's infamous vulpine grins. "Don't keep me in suspense, old friend. What trick do you have hiding up your sleeve?"

"The American President, the Secretary of State, and the Director of National Intelligence are traveling as a contingent to Turkey."

"Warner is feeling the pressure. This will be his first face-to-face meeting with Erodan, and he's leaving his ivory tower to do it," Petrov said, narrowing his eyes. "Hmmm, how to make a mess of this . . . Maybe we drop some bombs on the Kurdish rebel camps in Syria before the meeting. That will make Erodan happy and infuriate Warner."

"It will also infuriate the Kurdish rebels, motivating them to retaliate and make a statement to the world."

"What type of statement did you have in mind?" Petrov asked, leaning in on his elbows.

Arkady laid out his plan, and when he was finished, he met the President's piercing blue-eyed gaze. Most men wilted when confronted with Petrov's cold, silent judgment, but not Arkady. This was *his* tactic, but Petrov probably didn't remember the lesson thirty years removed. He was so good at intimidation now . . . so good at being Tsar.

Yes, it was an audacious plan—a false-flag operation that five years ago Arkady himself would have called madness. But the world was a different place today. The Kremlin's propaganda machine had flooded the world with the same techniques developed and honed over decades to manipulate, disenfranchise, and control the beliefs and opinions of its own populace. The demon soldier known as Fake News was the best thing that had ever happened to clandestine operations. When the populace loses the ability to discern truth from fiction, eventually they give them equal weight. Apathy supplants anger, disinterest usurps disapproval—these were the Kremlin's objectives.

The resulting chaos, especially in America, had exceeded expectations. The operation Arkady had just proposed in Turkey would be the perfect litmus test to gauge America's strategic response to a false-flag operation designed to undermine one of its most important relationships. Geographically, Turkey was the crossroads of the Eastern Hemisphere, positioned between Asia, Africa, and Europe. Because of this, it served as an economic, cultural, and strategic bridge. Trade goods, oil and gas, weapons, money, and human capital flowed like a superhighway through the country, making Turkey a nation that America simply could not afford to lose sway over. As the NATO member with the second largest military, Turkey was a crucial strategic deterrent to Russian intervention in the region. But if they could succeed in turning Turkey against the West, then the stage would be set for the War of Russian Reunification to begin in earnest.

He decided this point was probably worth emphasizing with Petrov . . .

Petrov waved a hand. "Crimea was the litmus test and all the proof we need. They are sheep, Arkady, feckless and afraid to act. We can do what we want, whenever we want."

"Careful, Mr. President. Crimea was different—lower stakes, lower political capital and influence. Operations against and inside a NATO member nation will garner a different reaction. You and I have talked at great length about orchestrating 'secession from NATO' campaigns in target nations prior to overt interventions. We have made good progress with Turkey so far. Why not push harder?"

"I don't see how a *failed* attempt to assassinate the US President in Turkey accomplishes this. If anything, it will unite the two countries."

"No," Arkady said with a grin. "It will have a destabilizing effect, further amplifying the mistrust and ill will already brewing between them. So long as there's no dead president to serve as a martyr and rally the American people and Congress into action, the event will reinforce the sitting administration's doubts about the stability and reliability of Turkey. But there needs to be dead bodies and blood in the streets to draw attention to the divide between Warner and Erodan over terrorism and the Kurdish separatists. We can, perhaps, even come to the rescue, taking out those responsible and claiming a victory over terrorism in Turkey that the Americans failed to prosecute themselves. We pressure Erodan to suspend NATO operations out of Incirlik indefinitely, and we lend military support to his operations in Syria. Isn't that worth the risk? Wouldn't that be a victory?"

"Bah, Turkey will never leave NATO. It is Erodan's safety net. He's like an unfaithful husband married to a rich and powerful woman. Russia is a fine enough mistress, but he will never leave his wife."

Petrov stood and walked over to his office window overlooking the courtyard below. "I don't like Warner, but assassinating a sitting President . . . It is too much, Arkady. You overstep."

"An assassination *attempt*. The mission is meant to fail."

"I think the answer must be no," Petrov said, but he was stroking his chin, deep in thought.

Arkady smiled. He had him.

"And who would actually die in your assassination attempt?" Petrov asked, turning back to him from the window.

"Perhaps the Secretary of State?"

"Ambassador Lukin likes him. He says Baker is driven by ego and self-interest and is someone we can manipulate."

This was, of course, the answer Arkady had expected. But he couldn't very well unmask his real target with too much zeal.

"All right, then that leaves the Director of National Intelligence, Kelso Jarvis."

Petrov laughed and turned to face him. "You're one cold bastard. They just lost their DNI to assassination last year and you want to do it again?"

"Different man, different time," Arkady said wryly. "And more importantly, Catherine would get another opportunity to ascend to DNI."

"Fine, do it," Petrov said, marching back to his seat. "But don't get caught, Arkady, or you will find your desk relocated to a nice office in the basement of Lubyanka."

Spoken like a true Tsar.

The President's thinly veiled, ironic threat made Arkady smile. When this was all over, if he survived the coup, Petrov would be the one who found himself in the bowels of Lubyanka. They were entering the endgame now. Petrov was the face of Russia. Only Petrov could launch the Reunification Campaign. But once that campaign was over, his days as Tsar were numbered. Petrov didn't know it, but he would be the scapegoat for the coming war, no matter the outcome. Arkady would see to that, even if it was his last act on earth.

Petrov's desk phone rang. He picked it up. *"Da,"* he said, fixing his gaze on Arkady and then dismissing him with a wave.

Arkady nodded, finished off the remainder of his coffee in one long swig, and then walked out of Petrov's office without a backward glance. The Russian President's arrogance didn't bother Arkady, and neither did getting booted from the meeting like he was some busboy at a restaurant. Nothing offended Arkady. He was above posturing and gamesmanship; the objective was all that mattered. Besides, he was too old for arm-wrestling matches. Arm wrestling was boring. Chess, on the other hand, that was still fun. Unfortunately, he hadn't had a worthy opponent in a very long time. Catherine reported that Kelso Jarvis was a brilliant man and had already made great strides salvaging the sinking ship that was the American intelligence community. Maybe in Jarvis he would finally find an adversary worthy of the title.

He smiled, thinking about the conversation he needed to have with Valerian. Time to set up the board and make the first move.

Let's hope you're smart enough to save yourself, Kelso Jarvis, because I'm fucking bored, and I'm coming for you, my American friend.

CHAPTER 28

Terrorist Compound
Manbij, Syria
2130 Local Time

Valerian Kobak sat cross-legged on the floor, his back to the wall, his mind deep in thought. He'd chosen the room directly on the other side of the cell where Amanda Allen was being held to serve as his temporary quarters. He wanted to be close to her. He enjoyed being close to her. The last time he'd checked the live camera feed, she'd been sitting in her corner, huddled under her blanket and fretting over her betrayal. He imagined her now, back pressed against the opposite side of the wall, their flesh separated by a mere six inches of wood and plaster.

Of all the aspects of his job, he liked interrogation most, and he liked interrogating strong women especially. Gender and sexuality made the duel so much richer and more stimulating. With this woman in particular, every encounter was a novelty, every interaction a coy flirtation. She was clever and brave and enchanting, this American spy, despite her inexperience and naivety. In fact, were she more seasoned, he imagined he'd already be breaking fingers. Captives who imagined themselves as hard-asses took the fun out of interrogation, like a dinner date who demanded they skip drinks and entrées and go straight for dessert. As it were, this interrogation would go down as one of his all-time favorites.

And to think I almost tried to talk Arkady out of giving me this assignment!

He was fantasizing about the next interaction when the encrypted satellite phone stuffed in his go-bag chimed. With a heavy sigh, he got to his feet and retrieved the phone. He accepted the call and then walked to the opposite corner to answer.

"Prime," he answered, stating his code name in Abzhui, the Russified dialect of Abzkaz. Despite being an official language of Abzkazia, few people spoke Abzkaz anymore, with most of his countrymen choosing to converse in Georgian or Russian out of both convenience and necessity. Two or three more generations, and the language would go extinct, but that hadn't stopped Arkady from learning to speak it. He claimed tradecraft as his motivation for doing so, wanting a rare, cryptic dialect they could freely converse in without being understood by eavesdroppers. There was some truth to this, but Valerian recognized the other unspoken truth. Arkady made this great effort as a gesture of mutual respect. Very few people understood how Arkady's mind worked; even fewer understood his code. Effort, competency, communion, these were the currencies that Arkady Zhukov traded and negotiated in. These were the only things that mattered.

"How is the game going?" Arkady asked, getting straight to the point.

"We are in the middle game," he answered, using Arkady's preferred universal chess metaphor to convey a tremendous amount of information in a single sentence. The Russian spymaster likened all complex processes to the three phases of chess: the opening, the middle game, and the endgame.

"How did you open?"

"Pawn to e4."

"And how did she counter?"

"With the Sicilian."

"She's aggressive *and* competent?"

"Yes, very much so."

"How much longer until the endgame?"

"Sometime tomorrow," Valerian said. "She still thinks she can win. She's fighting hard to defend the pieces she has left, despite her losses so far."

"In that case, I'm sorry to have to do this, but there's been a change of plans," Arkady said. "We're moving Allen to a black site in Grozny. You have a new assignment."

Valerian felt a surge of white-hot anger, and he clenched his jaw shut for a beat to stop himself from cursing at his boss. "But I'm not finished."

"I know," Arkady said, "and I know it is upsetting to have to hand your work over to be bungled by lesser men, but unfortunately, that is the nature of our business. There's only one Spetsgruppa Zeta in Russia, and only one Zeta Prime, which means you are a man in high demand—a soldier whose assignments and priorities are ruled by the whims of fate."

"But I'm not finished yet," Valerian repeated, scanning the room for something to break.

"Find your center," the spymaster said, his tone now that of a patient father calming a raging child.

"This one is special," Valerian said, starting to pace. "We have a bond. There is communion. I need to see it through."

"I'm sorry, but the answer is no. You have one hour to play with her and get your head to a place where you can walk away from this. But understand—she must be alive, ambulatory, and able to speak when you're finished." Arkady's voice was a hard line. "That is an order."

"Yes, sir," Valerian said, collecting himself. "Where and when is the handover?"

"A Screen unit is en route to pick her up as we speak. Barring complications, expect them in two to three hours."

"You're sending a Zaslon team here?"

"My options were limited."

"I understand, but it's not a good idea."

"Why?"

"Because the people here hate Russia as much as they hate the Turks and the Syrian regime. Two days ago, a MiG-29 dropped bombs on their encampment in Afrin. They are hot about it. The Malik legend was carefully curated as a Chechen terrorist who despises Russia. If these Screen guys come in swinging their dicks and talking Russian when they think no one is listening, we are fucked."

"You don't have to worry about that. They are professionals; Zaslon is the best SOF unit in GRU. This unit has been operating undetected in the region for months."

"You of all people know better. You're the one who beat into my head that I can only rely on other Zeta operatives. That everyone else is sloppy, and it's true. I've seen it again and again."

"You're right, of course you're right, but my options were limited. I need you and your team in Turkey ASAP. Which means you need to manage the handoff effectively and expeditiously. If you're worried, use a standoff. Drive her out alone and hand her over yourself. I trust you to make the right decisions. You have full authority and autonomy. You're Prime. Today, Zaslon works for you."

"Copy," he said. "What about the ORDMOD?"

"The mission package has been saved as an attachment to a draft email in a newly created Yandex account. Delete after reading. It will remain active for two hours, that's all."

"Username and password?"

"Selected from your serial list. Combination A7 B4."

"Copy. Anything else?"

He heard Arkady exhale heavily on the other line. "When you read the orders, you will be upset. You will want to contact me and tell me that it is impossible, that it is insane, and that you need two months to plan . . . so I'm going to head off this conversation now. Yes, the mission is impossible. Yes, it is insane, and yes, you will probably fail. All of this is okay. The objective is to create chaos, doubt, and fear. Success requires a degree of failure, as you will see. I have our best planners moving the pieces into place as we speak. All you have to do is get yourself and your Kurdish friends to Istanbul. Niko will meet you there and help you manage final logistics and provide your team with weapons and explosives. Good luck, Prime. Make me proud."

The line went dead.

Valerian closed his eyes. He focused on his breathing—inhaling through the nose, exhaling through the mouth—noting the rise and fall of his diaphragm, the expansion and contraction of his chest. As he centered himself, the hurricane of corrosive, chaotic, and destructive thoughts and emotions he'd been feeling during the phone call began to wane—losing their fury and influence over him.

I am stillness. I am focus. I am a blade—honed for a single purpose.

I am the mission.

I am Zeta Prime.

He opened his eyes; the moment of weakness had passed. Renewed and focused, he set a timer on his watch for fifty-five minutes. Then he retrieved the notebook computer from his go-bag and logged in to the Yandex account using one of ten usernames and one of ten passwords he had committed to memory, giving them one hundred unique log-ins to share information before a new set would need to be generated. He read the OPORD, and when he had finished, he laughed. And when he was finished laughing, he left his room to find Samir and Mutla and brief them on the new opportunity, albeit with one critical misdirection. As far as his Kurdish friends were concerned, Warner and Erodan would be the targets of the operation. To his astonishment, the Kurdish terrorists did not balk.

"Why now?" Mutla asked, eyeing him with both curiosity and concern.

"I never ask why," he said. "That's not how my business works. That is the difference between you and me. I'm an opportunist; you're a terrorist. You want to change the world . . . Me, I just want to profit from it."

"We're not terrorists," she said, glaring at him. "We're fighting for an autonomous Kurdish state. A place where we can be free from persecution and genocide, something I wouldn't expect you to understand."

He unloaded a flurry of Chechen curses on her, none she would comprehend, but instead for effect. Then he took a deep breath and looked into her eyes. "I'm a Chechen. I understand what it means to fight for autonomy. I understand what it means to have my friends and family hunted, persecuted, and murdered."

She nodded at him, her expression softening a little.

"I had to leave that life behind," he continued, becoming pensive. "Too much pain . . . too much loss. I became what I am because . . . It doesn't matter anymore. You and Samir are fighting for a cause that is noble. I respect that, and it is why I trust you. This operation is too dangerous and too important to be left in the hands of hired guns."

"What do you think?" Samir said, flashing Mutla his broken-toothed grin.

Successful manipulation was generally a function of the target's intelligence and naivety. None of this impassioned, soul-baring, emotional flip-flopping was necessary to convince Samir. The opportunity itself had been sufficient to sway the big brute. Mutla, however, was a more difficult walnut to crack. He suspected she needed to see this side of him before she'd be willing to take the next step.

"I think," she said after a long beat, "that this is the opportunity we've been waiting for. The other two attacks were symbolic victories, but this . . . This will change the fate of our people. These two men are responsible for my husband's death. These two men are responsible for the continued genocide of our people. Erodan for pursuing it, and Warner being the one man powerful enough to stop it but instead choosing to turn a blind eye."

"How do we cross the border back into Turkey? Security is tighter now than ever before," Mutla said.

"Leave that to me. It's already been arranged. Gather your things and prepare to leave."

"What of the American woman? Are we going to kill her? Take a video and give credit to ISIS?"

"Don't be stupid," Valerian said, his voice hard. "She is worth nothing to me dead. Now that I've learned what I needed to know, I'm selling her. This morning there was an auction. The winning bidder is coming to get her as we speak."

"Who?"

"That is none of your concern. All you need to know is that the sale price was significantly higher than I anticipated, which means I can afford to pay you a bonus. Once I receive payment, I will wire one and a half times our negotiated rate into your accounts. And I will pay two times what I paid for the Adana job for this next operation."

"Three times," Mutla said, "and payment must be issued in advance. It is unlikely that we will survive the aftermath of what we are about to undertake. We may die, but the cause will live on, and the cause needs that money."

"This is not a negotiation. I will pay two times, wired in advance, end of discussion," he said and turned his back on them.

"Fine, we accept," she said.

"Good. Now gather your things, Mutla. You and I are leaving together. Samir will stay to oversee the handoff and then join us later."

"How long do I have?"

"Ten minutes," he said. "I need to have one last conversation with the American. Then we go."

CHAPTER 29

Amanda stopped writing and set her pencil down.

It doesn't really qualify as a pencil, she thought, looking at it. The only suitable noun for the writing implement the Man not Malik—that's what she'd taken to calling him in the private monologue in her head—had given her was a *nub.* He'd done it on purpose. You couldn't stab someone with a dull nub of pencil three centimeters long. It was so small she could barely maintain a grip on it. Writing with it was nearly impossible; her fingertips ached from clutching the damn thing so tight for the past hour.

Aching fingertips. She laughed. *That's the least of my worries.*

If she wanted something to fret over, why not fret over the stacks of bullshit she'd handed over to the Man not Malik during her last three confessionals? That little game had bought her a reprieve, but certainly whatever state actor the Man not Malik worked for was feverishly vetting the information now. It wouldn't be much longer before the word came back that the names and descriptions she'd provided were not checking out. When that happened, boy, would she be in trouble. She did not want to see the Man not Malik mad . . . yet a weird, perverse part of her kind of did.

That's disturbing.

All this fucking with her headspace was starting to get to her.

She picked up the empty can of Coca-Cola, put it to her lips, and tilted her head back. She knew it was empty. She'd already done this exact thing three times, but just one drop . . . just one drop of sweetness on her tongue was all she wanted. No drop came. With an irate scowl, she threw the stupid can and watched it clatter across the tile floor. Her blanket slipped off her shoulders and fell to her waist. Sighing, she rewrapped herself and was hit by a waft of body odor.

God, I stink . . .

I hate this place. I hate these people. And I'm so damn thirsty!

"Can I please have some fucking water?" she screamed, surprising herself. She hadn't done anything like that before. Not once had she beckoned her captors. Why had she done that?

Because I've become dependent on them . . .

No one answered.

No one came.

I'm running out of time. I need to work on my escape plan . . .

She looked around her cell. No windows. Only one way in or out—a solid wooden door that locked from the outside and had no handle on the inside. Further complicating matters, the door was hinged as an inswing slab, which meant she couldn't kick it down because it shut *against* the frame.

That certainly does not meet fire code. I'm going to have to complain to management.

She scanned the ceiling and the walls looking for other vulnerabilities. No conveniently sized air ducts she could crawl through like in the movies. In fact, there wasn't a single supply or return air register in the room. The situation was both grim and obvious. To get out of this room, she would have to egress through the door, which meant she would have to overpower and kill one of her captors. Her escape would be one of opportunity, which meant she needed to be ready to exploit any opportunity when it presented itself. She scanned her cell again, this time looking for something, anything, she could use as a weapon.

I could always poke someone with my nub, she thought, her eyes settling on her pencil and paper once again. *I could give them a nasty papercut . . . I could smother them with my blanket . . . I could bonk them on the head with my empty Coke can . . . Oh wait, I know, I can drown them in my pee pail!*

This last thought sent her into a punch-drunk laughing fit, which was cut abruptly short by the click of the door latch. A half second later, the door swung open, and the Man not Malik was standing there.

"What is so funny?" he asked, fixing her with a curious smile.

"Nothing," she said, all the color and life draining from her.

He stepped into the room, carrying his little stool in one hand and a small duffel bag in the other. The door swung shut behind him, locked by someone on the other side.

"Something was funny. I heard you laughing."

"No, just me losing my wits from starvation and dehydration. Hilarious stuff—sensory deprivation and torture."

"Mmm-hmm," he said, taking a seat on his stool. "I've been there before myself."

She eyed him.

"Don't look so surprised. Why do you think I'm so good at this? I've been in your shoes—well, in your blanket," he said with a wan smile, "a few times before."

"So what? Is that supposed to make me respect you? Make me feel some sort of bond with you? This isn't happening to me by accident. *You're* doing this to me," she scoffed. "So fuck you."

His smile disappeared. "Give me the papers," he said, pointing to her latest assignment on the floor.

"Get them yourself," she said, tightening the blanket around her.

"I see you have fire left inside. Good . . ." he said, getting off his stool and then picking up the three pages of her hand-scrawled notes, "because you're going to need it."

"Is that a threat?" she asked, contemplating kicking him in the face. She could do it. His face was right there, in perfect range . . .

He sighed and looked at her. What she saw in his eyes disturbed her.

Was that pity?

Something was about to change, and for her, change was bad. Change meant new suffering. Change meant new pain. Kicking him in the face was not a smart idea. She retreated without actually going anywhere, and the Man not Malik went back to his stool.

The assignment he'd given her on his last visit had been different from the previous demands. This time, instead of asking her to reveal CIA personnel, methodologies, strategic objectives, and state secrets, he'd instructed her to write about her childhood and her father. At the time, she had rejoiced at the assignment—finally, something she didn't have to lie about. She'd written feverishly, filling all three pages front and back in a stream-of-consciousness, soul-baring exercise that was both easy and liberating. But now, watching him read it, she felt uneasy. She'd given her private self to him without hesitation. Willingly. Foolishly. Shame washed over her as she watched him read. He was engrossed . . . engrossed in her private self.

"This is very good, Amanda," he said, his gaze still transfixed on the page. "Exactly what I was hoping for."

She looked away, waiting for him to finish. Finally, he broke the silence. "Get up."

"What?"

"I said, get up."

Fear blossomed in her gut as she got to her feet, careful to keep the blanket wrapped around her.

"Give me the blanket," he said.

"No," she said.

"Give me the blanket, Amanda," he said, his voice a hard line.

"Please . . ."

"Now!"

Steeling herself, she unwrapped the blanket, balled it up, and threw it to him. Unlike before, when she'd stood bare, brazen, and defiant in front of him, now her nakedness unnerved her. She felt weak, ashamed, and vulnerable. The blanket had done its work, and she wanted it back. Desperately. She felt his lascivious gaze on her, crawling over her skin like a thousand ants. She shuddered.

"Just get it over with," she muttered.

"What are you talking about?" he asked, getting to his feet.

"Whatever you're going to do to me, just do it," she whispered, looking anywhere but in his eyes.

He reached up and gently caressed her cheek. She heard his respiration rate picking up. She saw his posture stiffen. This was it. It was really going to happen this time. She forced herself to look him in the eyes. This time, instead of pity, she saw anger and something else . . . *restraint?* He turned abruptly and walked to get the small duffel bag he'd left on the floor next to his camping stool. After unzipping the top, he pulled out a folded stack of clothes and walked back to her.

"Here," he said, handing the clothes to her. "Get dressed."

A wellspring of hope blossomed inside her. "You're letting me go?"

"No," he said. "Unfortunately, our time together has come to an end."

"What?" she said, an insidious black dread usurping the hope she'd felt just a heartbeat before. "I don't understand."

His expression turned grim. "Another party has taken a controlling interest in your fate, and I am sorry to say that as unpleasant as your life has been for the past several days, it is about to get much, much worse."

"No," she heard herself say, clutching the clothes to her chest. "I don't want to go."

He turned away from her and began to pace. "Get dressed, Amanda."

She was trembling now and hated herself for it, but it was the fear. It was automatic. She looked down at the clothes and realized they were not *her* clothes—just a dirty pair of pants, a light sweatshirt, a wool cap, and a pair of shoes.

"These are men's clothes," she said.

"I know. It is all I could find that would fit you."

"But what about underwear?"

"Your undergarments were destroyed," he said, still pacing. "I'm sorry."

She stood frozen with indecision. Was this her last chance? When he knocked on that door to leave, should she try to kill him? She looked at his V-shaped torso, at the form and breadth of his shoulders. The Man not Malik was no brutish hulk like the man with the broken tooth, but he was powerfully built. In fact, the way he carried himself, his movements and posture, belied a military bearing. In a fight between him and Samir, something told her he would be the victor. There was no way she could best him, even with a weapon. Even with the element of surprise, he would dispatch her as easily as if she were a toddler.

"Get dressed," he snapped, this time the slightest hint of a new accent flavoring his English.

She did as instructed, quickly getting into the clothes, slipping on the shoes, and even donning the wool cap, although she wasn't sure why. "Okay, I'm dressed."

"Good," he said and then retrieved three more items from his bag: a bottle of water, a Ziploc bag with dried figs and walnut pieces, and a black zipper case. He handed her the water and the bag, but the black zipper case he stared at for a long moment before walking away from her and unzipping it. She craned her neck to see what was inside, and the contents made her heart skip a beat—glass vials, a hypodermic syringe, and aluminum blister packs. He withdrew a single blister pack, zipped the case closed, and hesitated a beat before turning to her. "Inside this packet is a suicide pill. I offer it to you now as my parting gift."

A lump the size of a golf ball formed in her throat. "You want me to take this now?"

"No," he said, shaking his head. "When the time is right, you'll know."

"I don't understand."

"The place where you are going, Amanda, there is no coming back from. The people who will finish your interrogation will desecrate you. They will mutilate your body and soul, and I can't . . ." He closed his eyes and exhaled. "I give you this as a mercy."

He held out the little metallic packet.

She accepted it.

"Why? Why are you doing this?"

"You chose to play the world's most dangerous game, and you did it for what I know were noble reasons. Unfortunately, your handlers did not dissuade you of this egregious miscalculation. They sent you, naive and unprepared, into the sewer to battle monsters you were never equipped to challenge. I am not a moral man, Amanda Allen, but I do follow a code."

"How does it work?" she asked, not believing she was contemplating what she was contemplating.

"There is a glass pearl inside the blister pack. The pearl contains a lethal dose of liquid potassium cyanide. All you have to do is put it in your mouth and bite down. The poison kills quickly, stopping your heart within seconds of exposure. But be careful. If you swallow the pill without cracking the shell first, it will pass through your digestive system without incident. The pearls are designed that way on purpose, to give the operator the ultimate choice in the moment. But choose wisely, because you won't get a second chance."

She nodded and tucked the little blister pack in her right pants pocket.

He returned the black zipper case to the duffel bag and walked to the door to leave.

"Wait," she said as he rapped his fist against the door. "Tell me your name."

He looked back at her, considering for a beat. "You can call me Prime."

CHAPTER 30

Two Blocks South of the Target Compound
Manbij, Syria
May 8
0020 Local Time

Dempsey watched with approval as Amraz Demir checked over his weapons and kit in the dim light of the garage. Raz was kitted up like a professional soldier, not like some street thug or foreign militia fighter. Dempsey had seen the kid in action—he had a reasonable partner for this assault.

And a reasonable weapon in the up-armored BMW.

"This is going to be fun," Raz said with a white-toothed grin.

"I don't think 'fun' is the word I'd use to describe what we're about to do," Dempsey said, remembering what happened the last time he'd tried to rescue Allen.

"Yeah, well," Raz said with a chuckle, "I've done eighteen assaults since coming to Manbij, and all of them alone. Just having another shooter in the car makes it fun."

"My team will be on time on target as we arrive. There'll be more firepower than you know what to do with. But listen, Raz, you make a point that I want to talk about. You've had a couple of years of riding solo, and being a cowboy has kept you alive. This operation is about precision. As part of this tactical team, I need you to follow commands. If we all work together, we can be in and out in minutes, but if you're off doing your own Lone Ranger thing, then I guarantee someone will get hurt who shouldn't. Okay?"

"Check," Raz said. "I was a Marine medic, remember? If there is one thing we do well, it's follow orders and rules of engagement."

"We cover each other, fire and move together; I'll relay comms to you as they come to me."

"You're the boss," Raz said.

Dempsey nodded, satisfied. Their scouting mission earlier in the day and the Reaper surveillance had confirmed with a high degree of confidence that Amanda Allen was being held in the compound Raz had identified. After that, Adamo and Smith had moved into place all the chess pieces necessary to try again. The plan was simple: Dempsey and Raz would crash the front gate in the armored BMW, drawing fire and attention to the front of the compound. The rest of the Ember team, currently inbound on an Osprey from the USS *Ronald Reagan*, would arrive thirty seconds later. The pilots would drop Grimes on the roof of the outbuilding and then hover just long enough for the rest of the assault team, led by Munn, to fast-rope down inside the compound wall. Munn's team would breach the rear of the compound while Dempsey and Raz entered from the front. If everything went according to plan, they'd have Allen out in less than three minutes, with everyone EXFILLING on the Osprey.

He looked at his watch, then patted the dirty, dimpled hood of the BMW. "Let's get this beast into position."

He let Raz slide into the driver's seat, resisting the almost overpowering urge to take control of the vehicle, then slipped into the passenger's seat, his assault rifle cradled in his lap. The engine roared to life. Dempsey looked at Raz. The smile on the kid's face eclipsed mere pride.

The BMW was more than just a car to him; it was his guardian angel—a partner in crime that had saved his ass countless times in countless impossible situations.

Dempsey laughed.

"What's funny?" Raz said, a bit defensive.

He shook his head and held up a hand. "Nothing . . . or maybe the whole damn thing. I did some pretty insane stuff when I was a SEAL—even more insane stuff since I joined this team—but nothing like crashing through the gate of a heavily guarded enemy compound in a luxury sedan riding next to your crazy ass."

Raz smiled and put the transmission into drive. "In the immortal words of John McClane—yippee-ki-yay, motherfucker!"

"Let's go save this girl," Dempsey said, clapping Raz on the shoulder.

They pulled out of the garage and onto the dark and empty nighttime street.

"We have you on the move, Atlas," Baldwin said.

"You're five by, Olympus," Dempsey said. He looked over at Raz and gave him a thumbs-up. "We have comms and they have eyes on us."

Raz nodded.

"Banshee is inbound, on schedule," Baldwin reported, referring to the inbound Osprey by its call sign.

"Atlas, Titan One," said Munn's voice on the line. "It's good to finally hear your voice, man. You good?"

"All good. Moving into position," he said. "Really happy to have you guys onboard this time around."

"Roger that, brother," Munn said, and Dempsey could practically hear the grin on his face. "I'll call us at the IP and then call your hit. Once you take the gate, we'll be on the slide in ten seconds."

"Check."

Dempsey tapped the side of the trigger guard. In a few more minutes, it would be over. Amanda Allen would be safe, he would be back with his team, and they would all be on a bird heading home.

CHAPTER 31

Amanda paced the tile floor, fingering the small glass pellet in her pocket and trying not to think about what was next. They were moving her, and if the Man not Malik was to be believed, the fate awaiting her was worse than death. But she would not let it come to that.

She looked at the heavy wooden door to her cell.

The sands in her hourglass had run out. The next time they opened that door would be her final opportunity to escape. Frantically, she scanned the room for the millionth time, looking for something, anything she could use as a weapon.

There's nothing . . . fucking nothing!

Then her eye caught a glint of silver behind her piss bucket, and an idea came to her. She ran to the bucket, picked up the Coke can, and then, grabbing the top in her right hand and bottom in her left, she began to twist—twisting and twisting until finally the two halves pulled apart, leaving a short jagged spiral of aluminum.

It was something.

She noticed a thin red line appear across her middle knuckle where an edge had cut her and she hadn't even felt it. She walked to the center of the room. Whoever came for her would have to enter the room to get her, and she prayed they'd be lazy and leave the door open. She stood waiting and staring at the door, her mind running over memories from a class at the Farm where they'd taught her how to use and apply lethal force. She remembered wondering at the time why someone like her, someone tasked with intelligence gathering from an office, would need to know how to kill a person. But now here she was, desperately needing to remember. The twisted aluminum would not penetrate the temple, for sure, nor could she jam the thin edge up into the hole at the base of the skull, the perfect place to instantly incapacitate an attacker as their brain becomes separated from their body. No, the aluminum wasn't rigid enough to stab, but her bleeding knuckle was proof it could cut.

The throat, then.

She held her impromptu weapons, one in each hand, behind her back and talked to herself as if her Farm instructor were in the room with her: *The carotid arteries are deeper than you think. You need to penetrate an inch or two, more in someone with a thick neck, to sever them. Once you're in the neck, you need to twist your blade around to shred the artery. If you just slice it, the muscular wall of the artery contracts, and the bleeding is much slower. Open one artery and then the other, and blood flow to the brain all but stops.*

She heard a click.

Her heart rate picked up. Next came the sound of wood scraping wood as the door was opened. She tightened her grips on the two halves of the shredded Coke can.

I'm leaving here free or in a fucking body bag.

Suddenly, the thought of dying didn't frighten her nearly as much as the thought of having that fucking black hood thrown over her head.

Hinges creaked and the door opened.

The broken tooth man came in, his face dark and unhappy. He had the hood in one hand and a flex-tie in the other. He barked at her, his hands gesturing for her to come to him. She didn't move, her head hung in submission and eyes down. The more she looked beaten, the less he would expect what was coming.

He barked again.

She stared at the floor, still frozen.

She could feel him moving toward her and then saw his feet.

He grabbed her left arm.

She readied herself, tightening her core and visualizing the strike.

Outside, she heard shouting. A heartbeat later, an explosion rocked the compound, followed by automatic weapon fire. She felt the broken tooth man's grip on her left arm loosen as he looked over his shoulder and hollered into the hall. Instead of pondering what was happening, she simply exploited the opportunity. Her gaze ticked to the left side of his neck, and with every ounce of weight and strength she possessed, she drove the jagged spiral of aluminum into her captor's neck. The razor-sharp metal pierced his flesh, and as it did, she pressed it deeper, twisting her wrist. The man stumbled backward, tripped, and fell. But he pulled her with him, and she landed on top of him. The back of his head smacked the tile floor with a resounding thud. Blood sprayed from his neck, spattering the side of her face as she scrambled to straddle his chest. She struck with the other shard, this time going for his eye instead of the neck. This strike connected as well, and he bellowed with pain and rage. She struck again with her right hand, targeting his other eye, then just his face in general—striking faster and faster, harder and harder.

Screaming and slicing.

Slicing and screaming.

Again and again . . .

And again.

Beneath her, he made a gurgling sound and feebly pawed at his blinded eyes and ruined neck. Outside, she heard more shouting and more gunfire. She climbed off his chest and stood above him—the hulking killer, rapist, terrorist whom she'd somehow just vanquished—and watched the blood pour from his eviscerated face and neck. Then she heard a voice in her head, not her voice but the words from her instructor at the Farm, a former Green Beret.

This tango is down. Time to move.

She spat on the bastard's corpse. "Fuck you," she growled, wiped the blood splatter from her face with her sleeve, and then moved to the door. Her focus suddenly sharpened, and she became aware, as if for the first time, that an intense gunfight was raging outside. Could this be another rescue attempt? Her heart fluttered in her chest. Perhaps she should shelter in place and wait?

No! I'm not waiting for anyone to come for me. I'm not a prisoner anymore, not now . . . not ever again.

Amanda crouched beside the door and peered into the hallway. She looked left, then right, and finding it deserted, she stepped out of her cell. She dashed across the hall and pressed her back against the wall. Then she sidestepped until she reached the cased opening leading into the next room. She peeked around the corner for a quick look and pulled her head back. The room on the other side of the wall appeared to be a sitting or gathering room with a tile floor and two small sofas facing each other with a coffee table between. She tried to remember the path she'd taken when they'd dragged her into this place, but she'd been wearing a hood and had been disoriented. She was pretty sure she'd walked across that tile floor. Yes, she was almost positive she had. Gunfire reverberated outside as the battle raging became more intense with each passing second. Her plan was simple: get out of the house where the Americans could see her and she could see them. Hopefully they would then provide cover fire while she ran to one of their covered positions. She exhaled, steeled her nerves, then dashed around the corner.

The room had been unoccupied on her last look, but not now. A lanky young man was backpedaling into the space, firing an AK-47 at a target in the opposite direction. Her brain performed a split-second calculation and realized that turning around and running away was a nonstarter. So she did the only thing she could do—dropped her shoulder and slammed it into the small of his back. He arched under the blow, lost his two-hand grip on his weapon, and sprayed the walls and ceiling with bullets. She didn't have the mass or power to take him down, but she used her momentum and the power of her legs to drive him forward and smash him into the opposite wall. Without missing a beat, she drove her right knee up and between the man's legs from behind, smashing his groin. He cried out and dropped his weapon as she kneed him a second time, but before she could land a third strike, he whirled and tackled her to the floor. She hit the tile hard, the impact knocking all the breath from her lungs. Time slipped into slow motion as his hands found her neck. She beat against his forearms as he began to choke her, but it was pointless. His grip was like iron. Then she remembered the cyanide bead in her pocket. Her right hand flew to her pocket, and her fingertips found the little glass sphere. As black clouds appeared in her peripheral vision, she reached up and tried to put the bead in his mouth, but his lips were pressed shut tight. In desperation, she dug her left thumbnail into his right eye. He screamed, and she put the glass bead into his open mouth. Then, in an adrenaline-surged last moment of consciousness, she drove the palm of her hand into the bottom of his chin, slamming his jaw shut and praying the fragile glass sphere would break.

If it didn't, she would be dead.

Blackness eclipsed her vision, and she felt herself slipping into unconsciousness . . . Then the pressure on her neck disappeared. She gasped, sucking in a breath and hyperventilating as the world came back into focus. Above her, the terrorist arched his back and began to shudder. Then his eyes went wide and all the muscles in his body began to contract violently. Amanda pushed out from under him, crabbing backward on hands and feet, as he spewed frothy foam tinged with blood from his mouth. He began to seize, and she watched him tip and hit the ground like a log. After two or three seconds of twitching, he abruptly stopped, became rigid for a moment, and then lay still.

Outside, gunfire continued to rage, but between volleys she heard the unmistakable thrumming of helicopter rotors. And the sound was getting louder. Emotions swelled over her, hope and anticipation, as she rose on shaky feet. With bolstered resolve, she picked up the assault rifle from the floor.

"They came back for me," she murmured, bringing the weapon up. "And this time they're not leaving without me."

CHAPTER 32

Target Compound Courtyard
Manbij, Syria
0035 Local Time

"Were you expecting this kind of resistance?" Raz hollered at Dempsey from his crouched position behind the BMW.

"No," Dempsey shouted as another wave of rifle fire ricocheted over the hood of the armored car that was the only thing keeping them alive. He shifted low and left, popped up, and fired several three-round bursts at the line of shooters crouched behind a cluster of vehicles in front of the main house. His rounds didn't find a target.

Damn, these guys are good.

Less than five minutes before their planned assault, Baldwin had observed and reported that a convoy of three vehicles was arriving at the compound. This unexpected complication was simply par for the course as far as the Amanda Allen rescue endeavor was concerned. *Of course the terrorists were moving her again. And of course they'd brought lots of extra shooters to help out and spoil the raid again.* With the Ember assault team on an Osprey en route from the *Reagan* and no FARP nearby to fall back on, they had no alternative but to stick to the plan and timetable as briefed. Dempsey and Raz had breached the front gate successfully and killed three tangos, but after that, things had gone to hell. Instead of quickly gaining the upper hand and dropping the rest of the insurgents like plinking cans, the remaining guys they were up against moved and shot like experienced operators.

"These guys must be YPG fighters," Dempsey yelled at Raz.

"No, I don't think so. YPG doesn't have vehicles that nice," Raz shouted, referring to the three black SUVs parked in a defensive semicircle by the compound's front entrance. "And they're not dressed like YPG guys."

"Titan, Atlas, we're pinned down," Dempsey barked. "SITREP?"

"Atlas, this is Titan One" came Munn's voice. "Overwatch is in place on top of the garage north of your position. But after dropping Zeus, we encountered heavy direct fire and couldn't get the team on the rope. Our pilot is looping around and will insert on the other side of the compound—east of you—so we can try to flank the shooters you have engaged."

"Check," Dempsey said, drifting toward the center of the BMW.

Fire . . . move . . . fire . . .

He popped up again and fired, but all the targets had repositioned since his last look. He dropped down again as bullets and tracers pounded the Beemer.

"Atlas, this is Zeus," Grimes called into his ear. "I'm up. I have range and angles to cover your six and anything between you and those black SUVs."

"What about the assholes behind the SUVs?"

"Negative, they're dug in like ticks, and the way they parked is blocking my LOS. If only I had more elevation. I can put holes in the vehicles and give you cover fire."

"Check."

"Stand by. I'll call your next shot."

Dempsey looked over at Raz and smiled. "Help is here. Pop up and fire on my mark. We're about to get a few seconds of covering fire from the north."

He listened to Grimes's whispered voice on the open line: "Three . . . two . . ."

On "one," he heard the first shot ring out from her .300 WinMag. On "zero," he called "Now" to Raz and they popped up. Dempsey sighted on the closest SUV as Grimes's second and third rounds slammed into the vehicles, his red dot traveling across the hood. A shooter popped up, aiming at the rooftop where Grimes was working. Dempsey placed his red targeting dot and fired. The bullet tore through the man's neck, and two other shooters trying to engage disappeared like gophers down a hole.

"Titan is a three-man team," said Munn in Dempsey's ear. "On the ground now, moving fast to the northeast corner of the main house to put your tangos in a cross fire."

"Take your time and clear," Dempsey said, not wanting any casualties today. "We have them pinned down."

"Check."

"Olympus, Atlas—report thermals. Do you have eyes on the package?"

"I have three thermal signatures in the house," Baldwin said, a strange hesitancy in his voice. "Two down and one moving. There was a prolonged struggle, but we are optimistic that the ambulatory signature we're watching now is female."

"Translation: we think Amanda Allen is in the fight," said Adamo's voice.

Dempsey felt his heart swell with excitement at the news, but then the feeling quickly morphed into irritation. "So she was fighting for her life in there and you didn't tell me?"

"Check," said a new voice, Smith this time, the unspoken implication obvious: *We didn't want you charging in there, hair on fire, without backup and getting yourself shot.*

But wasn't that his call to make? When they got home, this matter of withholding pertinent data might warrant a conversation.

"Olympus, Titan. How many assholes do you hold behind those circled wagons?" Munn asked.

"Five shooters and one KIA," came Baldwin's reply.

"They move and shoot like us. Who the hell are these guys?"

"I'm recording images of their vehicles and faces as I get them, but no recognition pops in the database so far," Baldwin said. "And I agree. Their performance rebuffing our assault has been impressive to say the least."

"So glad you think so," Munn said. "How about you offer me some guidance on the best position for my team so we can shoot these very impressive motherfuckers?"

"Of course," Baldwin said, unfazed. "There is a maintenance shed ten meters northeast of the northeast corner of the house. Perhaps you could divide your team, one of you taking the corner of the house, the other two taking positions behind the shed to widen your field of fire."

"Roger. Two, you and me," Munn said.

"Atlas, you have a single tango trying to flank you from the south," Baldwin reported. "Roving patrol, I believe."

"I got him" came Grimes's cool voice in Dempsey's ear.

Dempsey spun around, pressed his back against the BMW, where he felt the vibration of another volley of enemy fire against the heavy sedan, and scanned the expansive wooded yard to his right. He saw a figure, arms pumping and a rifle in hand, charging toward him. A crack echoed from Grimes's WinMag, and the man crumpled to the ground. The last member of the compound's four-man roving patrol was now down. That left the five tangos dug in behind the vehicles and Amanda Allen inside. The problem was, this was taking too long. They should have been on the EXFIL already. If they didn't wrap this up, they were going to have every bad guy in Manbij pouring in to join the fight.

"Olympus, Atlas. The back of the compound is clear, correct?" Dempsey asked.

"Affirmative."

"All right. I can't do shit from this position. I'm going to try to loop around south, breach the compound from the back side, and extract the package. Titan and Zeus, you'll need to keep these assholes up front busy."

"Roger that, Atlas," said Munn. "Titan will be in position in less than one mike. Once you secure the package, we'll egress south to join you for pickup by Banshee One behind the compound."

"Roger that," Dempsey said.

"Call the covering fire," said Grimes in his ear.

"Check," Dempsey answered.

"Titan in position."

Dempsey turned to Raz. "You're coming with me, bro. We're gonna make a run for the house."

"You go," Raz said. "I'll help cover from here."

Dempsey shook his head. "I can't leave you here with no comms. We have to stay together. My team will keep these assholes pinned down while we loop around to the back. We grab the girl, egress, and get the hell out of here by air."

Raz pursed his lips. "What about my wheels? I can't leave my car."

Dempsey suppressed a tight grin. "I'll get you a new car, Raz. I promise."

"It has to be armored," the young vigilante said.

"Of course."

"And black."

"No problem."

"And a BMW . . ."

"Whatever you fucking want, bro. I promise."

Raz nodded, and together they crabbed toward the rear of the BMW as a maelstrom of bullets pounded the opposite quarter panel. Dempsey got into a ready position, like a runner in the starting blocks. Raz did the same.

Dempsey tensed, waiting at the ready.

"Covering fire," Grimes said in his ear, and suppressing fire from all his teammates reverberated in the night.

"Go," he shouted, and then he and Raz took off in a sprint for their lives.

CHAPTER 33

Clutching the AK-47, Amanda moved toward the front of the house. When she got to the front door, she dropped to a knee and peeked outside. To her left, she spied three black SUVs grouped in a crescent. Sheltering behind the vehicles were five operators dressed in coyote-gray cargo pants and black long-sleeve shirts, tucked in. They were shooting at the broadside of a car—a battered BMW that appeared to have crashed into a hedge just inside the smashed front gate. Behind the car, she caught a glimpse of a large man, filthy, with a full beard and long unkempt hair. He appeared to be wearing a heavy vest—a suicide vest perhaps—and he was shooting at the operators behind the SUVs. Beside him, a dark-skinned fighter with a full black beard popped up and fired a volley before they both dropped from sight and couched at the rear of the sedan.

Those are the bad guys for sure. The operators with the SUVs have to be the Americans. It's a Special Forces team come to take me home.

Amanda belly-crawled out the front door and stopped behind a heavy porch railing with concrete balusters. She got to her knees, raised the rifle over the top of the railing, and aimed at the big man behind the

BMW, her vantage point giving her a better angle than the Americans pinned down behind the SUVs. Her finger tightened on the trigger—

The roar of automatic weapon fire erupted to her right as a firestorm of bullets pounded the SUVs from the opposite direction of the BMW. She shrieked and dropped back to the ground. Loud cracks punctuated the machine gun fire. She peeked through the gap between two balusters and watched as her rescuers took cover from fire targeting them from two directions. She glanced at the BMW and saw the big man and the other bearded fighter sprinting toward the back of the house and then out of view.

Oh shit, they're going tocome in the back and ambush us, she thought and began crawling toward the northernmost corner of the porch. *I have to warn the American operators . . .*

CHAPTER 34

Dempsey ran, arms pumping, legs churning, waiting for the round to his temple that would end it all . . .

The bullet never came.

He passed the southwest corner of the house, slowed, and pressed against the wall. A half second later, Raz slammed into the wall beside him, breathing hard and laughing. "See how fun this shit is when you don't have to do it alone?"

"Yeah, this is one helluva party we crashed," Dempsey said, shaking his head. "All right, let's sweep around the back, breach the rear door, and grab the girl."

"Hold, Atlas," said Baldwin's voice, halting them in place. "We have a small problem. The package has left the house."

"What?" he barked.

"She's on the porch," Grimes said. "I can see her. She's crawling *toward* the shooters."

"What the hell is she doing? She's going to get herself killed," Dempsey said and then added, "Cover fire. I want to take a look."

Grimes started shooting, and the gunfire from Munn's three-man team increased its tempo. Dempsey dropped into a combat crouch and crept around the corner of the house, exposed just long enough to peek onto the front porch before darting back. In that instant, he made eye contact with Amanda Allen. She was battered and bloodied, dressed in men's clothes, and she looked over her shoulder as she crawled straight toward the SUVs. He'd committed her face to memory, and the woman on the porch was definitely Allen.

"I'm here!" he heard her scream from the porch. "I'm over here!"

"What is she doing now?" Grimes said on the line.

"It's me, Amanda Allen!" she screamed.

"Zeus, cover fire. Keep those shooters down! Keep their heads down!" Dempsey yelled, and when he heard the first round from the WinMag, he popped out around the corner again. "Amanda Allen!" he shouted at the porch.

She spun toward him, but instead of greeting him with relief, she raised an AK-47 at him, arms trembling. "No!"

He ducked.

She fired.

The bullet missed, blowing a chunk out of the concrete railing a foot above his head. Then she dropped the rifle and vaulted over the front railing.

"What the fuck is she doing?" Munn said. "Atlas, she's running *to* the bad guys."

"Amanda, no!" Dempsey screamed.

She froze and then spun around to look at him. Realization spread over her face as she recognized her mistake. Dempsey watched in horror as one of the enemy shooters intercepted her, wrapped an arm around her waist and another around her neck. She shrieked, her voice a dying animal, as the man dragged her toward the cluster of SUVs. Dempsey brought his rifle up and surged forward in a combat crouch. He watched Allen get thrown into the back seat of the middle SUV while the other shooters unleashed a barrage of heavy counterfire in three directions: at Grimes, Munn's team, and him.

He twisted, dove right, and landed painfully on the brick steps leading onto the porch as enemy bullets whizzed past all around him. "Take them!" he shouted to both Munn and Grimes as he rolled and popped up to a kneeling stance, sighting through the concrete balusters and searching for targets. The shooters were disappearing, one by one, into their vehicles.

"We're advancing from the east," Munn called, raining bullets on the enemy position.

"Zeus, Atlas—disable those vehicles," Dempsey ordered. Then he popped to his feet, spun right, and sprinted up the brick steps onto the porch. He ran three meters, took a knee, and sighted in on the only remaining target he saw—a man with close-cropped hair slipping into the passenger seat of the lead vehicle. He squeezed the trigger and the man pitched sideways, his bloody head slamming into the B-pillar and then his body collapsing to the ground. The middle car started backing up, freeing itself from the other two.

He heard two cracks from Grimes's WinMag as sniper rounds slammed into sheet metal with seemingly no effect. Dempsey unloaded the remaining twelve rounds in his magazine at the driver's window, which starred multiple times, but no rounds penetrated.

Fucking ballistic glass.

"They're armored," Grimes reported. "I can't stop them."

He dropped the magazine from the rifle and slammed another one into place. He fired at the driver-side door, but it was useless. All three SUVs were on the move now and exiting the compound. "They're getting away," he growled, his voice a furious thunderstorm.

"C'mon," a voice called to Dempsey's left. "Let's go!"

Dempsey turned to see Raz sprinting back to the BMW. With a crooked grin, Dempsey vaulted the porch railing, landed with a thud, and charted toward the front passenger door.

"John, wait," Munn called. Then to the pilot he said, "Banshee One, we need immediate pickup."

Dempsey was at the car now, pulling open the passenger-side door and sliding in.

"Atlas, stand by. We have air support picking you up and we are tracking the package."

Raz was in the car now, turning over the heavy engine with a grumbling, throaty roar.

"Go?" the former Marine asked, looking at him.

"Go!" Dempsey said and slammed his door. "Titan, complete the pickup, grab Grimes, and check in with me. We'll pursue by ground; you pursue by air. We do whatever it takes. No way in hell I'm letting her slip through my fingers a third time."

CHAPTER 35

Amanda Allen stared at her blood-soaked hands, defeated.

Tears streamed down her cheeks and dripped in pink drops from her chin. She watched as one landed onto the back of her left hand. It seemed to hesitate a moment, as if deciding which way to fall. The car swerved and the tear slipped right, running between her thumb and the meaty part of her hand.

I'm so fucking stupid . . . so stupid, she thought, closing her eyes. *I ran to the wrong people.*

She wanted to scream. She wanted to savage the operator sitting beside her, savage him like she had the man with the broken tooth. She wanted to do these things, but she didn't. She couldn't. Because it was over. She had accepted that now. Fate or God or whatever cruel force of the universe was plotting against her had, yet again, turned the tide inexplicably against her. She would never be free again. Her escape had been pointless. Meaningless.

No, she corrected herself, *not meaningless.*

She'd triumphed over the broken tooth man. If that was to be her final act of courage, defiance, and self-preservation, it was a good one. If only she could have killed the woman terrorist, Mutla, as well. There was a special place in hell for people like her—a woman who would watch and even condone the torture and rape of another woman.

"Sunt in spatele nostrum!" said the passenger in the front seat, glancing over his shoulder and out the back window.

She didn't recognize the language, but it sounded Slavic.

The man beside her leaned forward and smacked him in the back of his head. *"Kes Sesini!"* he said and then glanced at her.

That was Turkish, she thought, *my chaperone telling the other guy to shut the fuck up.*

She twisted in her seat and glanced over her shoulder out the rear window. A pair of headlights winked at her, trailing their three-vehicle convoy and closing the gap. The driver jerked the wheel, slamming her into the door. She cursed under her breath. Then she eyed the brute sitting in the seat next to her. Caucasian, short-cropped dark hair, military bearing, and unmarked tactical clothing. He looked like an American operator.

But he didn't talk like one.

The filthy guy with the beard and the vest, he had been the American sent to rescue her. If she had just stopped and used her head. If she had just listened to the sound of his voice, she would have recognized him as the same man who had tried to rescue her from the first compound. But the wild-man appearance and the intensity in his eyes had terrified her. She'd actually tried to shoot her knight in shining armor.

I'm such an idiot.

Finally feeling her stare, the operator beside her turned and met her gaze. His face was a mask. His eyes were ice. After several long seconds of playing "Who's going to look away first?" he put a hand on her face and pushed her chin away.

These guys are Russians. Man not Malik sold me to the fucking Russians!

A wave of nausea curdled her stomach. Her mouth began to salivate, and she was positive she was going to vomit. The last time she'd vomited was when she'd gotten completely wasted at a party her sophomore year in college. She'd never drunk like that again. Ever. She hated the feeling of being hungover. But more importantly, she hated feeling out of control.

Just like this.

The nausea passed.

Another tear dripped from her chin.

She thought of the glass cyanide pearl the Man not Malik had given her. He'd called it a gift, and now she understood why. She would give anything to have that little glass pellet back—anything to pop it in her mouth and laugh at these Spetsnaz assholes who'd risked their lives to retrieve a dead girl. If only she hadn't used it to kill that terrorist who tried to choke her. But if she hadn't, then she'd be dead right now.

She glanced again at the Russian operative beside her, and he fixed her with a malevolent glare.

Yes, death would have been better than the fate that awaited her now.

CHAPTER 36

Dempsey glanced at the speedometer and saw that Raz was doing 100 mph, rapidly closing ground on the convoy of SUVs speeding through the streets of Manbij.

"Shit, he's turning, bro," Dempsey hollered.

"I see him," Raz said, braking hard as the last vehicle in the convoy abruptly turned left down a side road.

"Olympus, which vehicle is Allen riding in?"

Dempsey was almost certain she was in the rear vehicle, but the drivers had been changing positions like a street hustler playing "hide the marble" in a three-shell shuffle game. These guys knew what they were doing.

"Thermal imaging shows three bodies in that vehicle and only a driver in the others, so unless she's driving one of the escort vehicles herself, there's a ninety-nine percent chance—"

"She's in the last SUV," Dempsey shouted, cutting Baldwin off. "Turn now!" He braced himself against the dashboard as Raz jerked the steering wheel left, the heavy BMW tipping up on two wheels momentarily.

"What do we do?" Raz asked. "This street is too narrow to pass."

Tiny one-story houses lined both sides of the street. The road could barely accommodate two vehicles passing each other north and south, and the target vehicle was hogging the middle of the road.

"That four-by-four is up-armored and has ballistic glass just like the Beemer. There's not much we can do except try to force them off the road."

"If I could just get beside them, I'd have them stopped already," Raz said in frustration.

"The second escort has just turned north, parallel to you and six blocks east," Baldwin said in his ear. "Wait . . . The third is doing the same, one block further east."

Dempsey scowled, visualizing a bird's-eye view of all four vehicles on a city grid. He knew exactly what these assholes were doing because it was exactly what *he* would do. The two escort vehicles were positioning for an ambush ahead. They would straddle the road, creating a kill zone between them. The target vehicle would turn east any minute now then sprint toward the trap, trying to create separation. The target would shoot the gap while the two escort vehicles unloaded on Dempsey and Raz. But these guys knew the BMW was armored . . . which meant they must be packing something heavier.

"They're turning east," Raz said, confirming Dempsey's suspicion. A beat later, Raz whipped a right turn so hard that Dempsey almost landed in his lap. "This road is wider. You want me to get up beside them?"

"Not yet," Dempsey said.

"Atlas, the other two vehicles have stopped and repositioned," Baldwin said. "They are bookending the intersection a half mile ahead."

Of course they are.

"Pickup complete. Titan is heading to you, Atlas," said Munn, his voice cold steel. "Five mikes, maybe less."

"Is that a spec op variant Osprey you're flying?" Dempsey asked.

"Roger that, Atlas" came Munn's reply.

Dempsey flashed Raz a devious lopsided grin. "Gonna need your Banshee gunner to put some fifty rounds into these assholes' armored SUVs."

"We can do one better. The pilot tells me our bird has an upgrade package," Munn said. "Three mikes out."

"We still need to stop this asshole in front of us somehow," Raz said, piecing together Dempsey's conversation. "Maybe they can put some rounds in the engine block."

The thought of riddling the target vehicle with armor-piercing rounds with Amanda Allen sitting in the back seat seemed too risky, but what other option did they have? "You may be right," Dempsey said.

"Shit, RPG!" Raz barked and juked the steering wheel hard left. Dempsey smacked his head hard against the passenger window as a trail of white smoke zipped past the BMW. The projectile detonated beside them, impacting the ground exactly where they would have been had Raz not reacted so quickly. The force of the explosion almost flipped the heavy BMW, but Raz cut the wheel hard right and the BMW slammed back onto the pavement with an impact that sent an electric stinger down Dempsey's left leg.

The car skidded right in a screeching arc and came to a stop.

"Out, out, *out*!" Raz screamed.

Dempsey yanked the door handle, kicked the door open, and rolled out of the BMW as a second projectile hurtled toward them. The heat from the explosion engulfed him as the pressure wave bowled him over. His head and ears felt like they were stuffed with wet cotton. He forced one last complete barrel roll as bullets pounded the pavement beside him. Adrenaline and fury propelled him up into a kneeling firing stance; his weapon was in his hands a beat later, held steady and true by hands that had spent over two decades outgunning adversaries. His red targeting dot found the shooter's forehead and he squeezed the trigger. The shooter's head pitched sideways, smacked into the corner of the open door, and then the body crumpled.

Like the breath of God, wind buffeted his back as the CV-22 Osprey popped up over the buildings behind him, its giant nacelles turned vertical as the huge rotors kept the enormous bird steady in a low hover. A tongue of fire erupted from the GAU-17 Gatling gun as the pilot targeted the other escort SUV. The torrent of bullets cut a second shooter wielding a machine gun in half, the top half of his body spinning completely around like a figure skater before dropping and coming to rest beside the lower half. The CV-22 seemed almost to take a bow, rotating left again, and then a salvo of rockets streaked out from the launcher pod mounted to the cheek of the bird. The black armored SUVs erupted in sequential fireballs, sending burning hunks of debris in all directions.

"Stop the target vehicle before it gets away," Dempsey shouted, his voice dull and far away in his pressure-injured ears.

The SUV with Allen was accelerating through the kill zone, shooting the gap between the burning escort SUVs. Dempsey said a silent prayer as the Osprey rotated fifteen degrees clockwise, and a short burp of fire leaped from the turret as the gunner shredded the nose of the speeding vehicle with an expertly targeted volley.

"Oorah, Marine," he mumbled as the front of the SUV erupted in a cloud of steam and smoke and then drifted to a stop. The front passenger door opened a beat later, and the shooter inside popped out, dropping to a tactical crouch and bringing his weapon to bear on Dempsey.

Rounds whizzed past Dempsey's head as he placed his targeting dot on the shooter's forehead, dropped the man, then advanced in a combat crouch. An old back injury protested loudly, and his left leg felt dull and heavy. He felt the wind change as the Osprey pivoted yet again, this time rotating until the rear cargo bay was facing him and the ramp lowered, his Ember teammates visible inside.

Then the right rear passenger door of the crippled black SUV swung open, and Amanda Allen stumbled out onto the street. Her hair was matted and plastered to her head, her gray pants and shirt were caked in blood, and her face was streaked with dried gore. She stared at the ground, her arms limp at her sides. Dempsey stopped, steadying himself with his left foot forward, his hands tight and steady on his rifle.

"Amanda Allen!" he called. "We're American operators and we're here to take you home."

Allen did not look at him, keeping her gaze fixed on the ground. A heartbeat later, a hulking figure stepped out behind her. He wrapped a heavily muscled arm around her neck and pulled her into his chest. She didn't resist, and this time she didn't do anything rash. She simply stood there, a rag doll held up by invisible strings.

He placed his red dot just left of Amanda's right ear and onto her captor's forehead.

Then he exhaled and—

A puff of red exploded behind Allen, and the big brute crumpled to the ground *before* Dempsey pulled the trigger.

"Shooter down," Grimes called.

Dempsey glanced over his shoulder and saw Grimes laid out prone on the loading ramp, her WinMag set up on its tripod. She nodded at him, and he turned back to Amanda. Behind her, a shadow moved inside the SUV—the driver and last enemy fighter in the convoy.

"Amanda, get down!" he shouted and sighted over the top of her as she dropped to the ground. A head popped momentarily into view inside the vehicle. He flipped the selector on his rifle with his right thumb and advanced on the SUV, firing three-round bursts through the open rear door into the dark interior of the vehicle. He closed the gap quickly, his targeting dot dancing inside the cabin, looking for movement. Seconds later, he was peering into the vehicle where the driver was slumped over, chest and face covered in blood. Dempsey flipped the selector back to single shot and put one final round into the back of the driver's head.

"Clear," he reported and then turned back to Amanda, still on the pavement beside him, hands over her head. "Amanda, you're safe. I've got you."

She looked up, her face pale and slack.

Dempsey touched her cheek with his gloved hand. "Tell me again," he said and smiled softly.

The girl tried to speak, sobbed, and then closed her eyes tightly. She opened them again and looked him in the eyes. "I tried to save the ladybugs," she managed.

"That's right," he said. He felt Raz's hand on his shoulder but kept his eyes on Amanda and helped her to her feet. "Let's go home."

She collapsed into him, her arms around his neck, her chest heaving with emotional release. Beyond them, the Osprey hovered expertly with the open rear cargo deck a mere foot off the ground. He saw Grimes waving him toward them.

"Let's go, Atlas," Munn said in his ear. "We gotta get the hell out of here."

Dempsey turned to Raz. "Sorry about your car, bro," he said, grinning. "But she needed a new paint job anyway."

"So let's see," Raz said, grinning and rubbing his chin, "you owe me a new car, a lifetime of chiropractic care, and an unlimited supply of Budweiser."

"That's a bargain considering what you did for us. C'mon, let's get the hell outta here."

Raz shook his head. "Can't, bro," he said. "I'm not ready to go back. Which means I need you to expedite that fucking car because mine just got blown up. You have my cell number and you know where I live. We should be all set for delivery."

With that, Amraz Demir, the Kurdish American vigilante of Manbij, turned and walked off, heading west away from the carnage.

Dempsey heard sirens in the distance. He wrapped an arm around Amanda's shoulder and started guiding her toward the Osprey.

"It's over, Amanda. Time to go home."

"I think this is a long way from being over," she said under her breath. "For me, anyway . . ."

He didn't answer. She'd spoken gospel . . . The healing would take time.

Moments later they were on the ramp, and the tiltrotor aircraft was lifting into the air. Latif wrapped a blanket around Allen and led her forward. Grimes marched over and stood in front of Dempsey, arms folded across her chest, the sniper rifle slung over her shoulder.

"Pretty fancy shooting there, Your Highness," Dempsey said.

"Good enough to save your over-the-hill ass," she said and then wrapped him up in a hug.

Munn moved toward them as the ramp began to rise under their feet.

"You done, Rambo?" he asked, throwing an arm around Dempsey's shoulders as Grimes released him from her bear hug.

"Almost," Dempsey said. "We need to get back to that compound—see what we can grab off of the *X* to figure out who the hell these guys were."

"Agreed," Munn said.

"I'm afraid that won't be possible," Baldwin said in all their ears. "The compound is already swarming with what appears to be YPG personnel. But you have a bigger problem. I strongly suggest you turn north and head at low altitude toward the Turkish border with great haste."

"Why?" Dempsey asked, following Munn forward in the spacious aircraft. He passed the workstation where a door gunner managed the Osprey's weapons suite from a flat-screen monitor using what looked like an Xbox controller. He patted the man's shoulder in gratitude.

"Because I'm tracking a flight of two MiG-29s heading your way at very high speed," Baldwin said. "The airspace you're in now is not protected by our no-fly zone, and I'm assuming these are Syrian jets intent on your destruction. We have no permission to be where we are."

"Atlas, I have two F/A-18 escorts headed to you from the *Reagan* to take you through Turkish airspace back to the boat, but they won't be within a hundred clicks before those MiGs get to you." It was Smith's voice on the line now, and he sounded tense. "I have your Osprey pilots coordinating with the escort, and their orders are to fly north with God's speed."

"What about the Turkish no-fly zone?" Munn asked.

"Lesser of two evils, and despite Erodan's bluster, the Turks wouldn't dare shoot down one of ours," Smith said.

"Sure would suck to die now after all the hard work we put in trying to survive," Dempsey said, his face deadpan. After a beat, Munn and Grimes both busted up laughing and held out their fists to be bumped. He accommodated, then turned to look at Allen, wrapped in her blanket and seated alone against the bulkhead.

"I'm going to go talk to her," Grimes said, flashing him a knowing smile.

He nodded and watched Elizabeth take a seat next to the traumatized CIA agent and begin to comfort her. He couldn't hear them, but it didn't matter. He took a mental snapshot of the moment and filed it away . . .

Mission accomplished.

PART III

And remember: you must never, under any circumstances, despair.

To hope and to act, these are our duties in misfortune.

—*Boris Pasternak,* Doctor Zhivago

CHAPTER 37

Safe House
Qamishli, Syria
Two Miles South of the Turkish Border Town of Nusaybin and 250 Miles East of Manbij
May 9
1630 Local Time

Valerian sat at the simple wooden table, his legs crossed at the knee, and sipped the sickly sweet tea that those native to this region seemed to love. He watched Mutla pace back and forth, her own tea cooling on the table in front of the empty chair beside him. She was angry and upset. They both were. The compound had been hit by the Americans shortly after their departure. Everyone had been slaughtered, including her brother, Samir, and the Russian GRU extraction team. He didn't know if Amanda Allen had been recovered alive or dead; this little piece of intelligence he would have to wait for.

"How did you know?" Mutla stammered, eyeing him.

"How did I know what?"

"How did you know we needed to leave early? How did you know the Americans were coming?"

He laughed at this. "Mutla, they had already hit the first compound. I told you they were coming. We all knew this, which is why I arranged Allen's sale at auction so we could be done and move on to the next mission. We simply ran out of time, that's all. It could have been worse; they could have hit the compound before we left."

She mumbled something and then kicked a chair, toppling it and sending it skidding across the floor. So much passion in this one. She was simple, but not dim-witted. In another world or another time, she could have been much more valuable to him. But in this world, he needed her to be a good little soldier and do exactly what he said.

"Do you think the Americans are still hunting us?"

"Of course."

"Then why are we still here? We should move across the border where my people can hide us."

"I told you," he said patiently, "the border crossing is planned and scheduled. This is no small feat, and I cannot advance the timeline. I know you are upset about Samir, but I promise that those responsible will soon pay a very high price for what they have done. Now sit. Have some tea."

"I don't want tea. I want revenge."

He nodded, his face a mask of patience and empathy. "I understand better than most. I lost everything in Chechnya, and that is why—"

His mobile phone chirped on the table. He stopped midsentence, picked up the encrypted device, and looked at the screen.

"They're ready for me," he said, getting to his feet and pocketing his phone. "Wait here. Do not leave this house under any circumstance. When I return, we will depart for the border."

She nodded but continued to pace.

He grabbed her by the wrist and squeezed. She met his gaze, fire in his eyes.

"Do not do anything rash or stupid," he said, his voice hard and cold. "Do you understand?"

She nodded.

"Say it," he barked.

"I understand," she seethed through gritted teeth.

"We are the mission now," he said, releasing her wrist. "And we cannot fail."

He left her and the apartment, feeling very uneasy. He found the innocuous white sedan parked exactly where it was supposed to be. The vehicle was hot from sitting in the sun. When he climbed inside and started the engine, the air-conditioning chugged to life, and he let the cool air blow on his face as he clutched the steering wheel with a death grip. Feeling himself on the verge of losing control, he closed his eyes, focused on his breathing, and found his center. He pushed away the anxiety and worry about Mutla sabotaging the mission. He pushed away the desire to drive a blade through her right eye and be done with the trouble of having to deal with her. He needed her.

I am stillness.

I am focus.

I am a blade—honed for a single purpose.

I am Zeta Prime.

Feeling better, he opened his eyes, put the transmission in drive, and pulled away from the curb. He turned right onto Highway 23 and in minutes left the crush of buildings and people behind. Houses and businesses gave way to farmers' fields, and five minutes later, he turned left onto a dirt road heading north. He checked his watch and then eased off the accelerator.

Not too early, not too late. Everyone must be present when the end comes.

The low buildings of the old homestead on acres of fertile farmland came into view. As he pulled up to the gate of the farm, two men approached the car, both gripping AK-47 assault rifles. He rolled down the window.

"I'm Malik," he said in Kurdish. "I have business with Bayit."

The closer of the two guards nodded, almost a bow, as the younger man hustled over to open the gate.

"He is expecting you," the guard said and waved him through.

Valerian glanced at his watch. The timing was critical now; he had to execute down to the minute. He parked on the circular gravel drive in front of the house, grabbed his satchel from the passenger seat, and slipped from the cool cabin into the heat of the afternoon. Two guards stood beside the ornate door of the aged home. They did not address him but frisked him head to toe. Satisfied, they ushered him into the dimly lit foyer. A tall man, flanked by two armed fighters, approached Valerian, looking very much out of place in his dark suit compared to his traditionally dressed companions.

"Greetings, brother," the man said, eyeing the satchel hanging from Valerian's shoulder.

Valerian extended his other hand in greeting, but instead, the tall man embraced him like a brother and kissed his cheek. "It is an honor to finally meet the great Malik."

Valerian smiled. The sum of money he was about to transfer brought *great* honor.

"The honor is mine," he said, then followed his host into the large sitting room beyond.

Bayit, one of the three founding members of PKK, sat on an oversize leather chair flanked by two guards. The elderly man wore dark slacks and a simple white short-sleeved shirt, his legs crossed at the knees. When he saw "Malik," he set his teacup on the end table beside him, smiled, and stood. Like the tall man, Bayit embraced Valerian with a kiss on the cheek.

"Brother," he said, holding Valerian's arms in his hands, a broad, eager smile decorating his leathered face. "You honor us with your presence and with your generous gift."

Valerian bowed deferentially and returned the smile. "You have achieved two great victories in Turkey against the corrupt Erodan regime and the feckless Americans who praise your people in public but then do nothing to stop Ankara's policy of Kurdish genocide. They have used your people as bargaining pawns for too long. Our strategy is working. President Warner is flying to Turkey to try and mend the rift we have created between the two regimes, but with this next operation, the damage will be irreversible. The West will abandon Erodan, and then we can replace him with a ruler who will embrace a free and autonomous Kurdistan."

The old man clasped his hands together and then shook them over his head in victory.

"So do we have an agreement? I transfer the funds, and your shadow soldiers will see this next mission through?"

Bayit smiled. "I will see it done."

"Excellent," Valerian said. He opened his satchel and removed the laptop computer with a special carbon fiber case. He turned the screen so the man could see. "I wanted you to witness the money transfer in person so there could be no doubt of our alliance."

As the man's dark eyes studied the screen, Valerian executed the transfer on the encrypted computer. The sum was significant—likely the single largest lump-sum cash infusion PKK had enjoyed over the last fifteen years. The beauty of this deal was that the PKK account was in a Cyprus bank, over which the Kremlin held ultimate sway. When it was time to take the money back, it was as simple as picking up the phone.

"It is done," he said and then pointed to a small icon at the bottom of the screen. "If you open this application, you can message me in the dark web. The VPN connection on this machine utilizes a series of encrypted servers all over the world." He closed the computer and handed it to the old man. What he did not explain was that these messages would never actually reach him, nor that the computer was equipped with a GPS pinger and that its special case and solid-state drive were hardened to resist shock and extreme heat. No, he failed to mention these things, along with the fact that the computer contained hundreds of files detailing PKK's plans to subvert the relationship between the United States and Turkey by attacking Incirlik and unmasking the secret CIA base in Adana.

He glanced at his watch, smiled, and got to his feet. "I must depart. The timetable is short for the next operation, and I am needed."

"You must let us feed you," Bayit said, standing. "We prepared a great feast to celebrate."

Valerian smiled, hiding the anxiety he felt as his mind counted down the seconds. "Please, feast and celebrate our coming victory. Know I am here with you in spirit today and that I will return to take advantage of your hospitality after the mission is accomplished."

With a parting embrace, Valerian was escorted out of the house to his car. He started the engine and glanced at his watch. He was eighty-three seconds behind schedule, but he had incorporated a safety factor into the timetable. He drove without haste to the front gate. Only once he was on the isolated dirt road did he accelerate to make up some of the lost distance. As he turned right onto Highway 23, he scanned the skies through his windshield. After a beat, he sighted two black dots growing on the horizon. As the farmland began to fill with scattered buildings, marking his entrance into Qamishli, the two Russian MiG-29s streaked past like lightning—so low to the ground that they pulled funnel clouds of dust in their wake.

A moment later, the earth shook with thunder as the PKK compound was destroyed.

The talk of feasts had set his stomach to grumbling.

He pulled a plastic bag with walnuts from his pocket and popped a handful in his mouth.

Then, despite his best efforts not to, he fantasized about Amanda Allen as he drove back to pick up Mutla and commence the final phase of the operation.

CHAPTER 38

Air Force One, SCIF
On the Ramp at Andrews Air Force Base
May 9
1230 Local Time

"What do you have for me now, Kelso?" the President said, glancing at his watch in irritation and then at Jarvis.

Jarvis knew Warner was a stickler about respecting the clock and adhering to schedules. If there was one resource the President always had in short supply, it was time. This was the third "wheels-up" delay they'd had getting Air Force One on its way to Turkey for their scheduled arrival at 0800 local time in Istanbul.

"Sir, there was an attack on a compound in northwest Syria, just south of the Turkish border," Jarvis said.

"What kind of attack?" Warner asked.

Petra clicked the remote she was holding, and an image filled the screen behind her—only rubble and smoke remaining. "Two Russian MiG-29s hit this site near Qamishli."

Warner pounded his fist on the table. "What the hell are the Russians doing hitting targets in eastern Syria? I thought we had a back-channel agreement they were going to stay out of that particular sandbox. Why the hell are they hitting the Kurds today? Do we still have people there?"

"No, sir," Jarvis said. "Everyone's out."

Warner's shoulders relaxed a little. "Have you contacted the Kremlin about this?"

"Yes, sir."

"Did they pull their typical bullshit and talk in Russian riddles?"

"Actually, sir, on this they've been quite forthcoming. They say they had short-fuse intelligence that allowed them to target a PKK compound that they claim . . ." Petra paused.

"Claim what?" Warner demanded.

Petra glanced at Jarvis with her *You better take this one* eyes.

"Sir, they claim that this was the command center for a PKK splinter faction responsible for the attack on Incirlik as well as the CIA base in Adana."

"They specifically mentioned the CIA base?" the President asked. "The *ultrasecret* CIA base that only a handful of people in the world knew about?"

"Yes, sir. They contacted us within the last hour with what they are calling a courtesy call. They wanted to let us know that they'd be making a public announcement that they succeeded in a mission to take out those responsible for the attacks. And, sir, they claim to have proof they will share at that time."

"What kind of proof?"

"Whether they have proof or not is irrelevant," Petra said.

"Explain?" Warner asked.

"This is a classic Russian maneuver. If they don't have proof, they will manufacture it. They didn't conduct an actual *investigation*. This is a propaganda campaign designed to make us look weak—like we were unable to anticipate and prevent an attack on our facilities inside a NATO country," she said.

"And then they paint themselves as the heroes who find and prosecute the responsible terrorists. Petrov gets to pat himself on the back while ingratiating himself to Erodan," Jarvis added, shaking his head. "Oh, and don't forget, he just made a show of blowing up a bunch of Kurds inside an area that was, as of only one week ago, coalition-secured territory."

The President waved his left hand, cutting him off. "This is bullshit. Kelso, who do we have in the region? Do you have a team nearby? We need our own eyes on this clusterfuck."

"We have several options, sir. We have OGA and Activity assets a short flight away in Iraq. We have an FBI counterterror footprint working in Adana, of course. And I have another asset not far as well."

The President turned to his Chief of Staff, who had been uncharacteristically quiet and was staring at the image on the screen. "Go find Secretary Baker and have him reach out to the Russian Ambassador and set up a call immediately with Petrov. Tell him we insist on a joint investigation at the bombing site. You're right about the propaganda, Ms. Felsk, but let's not make this easy on them."

"Yes, sir."

Jarvis was impressed. And he agreed. He couldn't quite make sense of all the colors and merging plots twisting around in his mind's eye, but hierarchies would eventually materialize, and when that happened, he would be better prepared for what was coming next. He considered suggesting, again, that this was the worst possible time for the President to travel to Turkey, no matter how secret their itinerary was kept. That advice had been rejected several times already, so Jarvis decided on another tack.

"Sir, may I suggest that, until we sort this out, I arrange to have Ember on the ground in Istanbul?"

The President looked at him and pursed his lips. "I trust the Secret Service, Kelso. Your guys are the best at what they do, but they're not the experts at presidential protection."

"I agree, Mr. President, but that's not what I had in mind. While Secret Service is watching your back, Ember can watch their back," Jarvis said, weighing his words carefully, "should something unanticipated happen."

The President screwed up his face. "Something like what, Kelso? What are you thinking?"

"I don't believe in coincidences, Mr. President. We've been one step behind on this thing since the beginning, and we're still playing catch-up. The Russians claim to have traced these attacks to PKK. We have not yet confirmed the link, but PKK was already high on our short list of groups who might be responsible. What if something else is coming? What if they're not done yet? I think it's prudent to have Ember close at hand as a precaution."

"Your choice," Warner said. "I trust you to make those decisions and won't micromanage you. And decide who you want on-site in Syria with the Russian investigation and make it happen."

"I'll send FBI's counterterror investigators. They're close and the best at doing a physical and forensic analysis."

"Whoever you think. Get it done. No more delays. Whatever happens next, we'll deal with it in the air. We need to get to Istanbul before this spirals completely out of control," Warner said.

"Yes, Mr. President," Jarvis said with a nod.

"If you need me, I'll be in my office up front. Update me on anything you uncover. If President Petrov is lying, I want him to do it to my face." With that, the President and his Chief of Staff left, leaving Jarvis and Petra alone in the SCIF.

"Do you really think the President is at risk?" Petra asked.

Jarvis nodded. "Yes, I do."

"Okay then, I'll get Director Smith on the phone and give him the bad news," she said. "That Ember has one more assignment before they can go home."

CHAPTER 39

CAG's Sensitive Compartmented Information Facility (SCIF)
***USS* Ronald Reagan**
Mediterranean Sea, Seventy Miles North-Northwest of Lattakia, Syria
May 9
2230 Local Time

"Tell me again, bro. Why is our rescued hostage here and not on her way home to Washington, DC?" Munn said, his feet on the desk. Dempsey sat beside him while Latif sat at the small table in the center of the room. Grimes was with Amanda Allen and Martin, having made a chow run to the Goat Locker, Navalese for the Chief's Mess where the NCOs gathered and ate. Everyone in the Navy knew that was where the best chow was on any ship—far better than eating in Officer Country.

"Shane wants more time to debrief her before she gets cut loose to the wolves at CIA," Dempsey said. "I get it. We won't get any information once she's gone. She was going to fly back with us and we were gonna soft interrogate her on the trip, but now, since we're going to Istanbul, that plan is trash."

Munn let out a groan. "Backing up Secret Service like some sort of security detail doesn't seem the best use of Ember to me—just sayin'."

"I agree," Dempsey said. "But so would Smith. So if the DNI wants us in Istanbul, then I think it's safe to say a shit storm must be brewing."

"Awesome," Munn said.

As if on cue, the large screen on the wall across from the table where Latif was playing some game on his tablet came to life, Smith filling the screen.

"Gentlemen," the Ember Director said.

"Hey, Boss," Munn said. "You got some gouge on what the hell is going on?"

"Not yet, Dan, but Adamo should be able to provide more definition for the team real soon. In the meantime, try to rest up. You guys look ragged, and I need you fresh tomorrow." Munn nodded while frowning and looking at his boots.

"JD, can I have a few minutes in private?" Smith said.

Dempsey looked up at the big-screen TV and then over at Munn, who stared at him with curiosity.

"We'll give you the room," he said and gestured with his head for Latif to follow him out. "Let's go, Army," Munn said, and Latif followed him out the door.

Dempsey watched them leave, wondering what the hell was going on that Smith needed privacy.

Smith smiled but seemed awfully serious. "How are you doing, John?" he asked.

"A little banged up, but good. How are you?"

"Worried," Smith said simply. "I wanted to debrief you in private about the solo portions of the Allen rescue operation."

"I included everything in the debrief," Dempsey said, confused.

"I'm not talking about the after-action report," Smith said. "I'm talking about your head, John. I'm concerned about what I saw."

"What do you mean, what you saw?"

"The decision to pursue Allen solo after the first failed engagement left us scratching our heads back here in Virginia."

"The mission dictated it," Dempsey said, suddenly feeling very much on the defensive. "Things were fluid—kinetic. I needed to pursue the terrorists after al-Bab, so I did. I fell in on another asset that I capitalized on, and we found the girl. The mission was a success. Adapt and overcome, right?"

Smith nodded. "I get it, I do. But I just want to try to understand your thought process. We lost comms, which meant you lost your QRF backup and your EXFIL option. Theobold was badly injured, and you sent him back to Turkey with just his terp. Then you decide to head east, pursuing Allen, but not really—because the truth is, you didn't know where in the hell she was. Did you ever stop to think, during any of this, what was going on with the rest of SAD?"

"I didn't, uh, give it a whole lotta thought at the time, to be honest," Dempsey admitted. "I suppose I just assumed that even though comms were down, Baldwin was tracking everything visually and that when the comms problem got fixed, you guys would put all the pieces back together and get me off the *X*. My mission was Allen, and when they decided to move her, I just couldn't do nothing. You know how these assholes operate, Shane. Once they feel the heat, they get nervous. They make rash decisions. I knew the one thing she didn't have was time, and if *I* didn't get her out, then she was as good as dead. I wasn't going to let that happen again."

Smith cocked an eyebrow at him. "Let *what* happen again?"

Dempsey set his jaw and didn't answer.

"Okay . . . What about when you forced Amraz Demir into hot pursuit from the compound in Manbij when we had an air asset and your full team right there on the ground with you. What was your thinking there?"

"Belt and suspenders, right?" Dempsey said. "It was an opportunity to work air and ground in tandem and not lose eyes on the hostage."

"But Ian had eyes on her the whole time."

"Yeah, but we had eyes in al-Bab, and we lost them. Again—just belt and suspenders."

Smith was staring at him from thousands of miles away on the big screen, larger than life. "Uh-huh" was all he said.

"Hey, hard to argue with a success, right, Shane? Allen is down in the Goat Locker right now. If you want, I can get her, and you can ask her how she feels about my decision not to abandon her," he said with a hard edge now.

"I'm not accusing you of anything, JD."

"Yeah. You said that. So what are you doing, Shane?"

"My job, JD."

Dempsey blew out a breath. "Did someone else express concern? Someone from my team?"

"No, absolutely not."

"Is this because of something Adamo said? The guy still has a long way to go operationally, Shane. He still doesn't get it like we do—like only a blooded operator can."

Smith frowned. "This has nothing to do with Adamo, John. This is about me making sure that everyone on the team has their head where it needs to be. And to make sure that you, as the Director of SAD, have the tools and confidence in your team to execute the mission without feeling pressure to take unnecessary risks to complete the objectives. If your going solo reflects a breakdown in either of these things, I need to know."

Dempsey let out a long sigh. He was so damn tired. "I did what the situation dictated, Shane. I have a great team, and I trust them completely. This has nothing to do with the team."

Shane nodded but clearly had more to say.

Dear God, just let this be over, Dempsey thought.

"I know it's been a process for you to trust the team we put together—for you to feel the same sense of brotherhood you had in

Tier One. Ember can never replace what you lost, but it can be family. It is for me, anyway."

"Me, too," Dempsey said. He thought back to what Grimes had said to him earlier, how she cared about him, that they were family, and the realization he'd come to when talking to Theobold—that Ember was as much a family as his Tier One SEAL team had been. He believed that. He let his anger and defensiveness dissolve, looked up at the screen, and gave Smith a tight smile.

"Okay, well, that's enough of that." Smith let silence hang in the air a moment, and then he said, "Do you think you could get Allen in here? I want you and I to walk through a debrief with her, and by the time we're done, we should have a good handle on our tasking for Turkey."

Dempsey fetched Amanda Allen, and the ninety-minute debrief that followed went about as he expected—thirty minutes of probing with kid gloves and then the dam break. An hour of crying, cursing, and confessing followed as the young spook worked through her shame, anger, and frustration—all the things a psychologically grounded person should feel after an event like this. All in all, Dempsey couldn't help but be impressed with Allen. The bad guys had rattled her psyche pretty good, but she'd managed to keep her shit together.

"Hey, guys, I need to take a quick break," Smith said, snapping Dempsey's attention back to the moment. "Back in five."

"Roger that," Dempsey said, then turned to Allen as Smith disappeared off camera. "Do you need a break, too?"

"Nah, I'm good," she said. "You?"

"Nah, I'm good, too."

As they waited for Smith to return, they sat next to each other in silence.

"Thank you," she said out of nowhere. "For what you did." She reached out and clutched the top of his hand where it lay resting on the table.

He turned to look at her, and with a tight smile, he said, "It's my job."

"Maybe the first time you came for me, but not the second. You didn't have to try again. After what happened at the first safe house, you could have checked the box and everyone in the chain would've been satisfied. No one would have ordered you to continue. In fact, they probably would have forbade it, given the risks," she said, holding his gaze. "But you didn't quit. You didn't abandon me. I owe you my life. I'll never forget what you risked for me . . ."

He let her hold his hand for a few more seconds until she released it on her own accord. He didn't say anything. He didn't know what to say.

The sound of a door opening and footsteps from the TV speakers shifted their attention back to the videoconference. Smith appeared in frame, his demeanor changed.

"Round up the team," Smith said. "Adamo has something potentially groundbreaking he wants to share. He'd like to get a dialogue going, see if we can't connect all the dots as a group."

"Roger that," Dempsey said, then pushed back from the table. He rolled his eyes after he'd turned his back on the monitor.

"I saw that eye roll," Smith called from behind him as he walked out of the SCIF.

Dempsey didn't acknowledge the comment, which he knew was just good-natured ribbing. The eye rolling, however, was grounded in actual irritation. Dempsey hadn't said anything, but Adamo's absence in the field bothered him. *Really* bothered him. Had Jarvis not been promoted and Smith were still the Ember Ops O, then you could sure as hell bet that Smith would have been in the field with SAD every step of the way. Wasn't that what the Operations Officer was supposed to be doing, coordinating Ember operations? But was Adamo here? No, he'd stayed behind in Virginia at Ember HQ without showing the slightest reservation or guilt. When Jarvis handed the Ember reins over to Smith, he'd left the care and management of the organization entirely in Smith's hands. For two weeks after the transition, the staff had wondered who would take over Smith's old role. Everyone had assumed it was going to be Dempsey, but Smith had surprised them by naming Adamo. In some ways, it had been a relief. Dempsey had dreaded the imagined conversation with Smith where he would have to turn down the role of Ember Director and outline his reasons for remaining in the field as the head of Special Activities. Luckily, he'd never had to have that conversation. The actual conversation had been something like:

"So you're making Adamo Ops O?"

"Yes."

"The dude just got here and you're making him your second-in-command? Why not Grimes? Hell, even Munn would be a better choice for Ops O than fucking Adamo."

In the end, Smith had defused the confrontation by resting his hand on Dempsey's shoulder and saying, "Right now, JD, with the needs and resources that we have, I believe it's the right decision."

And that had been that.

Since that difficult day, Dempsey rarely spoke to Adamo and saw him even less frequently than that. Simon Adamo was the busiest persona non grata that Dempsey had ever worked for. According to Wang, the former CIA spook was routinely putting in hundred-hour weeks, and Smith was always making comments like "Adamo's burning the candle at both ends, John. Why don't you cut him a break?" and "The only person I know who works as hard as you, JD, is Adamo . . . so there's at least one thing you have in common."

What the fuck Adamo was doing during those hundred-hour weeks was beyond Dempsey. He'd not noticed any changes to their workflow or success rate . . . except for maybe a little less lag time in access to critical information and a little better cooperation with OGA assets. He reluctantly had to admit that SAD wasn't spending nearly as much time being resource constrained as they had been when Smith was Ops

O. Okay, fine, maybe the dude was good for pushing paper and talking to bureaucrats, but he sure as shit couldn't run an OPORD.

Well, it'll be interesting to see what Adamo and the Ember Nerdery has come up with now.

Five minutes later, he was back in the SCIF with the rest of the team in tow. Everyone quickly found seats around the conference table. On-screen, the camera view had shifted from Smith's office to the Ember conference room, where Smith was now joined by Adamo, Baldwin, Chip and Dale, and Wang, who'd flown back to CONUS after the al-Fahkoury op.

"First let me apologize for the timing of this call. I know it's late over there and you all could desperately use some rack time, but this is a discussion that can't wait," Adamo began. "While Director Smith and Dempsey were debriefing Ms. Allen, the Signals team and I were running queries based on the names and details that she reported. As an aside, Ms. Allen, while I am allowing you to sit in as a courtesy, at the request of Director Smith, please know that all of this is SCI-level classified and compartmentalized to the highest level."

"Of course," Allen said softly.

"The most interesting development," Adamo continued, "concerns the name Malik. From conversations Allen overhead between her captors, she deduced that a man named Malik was the principal behind the operation to assassinate Ambassador Bailey and kidnap her. She also inferred that he was not a member of the PKK splinter faction we believe is responsible for the attack on Incirlik and the CIA safe house but may have been involved in a peripheral role—serving as facilitator. Functionally, he fits the mercenary/arms dealer/money broker role. Based on this information, we ran queries on the name Malik through the various IC databases and—"

"That's not exactly how it happened," Baldwin interjected, looking at Adamo. "If I may?"

Adamo frowned and pushed his glasses up on his nose. "By all means."

"Thank you, Simon. When I heard the name Malik, it immediately rang a bell—a church bell at noon in the middle of town square—because that was the name we identified in intercepted comms during the al-Fahkoury sting operation. Malik was the individual who al-Fahkoury was supposed to meet on the yacht. It's not an uncommon name, so there was a 31.43 percent probability this could be merely a coincidence. But when we queried INTERPOL and the Five Eyes databases, we discovered only one Malik of consequence, and he has been a very busy man over the past decade, with dozens and dozens of log entries: arms trafficking, drug smuggling, money laundering, terrorism, and human trafficking, though the latter to a lesser extent."

"Okay, so you're saying Malik was supposed to be on the boat to meet al-Fahkoury, but he was actually in Turkey with our terrorist friends planning the operation to kill the Ambassador and kidnap our girl here?" Munn asked.

"No, that's not what I'm saying, Dan," Baldwin replied with an all-too-pleased-with-himself smile. "Malik was definitely on the boat."

"But that doesn't make any sense. How could Malik be the one interrogating Allen if he was dead?" Munn turned to look at Dempsey. Then his gaze shifted to Allen, and he cocked an eyebrow. "What are you smiling about?"

"From our first interaction," Allen said, sitting up in her chair, "something felt off. I mean, I even started referring to him as the Man not Malik in my head because somewhere in my gut I knew that wasn't his real name. Like I was trying to explain to Director Smith during the debrief, my Malik was educated. He was worldly . . . not that a terrorist can't be educated or worldly. Heck, we've identified dozens of operatives who've matriculated through US and European universities, but this guy was no Islamic jihadi. Sure, he had the beard, the clothes, and the Turks seemed to accept him, but I couldn't swallow the idea of him being former YPG, PKK, or even some disenfranchised Peshmerga who decided to go into the mercenary business to support his brothers and sisters in the independent Kurdish state movement."

"But the contingent on the yacht spoke Chechen," Grimes said. "Which would seem to indicate Malik was Chechen, not Turkish or Kurdish."

"That's right, Elizabeth," Baldwin said. "And most of the intelligence on Malik confirms he was a Chechen separatist who fled after the last war but used his ties to Chechen terror groups and Russian criminal arms dealers to start his business."

"Do you think the Malik who interrogated you could have been Chechen?" Dempsey asked Allen.

"Yes, he definitely could have been. I mean, he didn't look Arab, or Persian, or Turkish. It's so hard to tell with people anymore. This part of the world especially is such a melting pot. If I had to guess, I'd have guessed he was from one of the Caucuses. So yes, he definitely could have been Chechen. In fact, I even had the distinct impression he was wearing brown-colored contacts because one time I could have sworn I caught a flash of blue at the edge of the iris."

"Maybe the Malik who Baldwin thinks we killed on the yacht was just a proxy and the real Malik survived?" Grimes asked.

"Anything is possible," Baldwin said, "but we have intercepts during the forty-eight hours after the op that demonstrate confusion in terror circles concerning Malik's true fate."

"Let me jump in here," Adamo said, taking the floor back. "I did some of my own digging on this, and what I can tell you from talking to some Langley contacts of mine and a close friend in Madrid at Centro Nacional de Inteligencia who specializes in arms smuggling and organized crime in the region is that there's been a good deal of speculation about this man over the years. The longevity of his operation, coupled with the fact that two attempts to penetrate his inner circle were foiled, leads me to theorize that Malik is a legend, and not just an ordinary run-of-the-mill legend at that, but rather a carefully crafted and curated evergreen legend."

"What's an evergreen legend?" Luca Martin asked.

"I got this," Dempsey said, winking at Adamo. "Let me put this in terms even a Marine can understand. You know there's been like nine different Batman movies, with five different actors playing the Bat?"

"Yeah," the young Marine said, trying to suppress a shit-eating grin.

"Batman is an evergreen legend. It doesn't matter how many different dudes wear the mask; the legend lives on and on and on."

"I understand why they do it in the movies, but why would a terrorist do that?" Martin asked.

"Because it takes time to establish a network. It takes time to establish underground relationships, a 'credit history,' and a reputation that you should be trusted and feared among the skittish criminal underground," Adamo said.

"Think of it as a corporate brand," Munn added. "Like Tide detergent or Snickers candy bars, except in this case the brand is Malik and his product is drugs, arms, money laundering, and sex slaves."

"Okay," Martin said, nodding. "It's totally fucked-up but makes sense."

"So to backtrack a step, we're saying that Malik is not a single person, but a legend that's been occupied by any number of people?" Allen asked.

"That's right," Adamo said.

"And the man who came to Syria and interrogated me had likely just recently inherited the job?" she continued.

Adamo nodded. "That's our working theory. To continue Munn's metaphor, every successful brand has a powerful organization supporting it. Behind Tide, you have Proctor & Gamble. Behind Snickers, you have M&M Mars. No low-level terrorist group or arms-dealing Mafia syndicate could successfully perpetuate, fund, and staff an evergreen legend like this. If I'm right, then only a state actor could be responsible—and when you start crossing off the countries with both the means and motive to run the Malik operation, the list gets really short, really fast."

"Iran and Russia," Allen said, narrowing her eyes.

Adamo smiled at her, then held up his notebook to the camera and showed her his matching short list. "But given recent events, I think we can confidently rule out Iran, or we would have caught wind of it during our prolonged investigation of VEVAK operations and Amir Modiri. On top of that, we have an open channel with the Seventh Order in Tel Aviv, and I pinged the acting Director, Rouvin, about this. He claimed to know nothing of the Persians running an evergreen legend with the name Malik."

Just the mention of the Seventh Order hit Dempsey like a punch to the gut. A vivid memory of Elinor standing at Tell Qasile, hands on hips, smiling at him in the morning sunlight, flashed unbidden into his mind. He took a deep breath and blew it out forcefully.

"Holy shit," Martin said, looking at Dempsey in solidarity and unknowingly misconstruing what had him rattled. "Are we saying the Russians are behind all of this? I mean, that's crazy, right?"

Dempsey shrugged. "Don't look at me. I've been a counterterror guy for almost two decades now, but that meant Middle East and Africa ops. That Cold War, KGB, Soviet Union shit is way outside my wheelhouse. All I know about it is the stuff I read in novels as a kid."

"Me, too, but I can tell you with one hundred percent certainty that those assholes we took on in Manbij in the black SUVs were definitely not PKK," Munn said.

"One of the men that took me slipped up when we were driving away and said something that sounded Russian," Allen said. "At the time, I was convinced I'd been handed off to the Russians."

"Then those shooters were Spetsnaz," Dempsey said, slapping the table. "The hardware, the tactics, their operational proficiency—all screams professional operators. It finally makes sense."

The energy and excitement in the room reached a palpable level as they pieced together what only minutes ago had seemed like an intractable puzzle.

"Which brings us back to the brilliant construction of the Malik legend," Adamo said. "Building Malik as Chechen is both pragmatic and convincing. It's pragmatic because it justifies regular communications into Chechnya under the auspice of using underground channels. These channels could be maintained by GRU moles either within the actual Chechen resistance or simply posing as such. Either way, it's perfect if you're a Russian handler on the project. Second, it's convincing because the story of a Chechen rebel forced to flee his homeland since he's being hunted by imperial Russians is a sympathetic one if you happen to be an Anatolian Kurd living in Turkey who dreams of a sovereign Kurdistan and the demise of the dogmatic dictator who is waging a war against your people."

"I can tell you from my time working with the Ambassador in Turkey that Kurdish independence is on Erodan's mind every day," Allen said. "He's been using the Turkish secret police to conduct covert raids against suspected Kurdish dissidents for the past eighteen months. Now he's using the Turkish military to overtly attack Kurdish settlements in Syria. Many people are concerned that he will eventually use the army to round up tens of thousands of Kurdish citizens and brand them enemies of the state, just like the fifty thousand supposed heretics and traitors he imprisoned after the failed coup."

"But why would Russia want to help the Kurds in Turkey when just across the border in Syria, Russian forces are bombing Kurdish strongholds?" Latif asked. "Sounds like one helluva contradiction to me."

"Because the operations serve completely different agendas," Adamo said. "In both Turkey and Syria, Kurdish factions pose a destabilizing threat. In the case of Turkey, the destabilization drives a wedge between Washington and Ankara, which Moscow supports. In the case of Syria, Kurdish activity threatens the stability of the current Syrian regime, which is aligned with Moscow. Syria is both strategically and economically important to Russia. They want to support their ally, who, like Iran, is an important buyer of Russian weapons systems. Geographically, Syria is the gateway for gas pipelines from the Arab states into Turkey, gas that would ultimately flow into Europe. To date, Petrov has used his relationship and influence over the Syrian President to stop the development of Arab pipeline projects that would compete with Russian gas. And strategically, Syria provides the Russian military with an important base of operations in the Middle East that Petrov sees as critical to counter US presence in the region. A Syrian alliance gives Russia a port for Naval operations in the Mediterranean that doesn't require regular bidirectional transit through the Turkish Straits. Now his Black Sea fleet assets can be reassigned and repositioned in advance of a potential conflict, especially planned operations that threaten foreign intervention, without worrying about NATO members blocking his access to the Med. Think annexation of Crimea. Before Moscow moved an air wing in, the US and Israel had uncontested control of the sky in the region. Now, Tel Aviv must think twice before it acts unilaterally against its erratic neighbor to the north. This is Petrov's ultimate goal—to create a paradigm of fear and doubt where the world believes that an attack on Syria constitutes an attack on Russia."

"That all makes sense, but how does this relate to Turkey?" Latif asked.

"Turkey is a NATO member," Allen said, jumping in, "and is the member with the largest standing military force on the continent, over six hundred thousand personnel, and second only to the US in NATO. Turkey geographically and symbolically functions as the gateway to Europe. Its strategic importance to the stability, credibility, and functional effectiveness of NATO is enormous."

"Which is why we need to view the recent PKK attack on Incirlik with a different lens," Adamo chimed in. It was as if Adamo and Allen had prepared the brief together; that's how well they were playing off each other. "The media is calling it a failed terrorist attack to obtain the B61 tactical nukes, and the Russian propaganda machine is promoting this perception. But the attack wasn't a failure. On the contrary, it was a resounding success—perfectly achieving its architect's objective."

"Which is?" Dempsey asked.

"To create panic in the public about terrorists trying to steal nukes in Turkey and then turn it into an international crisis that drives a wedge between Turkey and the US. From the beginning, the attack on the airbase was a suicide mission. Heck, I personally believe the PKK fighters knew this going in. The simple exercise of planning the op would quickly reveal it was mission impossible."

"Then why do it?" Martin asked. "Why martyr yourself for Russia?"

"First, I'm not convinced they knew they were working as Russian proxies," Adamo said. "But even if they did, a shrewd commander would see the brilliance of the plan. Pretend for a moment that you're a senior-level tactician in PKK and your objective is regime change in Turkey. But instead of weakening the Erodan regime, all your previous campaigns have had the opposite effect—only further concentrating his power. Then someone comes to you and explains that you're approaching the problem from the wrong angle. That the only power strong enough to oust Erodan is the United States and NATO. And this person goes on to cite examples like Saddam Hussein in Iraq and Kaddafi in Libya, and he tells you that the only way to get rid of Erodan is to paint him as a mad dictator with potential access to ninety B61 tactical nuclear weapons. In that case, the world will demand one of two things happen: either the nuclear weapons are removed, or the dictator is removed. Erodan will never willingly part with his nuclear deterrent, and so . . . There you have it."

"Then you reveal the presence of an unauthorized CIA base to stoke the fires of mistrust and paranoia in Erodan's mind. Make him think that his ally has been lying to him, that the US can no longer be trusted," Allen said. "Make him contemplate evicting the United States military and intelligence presence from Turkish soil."

"And then the nukes become an international crisis," Adamo said, finishing the thought.

Dempsey looked back and forth between Adamo on the screen and Allen sitting next to him. They were smiling at each other, and despite himself, he couldn't help but be impressed. Sure, this complicated Turkish destabilization plot, orchestrated by the Russians and using Kurdish proxies manipulated by an evergreen legend they'd developed, could be 100 percent wrong, but he didn't think so. These two spooks made quite a formidable analytical pair. He shifted his gaze to Grimes.

Sorta like she and I are on the tactical side of the house.

"So I suppose that only leaves one question unanswered," Munn said, turning to Allen. "Why did the PKK terrorists take you? What nugget of information did you possess that Malik and the Russians wanted to exploit?"

"I have no idea, and believe me, I've been asking myself that question. I just assumed it was because they pierced my official cover and knew I was collecting intelligence in country," she said.

"Were you looking into Malik?" Smith asked.

"No."

"Russian operations in Turkey?"

"Not specifically, no."

"What about PKK? Were you actively penetrating their network or maybe getting close to uncovering this plot so that the Russians decided they needed to get you out of the picture before you could sound the alarm bell?" Smith continued.

She shook her head. "I was certainly aware of PKK and, like I said before, interested in Erodan's fixation on the Kurdish situation in general. But I wasn't running an infiltration or deep-cover asset."

"Sometimes the answers to questions like that are not as satisfying as we might wish them to be," Baldwin mused. "In this case, the

Ambassador was the target. The objective was to commence the destabilization process by escalating tensions between the US and Turkey. Were Bailey still in play during this crisis, he'd be functioning as a stabilizing force, working to bolster trust and confidence between Washington and Ankara. Taking Bailey out of the picture beforehand was most likely a calculated move."

"And me? What about me? Why didn't they shoot me on the street that day?" Allen said.

"There could be several reasons," Baldwin replied gently, as if he were explaining a calculus problem to his favorite but slow child. "One thing I've learned over the years is that all villains are, if nothing else, opportunists at heart. We may never know the true reason for your abduction, and if I may be so bold, I think that sometimes not knowing can be a blessing in disguise."

"And just how the hell am I supposed to live with that?" she asked, her eyes suddenly rimming with tears. ". . . the not knowing."

After a long silence, Grimes said softly, "One day at a time, Amanda. Believe me, that's the only way."

Everyone at the table looked at their hands. Dempsey felt an urge to wrap an arm around the woman beside him but resisted.

Adamo broke the silence a beat later.

"My present concern is that this Russian operation to drive an irreconcilable wedge between Turkey and the US is not finished. Right now, as we speak, President Warner, the Secretary of State, and the DNI are flying to Istanbul to convince President Erodan just how important the relationship between the US and Turkey is. Does anyone here care to guess the total number of times sitting US Presidents have visited Turkey over the past fifty years? Five . . . five times in five decades, and President Warner is going now. So if there is any doubt in anyone's mind as to where we stand—this, ladies and gentlemen, is a full-blown international crisis."

"If I were Malik, or whoever the sonuvabitch is behind this op, this is the moment I'd be waiting for," Dempsey said, garnering looks from everyone in the room. "You've got the President, the Secretary of State, the DNI, and their Turkish counterparts all about to meet in the same place at the same time. If chaos, mistrust, and blame is the endgame, why not lob a grenade into the middle of this party and see what happens?"

"This was my thinking exactly. Which is why I put together this OPORD for Director Smith and called this all-hands-on-deck meeting," Adamo said with a nod to Dempsey. Then he turned to Smith and handed him a binder, which the Ember Director opened and began to page through.

"I need some time to review the details, but this operation is approved," Smith said, his eyes still scanning the document Adamo had prepared. Then, looking up, he fixed his gaze on Dempsey. "Time to get some rack, people. Wheels up in five hours. We'll brief you on the details en route. For right now, all you need to know is that Ember Special Activities Division is going to Istanbul."

"To do what exactly?" Munn asked.

"I guess we'll know when it unfolds," Dempsey said, looking over at Grimes.

"Not to worry, JD. After all, what could possibly go wrong?" she said and then flashed him the world's most sarcastic smile.

CHAPTER 40

US Navy C-2 from VRC-30 / Carrier Air Wing Five
Call Sign Provider Two
Over the Sea of Marmara
Forty Miles South of Istanbul, Turkey
May 10
0630 Local Time

Dempsey hated not being able to see out of the ancient rattling turboprop that served as the workhorse transport for the Navy. Other than the cockpit windows, there was only a single tiny porthole on each side of the fuselage, and he wasn't near either of them. He shifted right on the canvas bench as the C-2 slowed, and the engines seemed to groan in protest. He hated old planes almost as much as helicopters . . .

"This plane is a piece of shit," Martin complained, apparently reading Dempsey's mind. "It's uncomfortable, it shakes like hell, and it stinks like pig ass."

"It stinks because of *your* pig ass, Martin," Munn growled. "What did you eat in the Goat Locker before we left?"

"Scrambled eggs with cheese and Tabasco," the former Marine said, grinning with pride.

Everyone groaned, even Dempsey.

Then the plane flared, nose rising on the approach, and dropped hard onto the runway.

"Damn Navy pilots," Latif grumbled. "Atatürk International has a two-mile runway. Why does every Navy landing have to be a controlled crash?"

"Well," Munn said, unbuckling himself and standing as they taxied, "you know what the Naval aviators say about landing on a runway: 'Flare to land—squat to pee.'"

Grimes punched Munn in the back. "I squat to pee—you wanna take me on in a gunfight?"

Munn laughed and raised both hands in surrender. "It's all about risk management, and no, ma'am, I most certainly do not."

Dempsey chuckled at the locker-room banter while he unhooked the belt at his waist and stood as the old plane rattled off the runway. It was good to be back with the team. They gave him purpose. And drive. Ember was becoming a brotherhood to him, more so with each passing day. He couldn't imagine operating without them, and that's when his mind drifted to his last interaction with Smith. Hours removed from the heat of the conversation, he was better able to view the operation through an unfiltered lens. Why had he tried to be a lone wolf? Why had he thought he could rescue Amanda Allen alone? That wasn't him. That had never been him. He was a team guy. John Dempsey was a team guy, now and forever.

The plane seemed to taxi forever, with Dempsey hanging on to a piece of orange cargo netting like a subway commuter. When the old plane finally jerked to a stop, a flight suit–clad crewman maneuvered between them to get to the back of the plane, and a beat later, the rear cargo ramp lowered to the ground. Beyond, he could see two black

SUVs sitting on the cement ramp that reflected light from the flight line. The tarmac was wet, and he could smell rain in the air.

Dempsey slung his kit, his pack, and his assault rifle over his shoulder and checked the pistol in the drop holster on his right thigh. Then he followed Grimes out the back of the idling C-2A Greyhound. As he passed the young crewman, the kid said, "Thanks for flying with Provider Airlines. We know you have no fucking choice when you fly Navy, so thanks for riding VRC-30. Come again. Buh-bye, now . . . Buh-bye."

Dempsey chuckled at the kid's shtick and followed Grimes down the ramp and over to the waiting vehicles. Two men approached them, one from each SUV. The operator from the lead vehicle was a few years older than Dempsey and dressed in cargo pants, a plaid short-sleeve shirt, and a Punisher ball cap.

The man extended his hand. "Hey, I'm Ponch, and this is Tab. We're GRS sent to give you a lift and provide some security for y'all." He looked over the five-member Ember team, all carrying kits and rifles. "But I guess we'll just provide the taxi service. From the looks of it, y'all got the security component taken care of."

Dempsey shook Ponch's hand. "Thanks for the help, bro."

"Yeah, well, the boss said y'all are part of the team that gave our boys a helping hand and lift outta Adana, so we owe you. Y'all are Ground Branch or something?"

"Something," Dempsey said.

"Check," the man said with a grin. "I used to be part of 'something,' too. I'm Army, and Tab over there was a frogman."

Dempsey glanced at Tab and was relieved that the former SEAL didn't look familiar. He extended his hand, and Tab shook it with an iron grip.

"So," Ponch said, gesturing to the two SUVs at the same time, one with each hand, "we'll split into two vehicles. I understand we have a drop-off for one of y'all inside the grounds of the Sarachane Municipal

Palace." His gaze went to the sniper case slung over Grimes's shoulder. "I'm guessing that someone is you?"

She tipped her chin at this.

"Okay, just so we're clear, Gendarmerie will be escorting you into position on the roof, not American Secret Service," the contract CIA security agent said, referring to the paramilitary branch of the Turkish Armed Forces responsible for counterterrorism and counterinsurgency operations. "You're the only person with permission to be on the roof . . . And don't be surprised if they give you a hard time, ma'am. Them Gendarmerie boys can be a little sexist. Not everyone is as evolved as Tab and me." He flashed her a big frat-boy grin and winked.

Grimes smiled coolly. "I'll be fine."

Ponch tipped his ball cap at her, then pulled a tablet computer out of his right cargo pocket and opened a map application that he showed Dempsey and Munn. "We'll set up our vehicles here at the corner of Sarachane Park access road . . ." He tapped a corner north and a hundred yards east of the long entrance to the Palace—which looked more office building than palace to Dempsey. ". . . and then here at the corner of Bukali Dede Sokak, the road behind the property to the east. This here"—he tapped on a square white building just past the corner—"is a driving school, so I'll sit us in the corner of their lot right at the intersection the Palace faces."

"I'm not loving that first spot," Munn said, looking at the map and frowning. "I don't want to get blocked in."

"We won't, at least not by vehicles. The Secret Service and the Gendarmerie will have the road closed several minutes ahead of the arrival, and we coordinated everything with the Turks, so we'll be right at the street at both locations. But so you know, there's gonna be a crowd. Civilian protesters have been mobbing the entrance to the IBB—the Palace—pretty much every day since the attacks. Half of 'em want the West out of Turkey 'cause I guess it's our fault they've been killing each other for over four thousand years. The rest are either protesting those protesters, or the Erodan dictatorship, or the right for a Kurdish independent state, or the Westernization of Islam, or maybe the new pomegranate-spice latte at Starbucks . . . The list is long and varied—kinda hard to keep track these days."

"Secret Service knows where we'll be, I assume," Dempsey said, ignoring the rant.

Ponch laughed. "Yeah, they know where you'll be, but they don't know who you are, and that has them pretty pissed off. They made it clear that you are not augmenting security and that they have no idea why you *are* here. I guess the order came from high up 'cause they didn't fight my brief, but they sure as hell don't like it. You cool with everything? Got any questions for me or Tab?"

Dempsey nodded. "It's all good. Thanks for the legwork."

"Yeah, man," the GRS operator said. "And we're two more guns for whatever 'not a security augment' tasking you got going on."

"We appreciate that," Dempsey said as they walked toward the vehicles. "Stay frosty, 'cause the way things have been going lately for us, we might very well need you."

CHAPTER 41

Vehicle Number Three
Presidential Convoy
Istanbul, Turkey
0830 Local Time

Jarvis looked out the thick ballistic glass at the metropolis that was Istanbul as the caravan made its way onto the E-5 Yolu highway. The route would loop them north around the airport and then bend east toward the historic Fatih district—the ancient city once known as Constantinople, long since swallowed by sprawl. Istanbul today was as vibrant and Western as any city in Europe, thanks largely to the policies and vision of Mustafa Kemal Atatürk, founder of the Turkish Republic and the country's first "secular" President. Once a people became secularized and accustomed to the freedoms, luxuries, and conveniences of the West, it was nearly impossible to turn back the clock, but in Turkey, Erodan was trying.

And unfortunately, he was succeeding.

"You're annoyed," Petra said.

He looked up at Petra, who sat across from him in the limo beside the single American Secret Service agent assigned to their vehicle.

"Yes," he said. "Having President Erodan riding with President Warner at the last minute just makes things more frustrating."

"Amen, sir," the Secret Service agent agreed, his six-foot-four frame hunched slightly in the seat. "Imagine how we feel."

"Be honest," Petra said, bemused. "What you're really frustrated about is that *they're* having a conversation and *you* can't hear what they're talking about. Don't worry, Warner won't give away the proverbial farm without you. He knows what he's doing."

"I know he does, but even the best of us need backup. He needs a wingman, someone to listen for subtext, watch body language, look for tells of insincerity or downright lies—I could be doing that for him right now."

"Yes, you could," Petra said, "but having you in the limo could also be a detriment. Your presence might cause Erodan to clam up, or maybe he would feel compelled to bring a second, and what could have been a productive, uncensored conversation becomes a chest-puffing standoff. Two-on-one or two-on-two is an entirely different dynamic than one-on-one," she said.

"Yeah, and that's why I hate politics," Jarvis said with a sigh. Missing out on the conversation in the President's limo wasn't the only thing he was upset about. During the transatlantic flight, he'd had a conversation with Smith and Adamo, in which the two of them had laid out their new theory of Russian involvement in the events of the past several days. This revelation had only stoked his existing concerns that this trip was a mistake. But despite his protest and adamant concurrence from the head of Warner's Secret Service detail, the President could not be swayed. The emergency summit with Erodan was happening, no matter the risk. "The United States," Warner had said, "will not yield its foothold in Turkey without a fight."

"In my experience," the Secret Service agent in their car said, "diplomacy occurs in car rides and over private meals. The summits and cabinet meetings are for photo ops and to squabble about the details."

Petra smiled at the agent. "Have you been with the detail long?"

"Oh yeah," he said. "I came on during the previous administration. But I prefer this one. He knows how to play the political game on TV, but he's typically no bullshit behind the scenes. I trust this guy. He might make mistakes, but he always has the best interest of the country at heart."

Jarvis considered the young man's words and reflected on his own evolving opinion of the President of the United States as they drove. Two years ago, his perception of Warner had been that of a self-serving politician with a penchant for talking out of both sides of his mouth at the same time. He still wasn't quite sure what Warner was truly capable of and how much of everything he did was for appearance, but he had grown to respect the man . . . more than he could say for most men.

"What's your name?" Jarvis asked the agent, breaking a long silence.

"Antonin Perez," the agent said. "The guys on the detail who think they're funny call me Tiny, but I'm Tony to my friends and wife. Recently, though, I got a new handle."

"What's that?"

"Dada, which also happens to be my baby daughter's first word."

"Congrats on being a new dad, Tony," he said, extending his hand to the agent. "I'm Kelso Jarvis."

"Oh, I know who you are, sir," Perez said, shaking hands and then settling back into his seat. "I have a younger brother serving with SEAL Team Ten, and he says they still speak your name with a holy reverence."

Jarvis smiled and was about to respond when the car began to slow. He shifted his gaze from Tony to out the window and saw the street ahead was mobbed with protestors.

"What the hell is this?" Jarvis said, his heart rate picking up. "The Turks assured us there would be a total media blackout about this summit. That's why we had it in Istanbul instead of Ankara."

"I don't know what's going on, sir," Perez said, pressing a finger to his earpiece. "But I'll try to find out."

Jarvis looked at Petra, and her expression spoke volumes.

I don't like this . . . I don't like it at all.

CHAPTER 42

GRS SUV
North Corner of the Özel Aysel Sürücü Driving School Parking Lot
Corner of Bukali Dede Sokak and Şehzadebaşi Cadessi
0845 Local Time

"This is bad, Ponch," Dempsey said, straining his neck and sitting up in his seat. "I can barely even see the entrance to the building. Is it always like this?"

The GRS operator pursed his lips. "Nah, I've never seen it like this. There are always a couple of groups of protesters milling around, but this is insane. Maybe it's because the two Presidents are meeting?"

Dempsey shook his head. "Can't be that. No one knows about this meeting. You wouldn't even know if you weren't working with us." Dempsey felt his heart quicken. "Unless it got leaked . . ."

"A leak? In politics? Never," Latif scoffed from the back seat.

"Eagle, this is Falcon One," Dempsey said aloud, now talking to the Ember TOC in Virginia instead of his escort. "You see what we're seeing?"

"A crowd that big is hard to miss, Falcon" came Baldwin's voice. "We've got good eyes on you and on POTUS, but the convoy has slowed to a crawl."

"The size of the crowd is what concerns me," Munn chimed in from the other SUV positioned across the street. "Why the hell didn't they cordon off access to the street today?"

"Because that would advertise the arrival of someone important," Smith said. "The fact that the street is open should be the best protection of all. They'll close it to car traffic at the last minute, just before the convoy arrives, but clearing pedestrians usually carries more risk than benefit, assuming no one knows what's up."

"Maybe somebody tweeted a picture of Air Force One landing at Atatürk International, and now everybody in the world knows what's up," Ponch said. "There's always that."

"Yeah, well, if they already know, we're screwed," Dempsey said. He looked over his shoulder at Latif, who was kitted up with his rifle across his chest. "June, hand me the black jacket out of my bag," he said.

Latif began rummaging through the bag.

"Falcon Two," Dempsey said, keying his mike. "Ditch your long gun and cover up with a sweatshirt or jacket. Pistols only. We need to check this crowd for threats."

"Check," Munn said.

Latif handed Dempsey a medium-length zipper jacket as Dempsey lifted his rifle over his head and set it on the floor of the SUV. Then he removed the drop holster from his belt and unsnapped it from his right thigh. He shoved the Sig P226 pistol into his waistband and donned the jacket. He pulled the extra 5.56 magazines from their pouches, making his kit far less bulky and noticeable under the jacket, and put them on the floor for later.

"Stay here," he said to Latif over his shoulder. He keyed his mike again. "Falcon Three and Four will stay with their respective vehicles. One and Two are moving to the street."

Two double-clicks told him the team understood.

"God, are you set?"

"Set," Grimes answered in a soft whisper, fully immersed in the sniper zone. "I have eyes on the property and the drive. I have the west approach and most of the east approach, except a short span, maybe twenty yards, blocked by the corner of the forward building."

Dempsey turned to Ponch. "I assume Secret Service is moving among the crowd."

The GRS agent shrugged. "Undoubtedly."

"All right," Dempsey said. "I'm betting we can spot them, but we need to make sure they know *we're* in the crowd with them."

"Falcon One, I'll work on deconfliction with Secret Service from my end," Baldwin said.

"Check," Dempsey said. "Two, I'll meet you near the north side of the IBB drive."

"Check," Munn acknowledged.

A beat later, Dempsey was out of the car, jacket zipped to his neck and nerves on edge. The sidewalk was all but unpassable, so he drifted into the street, careful to hug the curb in case a car came barreling down a road he couldn't see. The crowd was thick and loud. In some areas, people were shouting in the general direction of the government building beyond the wall to his left, and in others they were jockeying for position in front of television camera crews who had seemed to materialize from thin air. Many carried signs, further distracting him and impeding his view.

"This is insane," Munn grumbled in his ear. "I'm crossing the street now."

"The convoy is moving again but still making slow progress," Baldwin said. "They just turned north on Buyuk Resit Pasa. ETA is in three minutes."

"See anything, Two?" Dempsey asked.

"I see you now. I don't like being separated by this many people. We need to watch each other's backs in this quagmire."

"Check," Dempsey said.

"I have your back until then," Grimes chimed in.

Dempsey shoved and elbowed his way through the river of people, no longer trying to be gentle or polite, just trying to keep his footing as his torso was jostled left and right. The energy had a serpentine quality, with bodies sliding and slithering over, under, and around one another. From a tactical perspective, the situation was absolutely appalling, and he wondered how he could discharge his weapon effectively in this environment. Gritting his teeth, Dempsey crossed the street, eyeing a tight group of protesters shouting in cadence and pumping signs in the air.

"Hey," Munn said, sidling up beside Dempsey, panting from the effort of his approach.

"Maybe we should have stayed in the cars," Dempsey said. "Visibility is worse than I realized it would be."

"No, we had to do this. It's the only way to scan bodies and faces in the throng," Munn said.

"The convoy has reached the corner of Şehzadebaşi," Baldwin said, his voice still calm. "They're turning now."

"I see them," Grimes said.

Dempsey strained to see over the crowd but still could not spot the convoy. Despite two decades of Tier One operations, conducting missions in almost every conceivable environment, this was one situation he'd not faced before. In the crush of people, he felt powerless—the enemy could be everyone or no one. Then, thirty yards to the east, something caught his attention—two men and a woman right at the curb, holding signs but not chanting or pumping their arms in rhythm with the others. The woman looked in the direction of the presidential convoy, said something to her male companion on her left. She looked anxious. Then, despite the distance between them, she locked eyes with

Dempsey. Her face paled as she broke eye contact and addressed each of her companions in turn.

"Got something," Dempsey said to Munn. "Ten o'clock, two males, one female. Female is wearing a black headscarf. They're on the move."

Dempsey started pushing through the crowd, Munn at his side, closing on the trio.

"Falcon, this is God. I have them, three possible tangos closing on the convoy."

"Move!" Dempsey shouted, trying to pick up speed, knocking pedestrians right and left like a blocking fullback trying to clear a lane. "Tell Secret Service," he shouted, his right hand fumbling under his jacket to retrieve the pistol from his waistband.

"Roger," said Baldwin.

"They're converging on the convoy . . . splitting up, heading for multiple vehicles," Grimes said, her voice tight. "The woman is moving on Victor Two—she has a weapon."

"Shoot the girl!" Dempsey shouted.

"I don't have a shot," Grimes said.

An explosion rocked the ground and sent a shock wave through the crowd. Bodies scattered like tumbleweeds in a storm. Airborne, Dempsey tucked his head under his arms to protect his skull from a blow with the pavement. He hit the ground, rolling, pistol still clutched in a death grip in his right hand, and stopped with a thud against the curb.

With a groan, he pressed himself onto his hands and knees, when a second detonation knocked him back down . . .

CHAPTER 43

Vehicle Number Three
Presidential Convoy
Şehzadebaşi Cadessi, Half Block East of the Entrance to the Municipal Palace

The explosion shook the DNI's limousine with the impact of a Freightliner and slammed Jarvis into the corner between the door and the backrest. Fueled by an adrenaline dump, Jarvis instantly switched into tactical mode. He promptly drew the Sig Sauer P229 from the small-of-the-back holster he wore beneath his suit coat and scanned his colleagues for injury. Petra had slid low in her seat, her head below the window line. The Secret Service agent had been thrown into her lap and was righting himself when the second explosion hit.

"Jesus," Perez barked from the footwell after the second blast cleared.

Jarvis scanned the crowd through the ballistic-glass windows, looking for threats. "What have you got, Tony?" he barked.

Perez pulled a short-barreled MP5 machine gun from a door rack and scrambled back to his seat. "Sandman's vehicle is disabled," he reported, relaying information about the presidential limousine as he received it via the microtransceiver tucked in his ear.

"Is everyone okay?" Petra asked.

"No casualties," Perez said, "but Sandman is separated from the convoy lead, and neither vehicle is operational."

"We need to get them into our limo," Jarvis said.

"Hold on," Perez said, pressing a hand over his earpiece.

Outside the limousine, pandemonium ensued. Jarvis felt the chassis rock and heard wild, panicked screams as bodies thumped against the car. At first he thought the crowd was attacking the convoy, but as he watched, he realized there was nothing orderly or focused about it. They were a vessel bobbing in a turbulent sea of human chaos. He craned his neck to look forward through the windshield and saw the President's vehicle spun thirty degrees askew and drooping toward the front right quarter, where the sheet metal was mushroomed and the wheel had been blown completely off.

"They're trying to move vehicle four up to retrieve Sandman," Perez said. "We're instructed to sit tight."

"Bullshit," Jarvis said. "We're closer, and four won't get around us through this crowd. Tell our driver to advance, position our vehicle nose to nose at an acute angle to make a wedge—our front right corner to Sandman's front left corner. That will create a protected pocket between the rear doors and a corridor we can use to transfer occupants from their rear compartment into ours."

Perez nodded and relayed the plan into the mike at his wrist. Then, shaking his head, he said to Jarvis, "Negative. They want me to keep you protected."

"Goddamn it, Tony. Remember what your brother told you about me? Now pull this fucking car forward and let's EXFIL Sandman while we still can."

Perez nodded. "Yeah," he said. "You're right." He spoke again into his mike, this time giving orders to the driver up front, and immediately their limo began to creep forward. "I'm out first and covering the transfer. The agents in vehicle two will surround Sandman and the Turkish President and move them into ours. Vehicle four will follow and EXFIL the driver and the two other Gendarmerie dudes inside. Check?"

Jarvis nodded. "I'll cover you while you cover the detail."

"Stay in the car, sir," Perez said, but his voice said he knew damn well that wasn't happening.

The car jolted to a halt as the right front corner bumped the front of the presidential limo.

Jarvis handed his pistol to Petra and then reached across Perez and pulled a second MP5 from a bracket. "We do this together, or we don't do it at all . . . Now let's go save the President."

CHAPTER 44

Rooftop
Municipal Palace

Grimes peered through her scope at the chaos in the streets below. She saw the Secret Service agents setting up a perimeter around the disabled limousine, scanning over their weapons for threats. She'd lost Dempsey and Munn in the melee and prayed to God they were not among the fallen, an arc of lifeless, unmoving bodies surrounding the convoy like dropped flower petals.

Baldwin relayed the Secret Service team's plan to transfer POTUS and the Turkish President into the limo Jarvis was riding in. She watched as the number three limousine bumped nose to nose with the President's limo, creating a wedge. A beat later, the right rear door of the third vehicle opened, and a Secret Service agent emerged, followed by Petra and then Jarvis.

"DNI is in the open between the vehicles," she called, watching Jarvis moving in a combat crouch like a twenty-five-year-old operator, scanning the crowd and clutching a submachine gun as people streamed past the vehicles. A heartbeat later, the left rear door of the second limo opened, and a gaggle of people evacuated en masse—three agents, guns raised, with Warner and Erodan hunched low between them. Without warning, the agent guarding their right flank pitched his head back and crumpled to the ground. She zoomed in. The agent was dead, a gaping wound in the side of his head.

Sonuvabitch—we've got a sniper.

Grimes tensed as a pit of dread formed in her stomach. She'd never faced off against another sniper before. She pulled back from the scope and scanned the area for sniper hides. In her peripheral vision, she caught a muzzle flash from the only high ground with angles on the horrific scene unfolding below. She looked down in time to see the agent beside Jarvis grasp his chest and collapse against the side of limo number two.

"We have a sniper in the minaret of the Prince's Mosque across the street," she relayed calmly, her cheek once again kissing the stock of her WinMag.

She had only seconds to act. The President was moving between the two limos, heading toward the rear door of vehicle three. He was vulnerable. She spied a small open window in the side of the ornate minaret tower. The shooter had to be in there. There was nowhere else. But all she saw was dark; the sniper was a pro, his weapon pulled back into the shadows. She had only one advantage over him—the element of surprise. If she missed with her first shot, he would quickly identify her position, and the scenario would either escalate into a deadly sniper duel, or he would flee.

One chance, one shot . . . That's all I get.

She switched her scope over to thermal, and he materialized instantly before her eyes, lying prone and set from the opening, his weapon supported in the firing position.

"I have the shooter," Baldwin said. "Moving the drone."

No time for that, she knew. *I'm the only one who can stop him before it's too late.*

She didn't have time to do proper range and bearing calculations or adjust for elevation and wind. So she performed a quick mental estimate and sighted on the sniper's head.

Exhale . . .

Squeeze.

Through the scope, she saw a puff of orange around the man's head. Then his body fell away from the rifle and was still.

"Eagle, this is God. Sniper's down," she reported.

"Roger, God," came Baldwin's reply. "Nice shooting."

She shifted her sight back to the street below and the chaos unfolding around the presidential convoy. A woman stepped off the curb, dressed all in black, moving deliberately toward the vehicles. Her hand rose. A pistol perhaps?

She wasn't taking any chances.

Exhale—squeeze.

The woman collapsed onto the pavement before inflicting harm, but how many more terrorists were out there? Grimes scanned the crowd around the presidential security detail.

Why is this taking so long? Just get in the fucking car!

She didn't know who she more desperately wanted to be safe, the President of the United States or the DNI, but all she could do now was pray that the answer to this question would not be written in blood . . .

CHAPTER 45

In the Crowd
The South Side of the Şehzadebaşi Cadessi

From his vantage point in the crowd, Valerian watched Mutla collapse. The US security sniper's headshot had been perfectly timed, dropping Mutla before she could fire a round. To make matters worse, his sniper was not responding . . . probably having been dispatched by the US sniper as well. That meant his four-person PKK team was down—the two suicide bombers had done their work well, but the primary and secondary shooters had failed.

That meant he was the mission now . . .

He scanned the high ground and quickly identified the most likely location for the enemy sniper. Once he fired, his position would be revealed and the sniper would probably take him out with a headshot, but he could not let the objective go unmet. Arkady's orders had been to kill the DNI, so that was what he was going to do. Arkady hadn't shared with him the rationale of the operation or how the death of the US Director of National Intelligence would benefit Russia, but Valerian didn't care.

He was Zeta Prime.

His job was to execute orders, not contemplate them.

He scanned the bodies littering the street until he spied a dead female civilian on the pavement a few meters from the convoy. His only chance for success now was to capitalize on the chaos and innate human empathy. A good acting job would hide him in plain sight, allow him to close range to the target, and buy him the few precious seconds he needed to pull his weapon and take the shot. Decision made, he transformed from a cold, calculating killer into a frantic, grieving husband and set off running toward his murdered "wife," who lay not fifteen feet from the American DNI.

CHAPTER 46

Jarvis scanned the chaos over the barrel of the HK MP5 9 mm submachine gun—people were running, screaming, and crying everywhere around them. The wedge formation of the two limousines had accomplished his goal. Like a boulder in a raging river, it broke the flow of the stampeding crowd and offered a sheltered safe haven between the vehicles. The Secret Service detail, with President Warner and the Turkish President bundled roughly between them, had managed to shoot the gap and pile into the back of Jarvis's limo. Two Secret Service agents, however, had taken enemy sniper fire. One from the President's detail was down and, from his pallor and glassy eyes, looked unlikely to survive. The other, Agent Perez, was slumped against the right rear tire of the limousine.

"Get in the car, Tony," Jarvis commanded.

"The President?" the wounded man gasped, bloody bubbles forming on his lips.

"He's already in. Your turn now."

Jarvis watched Perez pull himself weakly into the car, leaving a trail of blood on the pavement. Then, something in Jarvis's peripheral vision activated an alert in his brain. He turned at the same time as

Petra, his machine gun coming up as her pistol did the same. A man who had been wailing and crouched over a fallen body had abruptly pivoted toward them. He was kneeling in a firing stance, pistol pointed directly at Jarvis. Before Jarvis could bring his MP5 to bear, he saw the muzzle flash.

Time stopped . . .

Jarvis locked eyes with the shooter—meeting a severe glacier-blue gaze intent on his murder.

Then something blocked his view.

Petra's body stretched out in front of him like a diving soccer goalie, but instead of catching a ball, she was trying to catch a bullet . . . the bullet intended for him. She collided with his chest, and they both fell to the ground.

He heard her cry out.

The limo was backing up now, the President safely inside and everyone else secondary to that mission. With every ounce of strength he possessed, Jarvis shoved Petra up and through the open rear door of the limousine. Then, channeling the young badass SEAL he had once been, he dove through the door and onto the floor of the moving car.

The door slammed shut behind him as the limo accelerated.

Instantly, Jarvis was on his knees beside Petra. Her jaw was set with pain, but her eyes were clear.

"Oh, son of a bitch that hurts," she said, meeting his eyes.

"What the hell were you thinking?" he said, shifting his gaze to her torso. "Where were you hit?"

Petra pulled her hands away from her ribs, just below her right breast. Her palms and the starched white shirt beneath were wet with dark blood.

"Someone get me a med kit," Jarvis demanded. He looked around the once cavernous limousine, now crammed with bodies, including Presidents Warner and Erodan.

"I think I'm okay," Petra said, but her eyes betrayed her worry. "It's tight when I breathe, but I feel better than you'd think for getting shot."

"Sir, I think you're hit," a Secret Service agent said, pointing at Jarvis's chest.

Jarvis looked down and saw blood on his shirt just beneath his left collar bone.

"That's Petra's blood, I think." But as he spoke the words, he realized that his chest was burning.

Damn. I am fucking shot.

In confirmation, a bloody bubble formed over the hole through his blood-soaked shirt as he let out a long breath.

"You okay, Kelso?" Petra asked.

He looked down at her and realized—strangely, in that moment—she'd never called him anything but "sir" since she'd come aboard as his Chief of Staff.

"I'm good, Commander Felsk," he said, smiling. "But a little piece of advice for the next time you try to catch a bullet for your boss—don't forget to put on your vest first."

She gave him a weak thumbs-up at this, but her cheeks were beginning to blanch.

"Time to the airport?" he asked, urgency in his voice.

"The highway has been closed to all traffic but us. We'll be there in less than ten minutes," one of the agents said. "The President's surgical team is standing by."

"We've got docs waiting for you, Petra, on Air Force One," he said, taking her hand. "Just hang in there; once they get a chest tube in, you'll feel better."

She gave him a wordless nod.

A beat later, his own breathing began to feel a little tight.

Well, shit, he thought, settling in beside her, *looks like I might need a chest tube of my own.*

CHAPTER 47

Dempsey got to his feet, and he was pissed. This was the third time in as many days that he'd almost been blown up. As the stars faded from his vision, he did a quick check of all his pieces and parts, and finding himself without any new unwanted orifices, he looked for Munn. He found the doc pressing up from a knee and shaking his head.

"You okay there, lumberjack?" he said.

"I'm intact," Munn groaned. "How 'bout you, old man?"

A single gunshot rang out behind Dempsey before he could answer, and he whirled to face the presidential convoy. The shooter took off sprinting into the crowd as one of the two limousines roared to life and laid rubber.

"The DNI is hit. He's egressing with Sandman in vehicle two," said Grimes's voice in his ear. "God has no shot on the shooter. He's moving east in the crowd—there's too many fucking people."

"I see him," Dempsey said and took off in pursuit.

"He's headed east on Şehzadebaşi," Grimes said in his ear. "I just lost him at the corner."

"Eagle has good eyes," Baldwin said in his ear. "Secure, overwatch."

"Roger, Eagle," Grimes said.

Munn was beside Dempsey now, sprinting stride for stride as they chased the DNI's shooter. Dempsey shed his black jacket and dropped it as he ran. "How's the DNI?" he demanded.

"No word yet," Smith said in his ear. "Focus on the target."

Legs churning, pistol in hand, Dempsey chased the assassin through a crush of people, cars, and minibuses down Şehzadebaşi Boulevard. Colorful restaurant awnings, vibrant storefront signage, and a row of alternating palm and deciduous trees lined the bustling promenade. As he ran, a single word flashed into his head: *collaterals.*

There's no way we're getting through this without more collaterals.

If Dempsey were to imagine the worst possible place on earth to execute a capture/kill pursuit, the Fatih district of Istanbul was it. Tourists, locals, merchants, students, children—people of every race, age, and culture—milled about like a swarm of ants in this architectural imbroglio that was historic Constantinople.

"Dude, he's getting away," Munn huffed, sprinting at Dempsey's side.

"I know."

"Then fucking shoot him."

Dempsey gritted his teeth. The comment didn't even warrant a response, but Dempsey understood the genesis. Just like Munn, he felt the frustration, the aggravation, and the creeping unarticulated sense that the sonuvabitch who'd just shot Jarvis was going to slip away and they'd be left empty-handed. But enough innocents had already been slaughtered today; no one was going to lose their life to one of his bullets.

He picked up his pace. The thrill of combat was rising inside him—not bloodlust, but a primal drive that fueled and propelled him. His pulse was a war drum pounding in his temples, the burn in his muscles a fire blazing. And as he flew through the crowd, people stopped and stared at the human missile screaming past.

"Shit, tango is stealing a scooter," Munn barked, lagging behind Dempsey.

"For your information, it's a Piaggio BV350," Baldwin commented in Dempsey's ear.

"And your point?" Dempsey said, scanning for a vehicle of his own to steal.

"My point, Falcon One, is simply that you shouldn't confuse it for a thirty-year-old Vespa. According to the company specifications, the Piaggio's maximum speed is eighty-five miles per hour."

"Then we'll need motorcycles to catch this guy . . . but all I see are fucking minibuses," Dempsey growled. "Find me a bike, Eagle."

"Roger that . . . searching . . . found one, thirty-five meters at your ten o'clock. Heading northwest on Şehzadebaşi Drive, on the other side of the median."

Dempsey glanced at the shooter, who was sitting on the motor scooter and aiming a pistol at them. With two decades' experience facing enemy fire, his mind automatically calculated the firing trajectory.

"Look out," he shouted at Munn and made a leaping tackle as a gunshot rang out and a bullet zipped past overhead. Dempsey rolled off Munn and brought his own pistol up. He sighted, and somewhere behind him, a woman cried out in pain as the round intended for Munn had found a target of opportunity instead.

"Shit, too many fucking people," he barked as civilians young and old scrambled in and out of his line of sight, fleeing in terror at the sound of gunfire.

"Thanks, bro," Munn said and scrambled to a crouch beside Dempsey.

In his peripheral vision, Dempsey could see Munn looking over his shoulder, presumably at the woman who'd just been shot.

"We have to leave her," Dempsey said, knowing exactly what was going through Munn's head. "There's no time, bro," Dempsey added, driving the point home. "Local EMS will be here soon."

"I know," Munn answered, frustration in his voice as he returned his attention to the assassin, who was pulling away.

"Hurry, Falcon One," Baldwin's voice said. "You're going to miss the motorcycle."

Dempsey snapped his attention to the line of oncoming traffic on the far side of the median and spotted a black motorcycle with a black-clad rider. He popped to his feet and charged toward the bike, dodging southbound traffic. When he reached the median, he cleared a low decorative iron fence and a row of shrub roses in a hurdle that would have made an Olympic triple jumper envious. For a split second, he considered tackling the motorcyclist but settled for stepping into traffic and acquiring the asset at gunpoint. Tires squealed and horns blazed as traffic skidded to an abrupt halt behind the BMW motorcycle.

"Get off," he shouted, training his Sig Sauer at the rider, who he realized was a woman. The helmeted, black-clad figure hesitated a moment, then engaged the kickstand and climbed off the bike. A beat later, Munn was at his side.

"You know how to drive one of these things?" the doc asked.

"Uh, not really," Dempsey said, and it was unfortunately the truth. He'd ridden a motorcycle only once, and that had been over two decades ago when he was in high school. In the Teams, he had mastered tactical three-wheelers, which couldn't be that different. He could probably figure out the clutch and gears, but by the time he became marginally proficient, the shooter would be gone.

"The target is escaping," Baldwin said calmly in Dempsey's ear.

Dempsey looked at Munn, his expression a question.

"Looks like I'm driving," Munn said and climbed onto the bike. "You can ride bitch. Let's go."

Without a second's hesitation, Dempsey whipped his leg over the back of the bike and settled onto the pillion. Then, wrapping his left arm around Munn's chest, he said, "Don't fucking kill us."

Munn retracted the kickstand, twisted the throttle, and whipped a U-turn. The BMW sport bike screamed to life and accelerated with rip-your-face-off speed into oncoming traffic.

"Dan?" Dempsey said.

"Yeah?" the doc called back.

"Were my instructions not clear?"

"No—crystal clear, bro."

"Then your execution sucks."

Blaring horns and screeching tires drowned out the sound of Munn's laughter, but Dempsey could feel it in his friend's chest as they rocketed along a gap between a row of parked cars and the counterflowing traffic.

"I don't see him. Where did he go?" Munn asked Baldwin.

"Not to worry, I have him," Baldwin said. "He's on Vezneciler sweeping right, out of your line of sight. Be advised, Falcon Two, the divided roadway ends in one hundred feet. You will have an opportunity to cross at the intersection ahead and get back into the southbound traffic scheme."

"Roger, I see it," Munn said, accelerating rather than decelerating into the maneuver.

Dempsey wrapped his right arm, pistol clutched in his hand, around Munn's chest, too, and held on tight. He had a pretty good idea what was coming.

"There is a gap in traffic behind that tour bus you're passing. You can cross the intersection in three . . . two . . . one . . . Mark the turn."

As they cleared the rear bumper of the tour bus, Munn leaned right into the turn and swerved the motorcycle around behind the bus, shooting the gap between the back of the bus and an oncoming Fiat. Dempsey let his body fall in sync with Munn's, imagining he was clearing corners as one of a tandem pair instead of riding bitch without a helmet on this motorcycle ride from hell. No sooner had they cleared the Fiat than Munn braked and pulled the bike into a left-hand turn, effectively executing an S-maneuver through traffic.

A woman on the sidewalk beside them screamed.

A horn blared.

Dempsey looked up and saw the left rear corner of a minibus turning onto the road directly in front of them.

"Watch out for the minibus," Baldwin said, and then Dempsey was pretty sure he could hear Baldwin take a slurping sip of hot beverage—a theater patron watching the show from his balcony box.

Munn juked the BMW left just in time to avoid a fatal collision, but not quite far enough to prevent the side of Dempsey's right knee from clipping the corner of the bumper.

"Shit, that hurt," Dempsey barked.

"Sorry, dude," Munn said, twisting the throttle and spinning up the motorcycle's engine to resume the pursuit, passing three more minibuses caravanning in a line.

How many fucking minibuses can one city have? Dempsey thought as they zoomed past the moving traffic like it was standing still.

"Talk to me, Eagle," Munn said.

"The target, whom Chip and Dale have dubbed Rook, is now one hundred yards ahead of you. He just made the dogleg turn onto Darülfünun," Baldwin said. "And, Falcon, be advised, there appears to be a tunnel."

"Roger that."

"And, Falcon?"

"What, Eagle?" Munn said, exasperated.

"There appears to be an accident on the ramp leading out of the tunnel on the other side, which none of the eastbound traffic appears to realize yet. It must have just happened."

"Your point?"

"My point is that by the time you get there, it is possible that our friend will be boxed inside the tunnel."

Dempsey considered this. *If I were the shooter, I would turn this into an opportunity—by finding a concealed position among the stopped traffic to ambush and kill my pursuers.*

"Watch the exit carefully, Eagle," Dempsey said. "Rook may exit on foot or on the bike. He may hijack a vehicle. If it were me, I might just lay low and wait."

"The target has entered the tunnel."

The motorcycle screamed east on Darülfünun, and a minute later, the mouth of the tunnel came into view. Just as Baldwin had predicted, eastbound traffic heading into the tunnel was beginning to slow. The line of westbound traffic, vehicles leaving the tunnel, snaked away beside them as no new cars were exiting the void—the accident apparently blocking the westbound lane, too.

"Eagle, Falcon One report. Do you have a visual on Rook leaving the tunnel on the other side?" Dempsey asked.

"Negative," Baldwin said. "All traffic is stopped."

"What do you want me to do?" Munn asked, braking. "We could go in fast and hot using the left lane, or we could ditch the bike and pursue on foot."

"If I were him, I'd expect us to pursue into the tunnel on foot," Dempsey said.

"So what would you do?"

"Depends on EXFIL options and the kinetics inside the tunnel. One of three things: ambush us, turn my bike around and try to blow past us at high speed heading west, or squirt on foot east."

"Okay, JD. What if you assault on foot, keep him busy while I rocket in fast and try to get past him?" Munn asked over his shoulder, and Dempsey held on for his life. "If I can flank him, then we'll put him in a cross fire, and eventually one of us will get a clean shot. But if he tries to squirt past us on his bike, then I'll be ready to run him down."

"Works for me. Let's do it."

Munn braked to a stop for Dempsey to climb off. "Just make sure you keep him pinned down with cover fire so he doesn't pick me off on my INFIL. How many magazines you got?"

"Four," Dempsey said, hopping off the BMW and doing a quick check of the pouches on his kit.

"All right," Munn said, revving the BMW's engine. "Let's deep-six this sonuvabitch."

CHAPTER 48

Darülfünun Tunnel Entrance

As he braked for the traffic jam in the tunnel, Valerian found himself grinning. He should be angry, cursing his bad luck, but instead, he realized that he was enjoying himself. It had been a long time since he'd found himself in a life-or-death situation like this. The American operators in pursuit were the most capable adversaries he'd faced in a very, very long time. For years, his legends had immersed him in the criminal underground, where his assignments had him working with Middle Eastern jihadis, Baltic thugs, and European Mafia. In those realms, his foes were rarely more than petty criminals elevated to their stations by money and brutality, not talent. Arkady had once warned him that the greatest enemy he would face in his profession was himself. Now, in this moment of adrenaline-charged clarity, he finally understood what the old spymaster had meant. Here, now, in this tunnel, he at last recognized his true enemy.

Complacency.

The American operator with the steel nerves, the one who had stared down the barrel of his gun and not flinched, was exactly what

Valerian needed—what he craved. *A worthy opponent.* This man was not some goatherd-turned-terrorist; he was not some dim-witted, muscle-bound street thug with a gun. This man was a professional—a soldier with highly calibrated instincts and skills.

This man is an operator.

He is me.

Valerian moved along the right side of the stalled traffic, weighing his options. He could simply climb aboard one of the many buses idling in the tunnel and disappear in the crowd, or he could stow away in the trailer of one of the two delivery trucks ahead of him. But if they were stalled for a prolonged period, the Americans would be joined by reinforcements. The team would conduct a hard-target search and he would be found.

Besides, where was the challenge in hiding?

No, to win his freedom, Valerian would have to kill both the operator and his teammate as they approached. Then, and only then, could he exit in disguise. He would change more than his outward appearance; he would *become* someone else. He would adopt a new legend—one of opportunity—and he would slip away.

He ignored the profane shouts and occasional middle fingers as he "skipped the line," shooting down the narrow gap between the column of traffic and the wall of the tunnel—a gap through which only a motorcycle could fit. As he came upon a twelve-wheel delivery truck, he dismounted, dropped the Piaggio on its side, and then pulled the bike beneath the idling truck. Then he took a knee and checked the magazine of the 9 mm HK, confirming the rounds remaining. His brain had long ago assumed the task of counting his fired rounds without being asked. With the extra magazine in his pocket, he had more than enough to dispatch the Americans, deal with any unanticipated complications, and disappear.

He crept forward and took up a position at the bend in the tunnel—the perfect location to execute an ambush.

CHAPTER 49

Dempsey flashed Munn a lopsided grin over his shoulder as he paused thirty feet outside the tunnel entrance in a tactical crouch. The entry was the most dangerous part of the advance because he had to transition from bright sunlight to darkness inside the tunnel. This refractory period, the time it took his eyes to adjust, was when he would be most vulnerable. If he were Rook, he'd exploit that transition.

He quickly scanned both sides of the tunnel approach, just in case the assassin had doubled back and was trying to flank him. Seeing no one, he crouched lower and drifted along the driver's side of the row of idling vehicles waiting to enter the tunnel. He could feel multiple pairs of eyes on him, each and every vehicle occupant looking at him with fear and uncertainty as he passed them, fully kitted up and trailing the pistol in his extended right arm. At ten feet to the shadow line, he accelerated rapidly, advancing then ducking behind the back of a minibus—*thank God for minibuses*—and then he slipped over to the passenger side of the line of traffic.

He popped his head around the rear corner of the vehicle for a scouting glance then pulled it back. The light dichotomy was terrible, and he still couldn't make out anything beyond the first few meters in the tunnel, but hey, at least he hadn't been shot. He exhaled, slipped around the bumper, and advanced into the lion's den. He crossed the shadow line, entered the tunnel, and ducked behind a delivery van. He squeezed his eyes shut, trying to accelerate the acclimation process. After a beat, he opened his eyes and turned away from the glaring sunlight outside.

A silent count ticked down in his head: *Three, two, one . . .*

Body primed with adrenaline, he rounded the right rear corner of the van and advanced, scanning over his Sig. He passed three vehicles. Then four. Then five . . . His heart pounded in his chest. Upon reaching another minibus, he dodged to the left side of the column of traffic to check the inside sight line and make sure he wasn't being flanked. Not seeing his quarry, he crossed back and stepped around the bumper, leading with his Sig in a tactical crouch. His eyes were fully acclimated now, and this time he saw movement ahead. A crouching figure had just executed the same maneuver in mirror image. They faced each other—two dualists, weapons at the ready—a mere twenty paces apart.

Dempsey fired three rounds—bang, bang, bang. In synchronicity with his last two trigger pulls, a double muzzle flash lit up the tunnel ahead. Two slugs slammed into his vest a heartbeat later, impacting dead center of mass. He felt the double thump, but the kinetic energy of the rounds was largely absorbed by the antiballistic ceramic plate in his carrier. He swallowed down the sharp pain and pulled in a slow, agonizing breath, and then he kept closing—unloading a prolonged, furious volley. Trigger pull, trigger pull, trigger pull, trigger pull . . . Thunder roared and reverberated in the tunnel as he sent a barrage of metal at his target. The enemy shooter dove between two vehicles, but Dempsey kept closing.

Trigger pull.

"INFIL now," he barked over the comms circuit. "Rook is crouched three cars back from the white delivery van, midtunnel."

Trigger pull . . . Trigger pull.

The reverb of gunfire was soon drowned out by the high-pitched whine of the BMW motorcycle as Munn screamed into the tunnel down the vacant left lane like an F/A-18 Hornet on afterburner. As Dempsey continued to advance on the shooter's position, providing cover fire for Munn, thoughts flowed through his head in a live stream-of-consciousness commentary on the tactical scenario.

The way he moves, the way he shoots—this guy's no terrorist shithead; he's a fucking pro . . . He's not cowering behind a car bumper paralyzed with fear . . .

Trigger pull.

He's active.

He's aggressive.

Shit, he's me . . .

Trigger pull . . . trigger pull.

He retrieved a fresh magazine from his kit, ejected the spent magazine from his P226, and slammed the new one home.

You're about to get shot in the leg, dude, the SEAL in his head suddenly warned.

Dempsey dropped his shooting hand to the deck and squeezed off two rounds parallel to the ground, aimed under the chasses of the idling vehicles. At the same time, two slugs whistled past his feet, missing him by inches. He squeezed off two more rounds along the ground and then sprinted toward the next gap between vehicles.

He's going to roll out and shoot Munn on the reversal . . . It's what I'd do.

The squeal of rubber on asphalt echoed in the tunnel; Munn was making his reversing maneuver. Jaw clenched, Dempsey slid between the front bumper of an Opal and the rear bumper of a Mercedes CUV and dropped to a tactical knee. A gunshot rang out.

Damn it.

He was too late.

He sighted around the left rear quarter panel of the Mercedes crossover just in time to glimpse Munn tumbling off the bike thirty meters away. A second gunshot cracked, and the window above Dempsey's head exploded. He managed to squeeze off a round as a second slug grazed his cheek.

"Shit," he cursed, jerking behind the hatchback.

He touched the fleshy part of his cheek just below the bone, and the tips of his two gloved fingers came away bloody. The tip of his ear burned, too, which told him the bullet had clipped the outer rim of cartilage on its way past. Rage erupted inside him and he was up, sprinting behind the Mercedes and looping toward the passenger side. He swallowed the rage and reminded himself that anger was no ally. It would cloud his judgment, distract his focus, and get him killed. Dempsey felt his heart slow, and the tremor in his fingers faded. He rounded the vehicle and charged up the narrow lane between the tunnel wall and the line of cars.

A car door opened ahead, and someone began to get out on the passenger side. Dempsey squeezed off a round at the ground, and the exiting moron recoiled and slammed the door shut. Dempsey slowed and fell back into a tactical crouch. He scanned left, looking for the shooter through the windows and windshields of the cars while keeping his head below the rooflines as he advanced.

A flash of gray on the other side of a windshield caught his attention. In that split-second glance, Dempsey thought he made out the shooter running away. Was he squirting or repositioning? Would he try to put another round in Munn on his way past?

That's what I'd do.

Cursing, Dempsey accelerated and leaped onto the hood of a low-slung convertible. His boots made craters in the sheet metal with reverberating thuds as he gained the high ground. Sighting over the roof of the car in front of him, he saw the assassin sprinting toward the tunnel's east exit, and just like he'd suspected, the shooter was bringing his weapon to bear on Munn, still lying beside the toppled motorcycle.

"Hey, asshole!" Dempsey shouted as he fired a two-round volley at the killer.

The assassin glanced over his shoulder as at least one of Dempsey's rounds made contact. The shooter pitched forward, stumbling for two strides before catching his balance. He made to level his pistol at Munn a second time, but Dempsey sent another three rounds flying his way. The shooter's torso jerked and his pistol tumbled out of his grip, but he stayed on his feet.

Dempsey jumped off the car hood and hit the ground running. He vectored straight toward Munn, who was lying supine on the asphalt, clutching his neck. He shifted his gaze from Munn to the shooter, who was quickly opening the gap between them.

But I shot you . . . twice! the voice growled in Dempsey's head. *Bastard has to be wearing Kevlar; otherwise he'd be down.*

"Eagle, this is Falcon One. Do you copy?" Dempsey said over the comms circuit.

No answer came from Baldwin, but he did get a raspy reply from Munn: "Interference from the tunnel."

As Dempsey took a knee at his friend's side, he spared a second glance at the fleeing assassin, who was about to exit the tunnel heading east. He looked back at Munn, who was clutching the side of his neck, blood running through his fingers.

"Jesus, Dan," Dempsey said, his heart skipping a beat. He moved to pull the blowout kit from his vest.

"Save it," Munn said. "I got this."

Dempsey cocked a *You're shot in the neck. Are you freaking kidding me?* eyebrow at his friend.

"It's a zone one injury," Munn said. "Too low to get the carotid artery, and there's clearly no nerve damage. Dark blood is probably the external jugular vein, which is easy to control." Dempsey looked at the former surgeon like he was speaking Latin—which he supposed he mostly was. "It looks worse than it is—like your face," Munn said, locking eyes with Dempsey. "What the hell are you waiting for, JD? Go get that fucker."

"All right," he said, popping to his feet. "Hang in there. Help is on its way."

He jumped over the totaled motorcycle crumpled beside his wounded teammate and sprinted down the tunnel. As he fell into pursuit, he scooped up the shooter's pistol—an HK 9 mm variant—and stuffed it into his waistband at the small of his back. Something told him he was going to need it later. Sirens wailed behind him. He prayed that an ambulance was en route and not just law enforcement. He also prayed Munn hadn't been bullshitting him about the wound, but he suspected that this time the doc was playing it straight. Dempsey had seen plenty of severed carotids in his day—hell, he'd been the one who'd done the severing in most cases. If Munn's wound had been mortal, there would have been more blood—a lot more.

Up ahead, the shooter disappeared from his line of sight as he ran up the ramp leading out of the tunnel. Dempsey squinted, readying himself to have his vision washed out as he crossed from shadow to daylight. A few seconds later, he was out, temporarily blind as he charged up the incline toward street level. A police cruiser sat at the top of the ramp, lights flashing but sirens off.

Wonderful.

The last thing he needed was a run-in with some Turkish traffic cop who decided that today he wanted to put on his big-boy pants and play a game of stop the American operator. Well, today was not the day to fuck with John Dempsey. Today the American operator would not stop until he was standing with his boot pressed against the assassin's neck—dead or alive, Dempsey didn't care.

Then, just as he'd feared, a uniformed officer stepped away from the gaggle of people around the traffic accident and walked into the empty westbound lane in front of Dempsey. He held up his palm to Dempsey and barked something in Turkish.

Why do they never try to stop the first guy? It's always the second guy . . .

Dempsey kept running.

The officer's gaze flicked to the Sig clutched in Dempsey's pumping right hand, and his eyes went wide with panic.

Don't do it, dude . . . Don't be stupid.

Unfortunately for both of them, stupid won the day.

Flustered, the cop backpedaled, and his hand went to his sidearm.

Dempsey did the math in his head as he accelerated—he had the time to do it right.

The officer's weapon was coming out of the holster just as Dempsey arrived. Dempsey deftly disarmed the young officer, but the Turk managed to squeeze off a round in the process. The bullet struck the ground between them and ricocheted clear. Dempsey twisted, the officer's pistol now in his hand, and pointed the muzzle of his Sig at the other man's chest. The officer's hands shot skyward in surrender. Dempsey released the magazine from the policeman's pistol and kicked it clear with his boot as it fell. Then, he pitched the compact Glock 9 mm twenty yards back into the tunnel. The officer stood frozen, staring at him in wide-eyed terror.

"I'm an American operator on a joint counterterrorism task force," Dempsey said, meeting the officer's eyes. "*Counter*terrorism—do you understand?"

The officer nodded.

"Don't shoot me in the back," he said and then turned and sprinted up the ramp, praying the officer didn't have an ankle holster.

"Nicely done, Falcon One" came Baldwin's voice in his ears, "but it took you long enough."

"Falcon Two took a bullet in the neck. He claims he'll live, but he needs a damn CASEVAC. You copy?"

"We hear you Lima Charlie, Falcon," a new but familiar voice answered—Smith.

"Are you still tracking this bastard?" Dempsey asked, scanning ahead.

"Barely."

"Which way did he go?"

"North. Turn left ahead on Fuat Pasa. He's still on foot."

"How far ahead?"

"Approximately one hundred meters."

"Shit, there's no way I'll catch him," Dempsey growled, resuming the chase.

"Don't sell yourself short. Rook appears to be either very tired or wounded," Baldwin said. "His pace has slowed dramatically over the past minute. You might be able to catch him."

"Now there's a backhanded compliment if I've ever heard one. I've still got three more days until I'm over the hill, remember?"

"Falcon One," Smith said, his voice deadly serious, "I have a big ask, and you're not going to like it."

"What?" Dempsey huffed, heart pounding and lungs heaving.

"I want you to take this guy alive. Amanda Allen has identified him from satellite imagery as Malik 2.0."

A string of silent curses ran through his mind. *Unfortunately, Shane, that isn't going to happen,* he decided, but to Smith he simply said, "Check."

"The target turned just east on Ismetiye," Baldwin said.

"That doesn't . . . fucking . . . help me," Dempsey huffed between breaths.

"Falcon One, Eagle," Smith said, his voice calm and confident. "Turn right in ten meters. I'm going to see if I can cut some corners and put you on an intercept course."

"Check."

"Right at this intersection, Nargileci Street."

Dempsey rounded the bend and sprinted down the narrow one-way street lined with little merchant shops along each side. At the end of the street, about a hundred meters away, he saw a stone wall.

"It's a dead end," he huffed.

"No, it just looks that way from your position. It's an intersection. At the T, turn left and head north," Smith said.

Dempsey listened as a discussion between Baldwin and Smith broke out, both their voices more distant. "You think Rook is going to keep east on Vasif Cinar, or do you think he'll go north on Uzun Carsi?"

"If he wanted to disappear, he should have fled to the Grand Bazaar. Kapali Carsi is one of the largest covered markets on earth, with thousands of shops. We never could have tracked him in there," Baldwin said.

If not for the fact he was sprinting, Dempsey would have sighed with relief. *Cat-and-mouse chases and gun battles in massive covered bazaars? Been there, done that in Tehran. Not today, no thank you.*

"Maybe Rook doesn't know this area," Smith said.

"That, or he thinks the odds of making his planned EXFIL are better than going to ground and trying to survive the coming manhunt."

"Why not exploit the chaos while you can?" Smith said.

"Exactly."

"In that case, looks to me like Rook has two viable escape options: the highway . . ."

"Or a boat."

"Precisely."

"As fun as this is, just tell me where to turn?" Dempsey growled. His leg muscles were burning now with lactic acid, and he was beginning to get winded.

"Interesting, Rook stayed east on Vasif," Baldwin said, apparently ignoring Dempsey now.

"Does that alley go through?" Smith asked, still talking to Baldwin.

"Yes, I think so. If we turn John here, have him cut this corner, and we accelerate him, then he should intercept the target here."

"I'm not a drone, guys," Dempsey wheezed, wondering how much longer he could maintain this blistering pace.

"Let's do it," Smith replied. Then his voice became crisper as he said, "Falcon, there's a narrow alley coming up on your right in fifteen meters. Turn there and you'll cut the corner. If you can pick up the pace, you'll be right on the shooter's heels when you emerge."

"Check."

Maintaining speed was getting more difficult as he navigated deeper into the warren of shops and cafés. The narrow sidewalks were paved, but he couldn't use them because of the hordes of people and all the other crap strewn about everywhere. Baskets, luggage, boxes, wheeled shopping caddies, and display racks—stuff that should have been inside the stores—had migrated out onto the sidewalks, allowing the merchants to extend their "showrooms" all the way to the curb. The impassable sidewalks forced him to run down the center of the street, which was lined with cobblestones rather than asphalt, making him one loose stone away from a pursuit-ending ankle roll.

He spied the narrow alley ahead and banked right.

As he did, a little boy darted out in front of him, laughing and running from his mother. Dempsey spied the kid just in time and hurdled him without breaking stride. The Turkish man carrying boxes, however, did not fare so well. Dempsey sent the man and his boxes airborne.

"Careful, Falcon," Baldwin chastised.

Dempsey gritted his teeth instead of responding. Besides, he was too winded to talk anymore. He just kept his eyes forward, feet pounding the ground and arms pumping.

Don't think about the pain. You're a machine . . . a machine with one objective.

"You're looking good, Falcon," Smith said. "If you can keep your speed on, you'll intersect Vasif Cinar just behind the target, who is heading east. He just slowed to a walk and ditched the gray jacket he was wearing. He probably thinks he's clear . . . He's on the north sidewalk, in front of a six- or seven-story-tall apartment building."

"Check."

Fifteen seconds later, Dempsey reached the intersection where the alley merged into Vasif Cinar, and the crowd was much thinner. Here the shops seemed to be closed—their storefronts' corrugated metal roll-down doors or accordion-style, expandable metal grates closed to keep out looters. He rounded the bend without slowing and scanned for the shooter: *six-foot-tall male, lean, broad shoulders, dark hair—bing, that's him.*

As if there was a psychic link between them, the shooter looked over his shoulder and met Dempsey's eyes. Like a jackrabbit suddenly confronted by a coyote, the man took off, but instead of running away, he turned left and ran straight toward a six-foot concrete wall topped with a five-foot metal fence rimmed in turn with a spiral of wound razor wire that cordoned off a courtyard between two buildings.

I've got you, asshole.

What happened next defied the laws of physics—the assassin half ran, half climbed up the wall where it intersected the eastern building like he was a computer-generated Hollywood special effect. He planted his left foot on the vertical surface and propelled himself upward, then grabbed a round metal drainage pipe running down the corner of the building. He shimmied up the pipe as effortlessly as a spider monkey up the trunk of a tree—hand over hand, foot over foot—until he was above the razor-wire coil, then pushed off the corner of the building into a backward swan dive over the wire, executing a back tuck roll in midair. Dempsey couldn't see the landing, but the sound of footsteps pounding away told him the sonuvabitch had landed like a cat.

"What the fuck was that?" Dempsey said, standing there like an idiot, panting and gawking at the wall.

"That, if I'm not mistaken, was parkour," Baldwin said.

"No shit."

"Don't just stand there, Falcon; go get him," Smith said with the slightest hint of sarcasm in his voice.

"I'm a SEAL, not a fucking spider monkey," Dempsey said through gritted teeth. "Do you still have eyes on him?"

"The courtyard is packed with trees. We lost him under the foliage, but it extends all the way to the next block. You could—"

"I'm going around," Dempsey interrupted and took off running to intercept his foe on the other side of the block.

CHAPTER 50

Complacency and hubris . . .

Valerian had allowed himself to fall prey to *both* enemies Arkady had spent years warning him about.

The American operator was more than just a professional. He was a relentless machine. Valerian's initial assessment that he would have to kill the American to escape had been correct. Unfortunately, the American was not cooperating. Valerian had put two rounds in his chest and shot his teammate back in the tunnel, yet still the American pursued—appearing seemingly out of nowhere each time Valerian thought he was clear. This man was either a magician, a tactical prophet, or perhaps the Angel of Death incarnate.

The pain in his left side was both a liability and a comfort. He'd needed this reminder of his mortality. He needed this reminder that he was capable of far more than just cracking walnuts and inflicting psychological damage. His body was a weapon. The loss of the HK meant he needed to harness all his power, exploit all his talents. Like the American, he, too, could be a machine—relentless and deadly.

He scanned the courtyard for exits and options. The green space had many trees, their bases surrounded by mulch and brick, but the branches were either too high to grasp or too thin to support his weight. Hiding here was untenable, which meant executing an ambush was his only option. The American would be coming around the block from the right in a few seconds. He sprinted across the courtyard to the corner and looked up. A couple sat at a bistro table along the railing of a second-story veranda café. They looked at him, both curious and dismayed. He smiled, gave a cordial nod, and then picked up a brick and tossed it over the railing, where it landed with a resounding thud. He then backpedaled five paces, set his jaw, and sprinted toward the exterior wall of the restaurant. He leaped, climbed, and leaped again, using his hard, powerful body to exploit physics and defy gravity once more.

A split second later, he was perched on the balcony railing, holding the brick and ready to descend on his foe . . . a foe who was turning a slow circle in the street below, scanning everywhere but up.

CHAPTER 51

Dempsey spun in a slow circle, his weapon clutched in both hands, the muzzle held level at the ready position. "I don't see him, Eagle. Do you have a visual?"

"Negative, Falcon" came Smith's voice, followed a heartbeat later by "Look out, John!"

Dempsey whirled just in time to see a shadow descending from above. In that split second, his mind filled in all the relevant tactical details—the assassin had leaped off the second-story balcony of the café on the corner and was bringing a brick down toward the top of Dempsey's skull. Dempsey curled at the waist, ducking his head. The assassin landed and smashed the brick into the middle of Dempsey's back. The force of the blow drove Dempsey to his knees, accompanied by a loud, sickening thud. Dempsey grunted, feeling a twinge of pain in his spine, but quickly assessed that the blow had not fractured any of his vertebrae. He knew what a broken back felt like—been there, done that. For the second time today, the antiballistic SAPI plates in his kit had saved his ass.

Reflex took over and Dempsey rolled out of the engagement zone, then up into a kneeling crouch. He brought his Sig up to where the assassin had been, but his foe had repositioned and promptly kicked the pistol out of Dempsey's hand. The weapon flew five feet and clattered across the cobblestones into a puddle. Dempsey looked at his opponent in disbelief as a brick—yes, an actual brick—flew at his face. He juked left, and the brick sailed past him and hit the ground with a resounding crack.

For the first time, Dempsey got a good look at the killer. The man standing in front of him looked like, well, him. He stood the same height—six foot one, give or take an inch—and had the same cruiserweight boxer's build. They shared the same square jawline and dark hair and wore nearly identical beards. The only real distinguishing characteristic between them—other than a decade's separation in age—was in the eyes. Where Dempsey's Irish-green irises were flecked with gold, this man stared back at him with slate-blue eyes the color of an Arctic sea. As Dempsey rose to his feet, he performed a quick survey of the assassin's body, looking for signs of a bloody wound he could exploit in the imminent melee.

His adversary didn't give him time to finish the survey.

The exchange happened so fast, Dempsey didn't have time to think. The operator inside, the one with two decades of close quarters combat training and dozens of real-world engagements, took control. The guiding principle of close quarters combat was simple—use only lethal techniques to maximize damage and injury to an opponent as quickly as possible. Strike fast and first with one's hardest surfaces—fists, elbows, knees—into an opponent's most vulnerable anatomy, like the throat, groin, stomach, eyes, and kidneys. In the real world, Dempsey had never been in a hand-to-hand engagement that lasted more than a few seconds.

This one lasted eleven.

The assassin took a half step and then snapped a front kick at Dempsey's midsection, but Dempsey instinctively pivoted his hips away from the blow. Wasting no energy of movement, Dempsey used the rotation to throw his first strike, a right elbow, with lightning speed toward the assassin's neck. Too late, he realized that the killer had rotated the mirror opposite of Dempsey's own pivot, and the elbow missed. But the distance was close, and Dempsey grabbed the shooter by the vest and pulled him in and off balance while driving his knee up to strike the groin. The knee missed, connecting instead with the shooter's inner thigh. He threw a second knee, and this time the blow landed. His adversary huffed and buckled at the waist. Dempsey pressed in, putting all of his momentum into an uppercut that struck the assassin's jaw, plowing the shooter's head up and back. Dempsey spun in a half circle, his left elbow accelerating toward where the man's temple should have been, but instead, his breath exploded out of his lungs as the assassin's left fist struck deep into his abdomen. Dempsey's rhythm broken, the assassin followed with a quick snap jab that caught Dempsey square in the nose. Pain mushroomed and twin rivers of blood gushed from his nostrils; his vision blurred as his eyes flooded with involuntary tears. He blinked his vision clear just in time to see a second jab flying toward his face. He bowed his head, taking the punch on the top of his crown. On impact, he heard a loud crack. Despite the spike of pain he felt, Dempsey knew it wasn't his skull he'd heard doing the cracking.

Rage erupted inside him, and his right hand found the hilt of the SOG bowie strapped across his kit. *I'm going to fucking gut you,* he thought, unsheathing the knife. His gaze flicked to his opponent's face, which, in that instant, was contorted in pain as he favored his broken right hand. Dempsey thrust the knife straight at his opponent's left eye, hearing the primal grunt from his own throat as he drove his body weight behind the accelerating blade. The assassin slipped the strike, twisting his head right, but wasn't fast enough, and the blade opened a gash in his left cheek.

Dempsey locked eyes with the killer and settled into a combat stance as his opponent did the same, bobbing up and down on the balls of his feet. Instead of pulling a blade of his own, the assassin suddenly flipped backward, kicking Dempsey's right wrist and then executing an impossible half twist in midair. The killer landed incredibly on his feet, facing a quarter turn away from Dempsey, his fists up and ready for the next strike. Dempsey's knife arced through the air and clanged on the cobblestones a few meters away. Then, before Dempsey could launch his next assault, his foe turned and fled, sprinting east with astounding speed. Dempsey looked left to where his Sig had landed in the puddle and saw that it was no longer there. He scanned the blank faces of the handful of onlookers who had gathered to watch the battle.

"Where's my gun?"

No one answered.

"Who took my fucking gun?" he shouted, dragging his laser beam gaze across the circle of people around him.

Eyes averted, hands went into pockets, and backs turned. He could only imagine the sight he must be, a raving modern-day gladiator brawling in the streets, blood raining down from his saturated mustache and beard. A young Turk, no more than fifteen years old, hesitantly pointed at the street. Dempsey followed the boy's finger to a black handgun two meters behind him and opposite the direction where the assassin had knocked the Sig out of Dempsey's hand. Instead of his Sig P226, he saw the HK SFP9 lying on the cobblestone street, half swallowed in a pothole. Dempsey gave the kid a curt nod, then scooped up the weapon, which must have fallen out of his waistband during the melee.

"Falcon One, this is Eagle. We have your tango heading east on Sabuncu Han toward the Misir Çarşisi."

"What's the Misir Çarşisi?" Dempsey asked, his spent body churning like a lumbering locomotive engine being slowly brought back up to speed as he resumed the pursuit.

"A famous spice market," Baldwin said. "If he goes inside, we'll lose him."

"Check."

Dempsey's broken nose was still streaming blood, and the swelling and mucus filling his nasal passages made it harder to breathe. His eyes were still watering, and the top of his head and his neck ached. Chasing this sonuvabitch was hard enough when he'd been fresh, but now he was tired and battered. He pushed all thoughts of pain and fatigue from his mind and focused on his single objective—*stop the target.*

He dug deep, channeled his inner SEAL, and accelerated.

"Do you have a visual on Rook?" came Smith's voice.

"Yes," Dempsey said, locking his gaze on the fleeing assassin forty meters away, heading toward a throng of people milling about in the street market outside the Misir Çarşisi . . . *but not for long.* A commotion erupted as the killer plowed through the crowd, knocking unwitting pedestrians right and left. A heavyset man fell into a cart of open spice containers; a multihued explosion of yellow curry, orange turmeric, and red chili powder dusted everyone within a two-meter radius and sent people running and coughing. Dempsey inhaled before he hit the spice cloud and held his breath as he sprinted through the commotion. The assassin was slowing, forced to maneuver through the crowd, which stayed conveniently parted for Dempsey in the assassin's wake. The gap was closing.

The shooter disappeared around a corner, and Dempsey followed him through what turned out to be the final dogleg turn exiting the convoluted alleys and narrow intersecting streets that made up the market district of historic Istanbul. He emerged onto a massive open-air stone courtyard situated between the Misir Çarşisi and a six-lane coastal roadway that rimmed the Istanbul peninsula. Locals and tourists alike milled about—some watching street performers, others taking pictures of the Yeni Cami mosque and its iconic twin minarets—but the crowd density was manageable.

Dempsey raised his HK and took aim at the assassin's back, center of mass. But before he could squeeze the trigger, his adversary showed almost supernatural prescience by running into the middle of a tour group.

"Terrorist! Terrorist gunman!" Rook was screaming and pointing back at Dempsey. Pandemonium erupted as everyone within earshot panicked, screaming and darting this way and that, mirroring the chaotic action of the agitated flock of seagulls squawking overhead.

Cursing, Dempsey lowered his weapon and resumed chase as the assassin sprinted toward the highway. Horns blared and tires squealed as the killer crossed six lanes of traffic—dodging, jumping, and spinning over and around moving vehicles.

Who the hell is this guy? Dempsey thought as he followed into traffic, choosing to navigate the busy thoroughfare the simple, old-fashioned way—by stopping vehicles at gunpoint. When he reached the other side, he scanned the crowd for his target. In the distance, he heard police sirens wailing.

"Looks like you're about to have company," Smith said in his ear.

"Took them long enough," Dempsey said. "Do you have eyes on the target?"

"Rook is heading for Galata Bridge," said Baldwin, referring to the 150-year-old bridge that connected historic Istanbul with the Galata district on the other side of the Golden Horn waterway. "The top deck of the bridge is for automobile traffic but does have sidewalks. The lower deck is like a boardwalk—packed with cafés and restaurants. Rook went to the lower deck."

Dempsey scanned back and forth on both levels but didn't see the shooter. Dozens and dozens of amateur fishermen lined the upper deck on both east and west sides, casting their spinning lines off the bridge into the blue-green water below.

"I don't see him. Which side did he go?" Dempsey said.

"East side," came Baldwin's reply.

Tourists and pedestrians parted like the Red Sea as Dempsey charged toward the east side of the bridge. He took the concrete stairs four at a time, striding from landing to landing to landing, as he hustled down to the seawall level. When he reached the bottom, he sprinted toward the lower promenade, yelling for tourists and the army of shoeshine scammers to clear out of his way. Gunfire echoed as bullets raked the metal safety railing that spanned the length of the lower level along the water's edge. Dempsey dodged left, toppled an aluminum café table, and dropped in behind it.

It appeared that Rook had procured himself a new weapon.

Dempsey ejected the magazine from the HK to check the count: eight rounds, plus the one in the chamber. He slammed the magazine back home just as a new three-round volley sent bullets into the panicked crowd fighting for cover at a restaurant. A middle-aged woman took a round in the back and pitched forward, collapsing on the ground fifteen feet behind Dempsey.

That's two civilians this asshole has shot.

Dempsey popped his head out for a split second, looked down the lower-deck promenade, and spotted the assassin sprinting toward the middle of the bridge. Dempsey jumped to his feet and gave chase. After ten meters, he came to the body of a uniformed patrol officer, whose lifeless corpse lay sprawled across the sidewalk, glassy eyes staring at the heavens. Dempsey checked the holster at the dead man's side and found it empty. Dempsey pushed himself harder, digging deep into his body's reserves, not prepared to stop until he'd drained every last drop of energy he possessed. Ahead, the assassin was closing on a metallic, monolithic structure that rose like a tower two stories above the upper deck.

"What's that gray structure I'm looking at?" Dempsey asked over the comms circuit.

"Galata Bridge is a bascule-style bridge," Baldwin said. "There are four of these structures, which indicates to me they contain the mechanical equipment for the bridge's operation."

"What kind of bridge?" Dempsey said.

"A *draw*bridge, Falcon."

Each mechanical tower sat atop a concrete foundation surrounded by a sizable landing. A dozen people huddled and crouched in clusters of twos and threes as the killer spun to fire another two-round volley. Dempsey dropped into a tactical crouch as both rounds missed him, sailing wide right. He slowed to a shooting stance, took aim, and fired. The bullet missed, pinging off the metal tower structure as the assassin once again defied gravity, using the gaps between the metal fascia panels to rapidly ascend. Dempsey unloaded two more rounds at Rook as he flung himself over the guardrail and disappeared from view onto the upper deck.

"Damnation," Dempsey cursed, looking for a staircase.

A beat later, he found the switchback stairwell leading to the upper deck. He took the first staircase in a sprint, bounding up the steps two at a time. But instead of blindly making the turn upon reaching the first landing, he stopped. His gut told him the bastard had a sight line down the stairs and would shoot him dead the second he turned that corner. He crouched behind the waist-high metal panel that formed the railing wall between levels. At some point, the assassin would abandon his ambush position, but when?

"Eagle, where is he?"

"We don't have him, Falcon One. He has not emerged from the structure," Baldwin said.

Dempsey blew air through his teeth.

Five rounds left . . . I've only got one shot at this.

He aimed the HK at the ceiling inside the metal tower and fired two rounds. The gunshots echoed loudly, amplified by the metal structure around him. In that instant, he popped to his feet, but instead of rounding the corner, he leaned over the top of the rail and sighted in. The distraction worked and bought Dempsey a half-second reprieve as the assassin was momentarily distracted by the unexpected sound and trajectory of the two rounds hitting the metal floor beneath him.

Dempsey squeezed off two rounds before his adversary could adjust his aim and fire. The first round hit Rook center of mass, and the second clipped his left deltoid, causing him to drop his weapon.

With a fresh surge of adrenaline, Dempsey scrambled around the bend and charged up the stairs toward his fleeing adversary. He reached the top of the staircase a beat later and ran out onto the upper deck of the bridge, scanning right first, the direction he thought he'd seen the target go. Police cruisers with sirens flashing were converging from both directions on the middle of the bridge. In three minutes, they would be surrounded by Turkish police, and this engagement would be over whether he was ready for it to be or not. A heartbeat later, he found Rook—perching on a narrow concrete ledge on the wrong side of the safety railing, fifty feet above the water. Dempsey's operator doppelgänger turned his head and looked at him.

Dempsey raised his pistol.

One round left.

They locked eyes over the barrel of the weapon—one man on the receiving end, the other on the judgment end. Dempsey's right index finger shifted from the guard to the trigger as he aligned the iron sights on Rook's forehead.

No more body shots . . .

The assassin inclined his head—a wordless, conciliatory nod, one operator to another—and then slipped from view as the bow of an eastbound ferry emerged below.

"Noooooo," Dempsey bellowed and ran toward the spot on the railing from where the assassin had jumped. By the time he arrived, the stern of the ferry was emerging from the underbelly of the bridge. On the roof deck, a man struggled to his feet—a man who, save for the eyes, could easily be mistaken for John Dempsey. For a fleeting instant, Dempsey contemplated climbing on that railing and going for it, but the ferry was moving too fast. The only thing he'd catch was air on his way down to a big drink in the Golden Horn. He raised his pistol and sighted in. In response, the assassin squared his shoulders and presented Dempsey with his chest.

Behind Dempsey, sirens screamed, and a baritone voice ordered him to put down his weapon, first in Turkish and then immediately after in heavily accented English. He didn't even have to look; he knew there were at least a dozen semiautomatic weapons trained on his back. If he took the shot at the ferry, they would open fire. Even with his vest and SAPI plates, this was one engagement he was guaranteed not to walk away from. With an angry growl, he released his two-handed grip on the HK and moved his index finger off the trigger. With his back still to the Turkish police contingent, he slowly, very slowly held the pistol out to his side and lowered it to the pavement. As he stood up and raised his hands, he returned his gaze to the ferry and, to no surprise, found the roof deck empty.

"Looks like you've made some new friends, Falcon One," said Smith in his ear.

"Yeah, so it seems," he grumbled. "If I spend one night in a Turkish prison, I'm taking it out on you when I get back. You copy?"

"I hear you Lima Charlie, my friend. Don't worry, we got you covered."

"What about Falcon Two?"

"Ambulance already picked him up."

"Tell me you got the sonuvabitch" came Munn's hoarse voice on the line, the doc apparently having refused to give up his earbud and link to the team this whole time.

"Sorry, bro. Not this time," Dempsey said, staring at the ferry as it slipped from view over the horizon. "Not this time . . ."

CHAPTER 52

Three Days Later
Washington, DC

Grimes sat in the back seat of Dempsey's Tahoe beside Amanda Allen, lost in thought.

Allen had specifically requested that Dempsey be present for her homecoming with Chief Justice Allen. She'd probably thought it poetic or honorable to have the man who'd rescued her deliver her to her father. Dempsey, being Dempsey, had of course obliged the request but then later come to Grimes and asked if she'd ride along. Reluctantly, she'd agreed.

She and Dempsey had not spoken one-on-one since the conversation on the Boeing before he left for the rescue op. That was the first time since Crusader that she'd tried to talk to him about everything that had gone down. And that was the first time since Crusader she'd let *Elizabeth* have a voice. After Jerusalem, she'd locked *Elizabeth* in the closet under the stairs and let *Grimes* completely run the show. The postrehab, nine-month ass-kicker CrossFit training regimen—that had been *Grimes*. The decision to go to sniper school: *Grimes*. Cutting all alcohol, caffeine, and sweets from her diet: *Grimes*. Sniping too many men to count with precision headshots and without remorse: *Grimes*. Shutting down all emotions that don't serve an operational or tactical purpose: *Grimes*. Hell, she'd been *Grimes* for so long now, she was having trouble remembering that her alter ego once had a softer side. As for Kelsey Clarke, the girl she'd been before she'd joined Ember and adopted Elizabeth Grimes as her NOC, well, that girl might as well be dead and buried. How long had it been since she'd seen her parents?

A year?

Yeah, it's been a year . . . not since the anniversary of Jonathon's death.

She shook her head.

I never even told them that I'd been in the hospital. I never told them that their little girl died on the operating table. Probably a good thing, because I would have also told them that, for their little girl, there was no white light at the top of a magical staircase leading to heaven, no choir of angels singing hymns, no kindly bearded man in flowing white robes telling her in a comforting voice that her work on earth was not finished yet and that she needed to go back.

No, when she'd died, she had not experienced any of these things. Just darkness, coldness, and emptiness . . .

What she'd experienced was nothingness . . . hollow nothingness.

But that was not the sort of thing people wanted to hear. Nor was it the sort of thing people needed to hear. People needed encouragement, they needed empathy, and most of all, they needed hope. *Grimes* could not give Amanda any of these things, which meant that it was probably time to unlock the closet door and let *Elizabeth* out . . . if only for a little while.

Watching Amanda now, wringing her hands in her lap, Elizabeth felt a pang of pity for the girl. Of course, Allen wasn't really a girl. She was a woman—an incredibly brave and strong woman—who was only five years her junior. But right now, in this moment, she seemed very much a girl, and Elizabeth felt a maternal inclination to comfort her.

Maternal was probably not the right word—*sororal* was more accurate. She'd not had a sister growing up, only a big brother, so slipping into a big-sister role was not something she'd had any real experience with. She'd always found herself fulfilling the opposite caricature—the defiant kid sister trying to prove to everyone she was big enough, strong enough, and smart enough to do it . . . whatever "it" happened to be. It had been no different at Ember, but she'd finally proven herself there, hadn't she?

Watching Amanda, she wondered who Amanda truly needed her to be right now: *Grimes* or *Elizabeth*?

Who do I need me to be?

From the driver's seat, Dempsey let out a barely audible sigh—a note of irritation that probably only she noticed. For the past five minutes, they'd been parked along the curb in front of the Chief Justice's DC townhouse at idle. He cut the engine and leaned his head against the headrest.

"I'm not ready yet," Amanda said immediately, a defensive edge to her voice.

"It's okay," Elizabeth said with a warm, empathetic smile, pulling her gaze from Amanda's nervous hands to her face. "We're not in a hurry."

Amanda nodded and lowered her gaze to her lap. They were silent for a while, until she said, "I don't feel like me anymore." Her gaze went to the middle distance. "Is that normal for people who go through something like, um . . . like what happened to me?"

Elizabeth nodded. "Yes, it's normal."

"It's hard to explain," Amanda continued. "Before, there was just one me. But now, it's almost like there's different versions of me all trying to occupy the space in my head. There's the me from before, the one I'd been my whole life, but she seems very far away. Then there's the helpless me, the one who was abused and violated and basically got her ass kicked. And last, there's the rage-monster me, the one who ripped a Coke can in half and used it to slit a man's throat and gouge out his eyes . . . It's kinda hard to keep straight which me I'm supposed to be now."

Grimes shifted uncomfortably in her seat at the words—almost her own words, but coming from a relative stranger. She forced herself to again be Elizabeth and reached over and took Amanda's hand.

"I think when something traumatic happens, we become the person we need to be to survive. I think that new person, the survivor, often has trouble giving up control when—" She stopped, noticing Dempsey's eyes locked on her in the rearview mirror.

"When what?" Amanda asked.

"I was going to say, when life goes back to normal, but for people like us, life never goes back to normal. That's the fairy tale we try to tell ourselves, but the sad truth is, in reality, the threat level is the only thing that dictates who we get to be and when."

Amanda nodded slowly. "So what you're saying is, the old me is gone? This is who I am now?"

She was formulating her response when Dempsey surprised her by turning in his seat and saying, "That's right. You can't go back. And even if you could, in time, you wouldn't want to."

Grimes looked at Dempsey, whose usually hard eyes were compassionate and earnest. There was a lot more to John Dempsey than people thought. She wondered who, besides her, understood that.

Amanda's lips curled into a sad smile. "I guess, deep down, I kinda figured that."

"But know this—there is a place for people like us," he said. "A place where you can cut the umbilical cord to your past. A place where you can learn to harness your demons and put them to work for you pulling the oxcart. A place where trauma, angst, and loss can be channeled into purpose and forge the bonds of camaraderie with your teammates. We're the guardians of the gate, Amanda. That's more than a job—it's a calling."

Grimes felt a chill at the words that were meant for her as much as they were for Amanda—for all three of them perhaps.

"Interesting," Amanda said, narrowing her eyes at him. "I guess I should probably keep this *place* in mind when I get put on terminal leave."

Grimes shot Dempsey a *What the hell are you doing?* look, to which he responded with the universal clueless-guy expression: *What'd I do?*

Realizing she was still clutching Amanda's hand, Elizabeth gave it an encouraging squeeze and let go. At the same time, movement in her peripheral vision caught her attention, drawing her gaze past Amanda's shoulder and through the rear passenger window. Justice Allen had appeared in the front window and was staring at the Tahoe from beside a drawn curtain.

"Looks like he's waiting for you," Elizabeth said.

Amanda turned in her seat and looked out the window at her father. "What should I tell him? I mean, he's not read into any of this." Then her eyes rimmed with tears, and she started to laugh and cry at the same time. "Christ, he doesn't even know I work for the CIA."

"Tell him whatever feels right," Elizabeth said.

"But he's not read in."

"Actually, we took care of that with the DNI," Dempsey said with a nod. "You're cleared to tell him whatever you want, or whatever you need." He smiled that boyish smile of his. "Except about *us*, of course. We don't exist."

"Oh, okay," Amanda said, wiping her eyes and taking a deep centering breath.

"You can do this, Amanda," Elizabeth said. "Of all the people in the world, I promise, he'll understand."

"I know."

"Would you like me to walk you up?" she asked.

"No," Amanda said, taking one final cleansing breath. "I got this."

"Good luck," Elizabeth said and smiled as Amanda climbed out and shut the door behind her.

They watched together, Grimes and Dempsey—or in this moment, was it John and Elizabeth? She wasn't sure—as father and daughter reunited in a tearful, loving embrace on the front steps of the townhouse.

"Do you think she's going to be okay?" Dempsey asked.

"Yeah, do you?"

"Hell yeah," he said. "I saw her in action. She's a badass."

Grimes cocked a skeptical eyebrow at him. "Her? Fifty bucks says she can't do a single pull-up, dude."

"Give me three weeks with her and you're on."

"Hell no." She laughed as she climbed over the center console to get into the front passenger seat. "No prep work allowed."

He looked at her and grinned.

"What?"

"I just figured Your Highness would have wanted to stay in the back seat while I chauffeured her back to the palace."

She slugged him in the shoulder, proud that her blow made the former SEAL wince. "That's for calling me Your Highness." Then she slugged him again.

"Ow," he said. "What the hell was the second one for?"

"For trying to recruit *her*."

"I wasn't trying to recruit her," he said, fighting back a grin as he started the engine.

"Yes, you were, John Dempsey."

"Okay, so maybe I was. I'll tell you this—I underestimated Simon Adamo as Ops O. He does things differently from Shane, but I'm starting to think he was the right pick for the job."

"Okay," Grimes said, confused. "What the hell does Adamo have to do with Allen?"

"Well," Dempsey said, pulling away from the curb, "now that you're a sniper-operator SAD badass fully committed to watching my back, don't you think old Simon could use some backup, too? You saw them in the SCIF when we were piecing this together in the after-action debrief. They think alike. They had a synergy. Are you telling me you don't think she'd make a good addition to Ember?"

"I don't know—probably," she said. Then, quieter, "Maybe . . ."

She looked at him, watching him in profile as they drove away.

"John?" she said, not sure what she needed to say, only what she wanted to say.

"Yeah?" he said, glancing at her expectantly.

"Never mind," she said after a long beat, her gaze going out the window. Grimes shook her head. *Elizabeth* had done enough talking for one day.

CHAPTER 53

Virginia Beach, Virginia
May 16
0715 Local Time

"Okay, Shane, what's the big secret?" Dempsey growled. The light turned green and he went straight, crossing Northampton Boulevard, no longer needing to ask where they were going. "If we were headed to NAB Little Creek all along, why not just tell me instead of playing games?"

Smith sat in the passenger seat, grinning and looking out the window and not taking the bait.

"And anyway," Dempsey continued, "it's a piss-poor idea for me to be on Little Creek. I spent all of my years with the East Coast Teams here before I wound up at the Tier One JSOC team in Tampa. There's probably a ton of guys I served with who could be on station. There must surely be a better place for whatever this training is you have planned. The Farm is closer, and we wouldn't have had to fight the damn tunnel traffic."

Smith said nothing, and Dempsey rolled down his window as they approached the guard at the gate, who wore an M4 slung across his chest. Dempsey pulled out the contractor CAC card from his center console, the same one he had used to access the CIA base in nearby Williamsburg. On this ID, his name was Jeremy Burnett.

"Can I help you, sir?" the young Master at Arms asked.

"Morning, shipmate," Dempsey said, handing over the ID. The young man scanned it with his handheld reader. The device beeped cheerfully, and then the guard handed Dempsey his card back. "Have a great day, sir," the kid said, and they pulled through.

Dempsey hated using contractor CAC cards. Without a military ID, there was no reflection of rank—so he was "sir," a title loathed by all Navy NCOs, but nowhere more than in the Teams.

"Turn left," Smith said as they approached the first intersection, and Dempsey looked over and raised an eyebrow.

"Not headed to the dune?" he asked, referring to the oceanfront area where the Teams often did training.

Smith just smiled.

"Are we headed out to one of the EOD units?" Dempsey asked as they approached a small bridge over the railroad tracks.

Smith shook his head, still grinning. The road made a right-hand bend, and then Smith pointed left. "Park there," he said.

Dempsey pulled into the lot beside another Tahoe, black like his. He recognized it as Munn's when he saw the giant sun reflector in the windshield shaped like a large blue pair of sunglasses.

"Munn's here, too?" he asked, but Smith just grabbed his backpack and stepped out.

Dempsey resisted the urge to punch his boss in the back out of frustration and instead duly followed Ember's Director across the road and then down a short aluminum gangway onto the marina pier, where an assortment of speedboats, fishing boats, and two older sailboats sat in the still water of Little Creek Cove. Across the cove were the large gray shapes of two LCUs and a single row of three small-force utility boats.

He slowed as realization hit him.

"What the hell did you do, Shane?"

At the end of the pier, he spotted the team, sitting in the back of a gorgeous Bertram 570. Latif and Martin both had beers in their hands. "Captain Dan" was up at the controls on the mezzanine deck, shouting something and pointing to him and Smith.

Latif and Martin jumped to their feet, and then he saw Grimes and—to his surprise—Amanda Allen come up from below. As they approached, the four unfurled a long banner on which they had handwritten—poorly—HAPPY 40TH BIRTHDAY JD!! and began hooting, hollering, and clapping at him.

Dempsey resisted the urge to push Smith off the dock into the water and to spin on a heel and head back to his truck. He sighed, forced a smile, and gave a theatrical bow. A day of deep-sea fishing in open water, not the party, got his feet moving. He stepped off the pier and onto the big ocean cruiser. He hated birthdays and hugs, but today he would suffer both of them because he loved these guys and didn't have the heart to be that guy who ruined his own party.

"So we own a boat now?" he said with a laugh, turning to Smith.

"Don't be ridiculous," Smith said. "We are always good stewards of the taxpayers' dollars. However, a friend of Ember recently relocated to Tampa after screening for JSOC's new Tier One SEAL Team and left his group share in this beauty unsold. So here we are."

"Chunk," Dempsey said with a grin, thinking of the SEAL who'd come through for them last year on Operation Crusader. "I knew he was picked up by Tier One, but I didn't know how much I liked him until just now." He flipped open the cooler after knocking Latif's feet off it and pulled out a bottle of beer. "To fishing!" he said, raising his bottle to the group. Martin was already casting off the lines.

"Not just fishing—spearfishing!" Munn shouted from the mezzanine as he eased the throttles and pulled the Bertram expertly from the pier.

In that moment, on the water and among his friends—some old, some new—a foreign sensation washed over him . . . *happiness.* For the first time in a long while, John Dempsey was happy, and it felt really, really good.

"Spearfishing? Count me out," Martin grumbled. "It's bad enough being on the ocean, but being eaten in it . . . no thank you."

"You are the lamest Force Recon Marine I've ever met," Latif said.

"There's sharks out there, dude! I'll guard the beer."

"That's like letting a German shepherd guard the steaks at a barbeque," Grimes said with a laugh.

"Let's get you changed," Smith said, clasping Dempsey on the shoulders. "I took the liberty of bringing some trunks and a T-shirt from your cage at Ember."

Dempsey followed Smith down the short ladder well and into the salon.

"Nice, Shane," he said, stopping. Smith turned around to face him. "Seriously, dude. This is awesome. I didn't know I needed it until just this moment. This is a real brotherhood we've started here."

Smith nodded, but his face seemed clouded.

"What is it?" Dempsey asked, a lump forming in his throat. He'd had enough of these little talks with Smith over the past two years to know some sort of gut-wrenching news was coming his way.

"I need to tell you something," Smith said, sitting on the small couch by the galley.

"Ooookay . . ." Dempsey said.

"JD, were you thinking about going to Jake's graduation?"

Dempsey slapped his forehead. How in the hell had he forgotten? Jake was graduating from high school in two days in Atlanta. Before Croatia—which had turned into Syria, which had turned into

Istanbul—he'd wrestled with the question of whether to sneak a peek at his son's big day. Now he'd almost missed it.

"I don't know, Shane. I'm guessing you're gonna tell me that I can't take that kind of risk and I need to just let it go."

"Not this time," Smith said, keeping his voice low. "I trust you, JD. With all your training and experience wearing NOCs, if you can't breach security and blend in undetected at a high school graduation, you're in the wrong line of work." His friend and boss leaned forward, elbows on knees. "What I wanted to tell you—or I guess prepare you for is . . ."

"Good Lord, man, just spit it out. I know Kate is remarried, if that's it, and I'm fine. I've accepted it."

Smith smiled. "Well, that's good, but what I wanted to prepare you for is what's on the horizon for Jake."

"What do you mean?"

"Jake screened and was selected for BUD/S. He's signed on the dotted line. He's leaving for boot camp next month, and then on to eight weeks of prep school before heading to Coronado. In his interview, he said he wanted to serve his country and be a SEAL like his father. He's already a hero—engaging that terrorist in the Georgia Aquarium last year like he did. He's since come to believe that service is his destiny. From what I've seen, he may be right."

Dempsey took a seat. He didn't know how to feel. He was sure Jake's decision was killing Kate. First her husband, then her only son . . . How could it not? But how did he feel? Proud . . . lonely . . . resentful . . . terrified? There was no sense hoping Jake might be one of the 70 percent who didn't make it through, that he would land in a nice safe intel billet of some sort. He knew his son. If Jake had his mind set on the Teams, then he wouldn't wash out.

Dempsey thought about that little chubby-cheeked kid Jake had once been. He'd always been Jacob then—Jake didn't fit him yet. He was only three when he'd asked Kate why he couldn't read the books himself instead of having grown-ups read to him. They'd laughed and told him that three-year-olds didn't read—that he had to learn his letters and then his words, and that he wasn't going to kindergarten for another year and a half.

For weeks he'd watched Jake with some little blue reader thing his grandmother had bought him. You loaded a book on it and dragged a little pen across the words, and the device would read them to you. Day after day, hours at a time, little Jacob would drag that damn pen across every book that came with it. Less than a month later, he'd walked over to them on the couch, a book under one arm and a hand on his hip.

"There. Now I can read," he'd announced, his eyes full of fire.

And he could. He'd memorized almost every word in those books, and he sat down and read to them.

"You okay, JD?"

He looked up at Smith. "Yeah, man. I'm good."

"What are you thinking?"

Dempsey got to his feet, snatched the shorts and T-shirt from the table beside him, and forced a big fat grin. "I'm thinkin' I'm gonna shoot me a big-ass fish today," he said.

As he turned to change, Smith clapped him on the back. Then his friend and boss left him alone with his thoughts. Dempsey's mind was a mass of conflicting emotions, and as usual, he elected to ignore them all. He pulled on his Forged shorts and the T-shirt Smith had brought. Then he sat back down and pulled his phone off the table. He went to the web page for Jake's private school. He clicked on the "Graduating Seniors" tab and scrolled through the list until he reached the high school graduation picture of Jake Kemper.

Jake was anything but the chubby three-year-old he'd just reminisced about. His jaw was set firm. He'd cut his hair, which was near military now, but with a long and curly tuft in the front to remind everyone he was still at least a little cool. He looked strong. His face was lean. But the eyes—the eyes held that same fire Dempsey remembered from the couch that day fifteen years ago.

There. Now I can read.

If Jake Kemper had decided to be a frogman, then he sure as hell would be a frogman. For a decade, Special Warfare had spent a fortune trying to improve their ability to screen candidates for BUD/S and predict who really had the mettle to become a SEAL. After all the money and research, even after the Special Warfare prep school designed to better prepare candidates for the rigors of BUD/S, the attrition rate had not decreased. Why? Because you couldn't test for the fire he saw in Jake's eyes. You can't prepare someone to have the heart of a warrior—the heart of a SEAL. These things were forged in a man's soul, and no test or prep school could do that.

He smiled and, to his surprise, wiped a pride-filled tear from his cheek.

Over the past year, it had been difficult for him to resist keeping tabs on Jake. It would be doubly difficult now. He rubbed his freshly shaved chin. Maybe he would ask Chunk to follow Jake's progress and check in with the instructors at Coronado from time to time . . . just to make sure Jake was all right.

Yeah, I'm sure he'd do that for me.

Chunk was a Tier One SEAL now, and he was a friend—a combination that meant he could bear the weight of John Dempsey's most important secret.

EPILOGUE

The Artist's Colony
Peredelkino, Twenty-Four Kilometers Southwest of Moscow
May 18
1117 Local Time

Arkady settled into the chair behind the old wooden writing desk and leaned back. The antique chair and the fifty-year-old floorboards creaked in response, not so much in protest, but in satisfaction. It was an inanimate sigh—*The master has returned home, and now all is finally right in the world.* He caught Valerian smiling at him over his coffee.

"What?"

"A quaint dacha in Peredelkino, a writing desk that would have made Boris Pasternak envious, a wood-fired stove burning logs split by your own ax . . . I never imagined you such the romantic," the younger spy said, gesturing around him.

"All spies are romantics," Arkady said. "The good ones, anyway."

"Hmmm, an interesting supposition," Valerian said, "but I'm not sure I agree."

"You wouldn't. Your generation and mine are of different eras. I'm a dying breed . . . Not many of us left these days," he said with a wan smile. "Pop culture and the internet hastened our genocide."

"That, old man, I *do* agree with."

The younger generation was incapable of appreciating a place like Peredelkino. There was no modern analogue to what it had been when Arkady acquired his "quaint dacha" in the late eighties—a place where the Communist Party's most important bureaucrats escaped the politics and stress of their jobs for periodic summer respites. Nor could they appreciate the place it had been when Pasternak—arguably the most famous literary Muscovite—had written *Dr. Zhivago* in the 1950s. Then, Peredelkino had been a retreat for Moscow's artistic and intellectual elite—a place where thinkers contemplated the oppressions, pragmatisms, and intrusions of living in and under a communist regime. Now, it was something less parading as something more—a magic mirror for Russia's nouveau riche and oligarchy flotsam who couldn't afford French chateaus to validate their self-importance.

However, one thing about Peredelkino hadn't changed since Arkady's arrival thirty years ago, and that was him.

"Talk to me, Valerian . . . What's on your mind?" Arkady said.

"What's that?" Valerian asked, dodging the question and pointing to the framed piece of paper that hung behind Arkady's desk.

"Ahhh, that," Arkady said, craning his neck to look at his most prized possession. "That is a page from a ledger that contained the names of our countrymen and women purged by Stalin as dissidents and enemies of the state in 1937. Forty-four thousand Russians were liquidated, murdered by men just like you and me on orders from a leader not so different from the man we serve today."

"There's a handwritten note in the margin," Valerian said, squinting. "What does it say?"

"It says, 'Don't touch this cloud-dweller,' an instruction written by Stalin himself."

"Whose name is it next to? What lucky soul did he spare?"

The corners of Arkady's mouth curled into a grin. "Take a look."

Valerian stood and walked over to look at the paper.

"It says Boris Pasternak," Valerian said, his voice ripe with incredulity. "Is it real?"

"Of course."

"Where did you get this?"

Arkady shrugged. "When I started at the KGB, they didn't know what to do with me. I wasn't from an influential family. I wasn't tall or handsome, and I wasn't particularly well liked. Let's just say, I hadn't found my true calling yet. So they stuck me in records. That was a mistake. This was not the only little gem I found. Never give a smart man access to everyone else's secrets unless your grand plan is to become his subordinate. By the time they realized their mistake, it was too late. I was running the show."

Valerian burst out laughing at this revelation. "You never told me that before."

Arkady shrugged. "A spy who lacks the discipline to keep his own secrets would be a dreadful mentor, don't you think?"

"Yes, I suppose so."

"All right, enough of this bullshit, Valerian. Something is on your mind. I think I know what it is, but I want to hear it from you."

"I can't stop thinking about the girl," Valerian confessed.

"Which girl?"

"The American spy, Amanda Allen."

"Oh, I see," he said, frowning.

"It's a problem I have," Valerian said, pursing his lips. "When I encounter particular subjects . . . I sometimes have trouble letting go."

He nodded, pleased that his prodigy was being so forthcoming with his "emotions." This was a recent development.

"I want to see her again."

"That's impossible," Arkady said, narrowing his eyes.

Valerian stood and walked over to the window that looked out onto the stand of pines surrounding the modest summer cottage. “The Americans who took her back and killed every one of our boys, was that the same team that showed up in Istanbul?”

Arkady nodded.

“Tell me about this group. Why have I never heard of them?”

“Because they are us, only operating under a different red, white, and blue flag.”

“What are they called?”

“Task Force Ember,” Arkady said. “Very small footprint. Very black. Just like Zeta.”

“How do you know this?”

“I have a well-placed asset in the Office of the Director of National Intelligence. This asset is one of only a handful of people in the entire US intelligence community who knows about this group.”

“What about on our side? How many people know?”

“Three. The asset and the two people in this dacha,” Arkady said, leaning forward and setting his coffee cup on his desk. “And I mean for it to stay that way.”

“Understood.” Arkady watched him run the tip of his index finger over the long row of stitches on his left cheek. “The American operator who pursued me was good . . . probably the best I’ve ever encountered. If I hadn’t been wearing a vest, I’d be dead. Do you know who he is?”

“No. We have no intelligence on their personnel, save for one piece of valuable information.”

“Which is?”

“That the Director of National Intelligence, Kelso Jarvis, founded the group and handpicked its charter members. Jarvis was a JSOC Tier One Navy SEAL Commander before he transitioned to the dark side. He favors this group and protects them.”

Valerian turned back to face him. “Which is why Jarvis was my target in Istanbul?”

Arkady nodded. "With Jarvis out of the picture, my asset would likely gain access to Ember personnel files and, quite possibly, control over the activity itself," he said, sharing only half of the equation. No need to reveal more than he had to, even with a trusted asset like Valerian.

"Do they know about us?"

"Very, very good, Valerian," Arkady said, smiling broadly. "That is exactly where your head should be. This is the difference between a good spy and a dead spy. You must always make the flip." Valerian nodded, but Arkady could tell the expression was lost on him, so he continued, "The natural inclination is to think in terms of us versus them. It's how the human mind is preprogrammed, but I have spent my entire career doing the reverse—thinking in terms of them versus us."

"I don't understand."

"One of the more interesting axioms of quantum mechanics is the observer effect. Have you heard of this?"

Valerian shrugged. *"Nyet."*

"The observer effect simply holds that the mere act of observing an event impacts the outcome of the event. Every interaction with an adversary, even something as seemingly innocuous as observation, compels a change—sometimes a change in tactics, sometimes a change in strategy, sometimes a change in policy, and sometimes a change in all three. Do you see where I'm going with this?"

Valerian nodded.

"By deviating from your mission parameters in Istanbul, you have drawn our adversary's attention. Once your PKK operatives failed, you should have disappeared into the shadows. Either you misunderstood my orders or you misunderstand my definition of failure. Killing Kelso Jarvis was the objective of the operation, but not at any cost. By revealing yourself to Task Force Ember, you forced an observation that might not otherwise have happened. They do not know the details of our organization or even our nature, but you gave them a glimpse behind the curtain.

They have observed us, and that observation changes everything. Do you understand what you have done?" Arkady growled, the rage he'd managed to keep under control until now percolating inside him.

"Yes," the spy said, looking at the floor. "I've forced us to change our behavior."

"That's right," the old spymaster said. "Tactics, strategies, policies that were effective before are now vulnerable and subject to exploitation. You have made everyone's job much more difficult, my impetuous friend."

"So what do we do?"

"That is not the first question you need to ask."

"Okay," Valerian said, realization setting in. "What are the Americans going to do?"

Arkady nodded. "That's right. First we must contemplate our adversary's next move, then we can contemplate ours. So the board has been set. The players are seated at the table and the clock has started. Only one king—Zeta or Task Force Ember—will remain standing when this chess game is over."

Valerian nodded.

"Are you ready to play?"

"Yes."

"Very well, then. You're Kelso Jarvis, playing white. I'm me, playing black. You get to make the opening move. So tell me, Valerian . . . What will it be?"

AUTHORS' NOTE

We'd like to acknowledge *you*, the Tier One readers, for your earnest support and online reviews. Without your passion and enthusiasm for the characters and the series, we wouldn't be writing this acknowledgment today. You have embraced John Dempsey and the Ember Team and, in doing so, brought them to life. So thank you for the gift of your attention, your time, and your hearts and minds.

With the last novel, *Crusader One*, we closed out the first trilogy in the series. *American Operator* marks the beginning of the next installment, with Dempsey and the rest of the Ember team facing a new and rising threat—an old enemy resurrected and refashioned for the twenty-first century. As such, we've got exciting and gut-wrenching developments coming your way in the next two books, so stay tuned.

We're also very excited to announce that we are planning stand-alone shorts and novels tied to the Tier One universe and intended to spotlight other members of the Ember team. The first one will be coming soon, hopefully in 2019, and we can't wait to hear what you think. Additionally, we have two other stand-alone novels in development with new characters facing emerging threats straight out of tomorrow's headlines. For news and regular updates on all these, please join our mailing list at www.andrews-wilson.com.

Finally, we'd like to address a common thread we've observed in numerous reviews and mail we've received from you, the Tier One readers. Many of you have been moved by the service and sacrifice of these characters. Many of you have commented that you hope and pray that a "real-life" John Dempsey is out there, protecting American citizens abroad and at home. To this we say, sleep easy tonight—he *is* out there right now, embodied in mind and spirit by the thousands of courageous and committed men and women in the US Armed Forces and intelligence community who are forever and always watching your six.

GLOSSARY

- AFSOC—Air Force Special Operations Command
- AQ—Al Qaeda
- BDU—Battle Dress Uniform
- BUD/S—Basic Underwater Demolition School
- BZ—Bravo Zulu (military accolade)
- CASEVAC—Casualty Evacuation
- CENTCOM—Central Command
- CIA—Central Intelligence Agency
- CO—Commanding Officer
- CONUS—Continental United States
- CSO—Chief Staff Officer
- DIA—Defense Intelligence Agency
- DNI—Director of National Intelligence
- DoD—Department of Defense
- Eighteen Delta—Special Forces medical technician and first responder
- Ember—American black-ops OGA unit led by Kelso Jarvis
- EMP—Electromagnetic pulse
- EOD—Explosive Ordinance Disposal, the Navy's "bomb squad"
- EXFIL—Exfiltrate
- FARP—Forward Area Refueling/Rearming Point

- FOB—Forward Operating Base
- HUMINT—Human Intelligence
- HVT—High Value Target
- IAEA—International Atomic Energy Agency
- IC—Intelligence Community
- IDF—Israeli Defense Forces
- IED—Improvised Explosive Device
- INFIL—Infiltrate
- IRGC—Islamic Revolutionary Guard Corps. A branch of the Iranian Armed Forces
- IS—Islamic State
- ISIS—Islamic State of Iraq and al-Sham
- ISR—Intelligence, Surveillance, and Reconnaissance
- JCS—Joint Chiefs of Staff
- JO—Junior Officer
- JSOC—Joint Special Operations Command
- JSOTF—Joint Special Operations Task Force
- KIA—Killed in Action
- MARSOC—Marine Corps Special Operations Command
- MEDEVAC—Medical Evacuation
- MEF—Marine Expeditionary Force
- MOIS—Iranian Ministry of Intelligence, aka VAJA / VEVAK
- Mossad—Israeli Institute for Intelligence and Special Operations
- NCO—Noncommissioned Officer
- NCTC—National Counterterrorism Center
- NETCOM—Network Enterprise Technology Command (Army)
- NOC—Non-official Cover
- NSA—National Security Administration
- NVGs—Night Vision Goggles
- OGA—Other Government Agency

- OPSEC—Operational Security
- OSTP—Office of Science and Technology Policy
- OTC—Officer in Tactical Command
- PJ—Parajumper/Air Force Rescue
- QRF—Quick Reaction Force
- RPG—Rocket Propelled Grenade
- SAD—Special Activities Division
- SAPI—Small Arms Protective Insert
- SCIF—Sensitive Compartmented Information Facility
- SDV—SEAL Delivery Vehicle
- SEAL—Sea, Air, and Land Teams, Naval Special Warfare
- SECDEF—Secretary of Defense
- SERE—Survival, Evasion, Resistance, and Escape
- SIGINT—Signals Intelligence
- SITREP—Situation Report
- SOAR—Special Operations Aviation Regiment
- SOCOM—Special Operations Command
- SOG—Special Operations Group
- SOPMOD—Special Operations Modification
- SQT—Seal Qualification Training
- SSGN—Nuclear-powered cruise missile submarine
- TAD—Temporary Additional Duty
- TOC—Tactical Operations Center
- UAV—Unmanned Aerial Vehicle
- UN—United Nations
- UNO—University of Nebraska Omaha
- USN—US Navy
- VEVAK—Iranian Ministry of Intelligence, analogue of the CIA

ABOUT THE AUTHORS

Photo © 2012 Jennifer Hensley

Photo © 2015 Wendy Wilson

Brian Andrews is a US Navy veteran, Park Leadership Fellow, and former submarine officer with degrees from Vanderbilt and Cornell Universities. He is the author of three critically acclaimed high-tech thrillers: *Reset*, *The Infiltration Game*, and *The Calypso Directive*.

Jeffrey Wilson has worked as an actor, firefighter, paramedic, jet pilot, and diving instructor, as well as a vascular and trauma surgeon. He served in the US Navy for fourteen years and made multiple deployments as a combat surgeon with an East Coast–based SEAL Team. The author of three award-winning supernatural thrillers, *The Traiteur's Ring*, *The Donors*, and *Fade to Black*, and the new faith-based thriller *War Torn*, he and his wife, Wendy, live in Southwest Florida with their four children.

American Operator is the fourth novel in the Tier One Thrillers series. Andrews and Wilson also coauthor the Nick Foley Thriller series (*Beijing Red* and *Hong Kong Black*) under the pen name Alex Ryan.

Discover exclusive content and sign up for their newsletter online at www.andrews-wilson.com. Follow them on Twitter: @BAndrewsJWilson.